CITY OF MIRTH AND MALICE

ORDER AND CHAOS: BOOK 2

ALEXIS L. MENARD

City of Mirth and Malice

Alexis L. Menard

Developmental and Copy edits: Brittany Corley

Proofreading: Molly Spain

Map Design: Andrés Aguirre

Character Art Illustration: Bella Bergolts

Exterior cover design: Lichen and Limestone

CONTENTS

AUTHOR NOTE

Content Warnings:

City of Mirth and Malice is a new adult fantasy romance that contains strong language and content some readers may find distressing including profanity, tobacco and alcohol use, graphic sexual content, mentioned death of a parent and sibling, gaslighting family members, brief breath play, torture, violence, and mentions of suicide. If there is something not included in this list that you as the reader found distressing, please do not hesitate to reach out to the author so it can be added.

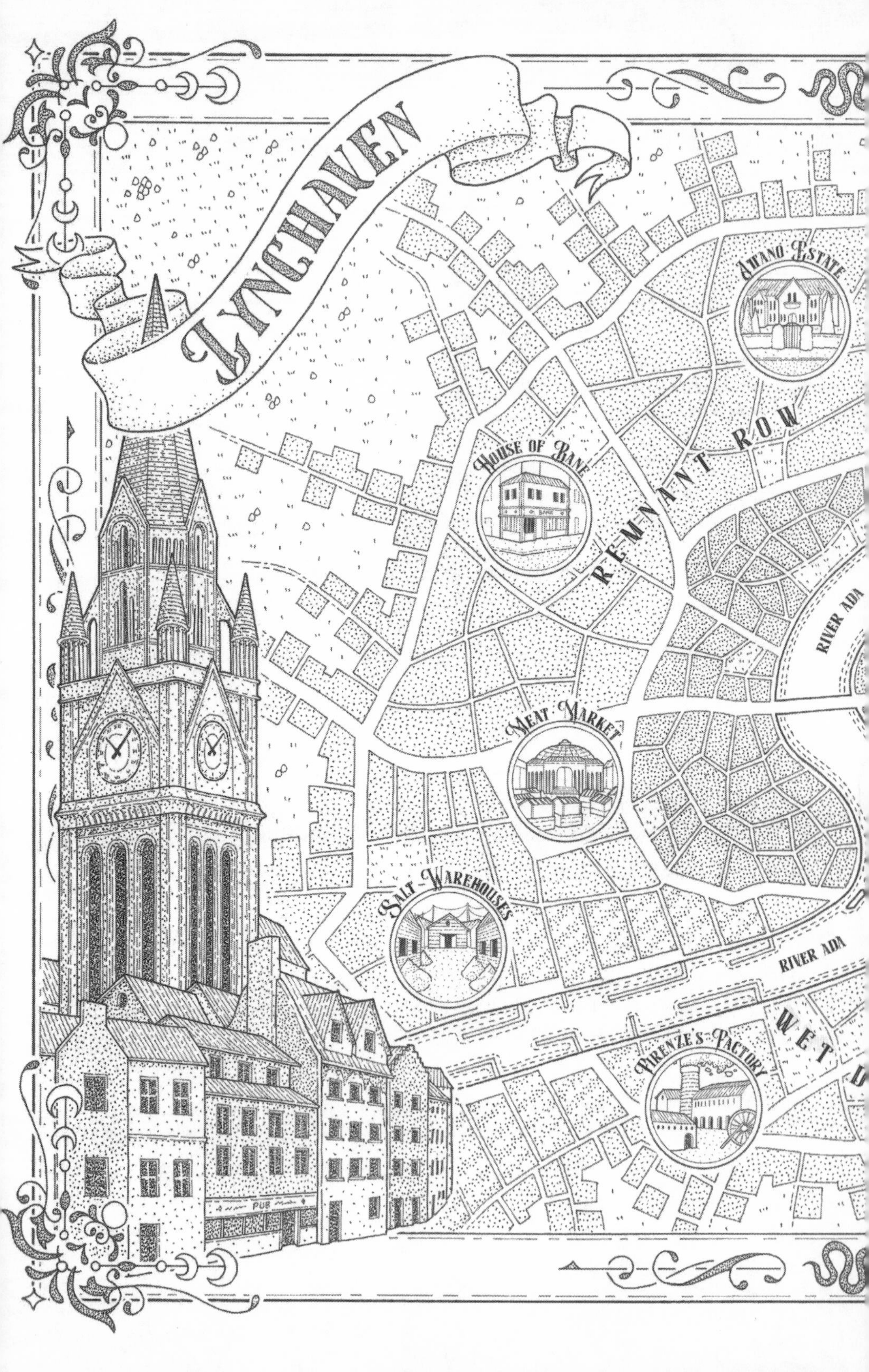

LYNCHAVEN
Awano Estate
Remnant Row
House of Bane
Bank
River Ada
Meat Market
Salt Warehouses
River Ada
Wet
Pirenze's Factory
Pub

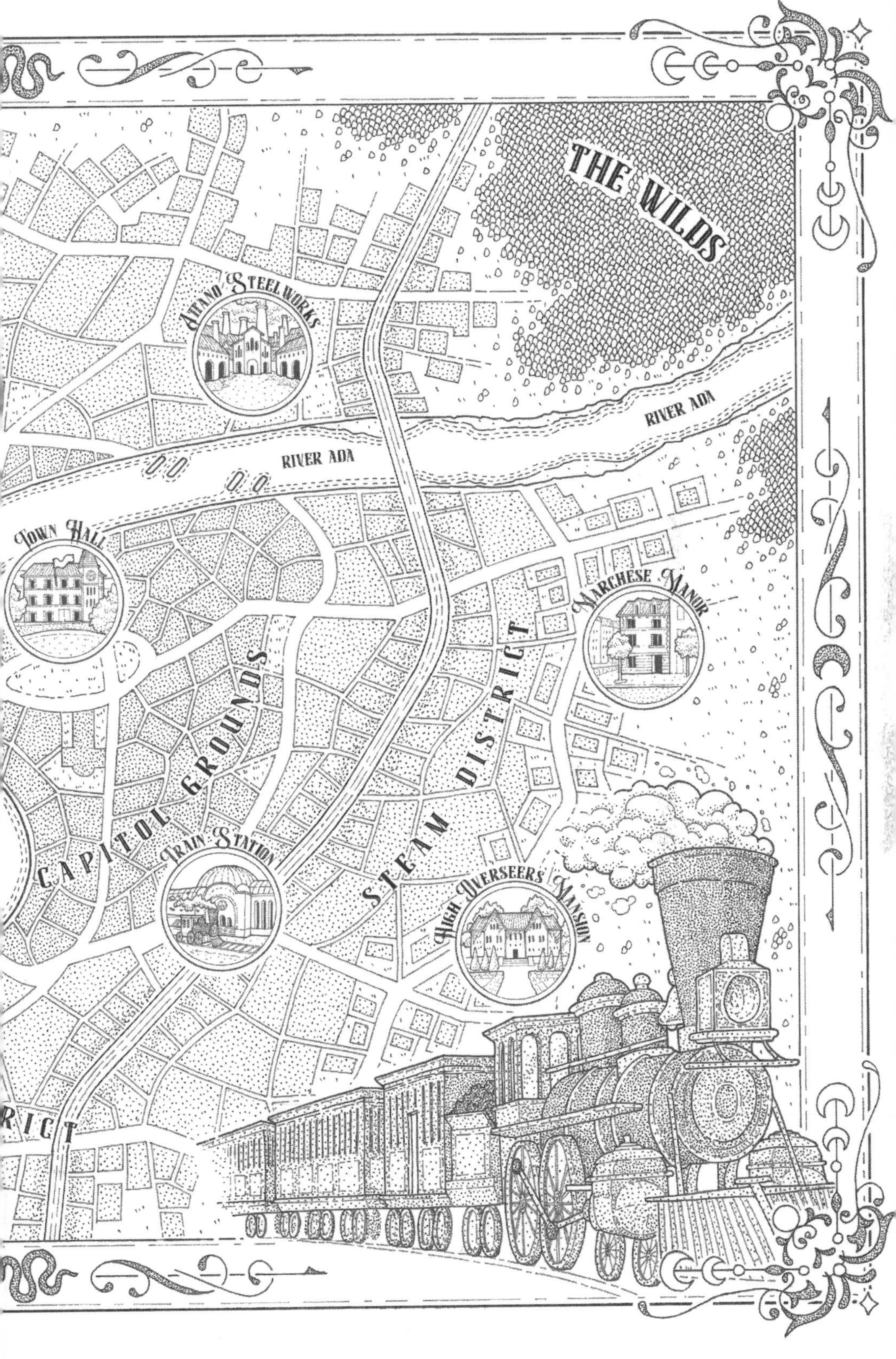
THE WILDS
ATANO STEELWORKS
RIVER ADA
RIVER ADA
TOWN HALL
MARCHESE MANOR
CAPITOL GROUNDS
STEAM DISTRICT
TRAIN STATION
HIGH OVERSEERS MANSION
RICT

The classification of the Remni and their descended

Bane

Benders
Darkthieves

Blood

Wearhs
Haelins

Mirth

Scolapa
Mentalus
Shifters

All mortals from the original age of creation

For my daughter, who taught me the true form of chaos. Don't let anyone steal your fire.

HOUSE OF BANE AND BLOOD
RECAP

Following the death of her father and becoming the sole heiress to a multi-generational railway company, Camilla Marchese is doing all she can to keep her family's business from slipping into bankruptcy. Striving to always put her syndicate first, even at the expense of her heart, Camilla concedes to the expectations of her four brothers and agrees to marry a local alchemist, Felix Firenze, in exchange for his investment into her company to clear their massive debt.

On the day of the wedding, Nicolai Attano, the leader of her family's biggest rival, crashes the ceremony with a deal she cannot refuse. Become his wife for six weeks and help him catch a serial kidnapper known as the Collector, who's been stirring unrest on his side of the city, and he'll clear her debts and shred their marriage contract. Camilla agrees to his terms and the significant freedom he offers, but not without cutting ties—and loyalties—with the very powerful alchemists.

Nico brings Camilla to Newport first to socialize at the races to begin their hunt, but when she catches him slipping away to the stables, she follows him, and witnesses Nico murder a man. She sneaks away before Nico catches her, but not before running into a group of blood-thirsty wearhs and getting bitten by one of them. Camilla waits for Nico back at their apartment and overhears him with a woman named Vanya Hartsong. They discuss breaking off their relationship. Camilla accidentally interrupts their conversation before she can hear more, and Vanya leaves. Before Nico can ask about her evening, the bite on her arm starts to burn, and she faints.

Days later, Camilla wakes at the Attano residence and meets her tailor, Sera, who's been sent by her brothers to relay any information she learns about the Attanos back to them. Camilla meets the rest of the boisterous family and admires their close relationships, unable to refrain from comparing her own family to her enemies. Later, Nico checks on Camilla to find her room empty and in disarray—kidnapped by the same wearhs that bit her at the races.

Nico kills the wearh that harmed his wife and breaks a sacred law between descendants. He takes Camilla to a guarded apartment to lay low until he can deal with the repercussions of his actions. Their hunt for the Collector comes to a pause, but Nico is meanwhile summoned to complete another job by the inspector of Lynchaven.

The inspector blackmails Nico into being his hitman. His list takes Nico to a city official this time. While heading home, Nico is caught by the Society, the city's law enforcement, and charged with the killing of the wearh and sentenced without bail. When Camilla hears of Nico's arrest, she heads straight into wearh territory to bargain with Sabina Bianchi, the leader of the Blood remnants and rival to the Attanos. She makes a deal to get Nico's charges dropped, but in exchange she'll have to fight in a Pit to the death with one of Sabina's creatures from the Wilds. Camilla faces the beast and is stabbed in the back, where the creature leaves a mark on her spine. The connection transports her to Oblivion, where she meets a messenger warning about Order being threatened by

Chaos. She awakens to Nico's family infiltrating the place. Nico drops into the Pit with the creature and Camilla, and with the help of his family, defeats the beast and takes her home.

Once Camilla is back on her feet, the pair make their way across town to investigate Camilla's unknown maternal lineage to try to make sense of the messenger's warnings. While in the heart of the Districts, they're spotted by the Firenzes men and attacked, narrowly making it out by jumping on a departing train. While they're stuck on a journey north, Nico confesses that he's working as a mercenary, but tells Camilla he has his own motivations on the job. The train finally reaches its destination and Camilla is shocked as they arrive at an old, unused shipyard and discover a ship is being built. A ship her train is carrying parts to, though she has no idea why. Nico has a panic attack while the pair are hiding from the workers, and Camilla kisses him out of distraction, but it reveals the attraction they feel for each other.

When they get back to the city, Camilla visits her brothers and inquires about the ship, but her brothers refuse information until she finds a way to cut off her marriage to Nico. She goes back to the Row with the Attanos, and Nico is summoned by the inspector for a final job, one he must complete the same night as the Salt Ball.

On the night of the ball, Nico tells Camilla they must act like they're in love to get the attention of the party. Things get heated in the alcove, but Nico leaves abruptly, leaving Camilla feeling rejected and confused about his intentions. When she goes outside for air, she runs into the inspector, who informs her about a rumor that the High Overseer is going to be killed later that night. Connecting what she knows about Nico and the inspector's warning, Camilla runs to catch up with him before Nico is caught in the inspector's trap.

Meanwhile, Nico finds the High Overseer waiting for him, and the leader of the city tells him the man he's been hunting, the one who killed his family, is none other than the inspector himself. The High Overseer poisons himself on his own wine as the city guard busts in. Camilla joins the fight but is stabbed by a magical blade, which drains her protective tattoo and releases a trapped power she never knew she had. The fierce magic destroys everything and everyone, allowing them to escape. Nico brings Camilla back to the guarded apartment where they confess everything to each other. They finally admit their feelings and make love, waking the next morning to an unexpected visitor. Sera tells Nico that his cousin was arrested, and when he leaves, she uses her mind controlling remnant to make take Camilla to her train, where her brothers are waiting to flee the city to the Continent across the Sea.

Nico meets the inspector on the bridge, who admits to being the Collector. Not to be outdone, Nico confesses that Vanya, the one who gave the inspector the list, fed the inspector the wrong names, and that Nico was killing his own enemies, not the inspector's. The inspector is arrested thanks to evidence left in the High Overseer's suicide note, and Nico is informed about Camilla's taking. He rushes to the departing train before she's gone forever.

Camilla's brothers inform her she is a descendant of Chaos, the only one of her kind. The Firenzes are part of a larger organization that are set on hunting her to destroy her power, so they're taking her away to protect her. But Felix Firenze hijacks the train, and

Camilla fights her way to the engine, using her newfound power, to take down his men and stop the train.

Nico takes on Felix as he leaps aboard the moving train until Camilla gets between them and says something to Felix that makes him stop fighting. Felix then shoots Camilla, and as Nico rushes to her side, Felix flees. Nico shoots at him as he enters a wall of fog, unsure if he hit his mark.

Days later, Nico is deeply grieving when he receives a note to meet on the train his family now owns. He discovers its Camilla's brother, Aramis, who informs him that Camilla is not dead. Sera was a shifter who pretended to be Camilla and died to trick Felix. However, the men who worked for Felix Firenze still completed the job, and now Camilla is trapped in Hightower prison. There, she faces another alchemist, one she recognizes from her past, and the testing of her volatile remnant begins.

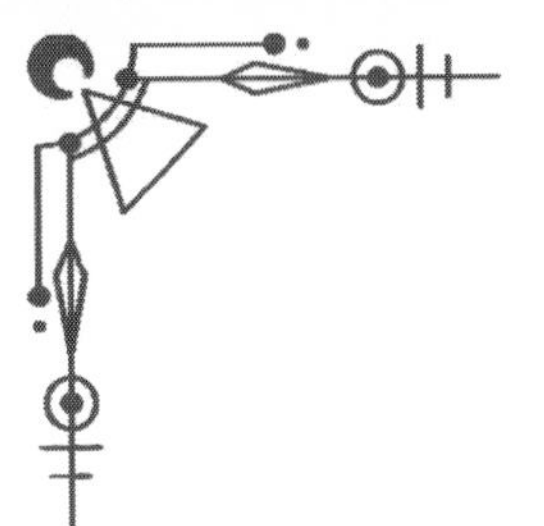
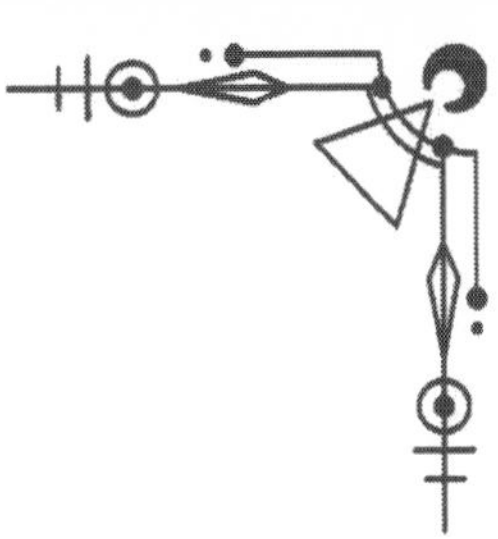

PROLOGUE

An unlikely visitor traveled to the foothills of the Falling Mountains, where ash and dust over the prison camp marked the entrance to the coal mines. A bitter stench coated his throat, even through the cover of his cowl pulled over his nose and mouth to filter the fumes. Black smoke rose from a water pump on the surface, draining the mine where the men worked underground, harvesting the island's primary fuel source.

Only the convicts worked the coal mines. The hard labor so dangerous, only the desperate and deprived could be forced into such hazardous conditions. Where rations were sparsely distributed, the workday was long and without break, and the poisonous gas and crumbling conditions usually killed a man before his time was served.

The guards showed him to the guardhouse, into a room where the warden met with prisoners if they needed a bit of motivation after not meeting their quota. Torturous acts were endured here, as

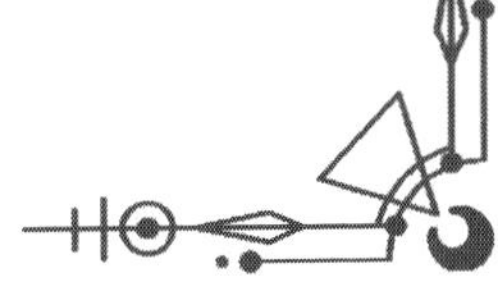

evidenced by the stains on the floor and the windowless walls. A pair of kerosine lamps lit the space from the desk where he sat, waiting.

A steam whistle blew in the yard outside, signaling to the workers that the day was done.

Chains slid across the dusty concrete floor. The prisoner he'd requested to meet wore shackles around his hands and ankles, bound securely per protocol. They locked him to a chair that was nailed to the floor in front of the desk.

He was shirtless and covered in similar filth. If the visitor hadn't know his natural hair was auburn, he'd assume it was grey, the way the mines had stained his features. When he locked eyes with the visitor, his grimy face broke out into a grin. Black coal lined the spaces between his teeth.

"*Giver and Greed*," Gavriel said, "it took you long enough, but I knew you'd come through. I told those treasonous bastards you'd come for me."

"Not enjoying your new accommodations, Inspector?" The visitor smirked.

He grimaced. "It's a kind of hell here. Some of these men remember when I sentenced them." He looked off; a shiver jerked his shoulders. "They do bad things to me when the guards go to sleep. And the mines"—he coughed as his breath rattled in his chest—"are darker than any place in this realm. Sometimes men will drop dead beside me, or a cavern will crumble on top of a team. I've watched men drown when the pumps stop working. The guards whip us for any reason at all—"

"I'm sorry to hear it." The visitor sighed. "Why don't you tell me how you got into this mess, and let's see what can be done about it."

Anger swelled in his eyes, recalling the memory. Gavriel then told him a story about how he appealed Nicolai Attano's prison sentence in exchange for being his hitman. It had all gone downhill from there. The bender, of course, had double-crossed Gavriel as he was known to do.

"That fucking Attano," he growled. "He fed me the wrong names, so we hit Niner sympathizers, not our opponents."

"You hired him to purge our leadership of those who oppose us, and instead gave him the opportunity to kill off our very valuable supporters?" the visitor asked.

The prisoner sputtered, "It wasn't my fault! He had help! And when I get out of here, I'm going to—"

"Calm down, Gavriel. You aren't going anywhere."

The man across from him shrank a size. "What do you mean? Haven't you come to release me?"

"Why would I do that?"

The old inspector swallowed hard. "I thought . . . I thought this was just temporary. To appease the law—"

"You *were* the law," the visitor hissed. "You knew exactly who Nico Attano was killing off and you let him. The others wanted to be cruel, Gavriel. They told me to leave you up here to rot after what you did. I disagreed. I thought you might want to know what the OIC decided—give you the opportunity to find some peace before the mines took you."

"After all I've done, the OIC would turn their backs on me? The Nine?" Calloused hands fisted around his chains. "All the remnants I caught and delivered to you! You would have none of them without me!"

"Who the fuck cares about a few descendants? We now have Chaos, *despite* you." When Gavriel's eyes widened, the visitor smiled. "That's right, Inspector. I caught the girl and cleaned up your mess. Next, I'm going to replace all the sympathizers you killed off, spread the influence of the Nine to every Third—from the Lowlands, through the Mez, to the Upper Notch—and when I'm finished, Order will be reestablished on the Isle."

"And what about me?" He jerked at his bindings, and the rattle of each link echoed through the space. "You'll leave me here? I still served the Order of Inner Courts for years. I found Hightower, where our patron saint split the void and gave us a precious source of power. What about what I've accomplished for Order?"

The visitor shrugged. "I suppose the OIC would let you come back. When you finish serving your time." He stood from the table, leaving the brief meeting. "Thank you for your information about the Attano. I figured as much but needed further insight into your arrangement with him before moving forward."

"Wait!" Gavriel cried behind him, pulling at his chains.

He ignored the prisoner, continuing out the door where a pair of guards stood watch.

"You're making a mistake! There are rats in the OIC!"

He paused at the door, sparing him one last look. "Don't waste more of my time, Gavriel."

"Hartsong!" he shouted. "Theo Hartsong and his daughter. They're the reason I'm in here." Gavriel cried. A well of tears spilled from the corners of his eyes and collected the ash soiling his cheeks.

"Hartsong?" he repeated.

Gavriel nodded his head enthusiastically. "Yes. Vanya was the one who gave me the wrong names. She conspired with the Attano to set her father up as the High Overseer."

This both surprised and pleased the visitor very much. "Good to know. Thank you for your time, Inspector."

"Firenze! Firenze, please, don't leave me here!"

Felix Firenze brushed down his coat and returned to a waiting carriage, with the information he needed, back to the city of Lynchaven.

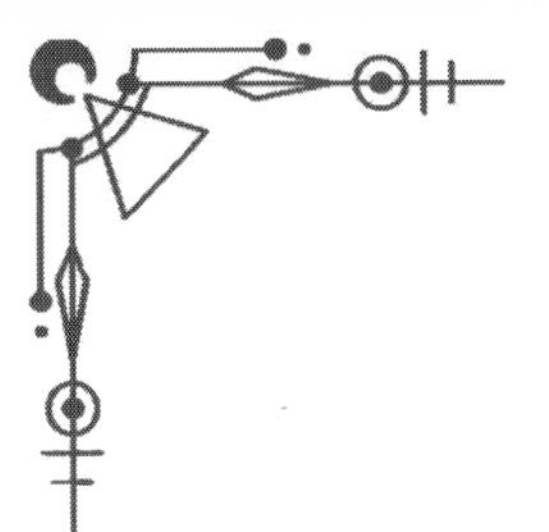
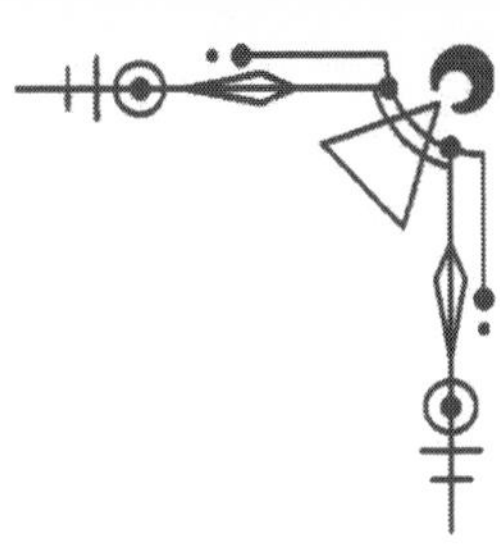

CHAPTER 1

NICOLAI

The air stilled.

Two Attanos in a room full of natives.

My remnant tugged at the collective hold of their breaths, my skin the weight of their stares. These people of power were my last hope to bring my wife home—and get her brothers the hells out my guesthouse. Yet we were nothing but a nuisance, the way they regarded us. Like snakes in their gardens.

They weren't entirely wrong.

The gathering was located along the back of the High Overseer's mansion, overlooking the grounds and sprawling gardens behind the estate. The rest of the OIC of Lynchaven sat around a long table, falling silent as my cousin and I showed our faces.

Neal Caldwell, the newly appointed inspector, led the meeting, seated at the head of the table to the right of Theodore Hartsong. The rest were commanders, donors, and wealthy business owners that paid to have a say in the workings of the city. Just a collection

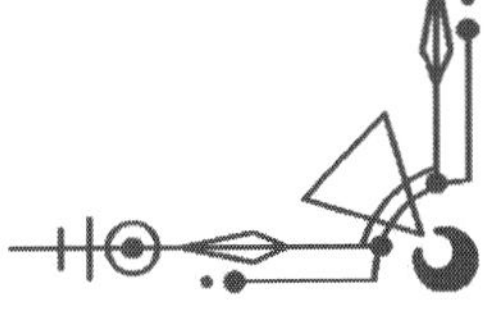

of old, native men and women that wouldn't live long enough to see the full consequences of the decisions they made in this room.

"Mr. Attano." Hartsong broke the stunned silence first. "I didn't know you were joining us today."

"Why wouldn't I be here?" I made a show of adjusting the lapels of my suit jacket, where the golden eagle sigil of the OIC had allowed me to pass the Watch standing guard outside. Theo had given it to me as a gift of good faith should I need anything after all I'd done to get him that seat over the city. He must have conveniently forgotten. "I represent the best interest of the Row, and I was under the impression when we spoke recently that you wanted to improve relations with your neighbors north of the river. Is that no longer the case?"

A muscle flickered along his jaw. Theodore had become the High Overseer by default, since the last one poisoned himself and left the seat open. Neal had been appointed in the week that followed, as the prior inspector had been arrested and thrown into the native prison thanks to my collaboration with Hartsong and his daughter. He wouldn't have long until the next election, a year tops, and I had challenged his loyalties to my family and to my side of the city in front of his incomparably precious voters.

"Of course it is, Mr. Attano. Why don't you and your guest have a seat, and we will give you the floor after the inspector has discussed his public safety plan. Might I ask who you've brought with you?"

"Luther Attano." My cousin bowed too low to be sincere. "At your service, Overseer Hartsong."

Theo's smile was tight. "Always a pleasure to meet more of the family."

We took the seats in the center of the room, near the aisle.

"Where were we?" Neal said with a crisp nod. "Oh, right. The drains. The Moselys filed a report, claiming the last freeze had caused some issues with the sewage backing up—"

His fucking rambling already gave me a headache. I pulled a cigarillo from the inner pocket of my coat and lit it on fire with the thumb of my false hand.

"We don't smoke in here," spat a man with a round face and small, dark eyes. His suit was a size too small, but the hate in his gaze was plenty enough to swallow me in his judgements.

I leaned forward and tapped the blaze over the rim of his glass, a bit of ash falling into his whiskey. "I'm not smoking."

The crease in his fat forehead deepened as he glowered. He reached into the front pocket of his blazer and pulled out a short knife wrapped in a leather sheath, placing it on the table. A blue glow spilled from the gaps. "And I don't have any weapons out."

"Is everything alright over there?" Neal asked. A row of heads swiveled in our direction. "Mr. Attano, we would hate to waste your very limited time. If you've come to discuss something with the cabinet, please take the floor."

I smiled at the man in front of me. He wouldn't be able to reach the blade before I put him on his back. Threats were empty without the reputation to give them merit. "That's very generous of you, Inspector. Thank you."

The chair made a harsh sound as I shot up from my seat and rounded the table to stand before the cabinet. At least twenty pairs of eyes settled over me, and I could almost hear their thoughts as if my remnant had descended from Mirth instead.

They didn't trust me.

Why would they? My name had been included in all kinds of rumors, though they had no evidence of the crimes they associated me with. The only other people that had been on that train—that knew what truly happened when everything went to hell—had disappeared or were dead.

Strangely, the Firenzes weren't here today.

My speech was rehearsed. I'd spoken the words a hundred times in the days leading up to this, despite my doubts. Appealing to the OIC was a long shot, especially when the leadership was dominated by natives. I wouldn't have come crawling to them for help unless I was truly desperate.

That time had come.

"Over the last few years," I started, "descendants, those who wield remnants that have been passed down from the Saints themselves, have disappeared across Lynchaven. The previous inspector admitted to being involved. He was found guilty of abusing his position to kidnap remnants of all variances—"

"And he's suitably detained until further notice," Theo said. "The OIC acknowledged his crimes and admitted Gavriel to the prison camps in the mountains, where he will live and work for the rest of his twenty-year sentence. Does this not appease you?"

"It doesn't." A flash of irritation widened his eyes. "It doesn't solve the actual problem. Hightower is not regulated by the OIC. You have no idea the treatment of the prisoners there. Which is why I've brought Luther here, as he can attest to the dangerous experiments they run on descendants and their remnants. I'm sure if you would listen to a firsthand account of the workings in that prison, you'll agree that operations on the island need to be investigated and the prisoners returned home."

The Overseer's face betrayed nothing, but the whispers of his company insisted on what I already suspected. They cared little for what Luther had to say.

"Experiments?" Caldwell asked. "This is the first I'm hearing of any experiments on prisoners. Do you have any proof of these accusations?"

"More like a lack of it. My cousin's remnant was destroyed as a result of their experimentation. Luther?"

Their pointed stares fell to him. Luther stood slowly, his gaze bouncing on each glare before settling on a spot on the wall like we'd practiced. He'd never been the kind of man to speak for anyone, granting me the privilege instead. Today, however, I could not speak for him, and he shoved his shoulders back to abandon his nerves.

"I was in Hightower for five years before the last inspector absolved me and my cousin of our illegitimate crimes. After a year or so, I was taken to a tower and repeatedly tested on, sometimes for days at a time."

"Who conducted these tests?" Hartsong asked next.

Luther shook his head. "A lady alchemist. She never shared her name or who she worked on behalf of, nor the purpose of the experiments, but I assumed they were interested in learning more about remnants and how they differ from each other. They seemed strangely interested in polys."

"Poly?" Neal leaned forward then.

"Polypotenia. It's when a descendant has multiple remnants in a certain class. For example, Nico can control the air, time, and light. All powers of the descended from the Saint, Bane. I could move sound and the air as well until—" He swallowed hard.

"Until what?"

Luther's eyes shut briefly. "They tried something different the last time they brought me into the tower. Something new. The guards there, I could tell they felt uneasy. What I can remember from the experience is being chained and drugged with glint—

always stuffed with the stuff to be honest. But the alchemist lady, she drew things on me. Symbols."

Neal cleared his throat. "Symbols? What kind of symbols?"

Luther's jaw quivered as sweat beaded above his lip. "I don't know. I've never seen anything like them. Lines and circles in geometric shapes. They covered my back, another on my chest, and a few on each of my limbs. That's the last thing I remember from the test." He drew a long breath. "When I woke up, it was like I had drowned in glint. Not an echo of my remnant remained. And I knew. I knew as soon as I felt that void in my bones, it was gone. Glint drains, but this . . . this destroyed."

Silence draped the room and Luther clasped his hands in front of his waist, stalling his fidgeting.

The new inspector squinted down at him. "Do you think they were trying to destroy your remnant, Mr. Attano?"

He quickly shook his head. "No. She was very displeased about the results."

Neal scoffed. "Well, you must have some idea of the reason for these tests. You were there frequently, as you said."

"I . . ." Luther's tongue stumbled in his mouth. His eyes lifted and found mine, and I offered a nod. He held my gaze. "I think they tried to harvest my remnant. I think the alchemist was trying to find a way to take it from me."

Smothered laughter filled the silence from the men seated at my cousin's side. Ridicule aimed to belittle his story, his experience, and his shoulders fell inch by inch with every disbelieving shake of their heads.

"Are none of you listening?" I paced up the length of the table. "Is there something amusing about any of this?"

Hartsong cleared his throat, sobering their smiles. "Of course not. This is no laughing matter. But if you are also a *poly*, Mr. Attano, why didn't you undergo any experiments?"

I took a calming breath and raised my left arm, pulling the sleeve of my coat down enough to reveal the composition of brass tubes and fingers forming my false hand. "I assume it was because I was already compromised, since they cut my arm off and left me to heal alone in my cell for the months following. The Collector took in plenty of prospects, all of which are still missing. Still locked up in Hightower, and the Order of Inner Courts has done nothing to bring them home."

"There is no evidence the missing descendants are in Hightower." Someone at the table spoke up this time. A woman with a ruby silk scarf tied around her neck and wide-rimmed spectacles magnifying her jade eyes. "Gavriel did not disclose this information—"

"Where else would they be?" My steps were lengthy, coming to stand in front of her. "He was the inspector! He could summon any descendant he wished, and they had no choice but to answer him. He'd stir up trouble just to have an excuse for a descendant to be arrested. He abused his position, and he sent those descendants to a place no one would ever question—where the OIC *doesn't look*."

Hartsong stood from his chair. "That is quite enough, Mr. Attano. The OIC takes these concerns seriously, and we will discuss—"

"I've heard enough." I whirled at him. "It's all you do here, isn't it? *Talk*. Meanwhile, there are families in the Row who are missing loved ones. If you truly gave a damn, you'd launch a full investigation and, at the very least, free the undocumented individuals sent to Hightower—the ones with no crimes attached to their place there."

"I have an idea," the man with the sheathed blade stood. "Why don't we come to a settlement? Send Mr. Attano back to Hightower and, in exchange, free these so-called blameless remnants. At least then justice will be had."

"Mr. Halloway—"

"Justice?" I arched my brow at him. "What crime have I committed, Mr. Halloway?"

He sneered. "Do you see the Firenzes at this table? No. They are still hoping their son recovers from your attempted murder. You shot him, and I'd bet all my reoles that you killed that poor Marchese girl and her family, just to take the Iron Saint for yourself."

A faint breeze wrapped around the room.

"*Boss*," Luther whispered.

I ignored his warning.

"You think I killed Camilla Marchese?" Just saying her name ripped open something inside my chest, releasing a beast my uncle begged me not to feed. "You think I *murdered* my wife?"

"I think it was all so convenient for you, Attano. That she died on her birthday, the same day her inheritance finally cleared, and that anyone who would stand in your way to taking her assets wound up similarly missing . . . or dead." He braced his large palms on the polished wood surface, glaring at me. "I will not support or aid someone like you. Whatever sad story you came here with is as much a lie as the life you lead. Your family only knows how to take advantage of others' success by stealing their livelihoods and pretending they earned it. You're nothing but a con."

Watchmen stationed at the doors stepped into a more active position. Their opinions of me were even worse than I assumed.

"I never claimed to have earned Camilla's assets. I didn't deserve anything she gave me." That was an undeniable truth. Not her company, and certainly not her heart. "But the remnants in

Hightower have nothing to do with me or my family. Whatever grudge you hold against me should not extend to them."

"My vote is no." He sat and plucked an empty glass from the tray in the center of the table, pouring himself a new drink. "I don't believe the claims of this man, nor do I think we should worry over problems that aren't our own. Our inspector will oversee the workings of Hightower and deliver fair and just treatment to the prisoners there, just as he oversees the treatment of native prisoners in the mines."

I doubted that very much. Neal Caldwell looked too fresh to be experienced with overseeing anything—especially not organizations as large and dynamic as the Watch.

Halloway and Neal shared a look. I suspected Neal was not his own man, but a placeholder for someone else—possibly several others—to decide behind the scenes.

Hartsong cleared his throat. "Mr. Attano, I would like to discuss something in private. If you would head to my office, I will be there shortly once we wrap up here."

"Overseer Hartsong—"

He shifted his attention toward Neal, murmuring something in his ear.

It was a punch to the gut, being helpless in a room full of powerful men. They could save Milla tomorrow, probably would if I could mention her name. But Aramis made me vow not to reveal she was alive. Gavriel might have been taken down, but his supporters were still out there—could be in this room if their apathy to help the descendants in Hightower wasn't obvious enough.

The watchmen kept their hands on the guns sheathed at their hip, and I tamed the urge to make a scene. I thought of destroying this room, these people, proving to them what true power looked like. But Milla's life was in their hands, and one wrong choice could burn the bridge that would one day lead me back to her.

For her, I swallowed what I truly wanted to say to these people and pushed down the remnant begging for release with a long exhale. "As you wish, Overseer Hartsong."

THE GUARDS ESCORTED us to a secluded part of the house not far from the meeting room. Hartsong's office was a modest-sized space with a single window overlooking a frozen garden. A pair of oiled leather armchairs waited in front of a dark-stained wood desk.

The place was exceptionally clean. The veneer of the desk was polished and smooth with not a fingerprint disturbing the gloss, and only a pad for notes with an eagle symbol printed across the bottom corner sat on the desk. No personal items marked the walls, leaving them bare and incomplete. Almost like he didn't even use this office. Like he'd never officially moved in.

"Want a drink?" Luther motioned to the bar cart in the corner as I circled the desk.

"Not yet." The top was clean, drawers locked. I wondered if he'd prepared to have guests in his office with everything filed away so securely.

Luther served himself, grabbing an amber glass. "That could have gone worse, I suppose. Uncle Sol wasn't optimistic about us coming down here. Not with the barricade still separating the Districts and the Row."

"We travel by train now, Luther. He shouldn't worry. If we don't give them a reason to arrest us, they'll let us pass through." Perhaps he was right. It could have gone worse today. At least we planted the seed. They knew what we wanted. It was all a matter of bargaining now.

A knock sounded at the door, and I quickly stepped around the desk to hide my snooping, but instead of the Overseer, another face appeared.

Vanya. Theo's only daughter and my former accomplice. "Nico, I didn't know you were coming today!" She flung her arms around my neck, leaning into my ear. "*We did it.*"

We had. Gavriel had never expected her to turn on him. His severed connection with the Nine Crowns had been our greatest weapon against him, and Vanya had seamlessly gotten every name of those who supported the Clemontes' acts of violence against remnants in a way few could. She was the perfect socialite, knowing how to make anyone she spoke to feel like they were someone important.

I hadn't seen her since she'd found me at the races over three months ago. Everything had changed since then, for both of us. Though, the rumors hadn't affected her opinion of me, by the way she wrapped me in an embrace that felt much different from the last time.

I patted her shoulder and quickly took a step back. "You should be careful greeting me like that, Vanya. I'm not well received around here. Wouldn't want to tarnish your reputation as the new Head of Public Affairs."

"Nonsense." Vanya waved her gloved hand. She untied the belt around her coat and sat behind her father's desk. "I just got back in from town, actually. It's already all over the Districts that you and your cousin were seen at the Main Station. I figured with the meeting today, that's where you were headed. How are you, Nicolai?"

That was a complicated question. I couldn't answer her

honestly, not with her father being the Overseer now. She might have worked with me in the past, but now that Theo had gotten what he needed out of me, there was nothing to ensure her loyalty. I settled on, "Busy, as usual."

"As usual," she repeated, still smiling. She glanced at Luther. "How do you do?"

"I'm just fine, miss." He lifted his glass in her direction.

Her grin faded a bit looking back at me. "I'm sorry about your wife, by the way. We didn't meet in the best circumstances, but it is still a shame. I attended a few parties at the Vasilli Hotel downtown, where her brothers hung about. The Marcheses were . . . interesting people. You have my sincere condolences."

I nodded and slowly sat back in my seat. "Thank you. I miss her very much."

"Do you?" She arched a thin, dark brow. She'd heard the gossip. A bigger question laced between those two words, wondering the same as everyone else in this city.

I swallowed and nodded, eager to put that vicious rumor to rest at least. "If I had to choose between that train and Milla, I'd trade that fucking locomotive in a heartbeat if it meant having her back."

Vanya inhaled slowly, nostrils flaring. "Well, she must have meant the world to you, if you would put her above your business pursuits. Be that as it may, I have an offer for you."

"What is it?"

She cleared her throat and glanced at my cousin before resting her gaze on mine. "I wanted to propose a union between us."

Luther choked on his drink.

My mouth hovered for a moment. Vanya had always been very direct, but this offer came out of nowhere. We'd never . . . I certainly never entertained any idea of our relationship going anywhere beyond its fundamental purpose: business.

"I know what you're thinking," she spoke in my silence. "It sounds ridiculous, even as I say it out loud, but think about it. A marriage between the leader of the Row and the Districts, we could make real change. You'd have an official position and the protection to use it. You married for business once, Nico. There's no reason you couldn't do it again."

There were plenty of reasons, but even if Camilla was dead like everyone believed, it was still a line I wouldn't cross.

"With all the respect for you in the world, Vanya," I said, "I will not marry anyone ever again. Not for business, certainly not for anything else."

"Why not?" she asked.

"Because no one will ever take Camilla's place, and that's all I will say on the matter." If she was hurt by my rejection, she didn't show it. "I'm sorry, but we'll just have to find another way to work the system, no matter how much it's rigged against us."

She opened her mouth just as her father burst into the room.

"Vanya, what are you doing in here?" he hissed.

His daughter leapt from the desk chair with a wince pinching her face.

"I was just offering my sympathies to Nicolai and his family. Relax, Daddy. I didn't touch anything." She rounded the desk as he stepped behind it, keeping the furniture between them.

The High Overseer released a long sigh. "I told you to stay out of my office. This is not a place for you to socialize. I have business to discuss with Mr. Attano, and you have duties to attend to yourself."

"Oh yes." She groaned. "Like organize the Women-Who-Vote For-Theo-Hartsong luncheon next week or visit the rich widows of the Steam District to very subtly ask for donations to the Theo Hartsong Foundation."

Luther stood awkwardly between them, loudly slurping a glass of whiskey.

"We all have our parts to play, Vanya." Her father's timbre dropped like he was chastising a child.

"I can play bigger," she said. "One day, you won't be able to kick me out of that seat, because it will be mine." Vanya didn't give her father a chance to reply. Instead, the door shut swiftly behind her.

Theo rolled his eyes and slowly lowered himself into the leather chair. "I'm afraid our previous business together has sparked the politician in her. She thinks she can do anything after taking down one little man."

"She did more than you," I told him. His expression hardened. "Vanya orchestrated the deal with Gavriel. Vanya infiltrated the Niners and got the names. You just reaped the benefits." Perhaps she did deserve to sit in that seat instead.

"Only because it would've been too suspicious for me to work with him directly." He motioned for Luther, who still stood near the wet bar, to sit. "But I didn't call you here to discuss the past, not when the future is more pressing."

I replied with a cynical smile. "I would love to discuss your plans for the city, Hartsong. Starting with what the fuck just happened in that cabinet." My grin fell. "Why did you not support my agenda like we discussed?"

He crossed his arms. "I told you—you could make an appeal to the OIC, but I never promised a decision in your favor."

I laughed at the nuance. "Is this how it's going to be? You're going to forget the ones who helped you get here all for a few votes? I'm disappointed in you, Theo. As are all the men and women sitting in squalor on the island."

"We need to wait until things calm down in the city. People are worried, Nicolai. Your family took over the steel business and now you control the Iron Saint. The Attanos are slowly taking over everything. The people of Lynchaven are afraid of you."

I balled my fist, my knuckles blanching. "Maybe they should be."

He looked at me like he didn't recognize the man who once worked for him.

"High Overseer." Luther leaned forward in his seat, taking his chance to speak after I had startled Theo into silence. "Did you receive the wine we sent over to congratulate you on your new seat?"

The question snapped his eyes wider, returning them to a bright green. "Why yes, Luther. That was very kind of your family. In fact, I do insist we open it now that we are all together to share the victory. Right, Nicolai?"

My smile was forced and tight across my face. "Wonderful idea."

While the Overseer stood to search for the bottle we'd gifted him last week, I asked, "Do you plan to maintain the blockade over the bridge?"

"For now, yes."

"Why?"

He popped open the cork before replying. "Why not? The Districts have been peaceful. Natives don't feel the need to leave home with dipped daggers or guns. The Square has seen more traffic now that the bridge has been blocked. Is there a reason the Row would need access to the Districts?"

"Besides the fact they have families here? Not everyone is afraid of remnants, Overseer. Honestly, there isn't a single reason you've mentioned that justifies keeping us separate. The Row runs off small businesses. Without the traffic you mentioned, they will fade and fall."

He sagged against the back of his chair. "The OIC will revisit the bridge next month when we meet again."

"Will we be invited, or will our invitation get lost across the river?"

Hartsong glared at me above the glass he poured, filling three crystal goblets with a generous amount of bubbly wine. "If you continue to cause anguish in my cabinet, you will not be asked to return. I will allow you to come back if you agree to leash some of your temper."

I raised the glass he offered me in the air in mock cheers. "To taming my temper and your fancy new seat, Theo."

He scoffed before taking a tasting sip. "What a strange concoction," he said. "The letter sent with this claimed it was a delicacy in your family, is that right?"

"My nonna has her favorites in the cellar." I smiled. "I have one more question for you, and then I will leave you be."

He took a deeper sip. "What is it, Nicolai?"

"Do you or anyone else in your *cabinet* plan to regulate the use of remnants more than the OIC already has? Beyond keeping us on one side of the city? Will you make it illegal for us to use our gifts in a way that helps us live and earn?"

He stared at me hard, leaving his face expressionless. "We would never seek to oppress descendants in such a way. We saw how that went on the Continent. It won't happen here."

Something like relief eased a weight off my shoulders—until the High Overseer choked on his words.

"*Saints*, excuse me, but I think I'm going to be sick." He set down his glass.

I set down my own without taking a single sip. I knew the stuff tasted foul. Had plenty of experience with Vex Veritas from my meddling grandmother, who took it upon herself to discipline her grandchildren. "We'll take our leave then, but I do hope you feel better, sir." I stood from the chair. "Come, Luther. We best return to our side of Lynchaven."

The Overseer did not see us out, and instead nursed the sickness spurned from his lie. This morning had been a failure on every front, and from what I learned, things would only get worse. We moved swiftly toward the carriages parked on the circle driveway in front of the manor.

"You're nothing, Attano." A voice stopped me in my tracks as a shadow stretched across the pavement.

I turned around, and Halloway loomed over me. "You can wear the nice suits and pretend you deserve to be in that room, but you will never belong here. No amount of money can change who you are—what you are. *Remnant rat.* If you dare come to this side of the city again, you'll find a different colored blade buried in your black heart."

"Niner blades are illegal, sir. Or did you not hear your Overseer's new decree?" I whispered.

"The Nine will rise again," he replied under his breath. "And when they do, they'll take this city back. Hartsong will either side with us or die with the rest of you."

I tilted my chin to stare up at him. Though he was a head taller and twice my weight, I made sure he realized who he threatened. Moments later, his cheeks paled. His chest convulsed as he struggled to gulp the air that I withheld from him. A delicious fear that satisfied some of my frustration glazed his eyes.

"Then I'll see you on the battlefield, Halloway. Bring your little blades. You'll need them."

I didn't release his breath until Luther and I were in the

carriage, though I swirled the air I originally took from his chest between my fingers. A vow like a ring around my finger, marrying me to a new cause.

"You know what needs to be done," I told Luther.

He nodded. Grim understanding drew the corners of his lips into a frown.

"Good. Make sure it's clear when you cross. I don't want any blood spilled today. Not yet."

When we reached the Main Station, I boarded the Iron Saint. Luther took the carriage to the Square, where the mouth of the bridge spilled into the business-lined streets. When the train set off and reached the viaduct crossing the River Ada, I stood and peered out the frosted window.

My family and the other descendants in this city didn't cross the Narrow Sea all those years ago just to face the same danger. We wouldn't be silenced, singled out, or sent away. This time, we would fight back when they came at our throats.

Three explosions blew apart the bridge connecting the Row and the Districts. The pieces of that connection and the threat of it fell into the Ada, swallowed by the deadly current.

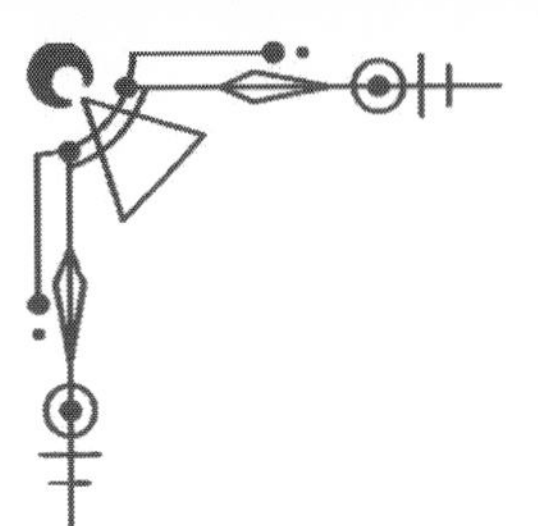
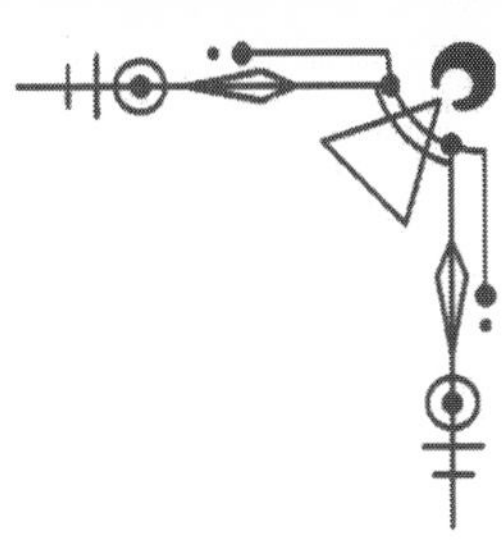

CHAPTER 2
CAMILLA

They chose blood this time.

My fingers, my toes, all the edges of my body had plunged in a frigid numbness. Exhaustion settled deep from the amount of blood they took when the alchemist had placed me under some kind of chemical spell. The effects of the drowsiness had worn off, and I could again sense the bone-deep cold of the cell floor and the bolts of pain triggered from the most minimal of movement.

They'd return soon. They always did after they drained something from me. At least it wasn't like the last round when they starved me for days. Left me with only sips of water sparingly until I could barely lift my head off the floor through the lethargy.

The floor trembled from a shift in the stone wall, and I braced myself for the coming of another session.

I didn't open my eyes to greet the guard, but the glare from the kerosine lamp burned anyway. The candle in my cell had long

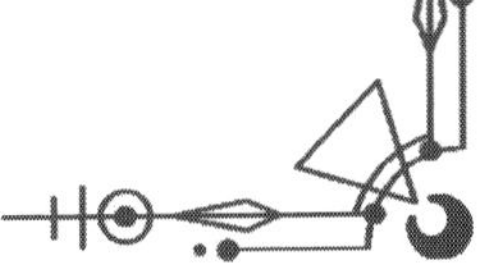

melted away, leaving me in darkness for the last several hours. Perhaps maybe even all day. Time passed differently in this place.

"Get up," a gruff voice ordered.

"I can't."

A steel toe nudged me sharply in the side, disturbing a broken rib. I winced at the lancing pain. "Then crawl."

I tried to lift my head from my threadbare cot on the floor and moaned. "Can't you drag me?"

Just rolling to my side to sit up was a tedious task, but the watchman made no move to help, regarding me rather like a sickly rodent to keep at arm's length.

"My orders are to never touch you."

"Unless it is to inflict pain or punishment," I spat. They touched me plenty when I didn't listen. Perhaps if I aggravated him enough, he'd concede and bring me upstairs, where the alchemist waited.

"You are an agent of Chaos," he muttered, as if it were a terrible secret. "Everything about you is dangerous."

"Chaos," I said with a dry laugh. Hadn't Nico always called me the same? He'd somehow known all along, had seen straight through me, even the parts of myself I ignored. Just the memory of him gave me a fraction of strength, enough to push off my cot and stand on trembling legs.

Part of me wanted to lay here until the end came. Wanted to concede to the taxing demands on my body, the pain pulling me under with every step. But hope was a stubborn force. Even the barest of it, the smallest chance of seeing Nico and my family again, flickered a dry flame awake in my heart. Perhaps that was all the fuel remaining that dragged each foot in front of the other.

"What's your name?" I asked. He was always the guard they sent to fetch and escort me. The whispered thud of his boots across the stone was his only reply. "You look like a Michael. I shall call you Mike." People were always less threatening when you knew their names, especially when they carried weapons of torture.

"Where are we going?" He didn't ascend the tower like usual. Instead, he gestured for me to take the hall that led outside.

"Delilah has something special planned today."

I could hear the smile in his voice, fluttering a fresh fear in my gut. At least I knew what to expect from the experiments. She'd take more blood, write strange symbols on my body, watch my mark bleed my veins black, just to suppress it with an injection. Delilah, the alchemist who'd somehow collected a startling framework of my concerning remnant, was keen to learn how to starve my power, but so far had been unsuccessful.

The hall was short, the way ahead shifting by the will of the watchman behind me. I still hadn't figured out how they controlled the stone without a remnant. Surely benders who moved the earth could manipulate this place—unless there were none here to test that theory. Maybe these watchmen were benders. Maybe they were traitors.

My time alone had given me lots of time to wonder about such things.

The sun had begun to set behind the prison as we emerged from the tower. Cool air, carrying salt from the sea, hit my face like a fond memory. It was the first time I'd been outside since I arrived here, the first I'd seen of anything besides the inside of my cell or the lab that had become some sort of sick reprieve. My eyes blinked at the sudden assault of light.

It wasn't raining, but there was a mist hazing the air, chilling my cheeks. Dew glazed the ground just as hard and cold as the floor of the tower. Algae and hardy plants that made their home in desolate environments such as this one covered either side of the walkway leading toward the main building in the distance.

He didn't lead me there, however. The watchman pointed to an open area between the tower and the main building, where a group of alchemists, guards, and Delilah waited.

Her demeanor since our first exchange had cooled. Our relationship shifted to one of scientist and specimen. I was nothing more than a creature to dissect—like all the others she locked in her alchemy tower. Instead of the lead smock she always wore during experiments, she sported a heavy cloak that seemed warm, considering the coloring of her cheeks. Her bloodred hair was covered with a cowl, but her hands still wore the same leather gloves. The ones laced with glint. The ones that burned when they touched me.

She carried a book tucked beneath her arm. Always carried that book.

We came to a large, circular platform smoothed into the jagged earth. Nine alchemists and a single alchemedis—my designated healer—stood in a line with Delilah between them. I wasn't the only guest, however. Another prisoner, obvious by his matching uniform to mine, stood on the other side of the circle.

"How is she?" Delilah asked my guard.

"Weak enough." The watchman nudged my spine with the hilt of his weapon, knocking me off-balance with the gentle probe. My knees cracked against cold obsidian, and I braced my hands in front of me so my face wouldn't suffer the same fate.

"We shall see." She cast a withering glance at me before barking an order at the alchemists. "Give her the salve and draw the barrier."

The watchman nudged me past a painted line drawn around the rim of the platform. Her associates scattered, each dipping their fingers into a pouch tied around their belts that stained them dark red. They drew something on the ground outside the circle.

"What are you doing?" I asked, my voice fighting against the wind.

Delilah stared into the bleak horizon with her hands clasped behind her back. "We have failed to suppress your power. It is not in your body, by the way it was triggered after we starved you of energy. It is not in your mind, as it was still provoked when we put you in a chemical sleep. And it is not in your blood, as we have already tested it for magical properties. And before you ask, no. It is not *your* blood we are using to create the barrier, as your remnant isn't found there."

"A Blood remnant's then?" I asked.

She nodded. "A descendant of Blood keeps their power in the same, which is why they become stronger when they drink it, enriching their own. Due to the magical property of their blood, we can use it for our own purposes."

Delilah loved to talk about her research, and I let her indulge me as often as possible. She was an expert in all kinds of magic, and she wanted to study my remnant almost as much as I did. Each experience as her lab rat allowed me to understand my remnant more exhaustively, and if I could somehow use it to save myself, then I'd let her reveal all the secrets Chaos hid within her dark magic.

"To find where your remnant is stored," she continued, "we need to see what it can do. There are no records of a Chaos remnant in history other than the record of Chaos fighting with her demon army in the First War. I'm curious how this power expresses itself in remnant form, if it is as powerful as Chaos herself. I have arranged three trials which should help us learn your limits, your source, and where it's hiding."

"Where is what hiding?"

The alchemist sealed her lips, refusing the information.

Her alchemedis approached with a jar in her gloved hands. "Don't move," she ordered. "I'm going to put this salve on your arm to annul the effects of the glint. If you harm me, you will be severely punished."

My eyes darted from the jar in her hands to Mike, unsure I trusted anything she put on my body. When I didn't cooperate quickly enough, the watchman snatched my wrist and shoulder with both his hands, burning my entire arm with the poison-rubbed leather.

My dirty skin quickly absorbed the cream she spread along my forearm, and as promised, my remnant flooded my spine with the warmth of its return. It filled my heart, racing my pulse with the surge of it all rushing in at once now that the door holding it back had been opened.

The pair quickly retreated over the line as I struggled to put a cap on the power seeking to escape. I needed to resist the mayhem in my veins and calm down—needed a source of distraction.

The man slouched on the opposite side of the circle stood motionless, his canvas clothes whipping in the breeze. The platform itself was large. Far enough, he couldn't possibly hear what we said as the wind carried our words in the opposite direction.

I asked Delilah, "Why is he here?"

Her smile was the most terrifying sight on the island—usually because it preceded something terrible.

"He is your first test. Today, we will see how you work as a weapon." She glanced at the descendant. "I offered him a deal. If he killed you, he could leave the island."

Her words carved me hollow, filling me with a fresh fear. She'd offered him his freedom. "And he . . . agreed?"

Delilah took several steps back until she was on the opposite side of the line. "He is a powerful Mirth descendant, Camilla. You are too weak now to physically fight him. You'll have to use your remnant if you wish to come out of this alive."

Every muscle lining my bones trembled violently in the damp wind. "I don't believe you'd let me die. Not after everything you went through to take me."

Her smile fell. "When the mortal spirit gets close to death, instinct takes over. I won't have to intercede before your remnant lashes out to protect you."

I clenched my teeth. "We'll see about that."

I had no intentions on hurting this man. If he realized that, he might have mercy on me as well. They couldn't do anything if we both made the choice to surrender. But with a prize as glittering and alluring as freedom in sight, could he see through her lies?

The last alchemist stepped away from her place on the line, finishing the final symbol. A milky blue glow lifted from the runes as static charged the air, lifting the hair on my arms as an iridescent wall wrapped the space around the platform, doming above to seal us within.

I'd never seen such magic made from blood and markings, and the idea of such a possibility unnerved me. What else could they do beyond creating more barriers between us?

"The boundary will burn you if you try to cross it. Only one of you will walk out of this circle, and only you will determine which." Delilah spoke loudly so the Mirth descendant would hear.

"She's lying!" I shouted. "We don't have to do this." Pushing slowly to my feet, I started toward him. "We have to show them they don't have power over us."

"Stop!" he warned. "Don't come any closer."

"It's alright." I lifted my hands in a show of surrender. "I don't—"

He attacked without warning. Though he hadn't moved a muscle, his remnant slipped into my mind, and suddenly I was no longer in control of my body. My feet halted, knees buckled from beneath me. I had only a heartbeat to be afraid before he canted his neck and snapped the joints.

He was a scolapa. A thought controller. And I'd just given him access to the greatest weapon in his arsenal.

My knees twisted, disobeying the rest of my body, and bending them so much the bones popped from the joints. I crashed onto the platform. Pain unlike anything I'd ever felt before consumed me. It shot through my legs, my spine, spreading until agony was so intimate, I knew nothing else. My voice was free to scream as my veins were burnished with fire—a fire I fought to suppress.

Tears swarmed my vision as I peered up at him.

"Please stop," I begged through gasping breaths. "I don't want to hurt you."

He responded by arching my back, bowing my spine until each notch of bone pressed together and the pressure threatened to split me in half.

"He's been here a long time, Camilla. His freedom is more important than anything." Delilah's voice was near, finding me through the ringing in my ears. "More than food to survive, more than air to breathe, more than goodness to live."

My hands clawed to gain purchase; the dark venom of my power had already spilled into my fingernails.

"He is not a man anymore. There is nothing you can say that will appeal to a heart the prison dredged from him. He will snap you in half if it means getting what he wants above all else. His humanity no longer controls him—he belongs to Greed."

Crack.

There wasn't much flexibility left in my spine. From my contortion on the stone platform, I stared at the descendant, whose stare was narrowed on me. Nothing existed in those dark eyes that resembled any kind of recognition of what he was inflicting. His image blurred as fresh tears brimmed my vision.

"Don't you want to know what you can do, Camilla? Isn't it time you explore your gifts in a safe, *controlled* environment?" Delilah coaxed me, stroking my power with her persuasive words.

But safe was the last word I'd use to describe anything on this island. I didn't want to find out what my remnant could do—not like this at least. Not at this man's expense. Though, the twist of my spine gave me little choice on the matter. He wanted his freedom—but so did I.

No one was coming for me. No one knew I was here.

The problem I faced concerned the uncertainty. I didn't know how to control my remnant. Whatever lashed out could hurt, kill, or annihilate. I reduced a man to vapor just a few weeks ago, and the bloody mist of his essence coated my hands every day.

Crack.

White-hot pain seared through my vision, and the world disappeared. The prison, Delilah, the other alchemists. It was just me and this agony, and the need to make it stop.

Anger swelled, overflowed inside me like a poison that tainted every drop of my blood. The Mirth descendant let go of my thoughts—or maybe I shoved him out. All I knew was that I could control my body, the parts left unbroken.

I rolled to my front and stared him down, blinking until my vision cleared and sharpened and dried of tears. My hands went black, flooded with inky darkness, and all at once my fury slammed open the door holding back my power. For the first time in weeks, there was no drug, no hesitation, no moral holding it back.

The rush of Chaos nearly pulled me out of my skin when I let it loose. Like I'd drilled a hole in a dam, not expecting the whole river to break through.

Thin black flames burst from my palms, crossing the floor and filling the circle in a sea of shadows that curled and flickered in the breeze slapping the island. The descendant took a step back, halted by the invisible barrier that somehow contained our remnants.

"Fire from Oblivion," Delilah whispered, something like awe in her voice.

He made a panicked sound as his unyielding composure cracked—but set his sights on me again. My flames reached his feet and lapped at his legs. His chest rose and fell in a rapid fluctuation, realizing his error too late.

I felt the push of his compulsion, the sharp turn of my neck as he tried to snap it.

"Stop it," I growled in a voice that didn't belong to me. This one too deep, too angry—a piece of thunder in a summer storm.

He didn't listen, but instead responded with the full force of his remnant to wrap my mind and squeeze. My wrist pressed and twisted against the floor, breaking with a loud pop. I cried out, my scream rolled from my chest and trembled the stone beneath me. The obsidian stone shattered, cracks spread through the polished platform like a web of fractures.

My arm pulsed with sharp, stabbing aches. I sucked a breath to tame the pain, a large inhale followed by a rushed exhale. The wind inside the barrier was unlike the gentle breeze outside. This wind—this storm—didn't come from the sea.

It came from my wrath.

My fire danced in the turbulence, shards of rock peeled in

treacherously sharp shards from the ground and were thrown into a cyclone of my mayhem. The descendant cowered, blinded by shadowed flames and upturned stone. His fear leashed some of the rage in my heart, appealing to the one still racing erratically against my ribs. My breath slowed as the anger shifted into shame, and the storm died with my fight.

The Mirth descendant peered up at me through the gaps of his arms that he used to shield his face, like a child facing a monster. And in that single connection of our eyes, his remnant slipped into my thoughts once more. This time, however, unexpectedly.

"What are you?" he asked through a mental bond.

Remorse splintered through my chest. *I don't know.*

His arms slacked at his sides. "I don't take pride in this, but I need my freedom. I have a daughter . . ." The image of a girl I recognized too well flashed in my mind, placed there by this man's memory. She was young, a mere child, but it was so obviously her.

Sera.

His face paled. "You know her?"

I choked back a sob and nodded. *She's my friend.*

I brought my memory of Sera to the surface of my thoughts. A recent one, so he could see the woman she grew to become. Surely, he would abandon this fight if he understood what his daughter meant to me—and I to her.

She'd been looking for him, and he'd been here. Why was he here?

The descendant was locked there, staring at me. His eyes focused on something beyond the perceptible planes of this world. "*Saints and stars*. She's so beautiful."

"Do you realize now who I put you up against, Camilla?" Delilah crouched near the barrier line so only I could hear.

The realization hit me all at once, recalling what I knew about

Sera and her father. What happened to him. This pairing had been intentional. My choice now would be more painful than any displaced or broken bone.

"Your father put his trust in the wrong people," Delilah said. "I asked my family in the city to figure out why the Marcheses would give one of his children a familiar, and they figured out the rest. With the help of the inspector, they discovered Marco Gallo and brought him here, where we too easily made him show us the memories he took from you."

I shook my head. It didn't matter. I was not his to protect. It had been my fault any of that happened, and now I could add Gallo's capture and imprisonment to a long list of consequences.

"It was him, Camilla. He betrayed your family, the reason your father is dead, why your brother is dead, and how I found you. You were your parents' best kept-secret, and he betrayed their trust." Delilah continued to dig her nails into my heart a little deeper. "That descendant is the cause for all the pain in your life, and now you have the chance to tear him apart like he did your entire life. You *deserve* this."

"No. No, it wasn't his fault," I murmured. Not to Delilah, but to myself. He'd only done what he thought he needed to protect his daughter. I tucked my broken wrist to my chest and flipped to my back, surrendering the fight.

"Finish her!" Delilah roared, at last realizing she wouldn't get to me. "What are you doing?"

I rolled my head to the side to look at him. His throat bobbed. "I'm sorry. I'll make this quick."

"*No*," I said. "No, please. Don't do this."

He froze my body into place and slowly strode to where I was sprawled across the broken platform. Broad hands braced either side of my face.

"I'm sorry," he whispered again.

His remnant slipped, having me just a neck-snap away from death. My life in his hands.

I snatched his forearm. "Me too."

The darkness from my hands seeped into his wrist. His skin rolled back, molting from his flesh where my touch connected us. Layer by layer. Skin, fat, muscle, tendon. His body stripped itself until there was only bone caressing my cheeks and the echo of his scream beating against the magic barrier, until even his skeleton eventually turned to dust like the rest of him. Nothing was left behind of Sera's father besides a red vapor that smelled distinctly like blood.

There was no controlling Chaos. It defiled anything it touched. Even now, as my disgrace festered, as it rose in my chest like the tide in a storm, so did the violence of the wind return within the barrier as it tore at my threadbare uniform. Closer than a kiss, slipping beneath my skin until its corruption stained my heart.

My eyes squeezed shut, and I clutched my broken wrist against the wall of my chest as bitter tears streamed down my cheeks. Sera would never forgive me. I'd killed her father. And for what? What had any of this accomplished? Had it fed something in Delilah's unsatiated curiosity?

Footsteps charged through the barrier. The watchmen carried shields coated with a glint mixture to buffer themselves against my power. One alchemist had followed close behind, a syringe in her hand. If she thought I'd fight her, she was wrong. I didn't want to feel this power any more than they wished me to have it.

I resented the remnant I carried, the mark on my back, and the day I ever let myself dream of becoming more than just a spoiled little heiress with a pretty train.

I had flipped sides. From being limited to knowing no limits.

Being powerless to having too much. What I'd give to be less than everyone again. What I'd trade to be not enough.

No one knew I was here. No one was coming for me.

I looked at the red vapor soaking the stone. Perhaps that was for the best.

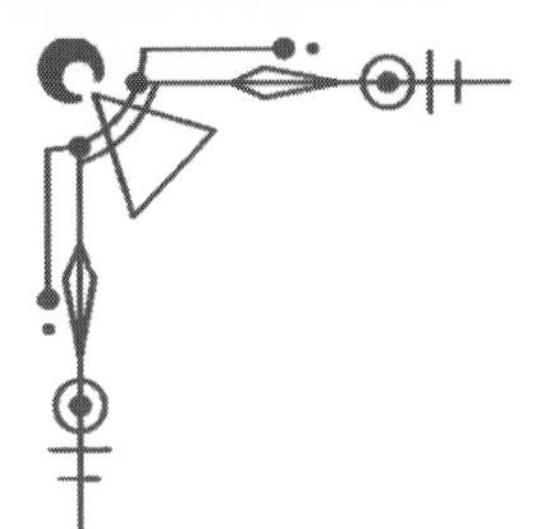
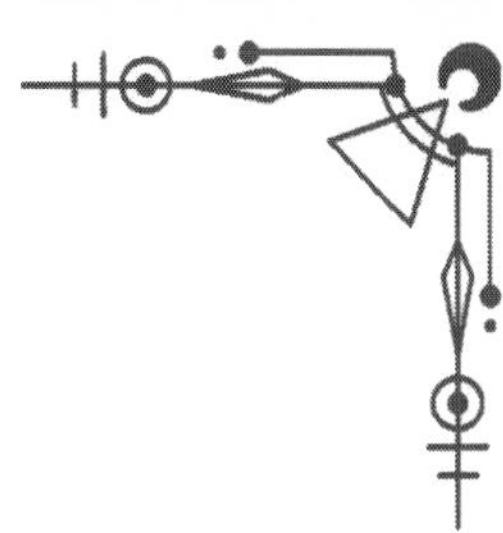

CHAPTER 3
NICOLAI

No sooner had my driver pulled the carriage down the side driveway than a loud bang came from behind the house. A line of smoke followed soon after, trailing from Esmerelsa's garage.

"Esme?" I called.

The all brick, two-story building at the far end of the gardens remained still, the origin of the smoke hidden from my view having only a side perspective of her workhouse. I sprinted around the frozen fountain to check on her.

"*Put that damn thing out!*" Esme's shrill voice scolded someone inside.

Relief eased some of the urgency in my strides, though her tone only doubled my concern—my cousin *never* shouted.

As I entered the garage, I found the Marchese brothers pointing between themselves and the overstimulated version of my cousin tending to a fiery mess on the opposite end of the room.

"What the hells is going on here?" I said to announce myself,

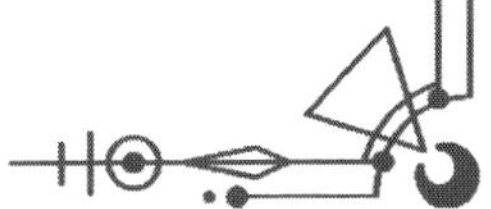

hastening between two aisles of various scrap metal—careful not to get the grease on my suit.

Aramis snapped his head at me, face glistening with a sheen of sweat and dust powdering one of his cheeks. "I have done nothing. It was him!"

"*Me*?" Jeremiah asked incredulously. The tips of his pale hair sizzled at frayed ends. "You're the one who ran into me! While I was holding an open *flame*."

"Would both of you just shut up? I don't understand why you were walking around with fire at all!" Esme shrieked. "Nico, would you help me put this out?" She gestured to a pile of scorched metal sitting on top of a welding bench. Gold and orange flames spilled from the twisted metal, billowing smoke through a cracked window.

Cupping my hands with my palms facing the floor, I sealed the burning structure by starving the fire. With no air to fuel them, the flames gradually receded, leaving nothing besides the steady drip of an oily liquid to the sullied floor. Esme quickly grabbed a drip pan to catch the mess.

"Do you always have to do the hand gestures?" Aramis asked, copying the motion.

"What?" My voice rose a pitch higher. "I—No, I don't have to do anything, it's just easier. Esme are you alright?"

My cousin yanked her welding goggles down off her face and gave me a look I understood too well.

Get them out of here.

"I'm fine. I'm just trying to work on recreating the sketches Aramis provided me of the ship engine. If I can replicate the design on a smaller scale, we could use it for all sorts of things. Unfortunately, *someone* who will remain nameless lit his cigarillo and caught my work on fire." She rubbed her eyes with the back of her gloves. "And now, I must start all over."

"It wasn't my fault," Jeremiah grumbled.

"To be fair, I *did* say no smoking in the garage."

Aramis nudged him. "She did mention it, Jer."

Her face forced a stiff smile. She pulled her leather gloves from her small hands and tossed them on a nearby table. "I think now would be a good time to take a break."

Good timing, indeed. "Meet me in the kitchen when you're ready. I have some things I'd like to discuss with the family."

Aramis quirked a brow. "Just the family?"

Family of Camilla was by law and by custom now family of mine—no matter my detached feelings on the association.

"Like it or not, Marchese, that includes you now." I glanced between them. "Clean yourselves up first. Nonna will beat your knuckles bloody if you dredge this filth into her kitchen."

Aramis looked down at his clothes, as if just realizing he was covered in fine grey dust. His black shirt sleeves were pulled up around his forearms. His hair was natural, wavy around his ears without any wax to comb it back as he usually styled it. Jeremiah was dressed similarly. Though he was a head shorter than his older brother and thin as a reed.

Esme tossed one of them a clean rag. "Get out of here, cousin. Saints forbid you get that pretty suit dirty." She winked to indicate her jest. I gave her the beginning of a smile, unable to offer anything more than that, before turning from the lot of them to head inside.

Winter had turned on the city with a vengeance. Small flakes of snow floated from a grey sky, covering the dormant garden with a thin layer of white. I shoved my gloved hands deeper into my coat pockets, enjoying the way the icy breeze nipped at my face, and burned the inside of my chest as I held down a large breath.

The sudden drop in temperature had been abrupt, and I wondered if it had reached the south tip of the Isle. Hightower was always cold from the sea and the stone it was built from. Winter was a different kind of brutal. I had hoped to have Milla back long before the first snow. The weather only insisted on how little progress I'd made of her rescue, and how much her absence was killing me—like the roses that had withered from the frost, leaving only brittle, thorny flesh behind.

Nonna and the aunts prepared dinner in the kitchen as I entered through the swinging doors. Luther hadn't returned yet, and a small part of me worried he had run into trouble taking down the bridge. Esme had weakened the metal infrastructure when relations between the OIC and the Row had broken down. With the rise of the new leadership, I wanted to make sure the descendants of Lynchaven were protected—even if I had played a part in showing that leadership to their seats.

"Nicolai." Nonna turned from her place by the stove to look me over. "You look like shit. When's the last time you've had a full night's sleep?"

A long damn time. Too much kept my mind awake. Too many troubles demanded to be worked out in the quiet hours of the morning.

"Do you think Milla has slept since she was taken?"

None of them spoke a word. My grandmother's gaze fell to the simmering pot she watched over.

"No," I answered for them. "I will rest when Milla can rest." And not a moment sooner. The Attanos were the only people who knew she was alive. The Marchese sons hadn't left the estate, remaining hidden within our walls in case the Firenzes gained word of their survival.

Luther finally appeared a minute later, shattering the awkward silence with a wild look on his face and Gideon beaming behind him. Adler joined a second later, snuffing out his cigarillo before Nonna snapped at him.

"Oh, *saints*. You three look too happy. What did you boys do now?" Fran asked, not bothering to hide her wince.

"*Blew up the fucking bridge*!" a voice shouted from the depth of the hall. Dread pooled in my stomach. I had little energy left to direct towards dealing with my uncle.

Lucinda and Ianthe regarded Luther like he'd just committed the crime of the century. They knew their son had killed men—and yet *this* crossed their moral white line? He blew them both a kiss before stealing a roll from Nonna's serving board. Carnage always gave him an appetite.

"Gideon," Fran barely whispered. "What is your father talking about?"

My cousin grinned and sat on a stool around the kitchen island. "For once, Mother, I had nothing to do with it. Adler and I were just the getaway car. Your daughter, on the other hand—"

"Don't blame this on me!" Esme's voice carried from the hall just as my uncle rolled in, his face flushed as his attention fell to me. Despite the accusations being thrown around the room, he knew this had been my doing. His anger was reserved only for me, as always.

"You did half the work!" Luther said.

"I only weakened the foundation enough so your bombs would be effective."

"They were very effective," Gideon chimed. "Luther blew up the whole thing in less than thirty seconds."

Luther smiled, his chin high. "And fucking beautiful, it was."

The Marchese sons lingered near the doorway, sensing they weren't quite family enough to get in the middle of our squabble.

Solomon rubbed his temples. "I cannot believe you all are being so careless about something like this. The bridge, Nico? Do you understand what you've done?"

"Yes." I leaned a hip against the edge of the kitchen cabinets. "Do *you*?"

A muscle tensed in his jaw. He braced his bare hands on the counter and took a bracing breath. "Apparently not. Please enlighten us all on why you would destroy the one thing that connects us to the Districts? Why have you threatened the peace between our sides?"

My gaze rolled over the rest of my family, who seemed just as intent on learning my motivations. I hadn't shared my plans with them, not that I needed their permission. I was head of Attano Steel, head of this family—besides Nonna—and the only one who had stepped up after my father died. Solomon didn't have to approve of my choices, but he'd have to accept them.

"The peace between our sides is an illusion. The OIC has no intentions to protect descendants. They refused to look into the conditions at Hightower, they dismissed the idea of releasing the prisoners, and they believe I killed the entire Marchese family and attempted to murder Felix Firenze as well."

"To be fair, they aren't completely wrong," Aramis murmured to his brother.

I shot him a glare but continued despite his interruption. "Later, after the meeting, I met personally with Hartsong where he lied to my face. He promised he wouldn't repeat what the kings on the Continent did to the descendants there. And you know what, Sol?" I leaned forward, looking him dead in the eyes. "He fucking choked on those words thanks to a little celebratory Vex Veritas we sipped on together."

"You drugged the High Overseer?" Solomon's voice rose a pitch higher, gripping the edge of the counter.

"I don't trust politicians, and he proved why I shouldn't." I pointed toward Nonna. "My grandparents and countless others crossed the sea in search of a safe place to be who they are. I will not have a few power-hungry bastards like Halloway and Hartsong and Neal fucking Caldwell subjugate anyone in this city—or this Isle."

"Nicolai." Nonna's voice was far gentler than I'd heard it in a long time. Not since I was a child. "Your heart, as always, is in a good place. But you do not have to fight everyone's battles. Not when you are already fighting one yourself."

I didn't tear my eyes away from my uncle, but I felt my grandmother's bony hand slip into mine. Her support stole some of the tension in my shoulders, letting them relax.

Solomon smoothed his face with a hand. "This is about Camilla, isn't it, Nico?"

"It is *always* about Camilla," I spat, hating the way her name always shook in my voice. "I did what you requested, Uncle. I tried to get her back the legitimate way, but because of who I am, none of them would even consider opening Hightower. When I get her back, when she returns home, it *will* be to a city where she is safe."

"What if we just expose ourselves?" Aramis spoke this time. "If the OIC sees we are alive, if we voice our support of your endeavors, perhaps they'd be willing to move forward."

I thought it over, but the same problem remained. "If the OIC finds out you are alive, there will be questions. Not to mention, the Firenzes have been silent since the train incident. They have influence and friendships with powerful people in the OIC, and if they want to take you down, they will find a way. As Milla's only remaining family, I will not let harm befall either of you. Stay dead to the world, and you'll be alive when it truly matters."

"We have to do more than just sit here, Attano!" Aramis argued. "My sister is a Remni. She's not just a descendant who's received a remnant from a Saint passed down for two hundred years. She's the *first* descendant of Chaos, which means she could be incredibly powerful. Do you have any idea what they must be doing to her?"

"Yes," Luther whispered, staring at his shoes.

Aramis glanced at him, something like regret squinting his eyes. "All I'm saying is that I don't mind risking my neck to get her out of there. As you said, we don't have much family left. I'll do whatever it takes to get my sister back."

He made a point I hadn't taken the time to consider. I was hardly the only one in this room who cared for Milla. I might have been at war, but I had a willing army to fight with me.

"We'll make negotiations with the OIC when the time comes. Another bridge can be built, but freedom is not so easily reestablished once it's taken." I looked at Fran, who was informally positioned as our social director. "That brings me to my next topic of discussion."

"How kind of you to include us this time," Solomon grumbled before pushing off the counter.

Ignoring him, I cleared my throat and said, "I want to assemble our own court. If descendants want any kind of influence concerning the future of Lynchaven, we need a seat at the table. We need representation. The OIC was shocked to see a remnant among their cabinet, but it needs to be commonplace. To do this, we need to have a remnant from each saint. A speaker, a leader, whatever the hells they want to call it. I want to meet with them and discuss what's coming."

"What are you talking about?" my uncle asked. "What's coming, Nico?"

"The war they asked for." I looked him in the eyes as I spoke. "I'm going to free every descendant in Hightower, and when we're done, we'll make this city a place where we can all thrive again."

"I hope you know what you're getting us all into, Nicolai," he said with a drawn-out sigh.

I hadn't a clue. Whatever happened next was out of my hands, but I'd be damned before I handed Milla's fate, and all the rest locked in that prison, into the spineless possession of Theo Hartsong. Without answering him, I pushed away from the kitchen and started toward the door.

"Where are you going, Nicky? Dinner's almost finished," Nonna asked before I could reach the door.

"Just going out for a bit. I won't be long."

Her lips puckered, and yet she leashed the words I knew hung on the tip of her violent tongue. Since Milla had been taken, some of the fight in my grandmother had gone with her. Nonna was fading, and like all the rest of the trouble in my life, I was powerless to stop it. The old woman seemed to have aged several years in the span of a month. Shadows clung to her eyes, a weariness in their grey gaze I'd never seen in them before.

The weather was twice as miserable when I exited out the side gate. The cold was a searing reminder that everything had its season and its turn, its life before death. And nothing—and no one—lasted forever.

THE IRON SAINT parked idle at the Industrial Station. Marcus, the Depot Master, was finishing up his books when I stepped into the small office overlooking the platform.

"Mr. Attano." He pulled his spectacles from his cheerful face. He always wore a smile, no matter the mood I met him with. "What brings you in so late?"

I sat in a chair in front of his desk. "What keeps you here so late? I'm surprised I caught you."

"Ahh." He waved a hand over the stacks of folders filling his workspace. "Just some housekeeping. Winter is hard on the supply. The snow shuts everything down and causes a mess for the schedules. Nothing you need to be concerned about, I assure you."

"I have full faith you could run this company better than me, Marcus." I pulled two letters from the inner pocket of my coat, turning them over in my hand. "Did the rest of the staff take the train home across the river?"

He nodded somewhat slowly, confirming my suspicions. The previous staff, all of whom were natives, had agreed to sign new contracts recognizing me as their boss, but that had been before this business with the bridge.

I sighed and sat back in the narrow, leather tufted chair. "When they arrive for work tomorrow, I want you to make me a list of everyone who wishes to seek employment elsewhere. I won't hold it against anyone who does not wish to get involved in the newly disturbed relations between the Row and the Districts. Attano and Associates will offer a twelve-week salary to cover any losses while they are searching for a new job—"

"Mr. Attano, if I may—"

"No, Marcus." I cleared my throat. "You repeat those words exactly to everyone employed. The same coverage is offered to you as well, though I'd hate to lose you."

The man smiled and passed a hand through dark hair peppered with grey. "I'm not going anywhere. I've been working for the Iron Saint since I was sixteen. It was my first job, and it will be my last if I can help it."

"Good." I nodded. Hopefully, the others would follow his lead then. "I have one more thing to ask of you, Marcus. You can decline, of course, but I'll pay you well for your trouble."

He scoffed. "I have no doubts about that."

He took the envelopes I offered out to him as I explained. "The black goes to the Overseer's mansion, explaining the terms of the bridge. The gold should be taken to the Vasilli Hotel. Show them the seal in the wax and they'll know exactly where to put it. The white is for you, as it contains your compensation."

He tossed the white envelope in a desk drawer, locking it shut. "Easy enough to remember. I'm not passing along anything dangerous, am I?"

"If you're asking if you'll get arrested, probably not." He shot me a look of concern that pulled a laugh from me. Brief and obnoxious in the small space, but a laugh, nonetheless. I didn't know when I'd last made the sound. "I'm kidding. Neither of these messages contains anything illegal. I can't send my own men, or they *would* be arrested."

He covered his yawn with his hand and nodded. "I suppose I could make a few stops before I head home tonight. Thank you for the opportunity. I'll get it done for you."

"Thank you, Marcus. Have a good evening."

I made to stand, but the train manager beckoned me to stop, holding the black envelope up in question. "If you don't mind me asking, how do you plan on fighting the OIC? You are a powerful man, Mr. Attano, but the combined influences of the Overseer and his board are too great for any one man to stand against himself."

A satisfied smile curled across my face. "The Iron Saint is the main transportation system for every good and service on this Isle. If they don't want their people to starve, their businesses to go under, or their resources to run out, they'll comply with what we want."

"And what is that?"

"Protection." I turned to leave him still sitting at his desk in the golden light of the gas lamp. "Money runs the world, Marcus. Remember that."

"Money might control the world, Mr. Attano, but do you know what I think?"

My steps paused. His perspective was interesting enough to listen a moment longer. "What do you think?"

"Love and kindness and loyalty." His voice went soft. "The things you cannot control, that cannot be bought, stolen, or negotiated, are the most powerful forces in this world. Over power, position, or money, love will win every time."

With my back still turned to him, I swallowed a thick knot in my throat. "I hope you're right, Marcus."

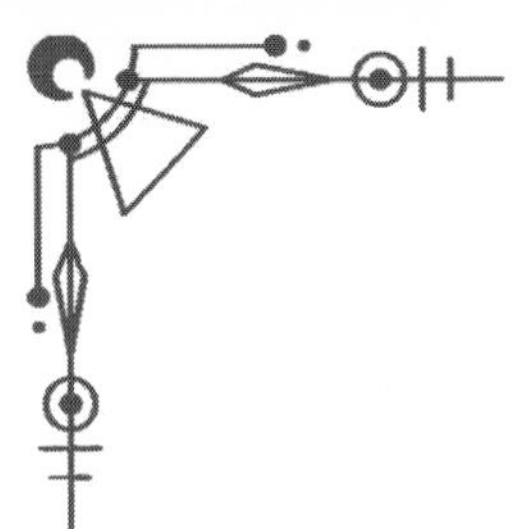
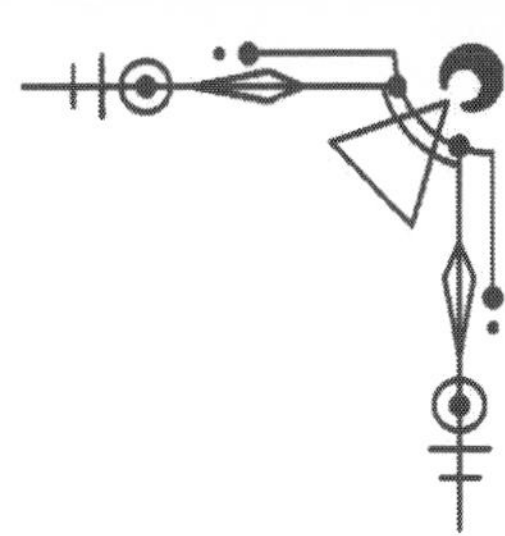

CHAPTER 4
CAMILLA

The tower was silent when Mike halfheartedly carried me back to my cell. I would have laughed at the irony that he had carried me anyway despite his initial refusal, but my head still swam in whatever the alchemedis injected in my veins. At some point, she tired of listening to my screams and sedated me from my suffering.

She reset my bones and taped my wrist straight. I vaguely remember choking on something they'd poured down my throat, and the muttered words, "*to speed up her healing*." Whatever it was, the effects hadn't worked yet. My body felt like I had been trampled by a racetrack worth of cruegers.

Mike laid me on my cot with surprising gentleness and left without a word. The stone slid shut behind him, stealing the light with his leave.

I slept for an intangible amount of time, until the drowsiness wore off.

"Milla?" My name slipped from the darkness, startling me awake.

"I'm still alive," I groaned. "I think."

"What did she do this time?" A deeper voice joined our conversation. "We heard them take you through the hall."

Vesper and Callow had been in the cells beside mine since the day I was thrown in here. At first, their voices seemed close enough that we shared the same cell. But I learned the pair were dark-thieves, and although their remnants were dulled by the glint, the shadows still carried their voice through the stone, enough so I had someone to talk to when the dark became a malevolent form of company.

"I don't . . ." I choked, recalling Marco's face when I grabbed him, when I flayed him into dust with a single touch. "I don't want to talk about what we did."

"That's alright," Callow said. "Let's talk about something else."

I curled my knees into my chest, wincing at the movement. "Have either of you been taken since I arrived?"

"No," Vesper replied, though she didn't sound proud about it. "Delilah has apparently lost interest in us."

My eyes stung, withholding the tears this place didn't deserve to take. "Did you ever go through . . . trials?"

"We went through experiments, but never trials." Callow answered this time. "She tried to bind my power to a watchman once. Ended up killing him, I think."

"Good riddance," Vesper hissed.

"Milla," Callow said slowly. "You've never told us, and we never asked after the first time, but—"

"You want to know what my remnant is?"

A pregnant paused filled his reply.

I sighed, wincing as each rib poked a sore place in my chest wall. If none of us were getting out of here, did it truly matter if I shared my secrets or died with them?

"Promise not to tell anyone?" I jested.

He snorted. "I dunno, me and Vesper are pretty popular here."

I smiled, though no one could see it. It was foolish, finding companionship in a voice. Trusting someone I'd never seen before, solely from the words passed between walls. They'd talked me through the panic spells, the recovery from Delilah's tests, the homesickness. I told them about Nico and my brothers, how I watched Giles die that day I was taken. They always listened and had something kind to say to put a bandage over the wounds in my heart.

And soon, they'd probably be dead. Just like the rest of the descendants who came to the tower. Just as I would, and I wanted someone to know who I was, even if this secret didn't survive beyond us.

"Chaos. I'm a remnant of Chaos."

Neither of them replied.

"Callow?"

Silence.

"Vesper?"

Nothing.

They didn't speak to me the rest of the evening, or the days that followed. Though, I was certain I heard their shadows crawl over my head and whisper between each other.

No one was coming for me.

No one knew I was here.

And now, even those that did wanted nothing to do with me. I longed for the next trial, if only to escape this empty darkness and the silence it carried.

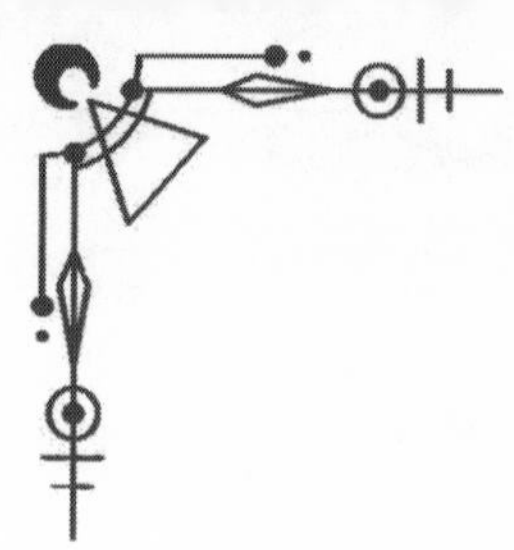
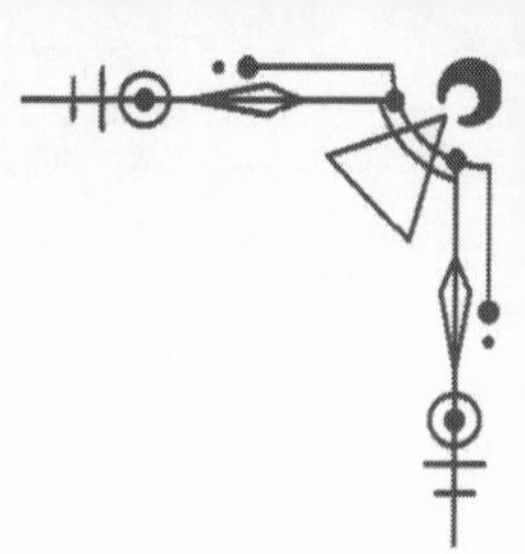

CHAPTER 5

NICOLAI

"They're waiting in the parlor."

Fran found me in the office down the hall from my bedroom. She had quickly gathered the right people—the right remnants—in less than a day. A task only my aunt and her extensive social contacts could have completed so efficiently.

"How did they feel?" I asked.

"Anxious." She rubbed the backs of her arms. "You could hear a pin drop in the room. I suggest you get downstairs before Sabina takes control of your meeting."

Naturally, the queen herself would show up in place of her sector and the Blood descendants. I folded a letter that had just arrived and hid it inside the pages of a book, throwing them both in a drawer for safekeeping. "Let's get this done, then."

"Nicky?"

"What?"

She licked her lips. "Sol asked to attend the meeting."

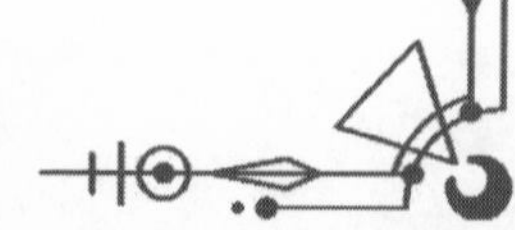

I almost laughed. "Of course he did."

"He's looking out for you."

"He doesn't trust me."

"You know that isn't true. He respects your decisions." She took a step closer, biting her lip. "He's just worried about your head. He doesn't want you making the wrong choice for the city just to—" She winced, knowing better than to finish.

"Just to save one woman." I arched a brow, but my aunt looked away.

"He doesn't want you do something you'll regret. A broken heart doesn't make wise judgements."

My head pounded between my temples. How many times had we had this same conversation with different words? I leaned over the desk, avoiding her stare. "I won't tell him where he's allowed to go in his own house, Fran. But eventually, he'll have to learn that I am not my father, and he cannot fix the past by compensating now for his previous silence."

He lived with the blame of my father's death. Sol had a feeling that derailing the train would be a bad idea, and yet he didn't stop my father. Afterward, he had to watch what became of holding his tongue. Not that it was his fault, nor had I ever accused him, but I knew well how the past liked to influence the present, and Solomon didn't want me to make a decision based on emotion. It was in my blood to be my undoing.

She started toward the hall but paused in the doorway. "Your father would be so proud of who you've become, Nicolai, but he would have never wanted you to take on the world without your family. We will do anything to help you get Milla back. So please, stop seeing your uncle and the rest of us as enemies when we're just trying to look out for you."

I waited until her footsteps were further down the hall before following her out, neglecting the guilty seed she planted until it shriveled dry.

THE PARLOR WAS STILL quiet as I entered, my uncle on my heels. Sabina took over the chaise, lounging on a hip with an amused look on her face, a glass of what appeared to be wine in her hand—though I had a strong inclination it wasn't *wine*. Regulus, the Mirth descendant skilled in shifting, paced in front of the hearth.

Three other descendants I was less familiar with stood near the windows overlooking the side driveway. One of the family haelens was in attendance—Ruth, was it? A younger man stood nearby with his hands clasped behind his back. His eyes were such a light blue, they were almost clear in the morning glare pouring between the curtains. Long blonde curls were tied in a loose binding behind his head.

The last descendant shielded herself in the shadows formed in the room's corner, stepping away from the natural light in favor of the darkness—the bender of shadows, a darkthief Milla was always so intrigued by. She kept her distance from the rest of us.

"Who are you?" I gestured at them both.

"Bree," said the darkthief. No further introductions needed there.

"Finnius. Finn for short." He bowed his head in a courteous greeting. "I'm a mentalus, a thought reader. I apologize, I didn't know you already had a Mirth remnant or I wouldn't have—"

"A little advice, Finn. Don't sell yourself short in the pitch." My inspection drew me closer. His suit was second-hand, the tweed worn at the lapels and wrists, but it was cleaned and pressed. A yellow handkerchief stuck out of his vest pocket. "You look a bit young. Where did my aunt find you?"

"She didn't." He winced. "Rook overheard from his contacts in the city that Mrs. Attano was looking for mind manipulators. He suggested the job to me personally, and I gladly offered to fill the need—for the right price, of course."

"The right price," I drawled. "Typical Canary Boy." I flicked the gold pocket square and smiled. I knew his type, where he came from and the streets he lurked.

A scolapa would have been more useful than a mentalus. Control gave us advantage, but so did information. I supposed I couldn't afford to be particular at this point. Regardless of his loyalties and the specifics of his remnant, he was here now, and he was willing.

"Alright, but if I catch you worming around in my head, Finn, I'll put a bullet in yours. Understand?"

He gave a quick nod.

"Good. Well, thank you all for coming on such short notice." I stepped away from the new recruit to claim a glass on the serving table and poured myself a drink.

Sabina sat up straight, her red lips in an ever-present smile. "When Nicolai Attano calls, it is best not to keep him waiting. Wouldn't want to be on the receiving end of those explosives your family is so well known for."

"It sounds like you came more out of curiosity than loyalty, Madame."

"Can you blame me?" She swirled her drink. "We want to know what the hells is going on. One day the OIC promises the ban will lift, the next the bloody bridge is in the river."

"The OIC promised many things they had no intention of

following through on," I said. In as few words as possible, I explained my meeting with Hartsong and the cabinet, told them what I knew and why we couldn't rely on the newly appointed officials to function in favor of descendants.

"So Hartsong lied, and you thought it'd be in everyone's best interest to destroy the last thing connecting us to the Districts?" Bree asked. "What if there was a reason he said what he did? What if you just made things worse?"

"No," Sabina said. "Nicolai was right to do it."

Her defense caught me off guard, so much so that my mouth slammed shut before I could respond to the darkthief.

"You're all too young to remember what happened on the Continent, but my mother never let me forget." Her gaze fell on something far away. "It started similar to this, with tensions high and descendants doing what they could to appease those without remnants, silencing themselves and their gifts to make others more comfortable. The kings on the Continent ripped away their rights to use their remnant soon after, all in the name of safety. But those who made the journey to the Isle saw it for what it truly was —control."

"Sabina is correct," Solomon said from a chair pushed near the hearth. "My mother doesn't speak of what happened on the Continent, but the kings were obsessed with order, enough so they took away the free will that the rest of us have taken for granted living here."

Order . . . The word sparked something in my memory. Weeks ago on the bridge, the morning I met Gavriel and brought him to his knees, he had spoken of something similar.

"Order will be reestablished when Chaos is destroyed," I muttered.

The weight of their stares fell on me. The bleeder queen stood slowly. "Where did you hear that, Nicolai?"

"Gavriel said it once when he thought he had me beaten. It made little sense then, but now—" I closed my eyes and inhaled a slow breath before I spilled Milla's secret. If Gavriel *knew* Milla's remnant was of Chaos, then the Firenzes and everyone involved in his plans might know as well.

Someone had turned on her family, and now Milla's enemies had her caged.

But why? If they wanted to destroy Chaos, why didn't they kill her when they had the chance? Why go through the trouble of sending her to Hightower? Unless they wanted something out of her specifically.

"Now, what?" Regulus asked. I had almost forgotten the shifter stood there, positioning himself behind Sabina's chaise.

I threw back the rest of the contents in my glass and set it down on a side table. "Now, Sabina has given me a better understanding about the OIC's vision for the future. Gavriel might be gone, but he wasn't alone in his cause. I'll need each of your help to undo the progress they've made so far."

"You want to raid Hightower?" Sabina asked. A question without even the hint of a smirk. It was the most serious I'd ever seen the queen.

I nodded. "Yes. Only once the prisoners are returned home can we begin negotiations with the OIC. Not a moment sooner."

Regulus released a long breath. "How the hells are we going to break into Hightower, much less free everyone inside? You've been there, Nico. I've only heard rumors of the place, but it doesn't sound very penetrable."

I strode to the hearth, where the fire inside was dying,

matching the energy in the room. "Do any of you have someone you care about in Hightower?"

Each of them nodded. The darkthief's shadows curled at her feet, slipping from the darkened corner.

"If you would let them rot in that hellish place, then get the fuck out of here. I don't have time to make a fancy speech to convince you why this is the right thing. If you'd like to be a part of something bigger than yourselves, if you're tired of letting powerless men make you feel powerless, then I will gladly accept your help."

"What do you need, Nicolai?" Sabina asked.

"It's very simple." I took out a cigarillo and lit the tip. "I need a way in, a layout of the place to plot our approach, and a way to move the stone composing the prison."

"What about a portal?" Regulus glanced at Bree. "Can't darkthieves use the shadows to create . . ." He gestured his hands in a circle.

She frowned. "It's not that simple. Spinning, the act of creating enchanted objects, requires shadows from the void. The shadows in this realm are already attached to something."

"How do we get you the proper shadows?" I asked. Never thought that sentence would come out of my mouth.

"Well." She canted her head with a sigh. "You can either wait until Magrahel, when the veil between our world is at its thinnest, or . . ."

"No time for that," I said. Magrahel was weeks away. "Or what?"

"Or you steal a shadow from someone who has just passed. It's incredibly illegal and unethical. If you go that route, I will not harvest the shadows myself. You'll have to find someone else to do it."

"What if I do the killing?" I asked.

Her face twisted in concern, having spoken like I had just offered to walk her dog instead.

"*Or . . .*" Sabina interrupted. "You could just buy some off the black market."

My attention flickered to the bleeder. "What black market?"

Solomon stood then from his chair. "Absolutely not."

"Oh, sit down, old man." Sabina waved her hand in my uncle's direction. "The black market in Anghor."

"Anghor, the ruined city?" I asked, skeptical.

"The very same. It's completely abandoned besides the black market that runs every night of the third week, if you know where to look."

Anghor was the remains of a city three hours down the river from Lynchaven. Not as large as the Isle's capital city, but it had a massive bridge that connected the north and south similar to the one I had just destroyed. There was another if one followed the river north to the mountains, but it would take days to journey up and around to reach the northside of Lynchaven.

"Do you know where to look, Sabina?" I asked.

She nodded. "Of course I do. When would you like to set up a visit?"

"As soon as possible. Tomorrow works."

"Tomorrow?" My uncle didn't hide his distaste for the idea by the way he shrieked the words. "You can't be serious, Nicolai!"

"I won't waste any more time." I pushed away from the hearth, pointing at him with the burning cigarillo. "I already squandered enough trying to get a fucking meeting with the OIC like *you* requested. This could have been done weeks ago."

He refrained from speaking again, though the glare he sent me insisted this wasn't over.

I ignored him and looked back at the other descendants. "I'll get your shadows, Bree, if you're sure you can make a portal."

"I can make a little portal," she said with a shrug. "How you'll get it into Hightower is a different story. There are two ends of a portal, an entrance and an exit. One will have to be placed in the prison before you can use the other to enter."

"I think I could be of some assistance," Regulus said. "It shouldn't be difficult to steal a watchman's face and sneak inside. I can plant the portal and activate it on my side. Nico and I are well experienced in shadow travel." He winked.

"That tentatively solves one problem." Sabina looked at Finn. "What can you do, boy?"

He sighed, lifting his cap from his head to pass a hand over his hair. "I suppose when we get inside, I could . . . interrogate a guard and get a map of the place from his thoughts."

"Brilliant," I said. "I'm starting to like you, Finn."

The beginning of a smile crept across his cheeks.

"And what about the walls, Nicky?" Luther had entered without me realizing. His hands clasped in front of him. "How we going to move them?"

The room fell silent. No remnant could control the walls of Hightower. The simple fact made it the perfect prison for people like us.

A nearby clock ticked away seconds before I spoke again. "I'll need more time to come up with something, but I'm looking into it. I'll contact the rest of you when I have more."

Gavriel said something else that bothered me . . . *the Remni and their descendants weren't the only ones who received powers beyond this world.* His voice had replayed on a loop in my head, like there was something more to his statement, the answer laced between his words.

What did the watchmen have that granted them power over the stone? It was a question that plagued my thoughts since the day I first saw them manipulate the walls.

"I'll send you a man to show you to Archie. He's my connection in Anghor. He'll make sure you're taken care of," Sabina said.

"Thank you, Madame. May I walk you out?" I offered my arm. The bleeder had a look in her eye that felt like she had something more to say. She smiled and bid the rest of the group farewell.

Sabina was quiet until we reached her carriage, but she stopped a short distance from her guards. "I have something for you." Her hand dove into her coat pocket and pulled out a folded piece of glossy paper. A picture. "I would have given it to you at the funeral when I saw you last, but given the situation when it was taken, I thought it poor taste."

Unfolding the picture, my breath lost its way from my chest. A photo taken of Milla when she was in the Pit. Someone in the crowd had taken it, possibly for the newspaper. She was staring at that demon creature. Her face was flat to hide the fear I'd felt trembling her body that day. In her hand was a dagger, thrust out in front of her like she held a sword instead.

Beautiful. Breathtaking. Seeing the details of her face and her body made me forget how to breathe.

It occurred to me only after I lost her, I didn't have a single picture of her. Nothing but my memory to recall her face and my dreams to haunt me.

"Thank you," I said to the bleeder, though my voice was thick and clung to my throat.

Sabina smiled. "If anyone can bring her home, Nicolai, it'll be you."

I steeled my face before it betrayed my surprise. "What are you talking about?"

Her crimson gaze narrowed. "Don't fuck with me, Attano. Camilla is alive, and she's in Hightower. That's the only reason you'd go through this amount of shit to get her back. You crawled to the OIC for fuck's sake."

She threw the hood of her coat over her long, silver hair and started toward her carriage. "Good luck tonight, and tell Archie I said *hello.*"

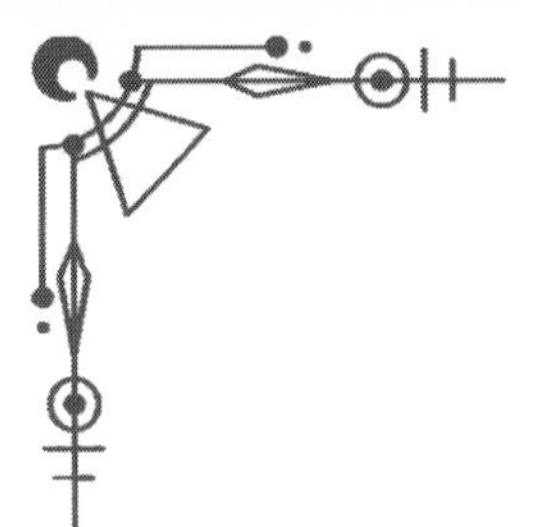
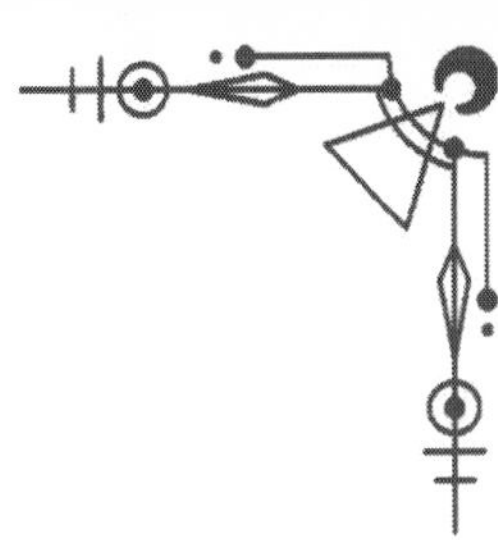

CHAPTER 6

NICOLAI

Sabina had rules if I was to use her contact to access the black market: take her carriage, don't bring anyone else, and—above all—*don't get fucking caught.*

I compromised, bringing Luther in case something should happen. The rest had been nonnegotiable.

Anghor was nestled in the curve of the river, just as it turned south to spill into the Narrow Sea. It was a three-hour journey from Lynchaven and, as expected, we weren't the only ones on the road. Every now and again, a speeding carriage would roll past, spraying the windows with muddy water as the wheels found every dip in the poorly maintained roads.

The ride was miserable, but Luther had learned long ago to sleep anywhere—in any condition. He sat on the bench in front of me with his arms crossed, head bowed as his nasal breathing joined the tick of his pocket watch propped in his hand.

I unfortunately had never learned the skill, and instead passed the time by staring out the muddy windows. The road dipped

when we came near the river, edging the outside of Anghor. From here, the old crumbling remains of the mill came into view. What served as the foundation of the city's infrastructure had turned into its downfall, like a cornerstone made of clay.

"Can you imagine?" Luther roused from his nap as the carriage slowed. His eyes focused on the remains of the city in the distance. "Hundreds of people trapped in there, burned alive."

It used to be difficult to imagine, but now, with the scene in front of us, it was a grim reminder of the cost of negligence.

Thirty years ago, a mill collapsed on its workers. The place had been built too cheaply to hold the machinery the new industrial era had pushed onto the work floors. It was said that when the building collapsed, it killed half of them instantly. While hundreds were trapped in the ruins, the place caught on fire, burning the remaining workers alive.

Apparently, the screams of the dying had echoed through the streets that day. The mill owners were put on trial but had not been found guilty due to the labor laws being so vague at the time. Since the mill was the city's main job source, most moved to find work elsewhere, too haunted by the ghosts of their loved ones. The city was eventually abandoned as the rest of the businesses went bankrupt.

"My father used to say the Anghor Mill was the reason he wanted to go into the steel business. To provide better work environments. Not just for descendants, but for the entire working class. He knew what it was like to work under those machines, and he wanted to improve the conditions in the factories, so what happened here would never happen to his family or anyone else."

My remnant pulled my false hand into a fist. He hadn't achieved that goal, but I would finish what he started.

"You both share that in common," Luther said. "The desire to put an end to the cycle of injustice."

I shrugged, uncomfortable with the comparison. "All change starts with one person pissed off enough to get their hands dirty."

"Well, I'd say your hands are properly soiled, cousin."

By the time the carriage came to a stop, the sun had dipped behind the horizon, casting the remains of the city in a golden frame. We emerged in front of a brick building several stories tall—a hotel, by the shape and the number of windows. We were let out beneath an overhang leading to a pair of black doors with brass handles. No sooner had Luther shut the cabin door than the driver pulled away.

"Guess we see ourselves inside," he murmured and glanced back at the empty driveway. In his hand dangled a briefcase Sabina had given to us.

I adjusted my coat and tie, smoothing out my appearance, before pulling open one of the entry doors.

The foyer was grand and well-kept, completely opposing the exterior of the building. We entered beneath a twinkling crystal chandelier holding dozens of blazing candles; a plush, cream-colored rug softened my steps. The rest of the floor was covered in a glossy marble tile, reflecting the candlelight where the rug didn't reach.

The room opened to twin staircases looping upward to the floors above. Brass bannisters complimented the bone-white pillars posted from the floor to the vaulted ceiling, where the sloped edges were painted to resemble a cloudy, sun-filled sky.

Everything in this place shone—despite the windows boarded up behind the navy curtains. Everything—including the gunmetal aimed at our heads.

Six guards, three on each staircase, stood with their rifles raised behind the bannisters.

"I think we're in the right place," Luther whispered beside me.

"Don't move," I told him. Whoever these men were, the color of our coats had no influence on them. They didn't care who we were, and I assumed they were an "ask for forgiveness before permission" sort of group.

"You must be a guest of Sabina's." A man appeared between the staircases; his words were slightly garbled from the cigarillo between his lips.

"You must be Archie," I said.

He nodded, opening his arms in a small bow. A grey tweed suit dressed his stocky stature with a matching cap. Frayed white hair spilled beneath the hat. Archie was an older gentleman with a wince in his walk that made it look like each step was a painful experience. He came to stand a short distance in front of us.

"Well, the Madame knows the rules. Did she bring what the dealer requested?"

Luther held out the case to the man, whose demeanor shifted once he felt the weight of the contents. His lips curled in a smile beneath a thick mustache. "Wonderful. Come with me."

We followed him past the posted guards and through the archway leading beneath the joined stairs. Gas lamps lined the walls, illuminating the thick darkness and dark blue wallpaper lined with golden foiled flowers. For a man with short legs and an unhealthy breathing pattern, he covered considerable ground, taking us down the main hall and through another pair of ornate black doors.

Velvet couches lined the walls, the fabric so dark it appeared black in the dim lighting. Two men and a woman sitting between them smoked something with purple smoke billowing from their lips. She giggled as one of them ran his hand up her thigh. The other sucked his cigarillo and blew the smoke into her ear, making her writhe between them.

"If I were you," Archie muttered behind his hand. "I'd hold my breath until we get to the ballroom."

Taking his council, I did just that.

The ballroom was similarly decorated to the rest of the hotel—chandeliers combined with gas lamps on the wainscoted walls to brighten the busy room. Platforms lined the floor, surrounded by crowds marveling at the displays. Some stages held objects. Enchanted statues that moved like the animals they were molded into. Another showed off a woman with a shaved head dancing while an inked creature resembling a fish swam across her bare skin. Familiars, like Camilla's, on sale for any one of the patrons here who had the coin for them.

"The main floor is where we keep the bigger displays," our guide explained. "There's a bar behind those curtains that sells potions and draughts of all sorts of compulsions. The rare stuff." He dropped his voice, forcing me to lean closer to catch his words. "The stuff *you're* looking for we keep in the back."

"How do you know what I want?" I asked.

His dark eyes shifted sideways at me. "You're here for business, not entertainment. Not like these folks. And Sabina never—*never*—sends anyone to us. Whatever you're here for, it must be important for the queen herself to send you."

Archie beckoned us onward. The crowded ballroom floor let us slip through, too enthralled with the displays to notice us. Some were hooded, others wore masks, and yet most preferred not to conceal their identities. A man in a starch white shirt approached, carrying a tray of flutes with the fang of a serpent sitting in the bottom. Luther reached for the glass he offered, but I slapped his hand away.

"Don't consume anything while we're here." I gave the server a look that told him to *fuck off*.

"Can't be worse than that homemade whiskey we made in Esme's garage when we were kids." He nudged my side. "It'll take more than a little poison to kill us now."

I scoffed at the memory. "Maybe. But it will only take a little vomit in Sabina's carriage for her to kill you herself."

His grin turned into a grimace. "Aye, true."

It took a moment to find Archie again, his stature disappearing in the crowd, before we continued to the back entrance of the ballroom. Four more guards stood at attention at the mouth of an archway. They barely glanced at our escort as he waved us through.

"Wait here," Archie barked, then took a hard right down a darkened hall. Curtained alcoves lined the inner wall opposite a row of windows boarded up behind thick curtains. Sounds of ecstasy, of skin slapping skin, slipped from the concealed spaces, and I gritted my teeth to ignore the warm sensation coiling down my spine. Milla was the last woman I had lost myself inside, and I wouldn't know pleasure until she could. Until she was back in my bed.

Luther cleared his throat to cover the high-pitched sighs, shifting uncomfortably on his feet. Thankfully, Archie appeared a few minutes later, no longer carrying the briefcase.

"He'll see you now."

Two more guards stood outside the door as we stood in the center of a dimly lit room. The lamps were left burning low, casting shadows across the carpeted floor from the various artifacts stored in their glass cages on display. The air was heavy in the room, like the pressure before a torrent of rainfall, and scented of sulfur and iron. The thickness of it filled with trapped magic and the power possessed inside various crystals and weapons.

"*Shitting saints*," Luther whispered. "Do you recognize what that is, cousin?"

He had wandered to the section of the wall that was completely bare. No wallpaper, no violent decorum, just bare obsidian. Smooth and polished to reflect my cousin's stunned expression as he reached out and skimmed his fingers across the plane of stone.

Of course, I knew what it was. I'd spent five years of my life surrounded by the same stuff, though none of it had ever been burnished like this one. My fingers curled into a fist, skimming the callouses across my hand where the stone had once bitten into my skin.

"Why is that here?" Better question—how? The slab was taller than Luther, over six feet high and approximately the same size wide. It had been sunken into the wall, so I couldn't determine the thickness, but regardless, it was still strange to see something so obviously out of place—even in a room of oddities.

"The same reason I acquire anything," a voice spoke behind us.

Turning, I met a well-dressed man standing in a three-piece charcoal tweed suit. A gold chain connected his pocket to the seam of his vest. His dark skin was nearly ebony in the outer reaches of the lamps, though the light refracted strangely in one of his eyes. The orb flashed, catching the light before moving out of its focus, returning to a pale white eye with a green iris, matching his opposite.

A false eye, and I wondered if it too was enchanted like the other objects in this room.

"It sells?" I guessed. He wasn't alone. A pair of women lingered behind him, just far enough to remain outside the conversation.

Thin lips tipped into a pleasant smile. "It intrigues. I enjoy the macabre and the strange, as do my clients. That piece you're looking at was donated to me by a certain inspector a few years ago in exchange for enough reoles to buy a new reputation—if you catch my meaning." He gestured to a sitting area arranged in the corner. "Why don't you sit down, Mr. Attano, and tell me what intrigues you so much to travel this far from Lynchaven."

Luther moved toward the chairs, but I stopped him. "Who are you?"

"Desmond York—or if you prefer—the Demon Dealer, as I'm more affectionately called."

I'd heard that name before but had never been desperate enough to seek his services, or his wares, until now. I glanced towards the sitting area, deciding it best to remain standing. Closer to the door that way.

"I need shadows, Mr. York."

His face remained passive. "How many?"

"Enough to make a portal."

The two women behind him giggled at my request. Desmond's smile grew steadily. "I can give you all the shadows you'll need, Mr. Attano. But I'll need something in return."

I swallowed down an uneasy feeling rising in my chest. "Was Sabina's donation not payment enough?"

He shook his head and laughed. "Exotic furs and horns are hardly worth that many shadows. Sabina gave you enough to get through the front door and a ticket to meet with me. You'll need much more if you wish to make a deal."

"A deal?" A muscle twitched in my jaw. It would've been convenient if the bleeder warned me to bring something more valuable to the merchant. This man wasn't after money then. He wanted a favor. "I'm assuming you have something in mind?"

Desmond turned to one of the women and nodded. His wordless command made her leave his side to retrieve something from one row of shelves lining the furthest wall. He looked back at me as he spoke again. "I need something moved across the river for a client. It comes from the South, and I cannot meet their needs without some assistance. Let me use your train, ship the materials for me, and I will give you all the shadows in the void."

"You are aware the OIC has checkpoints as well for stock moved through the city, correct?"

"Then I suggest you hide my goods well, because if it was legal, I'd do it myself."

I sighed a breath of disapproval. "I don't move drugs."

He held a hand to the space above his heart in mock offense. "I'm not a drug dealer, Mr. Attano. I have a reputation around here to uphold."

We had very different definitions of the word if he thought the smoke around here was natural. "What would you have me transfer, then?"

Desmond shook his head. "Now that, I can't tell you. My client demands full discretion, and I will honor their demands to get my full check."

Shit. If Solomon could hear this conversation now, he'd be livid. Worse, he'd give me that look like I was in over my head.

Don't feed the beast, Nico, he'd always told me.

Saints, it was far too late for that. I had nurtured my demise so much these last few weeks, there wasn't much room left for other options. I had successfully wedged myself into a corner.

"If I agree, I'll need the shadows now, before the job is complete."

"Then I'll need something from you personally, as collateral." Desmond clicked his tongue. His glass eye looked me up and down, searching for something he appreciated. "I like that hand of yours."

"Pick something else," I told him. "My cousin would murder me if I gave this away."

"I'll give it back when the job's done," he offered. His shoulders fell an inch. "Fine. I'll take *your* shadow then."

"My *what*?" I retreated a step, unable to help myself.

He shoved his hands in his pockets and shrugged, like it was the most casual thing in the realm, asking for a man's shadow. "You can live without it for a short while, as long as it remains in this realm. But if you fail, or if you go back on our deal, I'll—" His chin turned slightly toward the other woman standing to his right. "Well, Sinthia will give your shadow to the void."

"What happens then?" I asked, unsure if I wanted to know.

"You die," the woman spoke for her boss, soft voice null of concern.

"Cousin," Luther whispered. "I don't like this. Let them have mine."

"I don't want yours," Desmond said. "My deal is with Nicolai. His shadow stays with me until he completes the job. Only after may he return, and Sinthia will rejoin it to his person." The glass eye stared at me, like it could see through my flesh, straight into my mind. "I don't need money, Attano. I need reliability. It's a fair deal. One you'll have to take if you want your portal."

This bastard knew I was desperate. There was no use negotiating now, not when a good threat would do. "That's all fine. But if you don't return my shadow, my family will blow this entire hotel to the ground. My cousin here will kill you and take his time about it."

I took three steps toward him until he was only an arm's reach away. "Men like us, York, we go to the same hell. Double-cross me and I'll be waiting for you across the veil."

Desmond smiled. "Sinthia."

She stepped behind me, where my shadow had fallen across the carpet thanks to the angle of the gas lamps. I hardly felt it. A small tug in my chest was the only sensation as the darkthief returned to her master's side, holding a formless mass of darkness between the palms of her hands.

"Please put Mr. Attano's shadow somewhere safe, Sinthia. Wouldn't want to misplace something so valuable," Desmond murmured. He motioned for the other woman to hand us the box. Luther took it in his possession, and I was just as eager to the get the hells out of here now that business had been done.

"I'll send word concerning the transfer through Sabina. If you have any—"

A shudder rolled through the building, shaking the artifacts spread out on display. Glass cylinders buzzed, and the walls moaned as a tremble like a shockwave moved through the floor.

Desmond stilled, studying the sound and sensation. He barked a quiet order at his darkthief, and she disappeared through a pair of velvet curtains behind them.

"Mr. York—"

"Are you armed?" He grabbed a gun from the inside of his suit jacket.

Another quake shook the room, and I brushed aside the edge of my coat to grab the revolver sheathed at my hip.

Screams, gunfire, shattered glass, and splintered wood. Noise erupted outside the door, coming from the ballroom. The merchant cursed and snapped at the other woman, urging her to collect as many artifacts as she could carry and escape to the basement.

I pointed the barrel of my weapon toward the door. "What the hells is going on, York?"

"It sounds like we've been busted."

"The Society?" I asked, dreading his answer. Of course, the Watch would send the Society bastards to hit up the black market. The certain division of watchmen were specifically trained to deal with magic of all kinds, especially the monopolization of it. I doubted anything in this hotel was legitimate or regulated.

He nodded. "That stuff I need moved, men are looking for it," he shouted at us above the cacophony that grew louder the longer we stood there. He flipped a couch on its back, ducking behind the upholstery like it was a barrier. "There's a safe room beneath the hotel for situations like these, though we've never had to use it. Just follow the girls."

"Unfortunately, Mr. York, I need to make sure you stay alive." I didn't trust Sinthia with my shadow, and I wasn't confident in his ability to defend himself alone.

Wrapping the breeze, I lifted display cases with the force of my remnant and formed a thicker barrier around us. Fragile relics fell to the floor and shattered, rare metals and crystals littered the carpet as weapons fell from their racks.

Desmond groaned behind his velvet couch, but I figured he valued his life above his artifacts.

Just as the barrier settled, bullets ripped through the door. I ducked behind the short wall of display cases, the bullets tearing into the wallpaper behind us. The guarded door burst off its hinges, and I stayed low, watching through the cracks in the barricade to see six men fill the room. Each dressed similarly, golden pins flashing upon their lapels.

"Fucking eagles," York growled and shifted beside me to gain a glimpse of the visitors himself. "How the hells did they find me?"

They spread out across the room, unconcerned about coverage. The man in the center held a submachine gun, known on the streets as the Voidsender, a weapon that could shoot over a hundred bullets in a single minute. Only a handful were ever made before the OIC banned their production and sale, and the few that existed had become as valuable and sought after as any other treasure in this room.

"Desmond York," the gunner shouted. "Your deals are done. Surrender to the Society and we'll spare your life."

"Like you spared the others?" he spat. "Spare me your lies. You'll have to drag my cold, dead body out of this room if you want me."

"Happy to oblige."

He reloaded, the faint click of the magazine sliding into the port was the only warning we got before he sprayed the barricade with bullets. The noise was deafening, shots tearing apart the room and filling the air with smoke and shards of debris. Remaining low against the carpet, I let him unload his ammo before retaliating, though our wall wore thin.

"Boss," Luther called, still holding the box in the cradle of his arm, his gun cocked and ready in his opposite hand. "I'll cover you."

When the gunfire ceased to allow the man to reload, I stood over the half-wall, shoving the remains of the barricade toward the gunmen with a burst of air. Once the wreckage was clear and the watchmen focused on the furniture flying towards them, I stopped the time. A shot aimed at each man, though the bullets were caught in the corruption, suspended in time as they reached the edge of the intangible boundary containing my free movements.

An ache returned in my bones, a reminder not to hold the time for long or else risk weakening my remnant too much. Especially when I might need it. A few minutes was usually all I was granted until it became too much.

I let go. The furniture fell from its float in the air and colliding with bodies and wallpaper. The bullets found home in the chest of my targets, and each of them let out mangled cries as they fell to the floor.

Blood streaked the creamy carpet red. I turned from the lot of them when their sounds of suffering fell quiet, and started back toward Desmond and Luther, who were getting to their feet.

Desmond dusted off his pants while Luther inspected the box, making sure it was still intact. When he raised his head to look at me, his eyes went wide.

He pointed to something behind me. "Nico!"

Through a piece of glass that had once belonged to a display case, I caught the reflection of three more watchmen who had come behind the last ones. One of them lifted the Voidwalker from the corpse of the other, finger settling on the trigger.

Before I could lift my power, the wall behind us exploded. Luther's vengeful cry was a sound I hadn't heard from my cousin in a very long time. Wrathful, raw, an agony that tore into the heart in my chest, feeling the shred of his own as he unleashed something that had been pent up for years.

The stone sunken into the wall—the kind composing Hightower prison, the stuff Gavriel claimed had been pulled from the void—hurled itself over our heads and collided with the men behind me.

A deafening blast shook the room, thrusting me forward from the force.

Debris from the crossfire littered the air with a dusty haze, and splintered bits of masonry and wood framing were thrown from the damage.

I turned to follow his gaze—a gaping hole where the door used to be and the men who ambushed us crushed beneath the stone hurled twenty feet away down the hall.

"*Seven hells*, Luther." My voice was breathy, too astounded to speak with substance. My gaze returned to him. "How did you do that?"

He stared down at his hands, a wrinkle in his brow, then at the pillar he'd just ripped from the foundation and threw across the room. He shook his head, just as surprised as I was at what he'd just accomplished. "I . . . I don't know. One moment, I saw the bastard pick up the gun, ready to kill you. I just . . ." He swallowed. "Just put my hand out to stop him, and the stone followed."

Desmond surveyed the room, taking care to pick up anything left unbroken—which wasn't much if his whimpering and moaning was any indication.

Luther filled his empty hands with the box of shadows. His fingers fidgeted around the corners, a usual sign of his distress.

"Do you think it has anything to do with the experiments? Did they do something to you that could have given you the same ability as the watchmen in Hightower?"

He shrugged. I hated asking him about his time there, knowing how much he despised talking about it—but this was urgent. This could change everything.

"During the last test, the one where I lost my remnant," he said after a moment, "they had a guard involved. I thought they tried to bind my power to him, but perhaps . . ."

"Perhaps they bound his ability to you." I licked my lips in thought. "If they replaced your remnant with a different one, if what the watchmen wield is like a remnant, then you can move the stone the same as them."

His blue eyes widened, finding mine. "I can move the stone."

The significance hit us both at once. He focused again on the pillar of obsidian crushing the men in the hall and tested the theory. Without even a flick of his finger, the stone lifted.

Luther grinned.

"I'd say that solves our last problem, right, boss?"

A layer of dust settled over the bodies of the men still bleeding into the carpet. The symbol of an eagle, the sigil of the OIC, pinned to the lapels of their suits. If these men wanted whatever Desmond needed moving, then I was more interested than ever to oblige this wager with the Demon Dealer.

Even if it cost me my shadow—my life—I'd get Milla out of Hightower and make this city safe again.

"Two birds, one massive fucking stone." I grinned. "Let's get these shadows home."

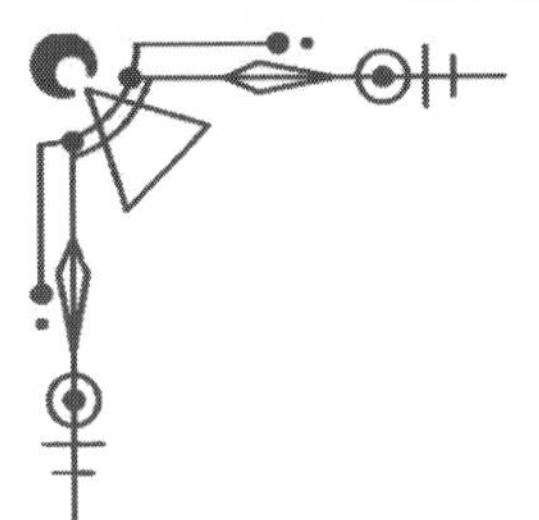
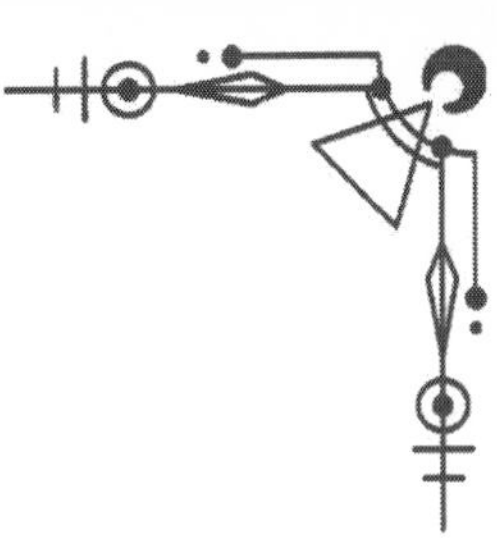

CHAPTER 7
CAMILLA

They left me alone for the days that followed the first trial, leaving no one besides the phantom face of Sera's father to lurk in the darkness. Occasionally, the alchemedis would come by to assess my wrist and knees. The cartilage had healed miraculously well thanks to the stuff she poured down my throat. Her treatments were a reminder of how quickly the past could be erased, forgotten, and yet the scars—the memories—remained long after the wounds were healed.

I ate my meal in the dark. Something with the texture of bread and tart-less fruit. The meat here was tasteless and tough, but it filled my stomach with something. When the stone trembled for the second time in a single day, I was thankful to have forced it down my throat.

"It's time for your second trial," my guard said.

"Hello to you too, Mike."

"Just get up."

His voice sounded more urgent today, like he was nervous

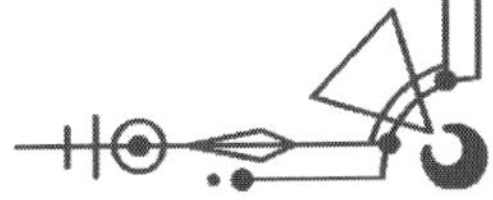

about something. When it took me a second to react to his command, he gripped the metal beater hanging off his waist to encourage a faster reaction—and I recalled well how he used it to offer a bit of extra motivation. Not that I needed much anymore. Where was the point of fighting? They'd get what they want out of me, eventually.

This place had taken a bite out of my spirit, a sure sign it was breaking me down. I missed the girl they took from her train, wished I could return to my old skin that had far fewer scars.

No one was coming for me.

I stood on rejuvenated legs, silently grateful the alchemdis's tonics had worked so well. The pain of the first day had kept me awake all night, and sleeping was the most productive thing to do around here. Better to be lost in a dream than picking away at my thoughts like a thread, unraveling my threadbare sanity more and more with every resurfacing memory.

And when I couldn't sleep, my thoughts returned home.

Of Giles and the way he used to drag me around town to every bar that served his favorite brandy. Simple memories of his laugh and his infectious smile. He was the only one who had been interested in my happiness concerning Nico. He'd have celebrated my moments of vulnerability when I finally fell for my husband, as he always celebrated the simplest achievements of those around him.

I shared a unique relationship with each of my brothers. Giles had been special, but I still hoped the rest of them shared a better fate. There hadn't been a chance to find out before I was taken.

I tried not to think of Nico when he unbiddenly ambushed my thoughts. I couldn't. There was enough pain in this place.

But *everything* made me think of him.

The grey of the sky was the same storm in his eyes. The feel of the breeze slipping beneath my tunic only lacked the charge of his remnant. The scent of smoke from the watchman a familiar blend.

I shook my head free of each reminder and focused on something else: the next trial. Another chance to learn more about myself and use it against the ones who took me from him.

We didn't return to the broken platform where the last trial had taken place. This time, my guard took me around the tower, to the border of the island, where black cliffs dropped into a restless sea. The only thing similar about this trial were the faces waiting for us. The same watchmen, the same alchemists, and Delilah.

I was already trembling in the violent wind slapping the side of the island and tossing my hair in every direction, which had long lost its curl from extended time lying on my cot and lack of access to washing it properly. Now, it hung dead down my back, lifeless and limp in the forbidding breeze.

"How is she?" Delilah asked Mike.

"The alchemedis approved."

"Good enough then." She looked me over. A cowl shielded her face from the elements. We met on a beaten path riddled with sharp stones that led back to the prison. Like the rest of the group, she wore tall boots covered in the mud that caked between my bare toes. The sun hid behind dark, wrathful clouds. Behind her figure, beyond the cliffs and white caps spraying the rocks, a storm thundered over the sea.

The alchemedis approached with her glinted gloves and slathered the salve above my wrist. Gradually, my remnant roused from a deep place, filling my spine until I stood a little straighter. My breath shuddered as I tamed it back, more prepared this time for the reunion.

"Your next trial will not be as simple as the first," she said to me then. "We realized your abilities as a weapon. This time, we will assess your skills as a shield."

"A shield?" I asked.

Her tone went flat. "There are three prisoners trapped beneath the cliff. Your task is to save them."

Something told me it wasn't as simple as the few directions she'd given me. "And if I don't? If I do not wish to be *studied* by you or your henchmen?"

She shrugged beneath the weight of her coat. "Then I suppose you'll let them die. Either way, they aren't getting back up here on their own accord."

Of course. Each trial would force my hand then. If I acted, I was an accomplice to what they learned about me. If I did nothing, I was worse—negligent to the lives of those who did not ask to be a part of this, no matter how insufferable our lives as Hightower's prisoners had become.

"Where are they?" I glanced at the mottled sky.

She pointed to the edge of the cliff.

Following her finger, I crossed the grassy stretch of flat land until it dropped abruptly into the sea. Below, a staircase jutted out the side of the cliff, descending to a piece of black shore being ravaged by the waves. The front of the storm churned the dark waters, filling the tide. Whoever was down there would be swept away before long.

"There are people down there?" I shouted over the wind at Delilah. When she nodded, my frustration morphed into anger. A sharper emotion, one with an edge to cut. "You're all fucking deranged. If you want to study me, then do your worst, but leave them out of it!"

"We tried," she said. "You didn't want to use your remnant, so

I thought it best to give you the proper motivation to figure out your power in a controlled and safe environment."

A maniacal laugh flew from a joyless home in my chest. *Safe.* That word again. She acted like she was doing me a favor, putting lives at risk just to give me a reason to use my power. Like she was helping me.

No. It felt more like she was *training* me.

She sighed dramatically. "The only way to understand your remnant is to use it, Camilla. You must practice letting it out if you wish to control it."

"I don't know how!" Shame fueled the anger in my tone, and I looked off into the gathering storm, avoiding her intelligent gaze. "I don't think it even can be controlled."

She pulled out her book from the inner fold of her coat, opening it to a section she'd marked off. "Chaos had a disorganized approach to her power. While most descendants pull from a place in their body where the remnant is stored, yours is not so tangible. The source of a remnant's power correlates from the part of the Creator their saint was formed from. Blood remnants are in the blood. Bane in the bone. Mirth in the mind. But Chaos? Chaos was formed from the Creator's soul. And since the home of the soul is the heart, I would expect you to find your power there."

My pulse bounded in my veins. My heart was made of nothing but blood and vengeful desires, neither would help me control my violent magic. "Learned all that from the book you're so attached to?"

She grinned. "I've dedicated my life to learning how to define remnants in the language of the Arcane. I want to define yours, but to do so, I need to know what makes you burn."

A rash of chills spread across my arms, and I tucked them close to my middle. She'd spoken of the Arcane a few times, a method of magic formed from science. Even being the source of her studies, the subject was still vague to me. "You can't control Chaos, Delilah. I would know."

She ignored my challenge, and instead looked at the sea.

"I think you'd better hurry, Camilla," she said in that dry voice I'd associated with pure evil. "The tide is rising."

My bare feet slipped across the jagged steps of a narrow staircase, each jutting out at odd angles, like they had been crudely carved in a rush. One slip could send me over the edge into frothy waters. The lack of uniformity forced me to focus on my steps instead of the incoming squall, where dark clouds gathered in threat. The first drops of icy rain pebbled across my skin, gradually wetting the grey, shapeless tunic that hung to my knees.

Before the mouth of a cave, the stairs stopped near a manual lift. Ropes and pulleys lined the wall of the cliff to lift the buckets cast aside near the entrance.

The mechanics reminded me of . . . a mine. But what were they collecting?

I stared into the cavern, hesitating for a moment. Returning to the dark so soon set my teeth on edge. Worse, it would be willingly, and I'd spent so much time in the darkness that I never wanted to linger there again, but a groan within that darkness shoved me forward. A familiar, agonized sound.

The cave was carved deep into the island, hiding from any source of light. Blinded, I used my hands to guide me along, skimming my fingers across the coarse wall of the tunnel. The air was heavy, humid, and reeked of sulfur—the same smell that wafted from Delilah's robes when she ran her experiments.

Before long, what little light existed behind me faded as the tunnel gradually descended into the island, curving slightly as if to return to the sea. I neared the first prisoner, their moans clarified into a single, raspy word.

"*Help.*"

There was no strength in their plea, barely louder than a breath.

"Where are you?" I called out. My voice echoed, returning to me in what sounded like a cavern. The wall beneath my touch angled, opening into a room of pitch darkness.

"Here! I think . . . I think I'm inside a cage."

As I stepped toward the origin of the voice, aware of how the sound reverberated around the space, my toes dipped into cold water. Nothing deep, a few inches at most. My steps sloshed in the shallow pool, ignoring the way it froze the blood in my toes.

"Keep talking. What can you feel around you?" I asked, still toeing my way towards the sound of the soft voice.

"Just bars around me, but the floor and ceiling are solid, and everything is made of stone, like the cells."

"Is there water?"

"There is now."

Right. The tide was rising, filling the chamber with the intrusive sea. I blindly held out my hands to feel for the cage, finding another wall instead.

"Lower," the voice said.

I sunk to my knees, and just as the woman described, felt the stone give way to tightly placed columns. My fingers skimmed over a hand clutched around a bar, trembling. I wrapped my own around them, savoring the first human connection in weeks, the comfort of skin to skin. A touch that didn't burn or bruise.

"What happened?" I asked her.

"I'm not sure. They brought me down here, and I thought I was just going to do my usual hours in the mine, but they didn't give me my usual supplies. One of the guards told me to sit, and they built this thing around me. They left after without an explanation."

Cold bastards. It hardly surprised me. The creep of the water line over my ankles stung deep, piercing the marrow in my bones and drawing a gasp.

She laughed then. "You know, I used to love the sea. Any form of water, really. Now they've stuffed me with so much glint, it doesn't feel the same. Can you imagine? A water bender, death by drowning."

"You're a bender?" I asked.

"Yes."

My heart twisted, wondered if Delilah had chosen her remnant specifically to make it more personal. "It's going to be alright. I'm going to get you out."

But even to myself, the words sounded unsure.

The bars stopped at my hips, forcing her to crouch in the cramped space. I shifted around the stone to study the shape of the containment, but there was no access to the inside beyond the thin spaces between the bars. A solid structure, smooth and formed like a pillar far beyond my reach towards the roof of the cave. There was no pushing it off with the weight of the cliff side balanced above it.

Water nipped at the back of my knees. Each lap of tide rose higher up my calf, racing my pulse with worry. If I didn't figure out how to break open the bars and set her free, she'd drown in there.

The panicked race of her breath in the still cavern indicated she understood the same.

But this cell didn't differ from the one above ground. The same porous rock that stood unmovable, unyielding to the inmates on the island. Yet the watchmen had the power to manipulate every inch.

"Why are they doing this?" she whispered. "What have I done?"

Delilah wanted me to use my remnant to see the range of its properties. First, as a weapon. Now, a shield. She wanted me to destroy Sera's father in a match to the death. This time, she put the lives of three prisoners in my hands to save, and not just their lives but possibly their freedom if I could pull it off.

A weapon to destroy. A shield to . . . protect?

A swell of the sea rushed through the cave, pushing the waterline up to my knees.

The trapped prisoner lost all composure and thrashed in her small cage, throwing her weight against the solid structure of stone bars and rising tide.

The salve Delilah had given me cracked a hole in my remnant, freeing from the glint's detainment. After releasing it twice now, once on the train and once on the platform, I was accustomed to its presence, how it filled my spine with molten steel and spread through my veins to lethalize my very touch.

I had killed—no, unraveled—two men now with my remnant. Peeled the fabric of humanity apart until it was nothing but a haze on the wind. If Chaos magic could reverse life itself, if I could return flesh and bone into the ash of the earth, then perhaps I could also apply the same fundamental to anything else in creation. Even the unyielding stone.

"Get to the other side of the cell, but don't touch the bars," I ordered. If I was to unleash the Chaos in my veins, I wanted to keep her far as possible from the flames so she wouldn't accidentally brush the fire from Oblivion.

When her ragged breath shifted to the other side of the containment, I braced my hands on the bars and focused on that liquid fire in my blood, let it pour from my fingertips and spread across the bars. I had no idea if it was working, the shadows hid my remnant from the prisoner and from myself, and I didn't know if I was thankful for their concealment or hindered by it.

But it forced me to focus on how much I let out, forced me to feel instead of watch, an approach I hadn't thought about before.

When the solid structure beneath my hands eroded away so quickly, I hadn't expected the loss of its support. My grip tightened on itself, gravel and coarse dust filled my palms as the remains of the bars fell into the rising tide lapping my thighs.

When there was nothing left to destroy, I focused inward. Let the pound of my heart soothe some as I took deep, calming breaths, drawing it back into my core where the flames originated. The darkness heightened my other senses, increasing the awareness of where my power retreated to rest.

Without thinking, I reached into the cage and found the prisoner crouched in the water, hugging her knees into her chest.

"I broke it! Come on." I peeled her arm from her body to pull her out. This newfound temperance—not something I'd quite call control—over my remnant, the knowledge that I had called it this time instead of being triggered to use it, seemed to put my power on a leash. A way to tame it.

No sooner had I pulled the trembling woman out than a hiss slipped from above. We both stilled to quiet our splashing, studying the noise. A deeper groan creaked from the ceiling just as a faint tremble rippled through the water. My legs were so benumbed from the coldness of the sea, I almost didn't sense it. But the prominent crack of stone above us was clear enough.

I must have burned through something fundamental, and now the cavern was moments away from collapsing.

"Get back to the tunnel." I tried to backtrack the way I'd entered, but a reverberant crack came from the same direction, followed by a rush of wind and the splash of falling rock, drenching us in salty swells.

"We're trapped," the woman beside me whispered, clutching my arm.

"No," I said, defiant against the truth. I frantically trudged through the hip-deep water, feeling the perimeter with my hands and edging it into memory. Even if there wasn't another tunnel, there had to be a way out. The tide found a way inside, after all. If I could break through the stone once, I could do it again. I just needed to find the side of the sea.

"Here!" I called out. "The water is coming from a break in the wall!"

A small gush streamed against my ankles, so faint I wouldn't have felt it if I hadn't been searching for such a sensation. My palms flattened against the side of the cavern, certain the open sea was just on the other side of this wall. Even as I focused on the waning retreat of my remnant, urging it back into fruition, the slam of a hard wave beat a powerful rhythm through the stone.

"Brace yourself." I took several hungry gulps of air myself. My power filled my veins, and my flesh rippled like bullets beneath my skin to my quickening pulse as if priming itself before release. I squeezed my eyes shut and lowered a fence guarding it back—a barrier I'd realized had come not from my will alone, but from my fear.

The wall, as it had before, crumbled to dust. Unmade by the remnant in my touch.

The wrath of the sea flooded the cavern, submerging us in its cold fury. I kicked and flailed, trying to claw my way toward the glare of light piercing the way toward the sky. The incoming surge shoved me further back, and I was tossed like the froth in the waves into the back wall. A hand found my wrist and pulled, dragging me with the motion of the sea.

In. Out. The trend of the tide tossed us. The prisoner swam beside me, guided my movements to work with the waves instead of against them. My chest screamed when we finally broke the surface and gasped for breath. Salt stung my eyes, blurred the focus on a patch of high ground. But my quivering limbs swam toward the smidge of land, thanking the lost saints as my fingers buried into sand.

A beach.

"Come on." The bender nudged my shoulder. "Let's get out of the water before we freeze to death."

I didn't realize how weak I was until her strong arm hooked around mine and pulled me to the highest point of the beach nestled in the curve of the cliffside.

"You did it!" A wild smile spread across her face. Seeing her for the first time, I discovered her to be young. Too young to be here, of all places. Her blonde hair, practically silver, stuck to her pale cheeks. "You saved us. How?" Her wide eyes wandered over me, trying to figure out how I had the power to burst through solid stone.

"It's complicated." Words were difficult. My lips heavy from the numbness, the draining of my remnant left my bones filled with lead. No matter how many breaths I took, the ache in my lungs would not be satisfied.

"Was anyone else in there?" I found enough strength to ask.

Her smile fell, shaking her head in denial. Worry kicked my heartbeat back into a frenzied pace. Had I missed someone? Delilah said there were three of them. I looked around, scanned the wide inlet filled with spires of jagged rock—and found another victim of the alchemist's trial.

Another woman was tied to a post in the middle of the sea. Her arms bound behind her, the waves drenching her form in a repetitious, unrelenting beatdown. Dark, wet hair curtained her face, but her head hung low, as if surrendering to the waves.

"There." I pointed. I stood on shaky legs and started down toward the edge of the beach.

"What are you doing?" the woman asked behind me.

"I've got to reach her!"

"She's at least thirty feet out there, you'll drown!"

As if predicting my fate, the moment I reentered the sea, a wave knocked me back, forbidding my passage. The swells were larger now and fiercer in turn. The impending storm was nearly upon us. So close—and yet impossibly far. If I had a boat or—better yet—the power over the sea, I might have been some help to the stranded prisoner. But I had nothing but my anxious heart and the sand between my clenched fists.

Sand.

The last time I had seen sand so fine was at Sabina's ball, when a descendant crafted it into a perfect glass rose. When he took grains of the earth, purposeless in their bare form, and created something beautiful to be admired.

If Chaos could unmake, could it do the opposite? Were there even rules bound to the disorder of my magic? Fire was used to destroy, but it could create under the right circumstances, and sand was a perfect raw material. I closed my eyes, blocking out the dying prisoner, the storm ravaging the sky. The sand filling my fists molded into something sharp, answering every question my anxious heart whispered.

You can do anything you want.

I'd kept every word Nico ever spoke to me and stored it in the deepest place of my memory, in that place where the heart kept the soul. Nico had seen my potential all along. Perhaps it was time I proved it to him—and to myself.

Every inch of my skin fevered as I let the shards of glass slip from my hands and into the sea. I dug my bloody and black fingers back into the grainy earth, pictured in my mind what I needed to get to the woman tied to the pyre.

A bridge. Whereas the deconstruction of the island's foundation and the human body had been the product of the fire I became more familiar with, it felt uncontrollable. Difficult to contain. The obsidian stone I'd let crumble into the sea would probably agree. But this—this felt different. This was fire in a different form, and I felt the reach and the heat of it as it rushed into the sand beneath the waves, as I demanded it to rise from its settlement on the seafloor and mold within the forge of my flames.

My heart slammed against my chest as I thrust the fire onward, past the wake of the water and straight into the sea. When I opened my eyes once more, there was still an open ocean and angry swells, but there was something else.

"Holy hells," the girl behind me whispered.

A bridge of black glass. Dry lightning flashed behind billowing clouds, reflecting a glaring reflection over the glazed surface. The sea calmed slightly as the wind ceased, as if the storm had taken a breath to marvel at my creation.

It wasn't perfect. There were parts of the bridge that spiked out at perilous angles, the walkway was far from flat. But it was a connection, from me to the stranded prisoner, and I carefully treaded across the smooth surface with frozen feet, taking care not to slip when a wave licked over the edge and slickened the path.

When I finally made it to the second prisoner, I pushed the veil of her wet hair out of her face. Dark eyes peered back at me. She trembled against the pyre she was bound against, her lips a frightening blue. Every inch of her was damp and freezing, but I made quick work of her bindings, catching her with my body as she sagged off the soaked wooden stake.

"I've got you," I said, hearing a new rasp to my voice.

The first prisoner waited on the beach, watching from a safe distance. Only once I pulled the second to her feet and convinced her to push through the pain lacing her body stiff did we make it down the bridge, safe and solid.

"Thank you." Her voice shook as she spoke. Both women huddled together in the sand, trying to find a fraction of warmth left in their flesh.

Meanwhile, I scanned the dark water for another prisoner. There was one left, and I had a feeling Delilah had saved the most challenging for last, once the stores of my remnant were dangerously low and I was lightheaded and sick to my stomach.

A whistle drew my attention upward, where a pair of watchmen stood on the edge of the cliff. Between them, a body hung limp, the hands and feet tied.

"*Saints*." I gasped. "They're going to throw her over." There was nothing but rocks and foam frothing between the teeth of the tide. No bridge would save this remnant. Nothing could save her from the impact of a fall that steep onto the sharpened shapes of the sea stacks.

To my dread, they threw her, forcing my hand once more, forcing me to commit to the first idea that came to mind. There would be no crash if there were no rocks. I thrust out a hand and begged for Oblivion to spread across the inlet, let it devour anything in the sea that would harm the falling prisoner.

It was a last, desperate decision. Lacking a regulation over the fire, the explosive nature of it consumed all the energy I had left. The last thing I saw were hungry black flames eating away at the spires of stone.

That, and the third prisoner who dissolved into thin air as she was devoured.

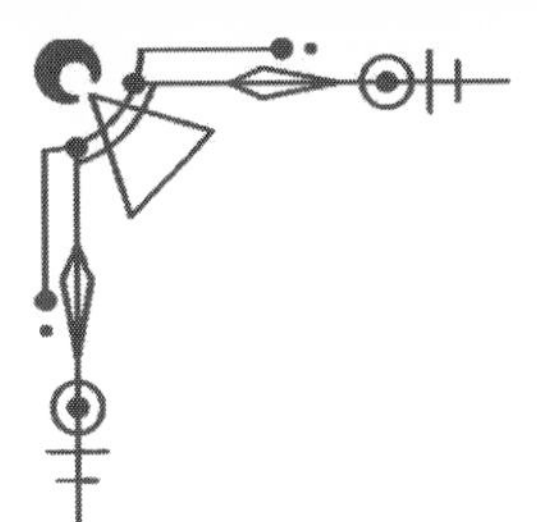
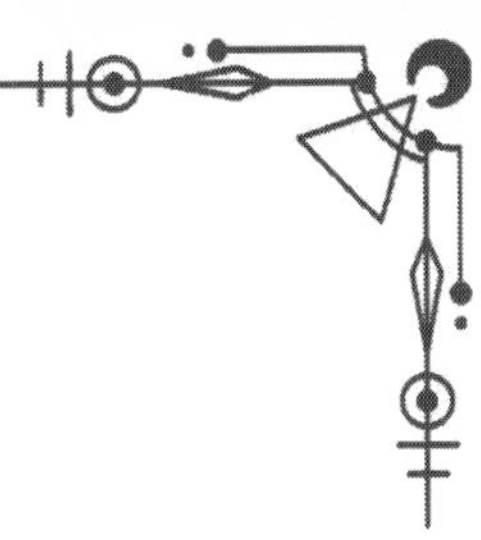

CHAPTER 8

NICOLAI

"Esme!"

A loud *thunk* answered in her place. My cousin rose from behind a workbench, rubbing the top of her head. Removing her welding goggles, her shoulders sagged as she saw me in the entrance of the garage.

"Oh, good." She sighed. "I thought you were Aramis for a moment."

"Has he been giving you trouble?" I asked.

She wiped her greasy hands on a towel hanging from her belt. "No. He's just . . . bored. And I mean I understand. He lost his brothers, his sister is in danger, and his entire way of life was stolen from him. I know you asked me to keep an eye on them but . . ."

"You need a break from babysitting?"

She winced. "Yes."

I circled her new project. An engine built on a smaller scale. Pieces of scrap metal littered the floor and cracked beneath my

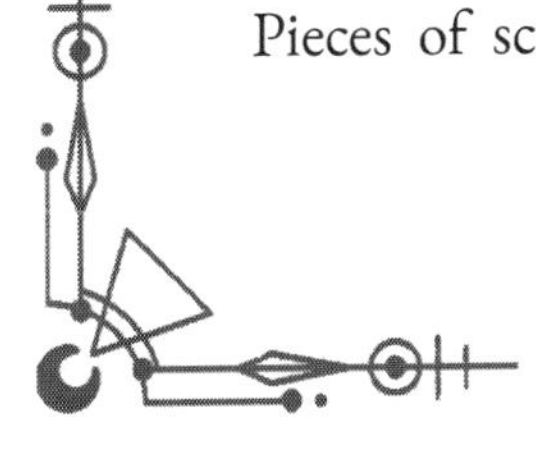

boots. "I'll find something to keep them busy, then. What are you working on?"

"It's a surprise." She grinned. "Though I suppose I can give you a sneak peek."

She strode to the brick wall behind me, where contraptions of all sorts hung from the wall. Daggers that could hide in practical clothing, a grappling hook I'd never seen her test, a cane sword Nonna had requested when her right side had weakened—which my aunts had promptly convinced her to reconsider given her poor eyesight and worsening cataracts.

She passed the wall and went to an object in the corner of the room covered with a tarp. Removing the covering slowly, she revealed what looked to be the frame of a bike with a much heavier build. The metalwork was flawless as I passed a hand over the aluminum frame, polished to reflect my image, marveling at her work.

"It's a . . . very nice bike, Esme. It looks like you've forgotten a few parts, though."

She snorted. "It's not just a *bike*. It's going to be automatic once I get the steam engine calibrated and running."

I looked back at the small engine, realizing where it was supposed to fit now. "A steam bike?"

"I'm still working on the name," she said. "But technically, yes. If the train and the boat can be operational, I figured, why not something used for more everyday transportation? When I'm through with it, you'll be able to travel faster than a horse. Maybe even as fast as a train."

I slipped my palm over the leather seat, golden-brown and soft from a recent oiling. Fast as the train? I slipped a breathy laugh at the idea. "Now that sounds fun."

Esme sighed. "Finally."

My gaze flickered from the bike to her. "What?"

"You're smiling. And not one of those asinine smirks you wear half the time. A true one." She threw the tarp back into place. "Who knew a new toy was all it took?"

I shrugged. "I'm in good spirits today. We've made considerable progress on getting into Hightower. Which is why I'm here."

"How can I help?" Esme turned serious at the mention of the mission.

"I have the shadows for the darkthief. However, she needs something to make the portal with. I was wondering if you could make something easily concealed that could sneak through the prison checkpoints, but large enough to be used as a portal." My hands buried in my pockets as she thought over my request.

"The requirements contradict each other."

"If anyone can find a compromise, it's you."

Her lips tightened, hiding her pleased smile. "Well, I suppose you're right. Though you should ask the darkthief to work her shadows here with me, so she can inform me of any special considerations she'd need for a portal."

"Are you actually asking to work *with* someone?" I asked, faking my shock.

My cousin smacked me with a thick glove she'd removed while we conversed. "If it means giving you the best chance to save Milla, absolutely. I'll step outside of all my comfort zones to rescue her."

My mood soured at the mention of her name. Six weeks had passed, and we'd officially been apart as long as we had been together. Somehow, the former felt so much longer.

"How soon can you have something ready?"

"Get your shadow bender here and I'll have something in a few days at the latest, depending on what we come up with. I'll work through the nights if I must."

Some of my nerves ate away at my ribs. I took a large breath to dissipate the feeling. "I'll keep the Marcheses busy as long as I can, so you can focus."

I turned to leave, but her hand over my shoulder stopped me short. "I'm proud of you, Nico. I know this is difficult, and you're trying hard not to show it, but I have no doubts you'll pull this off and get Milla back."

I tapped her hand but didn't push it away. The weight of it stole some of the burden stiff in my shoulders. "I wish I had your same faith in myself."

She scoffed. "You know, seeing your love for Camilla, it almost —*almost*—makes me want to find someone that loves me just as much. Then the Marcheses remind me why I enjoy being alone with my metal."

High praise coming from my cousin, who wanted nothing to do with a man, woman, or any form of cohabitation. "You have me, Esme. Always will."

"ARE you sure bringing them is a good idea?" Gideon asked as we drove to the station. I sat with him in the driver's seat, giving the cabin to Aramis and Jeremiah.

"They asked to help. Now that the bridge is gone and we can regulate who comes and goes to the Row, I feel better about letting them off the estate. This will be good for them." Besides, I hated dealing with Narcissa. Our history had been unpleasant from the start.

"What about the staff at the station?"

"Only a few of them work on this side, and the ones that do already know about the Marcheses. Marcus found Jeremiah and Aramis that day and helped them return the train home. They would have slipped that information to the Firenzes by now if they weren't loyal."

"I'd dare a Firenze to step foot in the Row," Gideon murmured.

I agreed. Had hoped for it, if only to fill them all with lead.

The Iron Saint was parked and idle, receiving maintenance after a long trip north where the cargo train had broken down. Aramis and his brother were silent as we jumped off the platform and proceeded deeper into the yard behind it, heading toward one of the empty boxcars stored off to the side. One of my men stood with a woman dressed in a tailored suit. Narcissa's form of security, I supposed.

"She's here?" I asked him.

The woman pulled out her pocket watch, hooked to a silver chain, to display the time to me. "You're late."

Gideon stepped forward and snatched the watch from her waist, snapping the chain from her vest. He smashed the glass with his fingers and twirled the minute hand until it was fifteen minutes sooner. He handed it back to her. "Check it again."

She shot him a glare and pursed her cherry lips. "Attano bastard."

"Enough," I said. "Ask your boss if it's alright if I bring some guests. They'll be the ones communicating with her over the next few weeks."

The boxcar rolled open with a grate and a slam. Narcissa stood in the gap, wearing a long fur coat that hung to her knees. Black lace tights led to bright red heels, the color of which matched her lipstick, a similar shade to her short hair.

"The more the merrier," she said with a smile. "Good to see you again, Nicolai."

The lie slid through my teeth easily. "Likewise, Summoner."

"YOU'LL NEED to be ready in three days."

The notes she passed me explained the timing. Aramis looked over my shoulder as I sat at a table with two chairs pulled up inside the boxcar. Narcissa sipped from a glass full of the ale she requested to have set up for the secret meeting.

It was a copy of the general's schedule, written in her own hand. She explained as we went through the notes. "The Watch disembarks down the river, where a small dock holds the boats they use to get to and from the island prison. A letter was sent to the general himself from Hightower, which I have also included."

"How did you get this information?" Aramis asked.

I nearly choked on my ale. "You don't know who Narcissa is?"

Seconds passed, and Aramis straightened. A touch of pink colored his cheeks. "Wait . . . You're *the* Narcissa? The one who owns the brothel in the Wet District?"

"The one and only." She smiled. "General Hughes visits me often, though we meet at a finer resort in the Steam District. Men like him are too refined to visit an establishment of sordid reputation. A little sedative after a romp puts him straight to sleep for hours. I went through his belongings while he was out and found a bit of information that would be of interest. Specifically, a letter from the prison." She looked at me. "You did request details on the traffic to Hightower, correct?"

"This is perfect." I skimmed over the details. Times and dates for the next launch. Even the names of requested watchmen. I'd give this to Regulus and let him choose his own victim. "Where is the copy of the letter from Hightower?"

She opened her briefcase and fished out another document, running an eye over the contents before handing it to me.

This one, I read slowly. Carefully. Letting no details go amiss. Aramis murmured something, finishing far quicker than I had while I got hung up on a section.

We are ready to proceed with the transferal. After running several tests on the Remni, we have discovered her remnant to be incredibly powerful and unstable. Extra hands are required for assistance in the last test. The Remni collapsed part of the island and eliminated several guards in the process, leaving us severely understaffed for the final procedure.

Their service to the Watch will be remembered and honored after Magrahel. Please see the attached list of recruits to replace them.

She killed a few guards. Had taken out part of the fucking island—the alleged impenetrable stone. The news swelled pride in my heart.

"That's my girl," I murmured.

Aramis grunted behind me.

"You can keep those," Narcissa said. "I'd rather not have copies of such sensitive information in my possession. I have a reputation to maintain." Narcissa finished her ale and stood.

"Thank you. It's certainly good to work with you again." This time, I meant it. She'd dug up gold with these letters.

"Better circumstances this time. Let's keep it that way. My girls are getting nervous, Nicolai. After you collapsed the bridge, they were worried their clients would find out who—and what—they are and take advantage of them."

I pulled a cigarillo from my jacket and let it burn, thinking. "If they are truly so afraid, send them to the Row. If they wish to continue their *nightly* business, we can set something up here. Sabina would be more than happy to work something out in her market, I'm sure."

Narcissa shook her head. "It's not so simple. They have families they cannot leave, children and debts they must pay for. Some bridges cannot be burned." The door slid on rusted hinges, groaning as she pushed it aside. "Protect my girls, and I'll keep the information flowing. Whatever you're planning, be safe. Many are counting on you—far more than you'd ever know."

I sighed as she left, closing the door behind her. Aramis sat in her seat, his brother joining him on the opposite side of the table. "Was my sister aware you were working with a courtesan?"

"Not entirely, no," I said. "But I have never indulged Narcissa's services, if that's what you're alluding. She was the one who summoned me when Gavriel needed to send me my next mark. Vanya Hartsong introduced us, a keen choice on her part. No one would ever question a man meeting with a woman like Narcissa."

"And now?"

I shrugged. "And now she works for me instead of Gavriel. The courtesans at her brothel are mostly descendants, which makes her entire operation in the Wet District illegal. Those women are practically her daughters, the way she cares for them. Which means her interests are aligned with mine."

"You said we were going to be in contact with her instead," Jeremiah spoke this time. His arms crossed.

"Correct. I can't be everywhere at once. Marcus will contact you when we receive word of another information dump. I'll trust you to keep me in the loop."

The younger Marchese rubbed his hands together. "Better than that stuffy garage, I suppose."

"Be grateful my cousin let you in at all," I reminded him. "I've asked Narcissa to look into the Firenzes next. They've been too quiet."

The conversation sealed itself with a long silence. Our business was finished, yet we lingered. A knowing realization settled between the four of us.

"Three days," Aramis sighed. "It all starts then."

I swallowed a dryness in my throat. Three days, and even that felt like an eternity. There were too many moving parts in this plan. If even one malfunctioned, the whole system would fail. "Will you come with me?"

The brothers perked, not expecting an invitation, apparently.

"Would you even need us?" Aramis asked. "We have no remnant to add to your crew."

Remnant or not, there was value in everyone if one knew where to look. "I could always use more guns. No one among us knows how to properly tend to a steam engine, either. If the ship you built is still there, I'll need someone to operate it."

Bree had informed me earlier that there weren't enough shadows to make a stable portal. It would get the lot of us there but wouldn't have the energy to hold as many travelers as we expected. If all thirty missing descendants were still in Hightower, we needed suitable transportation to take them back to the Isle. The Marcheses' ship had been taken by the Firenzes to take Milla to Hightower. I would bet it's still there.

The eldest brother let out a long breath. "I suppose we should tag along just to make sure you don't fuck this up."

Gideon shifted from the wall he leaned against to come to my defense, but I laughed. "Always appreciate the vote of confidence, Marchese."

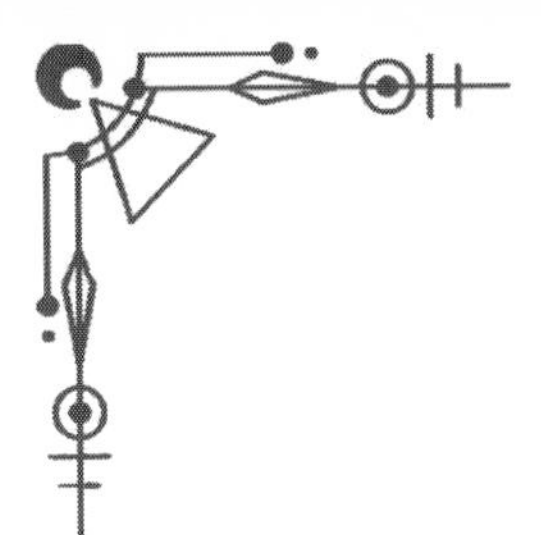
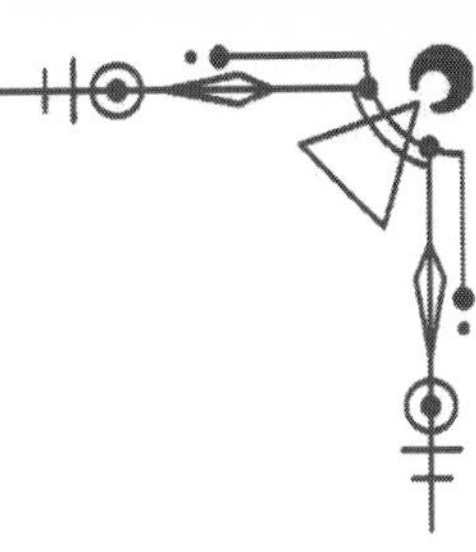

CHAPTER 9

NICOLAI

The sun hadn't even clipped over the horizon before someone banged at my bedroom door. I'd barely closed my eyes all night, unable to rest my mind enough to let it sleep. The plan rolled itself over and over again. Every step desired to be fine-tuned, flushed out, and foolproof.

"What the hells, Esme?" I rubbed my eyes to clear the haze of exhaustion.

"I need you to get something for me." The dark circles beneath the indentation of her welding goggles insisted she'd worked through the night as she promised.

"What is it?"

"Nonna's ring."

I frowned. "Did you ask her for it?"

She rolled her bloodshot eyes. "Of course not. She'd never give it to me after I've sworn off marriage. But you"—she gestured dramatically around me—"she'd let her favorite grandchild borrow it in a heartbeat."

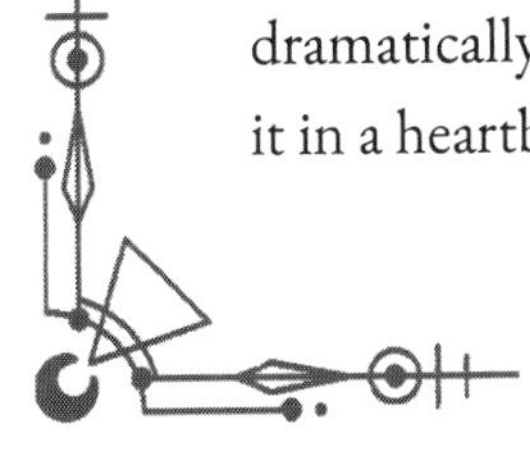

"I'm not her favorite."

"That's highly debatable." Esme frowned. "Look. I'm very tired, and I need the ruby in her ring to help Bree make a portal. You wanted this done fast, and we figured it out—"

"Alright, alright." *Saints*, it was too early for this. "Just . . . wait here."

Nonna didn't have her ring anymore. I would know, because it was currently in my end table, next to my bed. On the same side Milla had made herself comfortable that night she slept in my room. Meanwhile, I had been on edge, worried she'd look in the drawer where I kept Nonna's engagement ring and spoil everything.

The ruby was still in its velvet box, sitting prominently in a gold setting. Its cut was exquisite. Nonna claimed my grandfather had *worked his ass off* for a year, saved every extra reole he had, to buy her the highest quality gem in the shop. Even by today's standards, it was an impressive piece of jewelry. The sentimental value, however, made it priceless.

I reluctantly strode back to the door to hand it to my cousin. "What do you need with it?"

She pulled the ring from the box and held it in the gas light lamps still alive in the hall. "We've been testing ways to bend the shadows to make a sort of projection instead of a contained portal. A mirror is most common, since it's large and has a solid plane to attach the shadows to. But something small enough to sneak by the Watch required a bit of brainstorming."

A kaleidoscope of colors refracted across the ceiling tiles.

"If light can be collected and projected," Esme explained, "perhaps the shadows can be as well. To do so, we needed a rather large gem that had enough cuts in it to form a large enough projection for you to pass through."

Science had never been a strength of mine. I nodded along anyway. “If it gets Milla back, it’s worth risking.”

“I promise it shall remain in one piece. Our grandmother will never even know it’s gone.” Esme smiled and pocketed the box. Turning to leave, she made it five paces down the hall before her quick steps slowed to a stop. “Hold on.” She looked back at me over her shoulder. “Nico, why did you have Nonna’s ring?”

The look on my face must have said enough. I sighed, that ache in my chest pulsing with the slow beat of my heart. “Just keep it safe, Esme.”

She cleared her throat and answered with a quick nod, and I was thankful that, for once, she didn’t prod for once.

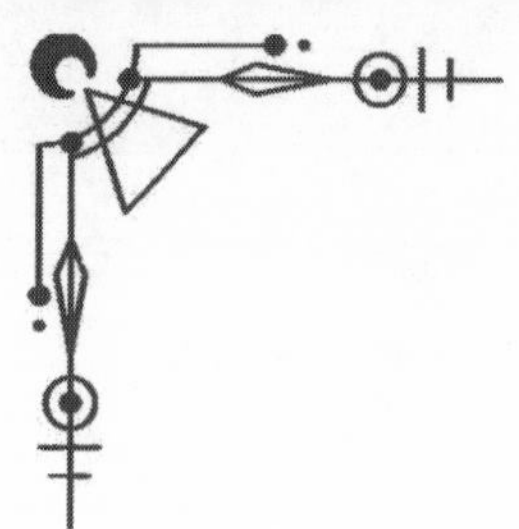
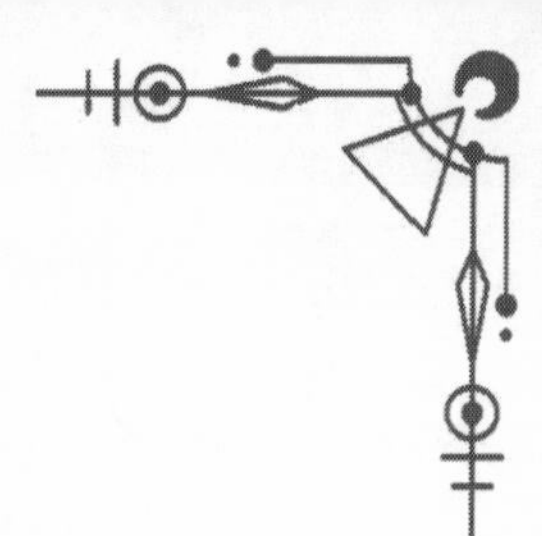

CHAPTER 10

CAMILLA

Heat woke me from a dreamless sleep like an old friend I had sorely missed. The crack of logs in a fire fluttered my eyes open, discovering the dance of orange flames in a hearth. I was lying on my side, encased in wool blankets with my hands stretched toward the source of heat as if they had unconsciously sought their own warmth.

My hands were no longer a bruised blue from the frigid sea, but a healthy pink. It was the first time in weeks I'd felt any measure of warmth, and I soaked in it, reveling in the way my blood practically simmered beneath my skin.

"The alchemedis said you'd die if we didn't warm you quickly. Fortunately for you, we still need you alive," Delilah hissed above me.

Turning to look up at her, my joints ached in protest at the slight movement. My bones were made of lead, heavy from a recent glint treatment.

"Don't get comfortable."

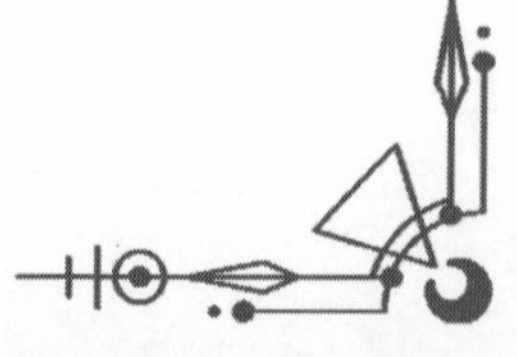

Her presence was enough to smother any contentment found in basic human luxury. I sat up off the floor to spite her, pushing through the rigid lock of my muscles.

"Why do you need me?" I asked, but my tongue was thick in my mouth, making it difficult to speak.

The alchemist didn't care. She lowered into an armchair pushed near the hearth, silent for a while. "The Remni were powerful beings, akin to warriors with divine blessing, when the Saints fractured and passed down their remnants. As one of Chaos, you not only wield the same destructive promise as her, but you can access the deepest hell in the void. A place created by Chaos to grow her army, and you're going to open it for me."

Oblivion.

"I don't know what you're talking about," I muttered. "I've never . . . the thought alone is ridiculous!"

"Perhaps." She opened the book she carried with her everywhere. She found a tab and smoothed down the crease of the spine to hold it open there. "But that's what the next trial will determine."

My jaw locked, forcing me to slide the words through my teeth. "I'm not going through another one of your trials."

Her thin lips tipped into a smile. "You won't have a choice this time. If you're worried you'll hurt someone else, don't be. We won't need to motivate you for this test."

My fists tightened on the blanket still wrapped around my shoulders. As much as I wanted to blame her for what happened, it hadn't been Delilah who killed Sera's father. It hadn't been her who turned the third prisoner into vapor. My choices ended the lives of two people. My pathetic lack of dominion over my remnant, the thing my father had wisely silenced, even more at fault. I despised that part of me more than anything else in my body.

"What about the other prisoners?" I asked. "I saved them. You said they would be freed if I—"

"I said they wouldn't return to Hightower." Her features settled into a glare. "And I was true to my word."

"What do you mean? What did you do with them?" My question came out in a whisper, unsure if I truly wanted to know.

"Nothing. The watchmen retrieved your body before the tide rose. They were not forced back to their cells, as was promised."

"You *left* them there?" On the side of a damn cliff with no protection from the elements, no way to scale the side of the island. A seed of guilt burrowed into my heart. I had saved them only to prolong the inevitable. No one could survive the sea and the tempest weather surrounding the island.

She shrugged. "Did you think I'd give them a boat ride back to the mainland? They are free. That was the bargain we made."

Her apathy snapped something in my heart. The blankets slipped from my fingers—and I lunged.

My throws were weak at best, but my nails were still sharp. I threw myself on top of her, tearing at her face, her hair, anything I could get to. She flung her arms up in defense. A squeal of surprise left her as my weight pinned her to the chair, my strikes hitting their mark. Hands gripped my shoulders and flung me off her.

While they wrestled with my arms, my legs remained free. I kicked my heel into her nose as a parting gift.

I hadn't even seen the watchmen standing in the same room as us; they'd been so quiet. They shoved me to the floor, pinning my arms behind my back while my face was shoved against a coarsely woven rug. From a rat's perspective, I watched Delilah pinch her nose to slow the bleeding from her face. Her hair was torn from its usual bun, hanging limply around her scratched face.

"You bitch!" she shrieked. "You're lucky I need you whole and well or I'd cut you apart for that!" She stood and knelt beside me as the watchmen pinned me to the floor, snatching my matted hair to pull my face off the ground.

"But know this, you wretched creature," she spat. "Once I've gotten what I need from you, I will destroy you and your remnant and banish your darkness from the world. I know what your power entails now. I know your weakness." She pulled my hair tighter, making me wince. "Most important, I know that even a Remni of Chaos has her limits. You are not all powerful like I once believed. If I can drain you, I can kill you, just like your mother."

As if she'd planned it, all my fight ceased at the mention of her. "You . . . killed my mother?"

Her cruel smile returned. "Oh, I did something worse." She released my hair and shoved my head into the ground, striking my temple against the stone. "Throw her back in the cell. Make sure the alchemedis keeps her healthy. We need her strong for the procedure."

My mouth dried at her orders.

The watchmen complied, and they dragged my limp body with their searing gloves. They didn't release me when we made it to the stairwell, the entire descent, not even when their grasp brought tears to my eyes from the burn of the glint in their gloves.

One of them, my usual guard, Mike, took me by both arms and tossed me against the wall of my cell. I scrambled to my hands and knees before he shut the wall of stone behind him.

"Wait!" I cried. It was just him, the other guards had left, but all I could see was my last hope. I had sunken to rock bottom, seeking a watchman's help. "Please . . . I don't know what Delilah has planned. I know you work for her, but you don't have to. Nicolai Attano, he's my husband and he'll give you anything you want if you help me get out of here. Please, Mike—"

"Shut your deceiving mouth," he growled. "There is nothing about you worth saving, Chaos. Power like yours shouldn't exist in the world. The sooner Delilah takes your key, the better."

"Key?" I asked, but the question hardened his face. He slammed the wall shut without another word.

Alone, I crouched over my cot, pressing my forehead into the thin canvas. My fist tightened, pulled at the strands of Delilah's red hair still caught between my fingers. The cold had returned, a reminder of where I was. I had no friends, no allies, no one to help me here.

No one was coming for me.

But the crack in my heart had opened just enough to let something free. The darkness he spoke of, a churning cloud that filled me with wrath and rage and revenge. Delilah had taken everything from me, and I wouldn't let her have anything else. Not another damn piece, including whatever key he mentioned.

Soon after, the guards brought me my first meal. A real meal. The meat was still warm and salted, and I savored every bite. I'd eat their food, drink their tonics to heal. I'd let them make me strong, let them regret it later.

No one was coming for me. That had been a mantra replayed in my thoughts every day since I'd arrived here.

No one was coming. So, I would have to save myself.

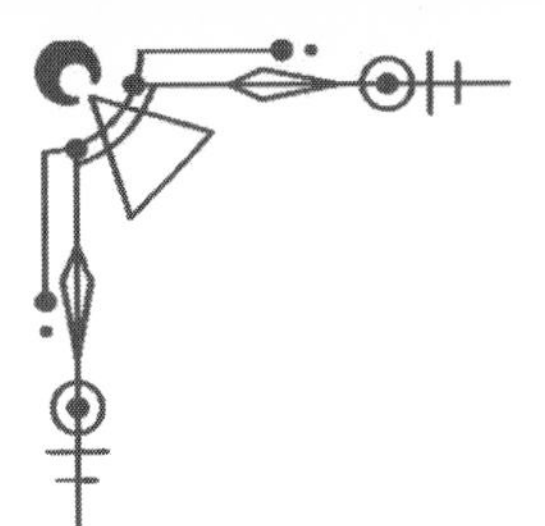
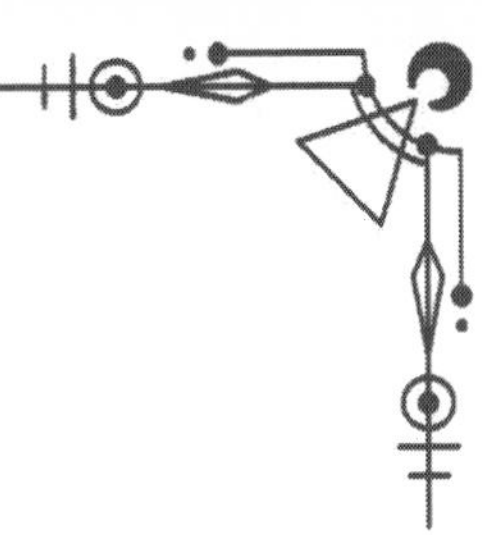

CHAPTER 11

NICOLAI

The day had come for Regulus to take the portal to Hightower. I trained my attention on the clock and the driveway outside the garage window. Everything was ready. The brick wall anchored our end of the portal, and a curtain veiled the shimmering surface of shadows. My cousins waited in their watchmen uniforms. We had laid our guns and equipment laid out on Esme's workbenches, cleaned and replenished with plenty of ammo.

All we needed was the sleezy Mirth descendant who, to my reluctance, held the fate of my wife in his dirty hands.

"Where the hells is he? He needs to meet the garrison before they head to the docks. If he's going to make it in time, he'll need to show up in—"

"Looking for me?"

I turned to find a mountain of a man standing in the doorway, twisting his mustache between two thick fingers. My cousins jumped to their feet with their pistols cocked.

"Who the hells are you?" Gideon demanded.

The watchman held up both hands, grinning ear to ear. "Commander Angelo Marden, at your service, Mr. Attano."

"Shitting Saints, Regulus." Luther sighed. "You can't show up here disguised like that."

"Right, because a member of the Watch would just tarry into the backyard of the most dangerous men in the city." Regulus rolled his brown eyes. "I just came by to pick up the portal. Nico said it was done."

"Why the fuck would you choose to impersonate a commander?" My strides ate the distance between us. "The entire ploy depends on you getting to Hightower without arousing suspicion, and you're playing the big man instead of an unimportant recruit. Are you an idiot or just that selfish?"

His smug smile fell. "I don't like your tone, Attano. This all depends on me, remember? I might be a little nicer to the one who's risking his ass to make this happen." Regulus's demeanor shifted to something more hostile. In the commander's skin, adding a few inches to his stature, he was more intimidating than usual. "I chose the commander so no one would give me shit. I've been pretending to be a fucking wash boy for the guard for the past week just to get his fancy pins, for shitting saints. You think I didn't think this through?"

"It doesn't matter what I think, does it?" I muttered. "There's no time now to change your identity. I trust you at least cleaned up after yourself?"

Regulus nodded with a locked jaw. "He won't be a problem. Now or later."

He looked me up and down, arching a brow at my own uniform. Narcissa had sent a trunk of old watchmen robes she acquired from the lost and found in her brothel. The courtesans had snatched articles while their patrons were otherwise occupied, playing foolish when they couldn't find their missing robes afterward.

"Where is it?" Regulus asked.

Esme approached from behind, the ring in her hand. Bree was at her side, ready to explain the disguised portal. She plucked it from Esme's outstretched hand and held it up for Regulus to see clearly.

"The shadows are trapped in here. The crystal is loosely fitted and easily twisted, just give it a spin to stimulate them. Once that's done, the portal will hit the back of the ruby and project a larger face on whatever you shine it on. A wall would be best or some other flat surface."

She lowered the ring to the space between them. The ruby sat high in the center on a setting Esme had fashioned. Beneath it, shadows swirled in a transparent crystal loosely trapped between the golden prongs.

Esme added, "Until then, keep it concealed."

"A little gaudy for my tastes, but I'll wear it." Regulus pulled off his glove. He slipped it on his pinky, the only finger that would fit. "When you asked for my ring size, I probably should have given you Angelo's hand."

My cousin rubbed her temples. "That would have been ideal."

"I'll drive you to the station," I said on my way to the door.

"Not necessary, Mr. Attano, I—"

"I wasn't being polite," I shouted, already outside. My boots crunched against the ice filming the lawn as I motioned the stable hand to ready the carriage. "Get in the damn car. We need to talk."

Regulus was silent until we pulled onto the main street. Before he could open his mouth, I asked, "What do want from me?"

He arched a thick brow. "What are you talking about?"

I tamed my nerves with a large breath. My heart felt frayed, worn from worry, of getting this all wrong. The closer the time came to rescue Milla, the less control I had over my temper.

"What can I give you to make sure you don't run last minute or turn on me later? I don't trust you, Regulus. You've always operated under the motivation of your best interest. What do you want from all of this?"

He had too willfully offered his assistance. Just because I worked with him in the past, didn't mean he was a friend. I still didn't know how the Summoner found him, or how much she'd told him about the inspector. He was damn good at what he did. His shift was flawless, from what I could tell. Regulus was valuable. He had to know that.

He pulled a cigarillo from a tin box and lit it. "Perhaps you aren't the only bastard the OIC has burned, alright? My services might be expensive, but you covered the costs. Now, I get something money can't buy."

"What is that?"

He took a hit before replying, blazing the tip of the cigarillo orange. "The Mirth community is small, but very close. When we heard one of our own was caught up with the Marcheses and the Firenzes, and subsequently had gone missing, we figured she was another victim of the Collector."

Understanding slipped through me like a cold draft. He knew Sera. He was going there for Sera, and she was long dead in my family's graveyard.

The unease in my chest worsened. "Don't let your vengeance distract you, I need you focused in Hightower."

He swatted the air like it was a ridiculous thought. "I'll get you in, Attano. That's my job, right?"

I didn't even mention the ring, didn't want to give him any idea of its importance to me. I'd cut it off his cold, dead fingers if he gave me any grief about it later. "Right. I'll bring you to the tracks. Cross the viaduct on foot. Narcissa said she'll have a driver waiting for you to bring you to the docks. They know her carriages and reckon you're heading to the island a satisfied commander."

"Wish that were true," he murmured.

I scoffed. "Likewise."

His stare turned curious. "She's there, too. Isn't she? Camilla."

No use lying now. He would see for himself either way. "Yes."

A barking laugh burst through the carriage, making me wince. His smile slowly faded. "But . . . I went to her funeral." Dark eyes shifted to look at me. "She was there, in the casket."

I licked my lips, beginning to regret this drive. "It wasn't Camilla in the casket. It was her friend. Her very good friend who died for her, to protect a secret about Camilla." My gaze never fell from his, ensuring what he obviously already suspected. "Her name was Sera. I'm assuming you knew her."

Regulus's shoulders slacked against the seat. His posture deflated, slouching. He didn't speak until the carriage rolled to a stop where the road came to a dead end near the river, where the viaduct that crossed it stood in the distance, hidden halfway in the fog.

"You fucking Attanos are the worst people on the Isle. You call me selfish." He scoffed. "But you'll use anyone to get what you want. To keep your pockets and your cock happy."

"Regulus—"

He slid down the seat and threw the door open. "I'll get you in Hightower. After this, don't ask me for anything, ever again."

WE WAITED.

All eyes rested on the mirror. Hours passed, and it took everything in me to sit down, to conserve my energy. I burned a cigarillo despite Esme's sideways glance, needing a distraction before I paced a trench across her garage.

"I thought we couldn't smoke?" A Marchese son broke the quiet. I shot him a glare.

"Nico is an exception." Esme sighed.

Solomon stood by Gideon and Adler, discussing something quietly with his sons. I watched their lips, read the words he spoke in a hushed voice. My uncle clamped his hand over his son's shoulder, told him how much he loved him, told him to get in and out, to come home. I looked away, feeling ashamed. Something burned in my eyes as my gaze returned to the mirror.

Solomon's cane tapped the concrete floor as he approached my seat. "Is this everyone?" When I confirmed his question, he sighed. "I wish you would have taken more men."

"More men would require more disguises. Once we break out the prisoners, we'll have all the men we need." It was a two-to-one guard to prisoner ratio. I liked those odds, but my information could be skewed if Milla's presence had drawn more guards than usual. I hoped that Regulus would overhear more information about this transferal happening on the island, and why Milla was the subject of it, before he found a quiet place to sneak us in.

It was my cousins, a handful of the best benders in the city, and Finn, the mentalus. Sabina offered her wearhs, but I denied them. Too many people knew about this plan to begin with, and with their recent involvement with the Firenzes, I'd never fully trust a single bleeder ever again.

"Nico," he said, voice low. "I want to tell you something."

"Yes?"

He shuffled, leaning closer to speak over my shoulder. "Please be careful. I know Milla needs you, but so does your family. Don't do anything overly reckless, alright?"

"Uncle, you think everything I do is reckless." I meant the words to sound lighthearted, though they just came out bitter.

He released a quiet sigh, and the disappointment in his breath made me regret my tone. "That's not true. I just . . . I just want you to value your life as much as you value everyone else's. I want you to come home. Your father—"

The mirror came to life, then. I stood, startled into action by the colorless haze surrounding the wooden frame.

"Hells," Adler murmured. "It actually worked."

"Of course it works," Bree snapped. "The problem isn't getting there, it's getting back. The portal won't be able to hold all the prisoners you want to free. It's not for bulk transportation."

Aramis adjusted the hood of his black robes over his head. "We'll find our way back fine. Just make sure the Iron Saint is parked at the docks."

"Marcus knows. He's well aware of the route," I told him. "Is everyone ready, then?"

Gideon stepped forward with a smile, hiding any reservation of this plan behind nerves of steel. He might have been the kindest cousin out of all of them, but he was also the most determined. Nothing was hard enough, cruel enough, to make him hesitate. "Lead the way, cousin. No more time to waste."

After weeks of planning and plotting, of careful collaborations and deals with demons, it was time.

Saints, it felt good to finally do something. I would bring Milla home, or I wouldn't come back at all. Either way, I wouldn't spend another day without her. The thought alone was enough to lift something heavy off my shoulders, permit me to take a full breath again. Let me return the smile my cousin knowingly sent me.

My fingers shook as I pulled a glove over my false hand, concealing it before facing the mirror. Luther stood beside me, and the shadows accepted my form, slipping around the arm I reached into the silver-foiled face.

"Let's go get your lady, boss."

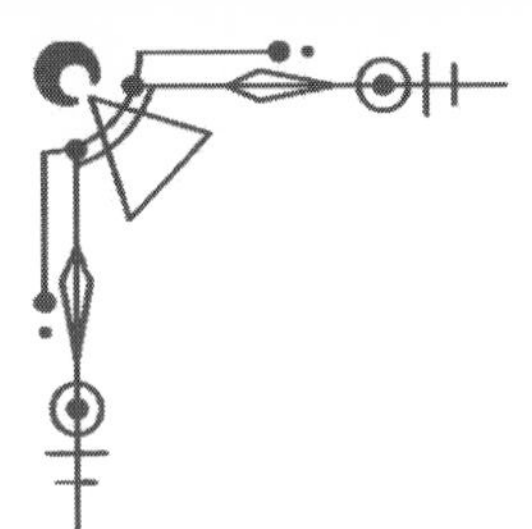
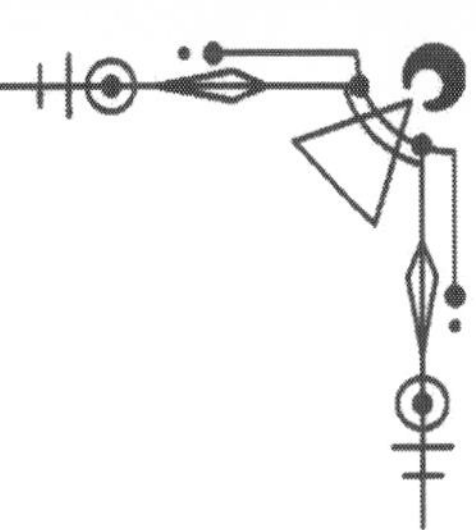

CHAPTER 12
NICOLAI

The commander's cabin was small, located off a wing branching from the main building on the island. Regulus and I went through his desk while the others slipped through the portal. It had been simpler than the mirror I used to infiltrate the High Overseer's mansion, having only one point of exit.

"Cozy." Adler arrived last after the Marchese sons.

I slipped a logbook found atop his desk in the back of my leather waistbelt holding an arsenal of sheathed knives. The front was embossed with an eagle spread across my stomach—the sigil of the OIC. The same symbol decorated the back of our robes. Once everyone was through, I pocketed the ring sitting on a stool still projecting the portal across a tapestry lined wall.

"What can you tell us, Regulus?"

Still wearing the skin of Commander Angelo, Regulus braced his hands on the black desk. The hem of a cloak draped his arms from silver shoulder gauntlets. He'd changed since I saw him last.

The new style of his robes appeared more like armor. "We were briefed before docking. There's a ceremony of some sort tonight, something in the tower. They moved the prisoners to new cells in the main building, and all staff besides those authorized for the ceremony must remain guarding the prisoners. No one is allowed out of their cells for any reason. They want the hole quiet—whatever that is."

I nodded along. "The cells are underground, hence the hole. Why are they clearing the tower?"

"I asked and was told those details were a need-to-know basis. Those who needed to know, already knew," he said. "There's a locker room down the hall, you'll want to update your uniform, Nico. Only commanders get into the tower. Get a helmet while you're at it. It's apparently the new style here." He grabbed a facemask made of shiny black metal. The only features engraved in the flawless sheen were two slits where the eyes should be.

"Do you know anything else about this ceremony? When is it happening?"

"Soon. They're sending all the guards down into the hole as we speak—"

A knock sounded at the door. Everyone stilled. I looked to Regulus, beckoned for him to answer, to say something to make the visitor leave. He only stood there with his mouth hanging open, taking far too long to choose his words.

"Angelo?" the visitor spoke through the door. Through the frosted glass of the privacy window, the outline of a guard appeared to cross its arms. If we could see his form, he might be able to see ours.

Regulus cleared his throat. "One moment."

I looked at Finn and nodded. He was too small in his watchman's robes to fool anyone. Even with the layers of uniform to thicken his build, the Watch would never take someone of his lithe stature. If he hadn't been essential to getting a quick map of this place, he'd be better classified as a liability.

Regulus started towards the door while I slowly slipped my revolver into my hand, eyes trained on the door. He opened it for the visitor, standing to the side so his body concealed the rest of the room. When the watchman was inside, his spine straightened to appear more alert.

"What's going on here, who are all of you? Angelo?"

Commander Angelo locked the door, pushed his towering frame between the other watchman and his escape. "They have some questions for you, Commander Seamus."

"Sit down," I said.

His eyes narrowed on the gun in my hand. "Put that down! We don't have time for this nonsense. I should report you all to Delilah and the Grand Commander. She'll have you all discharged from service for disregarding orders. I'll shout for aid right now—"

"Try it. I dare you."

His mouth opened to call for help, yet not a sound passed his lips. The air had been stolen from his chest, and it was then he realized exactly whom he had walked in on. Not a group of his comrades, but a gathering of vengeful descendants.

My gun fell as my arm slacked, hanging at my side. Luther and Adler slowly made their way to either side of the man, who glanced at them nervously. I gestured to an armchair in front of Finn. "I'll tell you again nicely. Sit down. Do as I say and you will be rewarded."

His steps were stiff, but he conceded to my first order, sinking into the worn leather seat. I smiled and released my remnant on the man, who inhaled a large gulp of air.

"Good man." I smiled at his obedience.

"Fucking *descendants*," he spat. "How could you betray us, Angelo?"

"Probably because I'm not Angelo, Seamus. Though I do hope we can still be friends after this."

Seamus didn't seem to reciprocate the sentiment.

I interrupted their exchange. "Enough. I need you to give us a map of this place. Where they are holding each prisoner, where the guards are stationed, how to get to the tower, all of it."

He gripped the arms of his chair as if to lunge. Luther pressed the barrel of his gun into the man's temple to make him still.

"There's not enough air in my lungs for you to steal to make me tell you anything. Fuck off, Bender." The veins in his forehead strained ash he spoke.

"That's fine. Do your work, Finn. Gideon, make a rough sketch of whatever he tells you."

"Ready," my cousin called from behind the desk, pen in hand.

"What is this?" Seamus asked as Finn stepped forward. The Mirth remnant cocked his head and concentrated on something I couldn't see, wincing as he shifted through memories.

"Alright, Finn?"

He nodded with a single jerk of his chin. "There's a lot to go through, and not all its pleasant to sift around. I'm almost there, though. He's trying to suppress the information."

"The first thing they teach us in training," the man said, teeth clenched with effort. "Is how to protect our thoughts from your kind." He struggled against Finn's intrusion, but resisting a Mirth remnant as it traveled through the mind triggered crippling headaches. If he was already squirming, Finn would break him.

"And you can't even do that properly," Finn said. "Alright, I think I found it. *Saints*, this place is massive."

"Keep it quick and general—we've got to move."

"Right, well, for starters, we're on the main level. There's a pair of doors that lead to the hole, which basically looks like it sounds. Corridors branch from a large pit. Prisoners are behind the walls, though it might be hard to find them. There looks like there is a marking on the walls outside of a cell, a symbol apparently for each kind of remnant, so they can keep track of what's occupied and what's empty."

"Can you find out how the guards move?"

It took him another full minute to answer. "Two in each corridor, only ten of them are used currently, though some stem deeper into the pit. Some of them are way down there, Nico. Seven hells, I don't know how they breath . . ."

"Focus, Finn. What else? What about the tower?"

He gulped. "Take the hall across from this one in the main room. There's a passage that brings you to an open space in front of a tower. It's straightforward from there. No one's stationed in front of it tonight since everyone is inside. You should be able to slip in unnoticed. Except . . ." He grunted. "You'll need to wear a mask like Regulus has. They're all wearing masks tonight in the tower."

"Fine. If that's all—"

"It's not." He sucked in a breath. "They're going to take something from a prisoner tonight. Seamus here thinks it's a bad idea, as do the rest of the guards. They talked. They sent word to a family—"

"Shut your fucking mouth and get the hells out—"

"They sent word to a family in the city to warn them." Finn raised his voice above the guard. "They didn't need extra men at all. It was just a ruse to send a message."

A family on the Isle. Most likely the ones that paid their pockets. The Firenzes were the Society's biggest donors, coincidently the same branch of the Watch that worked the prison.

If they'd sent for the alchemists, then the family could very well be here tonight as well.

"Where are those damn masks, Regulus?"

MY COUSINS TOOK care of the guard, killing him quietly and disposing of his body in a locker in the commander's office so he wouldn't tip off the rest. Regulus guided me to the small armory they kept, quickly showing me the right cape to adorn and how to wear the mask so I could still breathe.

"Keep the hood over your head. You shouldn't see any part of your skin," he instructed. "And be careful of the gloves. I almost blew my cover getting scalded by them. The inside is fine, though."

True to his word, I barely skimmed the leather and felt the familiar burn of glint. Slipping them on to complete the uniform, I felt like an ominously colored peacock beneath all the layers of platinum and black decoration. "Anything else?"

He looked me over once and gave a nod of approval. "You look like a commander. Should be good enough to let you in the tower, now that there's a space to fill."

We met the men back in the hall. I ran over the plan with Luther and the rest of my family and our men before splitting from the group. They'd follow Luther's lead and the map Finn helped sketch for them while the Mirth remnant hung back with Aramis. A few of our men would escort them to the docks and clear the way to the ship, then have it prepared for a quick escape if necessary.

Regulus stood behind the Marchese sons.

"What are you doing?" I asked. "We need you to help take down the guards in the hole."

"My job was to get you in, Attano. I'm not going to be left behind. Where the Marcheses go, I go. At least I know you'll watch out for them."

Gritting my teeth, I dismissed him. Every argument was just another wasted breath keeping me from the reason I came here. "Fine. Once I have Milla, I'll check on the main building and the hole progress. From there, all bets are off. Get everyone out as quick as possible, shoot anyone in your way, and get to the ship. Understood?"

Clear as fucking mud, the way none of them responded. I'd done my best to prepare them for what lay beneath the surface of this island. Hopefully, it would be enough.

Luther trailed me until we reached the end of the corridor, passing empty offices with darkened windows. The main building was empty. Whoever was to transfer from the tower must have already done so. Obsidian stone sealed shut the entrance to the hole.

My cousins pulled their hoods over their heads, and I fitted the silver mask over my face, hiding my identity. "According to Angelo's logbook, there are forty-seven prisoners in the hole, a few more than we expected. Make sure each one comes out."

Luther stepped before the wall which concealed the main hall leading into the hole. With a sweep of his hand, the stone lurched to the side, slipping into a pocket discreetly. He cocked his gun with a crooked smile. "Don't worry about us, boss. Just another day on the job."

The rest of the group followed close behind, weapons out, each one disappearing under the cloak of darkness. Part of me wished I could split myself in two, could be everywhere at once. I wished to join them, to protect my cousins, to make sure they walked out with the forty-seven as well.

Since the day Milla came into my life, I knew a time would come where I'd be forced to choose between my new family and my old. The choice wasn't easy but clear as the day I'd prepared to make it. I started down the opposite corridor.

It was time to get my wife back.

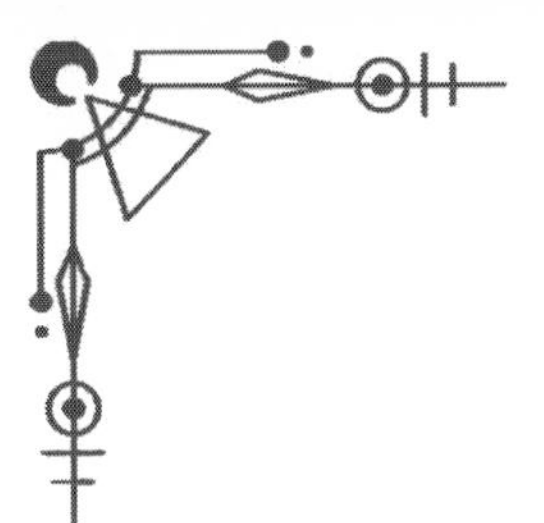
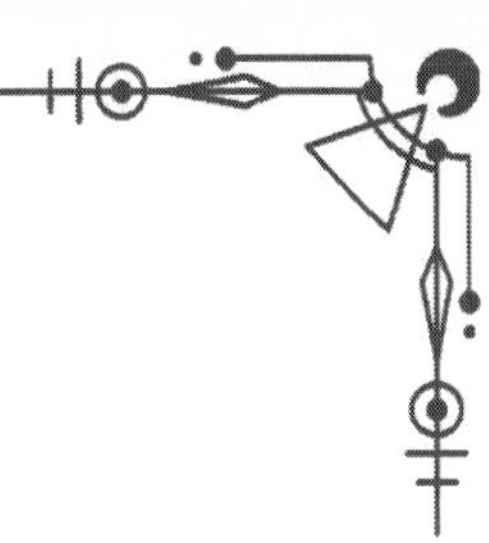

CHAPTER 13

CAMILLA

A strand of red hair twisted around my finger, cutting off the circulation back to my hand. They would come for me soon—had to be soon. I'd never heard so much noise in the tower. Stone grinding against stone, prisoners yelping as guards shouted orders, the crack of whips and beaters as they hit flesh and the cries they evoked.

"Vesper? Callow?" I whispered into the dark, hoping they'd hear me. "Are you still there? Please, don't ignore me if you are."

A pause followed, and I didn't know if they pointedly ignored me or if the guards had already dealt with them.

"We're still here, Milla."

It was Vesper who'd broken the quiet, the first time I'd heard her voice in weeks. Relief and bitterness fought for dominance in my heart. "Do you know what's happening?"

I looped the strand of hair once more around my finger, waiting for her to reply.

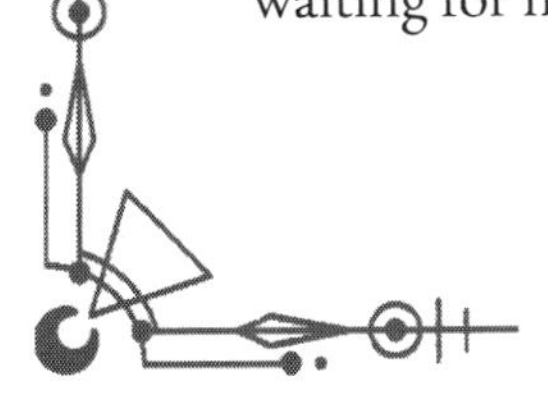
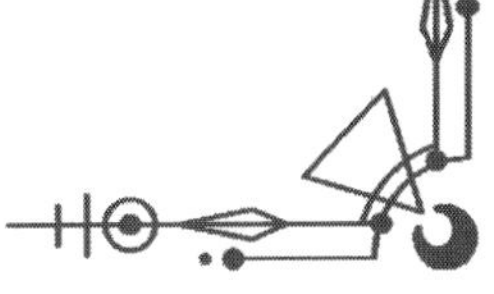

"They're clearing the tower for a ceremony. One of them said something about a third trial. Your trial."

I figured. Delilah had promised as much. Her confirmation only encouraged my plans, and I quickly set to work, forgetting the darkthief like she had me. Waiting until the noises grew loud enough to cover the sound of ripping fabric, I tore off a strip of cloth from the bottom of my left sleeve, pulling at a hole the rocks had torn in it during the previous trial.

"Milla?"

"What?" The word was muffled as I held the dirty strip between my teeth, trying to tie it around my upper arm.

"Just so you know," she said, her voice gentle. "We never meant to be cruel, ignoring you. It's just. . . we didn't think we'd ever find you."

My work ceased. "Find me?"

"Vesper, that's enough," Callow interjected. "We aren't safe to speak of it here. They could be listening."

"She might be about to die, Callow. Shouldn't she know?"

I would not die. Not today, anyway, if my plans meant anything. "What are you two talking about?"

"Your remnant," she blurted. "We've been looking for you. It's about—"

Vesper's cell opened, the vibration of the moving stone shuddered through the floor and severed the connection between us.

The intrigue she sparked inside me felt like hope, and I pushed it down before whatever was left of my optimism grew wings. There was no hope here to wish for better days, only the choices we made to ensure we claimed them. Vesper was a stranger, as unfamiliar to me as any knowledge of my remnant was to the world. She must have been mistaken.

No one was looking for me.

Before long, the few prisoners held here had been moved, leaving me isolated in my schemes. Though this time, I wasn't worried about what would come. My strength had returned little by little with every meal, just as Delilah wished. They even let me bathe by myself, though the water was freezing and the bath brief.

The alchemedis came shortly after for my glint treatment, shadowed by the guards. She didn't notice the tourniquet fashioned around my bicep where I tied the shred beneath the other wide sleeve of my tunic, coincidentally the same arm she administered the sedative.

When the stone rolled shut, I sucked as much poisoned blood from the puncture site as I could and spat it across the stone. Only once my blood stopped burning on my tongue did I pull the tourniquet loose. I hid the bloodstains with my thin cot, eliminating the chance for questions from the guards when they came to retrieve me.

It actually worked. A bit of glint still seeped through, dulling my remnant for a moment, but it wore off much faster than usual.

The one good thing that had come out of Delilah and her trials was the opportunity to learn more about my remnant and what it could do. She taught me how to destroy, how to feel it—and I would make her regret the trials she'd put me through. I had the will and the way to escape now, blow through the stone and send the whole tower crumbling down, but I wanted to wait until the right moment.

I'd wait until this last trial, until the guards and the ones who'd beat and tortured me throughout my time here, the alchemedis who drugged me senseless, the alchemist who kidnapped me. I'd wait until they were all in the same room—and I'd unleash all the wrath in my remnant on each of them.

I'd destroy Delilah and her staff, the guards, and purge the world of their cruel curiosity. Then perhaps finally some good would come of Chaos.

THE TOWER REMAINED NEARLY SILENT. I kept my ear to the floor, listening, trying not to shiver and conserve the strength I had collected from the last few days. The stone door of my cell rolled away, and I startled at the introduction of the first sound, sensation, and light I'd known for hours.

"Get up. It's time."

"Mike? Is that you?" I squinted at my guard. A black mask concealed his face, reflecting the light of the kerosine lamp he carried. "Is that a new outfit? You didn't have to get all dressed up for me."

"*Now*, prisoner."

I smiled. "And here I thought we were on a first name basis. Suit yourself, Michael. I'd hate to keep the bitch waiting."

If he objected to me slandering his superior, he said nothing. I didn't even know if Delilah was the boss here, or if she worked for the Watch. I supposed it didn't matter, as they were all on the same side, anyway.

He remained several paces behind me as I climbed the stairs to the Orbitarium, the top of the tower where Delilah's laboratory was situated beneath a glass dome ceiling. But when the stone rolled away, I discovered the roof was gone. Cold, salty wind filled my chest, something fresh instead of the stale and stagnant air in the cells.

The oculus had opened, revealing the night sky with not a cloud present to conceal the starlight. Guards, dressed in the same armor as Mike, stood around the perimeter of the room in front of the machines and instruments Delilah used in some of her tests.

I couldn't see their eyes, but I felt them as they followed me to the center of the room where the alchemist stood. She wore her usual garb, a heavy smock over simple clothes and thick gloves over her clasped hands.

"Now that we're all here"—she slid her gaze to a guard standing apart from the rest—"we can proceed with the last trial. How much glint did she receive this morning?"

The alchemedis stepped behind her, holding a clipboard. "Half a vial. Enough to hold her through the night if needed."

"Good." Delilah gestured to the guard behind me. "Chain her and expose the mark."

Two large hands braced my shoulders, shoving me to my knees where they hit the stone with a splitting crack that was muffled by the activity in the room. I hardly felt the dull throb in my bones while Mike clutched my arm to clasp each chain around my wrist, his gloves burning my skin. There was little slack to the new bindings. The weight of them dragged my hands to the floor.

He gripped the collar of my tunic and ripped it in half, exposing the length of my spine, the same fire licking the back of my neck. Cool night air brushed my bare skin, prickling my back with chill bumps, and I gasped at the assault. My arms fought the resistance of the chains to wrap around my middle, feeling vulnerable with so much exposed to their veiled stares.

"What does this have to do with my mark?" At this point, I wanted as much information as possible. Delilah knew more about me than I did, and she might be more inclined to share if she thought she had all her loose ends tied down.

"You were given that mark, not born with it." She adjusted her gloves and paced around me to view my back better. "How?"

I shrugged. "I fought a creature from the Wilds. The wearhs who caught it called the beast a demon. It pierced me and left the mark on my body."

"One of Oblivion's messengers then," she barely whispered. "Chaos must have sent it to you, which means it's truly time, then."

"And you think this mark is some kind of key?" I asked to keep her talking. "Does this have to do with Oblivion?"

Her displeased frown erased the satisfaction from her lips. "How do you know about the key?"

For some reason, I didn't mention Mike. "It doesn't matter. I have no key. Whatever you are trying to unlock, I cannot do it for you."

"It sounds more like you're hiding something." Her eyes narrowed. "I believe the demon realized what you were when it pierced your blood, then it delivered the key. I think Chaos sent it to find you, that it came to this Isle from the void to give you the key, knowing the time was coming to open Oblivion once more."

"You're fully deranged then, if you truly believe a word of any of that." How could a simple mark on my back open the deepest hell in the void? It was a sign of Chaos, a symbol of my curse, a burden I now had to carry and conceal. It did nothing but cause pain and grief and paint my hands bloody.

"Perhaps," she replied. "But if I'm right, I'll be the most celebrated scientist in all the realm. I'm willing to risk that possibility."

"Get the hells away from the Remni, Delilah!" A voice boomed from the entrance of the Orbitarium. I turned to find another guest, one I definitely wasn't expecting, filling the empty space where the stone was still set aside—and he looked *pissed*.

Felix Firenze.

"What are *you* doing here?" She came to stand in front of me as if to hide me. Felix stepped into the crowded lab, three of his men following close behind, pressing their backs against the curved wall.

Felix's cheeks were flushed, his thick neck covered in red splotches with perspiration glistening his brow. "I got word you were making the exchange today. Imagine my surprise when your last report mentioned nothing of the sort!" He huffed a breath. "You lied to me once about the Remni, and I had to learn from someone else that she was alive. I crossed it off as poor communication, but this? This will cost you, Delilah."

"I don't answer to you, Firenze. I am the Head Alchemist. Your family is only where they are today because of my sacrifices—"

"And you are only alive because my family protected you. Might I remind you, *Head Alchemist*, that my father was the only one who believed your claims among the Niners. If it weren't for him, you'd probably have been killed off by the Marcheses, like all the rest who learned their secrets. Your lab, your funding, your opportunities are all paid for by us."

Felix took another bold step forward, but none of the guards stopped him. Perhaps he did have the upper hand.

"It is time, Felix." Delilah's tone softened. "You might fund my projects, but this is *my* science and my life's work."

"We should wait for Magrahel, like the OIC plans. We can use the key then—"

"So they can take responsibility for the work we've done, the research I've put into this to study the Arcane? We do this now and Order answers to us," she whispered, as if sharing a secret. "With Gavriel gone, we have weak men in leadership, but that"—she gestured to my back—"will give us the power we need to outset them. We need to take the key for ourselves. It is the only way to ensure our place in the New Order."

Felix shook his head. "If one thing goes wrong, Delilah, you could ruin hundreds of years of work. The last time you tried to transfer power, you destroyed a man's entire remnant! You could destroy the key in that case, and what then? What makes you confident in your science now?"

Delilah straightened; her chin raised slightly. "Commander Lear."

She spoke the name like a request. A moment later, a loud, screeching sound filled the room. So harsh was the cry, I doubled over, unable to cover my ears with my bound hands. The sound ceased just as quickly but left behind an incessant ringing behind.

Sound. A native commander, one of the Watch, controlled *sound*. Delilah had taken a remnant and given it to a watchman—with science. Hadn't Luther controlled the same? Was his remnant tested here as well? The bloodstains on the tile suddenly held a new meaning.

"I didn't fail," Delilah said coolly. "I lied. Just like I lied about capturing the Remni. Men in power have taken from me before, but they will not take my accomplishments. The Society will become what it was always meant to be because of my discoveries."

"You are making a mistake, Delilah," Felix said. "We had one job—to study the Arcane—but you're going too far with this. Stand down, or the OIC will handle your deceit in ways I cannot protect you from."

"I'll take that risk." For the first time, she let go of the book she carried and handed it to Felix. "This was hers, written by Chaos in the days before she disappeared."

"Where did you get this?" He flipped through the book, his brows furrowing with interest.

"I have my resources." Delilah's lips thinned, like she was holding back a larger truth. "I've been using it to guide Camilla's training and testing to better define her remnant in the Arcane so I could properly link her power to me. If she holds the key, it should transfer."

"You'd take the power of Chaos?" Felix sounded unsure.

Delilah shook her head. "Chaos must be destroyed before we open Oblivion. That much she made explicitly clear. I only wish to connect us. When the bond is formed, I'll use a conduit, a Siphon, to take the key. Once I have it, we can be done with her."

"What is in Oblivion?" I asked them.

Felix turned his head slowly in my direction, letting his gaze hover for a beat. He stepped near the edge of the boundary, squatting in his wrinkled pants to catch me at eye level. "Hello, Camilla."

"Felix," I spat.

"Look at you." His dark eyes scanned my body. A smile formed across his oily cheeks. "Look at what's become of the Princess of Steam. Would you do it differently now, Camilla? Do you regret not choosing me?"

For a moment, I thought of letting go of the magic rolling within my core like an anxious thought, but I reined in the urge. His time would come. "I regret nothing, only that Nico didn't shoot you in your ugly face when he had the chance."

Felix shifted to reach into his pocket, and pulled out a single lead bullet. "I thought I got you, you know. I shot you through the stomach, left you on that train bleeding out and cold with your husband. But then, I realized . . . in no reality, would I have killed you before I could have you."

He reached for my cheek, stroking his finger across my grimace. What was he talking about, shooting me? The last time I saw him, he was being shot at on top of the train while I snuck to the engine.

A dreadful feeling unfurled in my belly.

Felix leaned closer, like it was a private conversation. "It was almost as if someone made me do it, like a remnant got in my head. Do you know any Mirth descendants who can control thoughts? Any shifters who'd take your place? There's not too many Mirth polys in the city."

I shook my head, but my slow denial stretched his slimy grin.

No. Not Sera. He couldn't be talking about Sera.

The scene, however much I denied it, played out in my head on its own accord. If she had pretended to be me and made Felix shoot her, he'd think I was dead. Everyone would. Just like Delilah had said. It's how she'd kept me here so long, her little secret project.

Felix lifted the bullet between us, a name carved into the lead. "Your husband got me good before I escaped. But I kept the bullet he left in me, and I carved his name right there, as a promise to return it to him very soon."

He stood, letting each line he whispered sink into my heart word by word. Sera was the only one on the train that day that could accomplish such a thing. And she had, if Felix's genuine surprise at my presence here was any indication.

My hands fisted, digging my nails into my palms to distract the pain in my heart with something more visceral, more tolerable, one that wouldn't draw tears to my eyes.

I hardly had time to grieve my friend before the alchemist resumed her trial. She motioned to the women behind her. "Proceed."

Delilah stepped around me, and I realized then, with my back exposed, I'd have to be quick. The Watch would notice my power priming as it fed the black in my veins. My exposure gave them warning. She turned away just as the other alchemists joined me in the center of the room. Three of them drew symbols on my body with a hot solution, melting lines into my skin.

I shrieked with every stroke, struggled against the chains anchoring me to the floor. One of them worked on a symbol over my shoulder, but I thrashed so hard against the bindings around my wrist that I knocked the brush from her hands.

"Stay fucking still!" Mike growled. His fist grabbed my hair and shoved me into the floor, pressing his knee into my spine to hold me down, making it difficult to breathe. I tried to push off the floor, to gain an inch for my chest to move and take a breath, but his weight was smothering.

The alchemists pinned my arms with a scorching grip. I burned everywhere they touched, sketched, dripped their boiling hot ink across my cold skin.

The guard on top of me twitched, and his grip loosened until he finally released my hair and slumped to the side, slinking to the floor with a clank of metal and the thud of dead weight. The women paused their drawing, allowing me to move again. I lifted my head and pushed off the floor to my knees, taking in a lungful of air.

Delilah screamed.

"What have you done?" Her eyes were wide on the bodies littered around me. I followed her gaze, studied the guard and the women on the floor, how the watchmen around the circle inched back.

Delilah fell to her knees and checked the nearest woman's pulse in her neck. She looked at me, green eyes filled with deadly reprisal. "You killed them!"

"I . . . I didn't do anything!" Truly, I didn't know what had happened. It was like they just fell over and died where they stood. I looked at my hands, but they were bare, insisting what I already knew. I hadn't killed them—but then, who had?

Wind wrapped the room, stirring a violent gust around the Orbitarium. A familiar spark skimmed my cheek, going against the breeze to slide down my jaw, then my neck. It was a feeling I had committed to memory, a touch I'd know in the dark.

It was impossible, and yet despite the odds, there was no doubt left in my body as my skin felt the charge of his remnant, the way it slipped through my hair and filled my lungs with power. *His* power. He was here.

Tears pricked the corners of my eyes and blurred my vision as I glanced around the room, searching the masked faces for the one who commanded the wind and my heart.

"What is happening?" Delilah roared. "You said she was sedated!"

"Because she is!" the alchemedis shrieked. "This cannot be her."

Delilah's sharp rage smoothed into a cool realization. She knew the range of my remnant, and it never extended to the natural forces of the world. She glared at the guards. "Show your faces, each of you!"

The commanders removed their masks as ordered, revealing one disturbed expression after the other. All but one, who waited until he had the room's attention. The last guard lifted his mask, confirming what I already knew, what I had felt with as much certainty as the breath in my chest.

"Nico," I whispered.

He smiled. Steel-grey eyes settled over me. "Hello, princess."

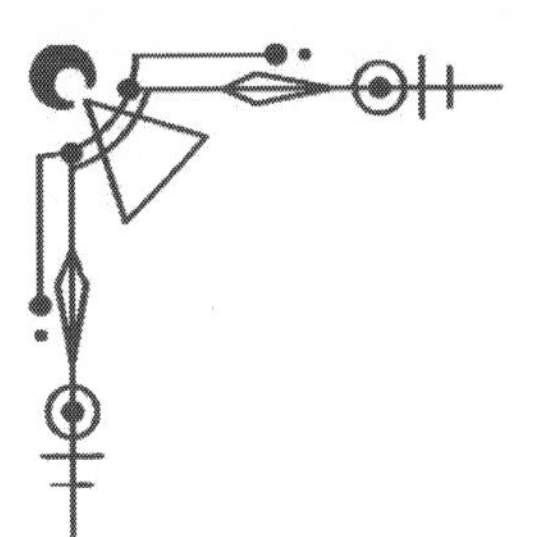
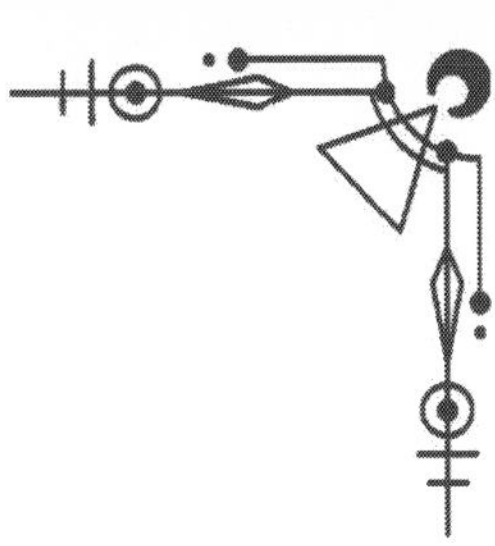

CHAPTER 14
NICOLAI

My face must have become notorious to these men, for as I removed my mask, each commander reached for their gun.

"Nico!" Milla shouted my name this time, and it made my smile widen despite the barrels of five pistols pointed in my direction. Despite Felix *fucking* Firenze and his cadre crashing the party.

I was about to use my remnant to stop time, but Milla's chained wrists filled with darkness, a warning sign of her remnant from what I remembered in my brief encounter with her Chaos. Black flames ate away at her bindings, setting herself free.

The alchemist, Delilah, cursed and flung herself behind a workbench. "Get the glint!"

With a whip of dark fire, Milla lashed out at the nearest watchman, slicing him clean in half.

There were four left before I could lift a finger to defend myself.

She snapped her head in the opposite direction, where Felix

and his men stood unaware, and thrusted her hand out. Her remnant followed, racing across the floor to travel up the wall as if the stone were just a tapestry. The wall crumbled with a loud crack, sending large, heavy rocks crumbling over their heads. They disappeared behind the falling rubble, finding coverage in the hall. One of the watchmen tried to run for it, back to the doorway to the stairwell—and was crushed instead.

Three.

I paused time just as the remaining returned their attention from Milla to me. They sent off their guns, and bullets hovered just inches from their barrels. Milla looked at one, golden eyes wide with worry. Not desiring to waste good bullets, I pulled a dagger from one of their belts, slashed each of their throats to finish them off.

Finally—*finally*—I crossed the remaining distance to Milla, nearly diving to the floor to kneel beside her.

I took a moment while she was still frozen in time to study her, ignoring the ache inside my bones as the strength of my remnant was tested. The sight of her made me choke on my breath, gathered a glaze over my eyes as I ran my thumb over a split in her bottom lip.

My goal had been to wait until we received more information out of Delilah. When Felix entered the conversation, my interest piqued, desiring to understand the dynamic between the alchemists. But when that Society bastard slammed my wife to the ground, I lost all interest in keeping anyone in this room alive.

She looked well for being in Hightower for the last several weeks. Her frame was thinner, her once flawless, soft skin now covered in various sizes and phases of bruising. But she was *alive,* and mostly, uninjured. More than that, she was fighting. Whatever this place had done to her spirit, it hadn't taken that much from her, at least.

I could have stared at her all night, amazed by her existence and her beauty and her power if not for the flash of warning from my remnant striking through my marrow. There would be time to bask in her later. For now, we needed to get the hells out of here.

I shifted in my crouch, giving her space, and released the second.

The commanders fell dead as their bullets hit the wall where I had just stood. Milla blinked, startling when she realized I was right in front of her.

"*You*," she whispered. Her eyes were saucers of golds and greens, glossy and red with stifled tears.

"Me." My voice cracked. "Isn't this great?"

She released a laugh that mixed with a sob, reaching for my face to take my head in her hands. Her fingers played up the line of my jaw, fixed themselves into my outgrown hair. "I can't believe it. You're really here. You're *real*."

My hands went to her arms, which slowly returned to her natural skin tone with the receding of her remnant. She flinched, sucking a breath in pain.

I cursed my idiocy and tugged off the gloves. "Hells, I'm sorry, Milla. For the gloves, for not being here sooner, for letting this happen. All of it."

"But you came for me," she said in a strained voice. "Delilah said—" Something shifted in her eyes, looking over my shoulder. "Nico, move!"

She shoved me back with surprising strength, putting distance between us. I spun around to face Delilah, who had crawled across the floor to retrieve the dark red ink from a dead alchemist to finish the symbols drawn in a circle around the floor. As soon as she closed the final loop of a symbol, a wall of milky light formed a circle around Milla, shimmering strange arcane symbols in the iridescent glow.

"Fuck," I hissed. "What is this?"

"A barrier," Milla replied, but she glared at the alchemist. "Once you cross it, you cannot leave unless the symbols are disrupted."

I dove toward the images—stopped by a sharp penetration near my spine.

"Nico!"

It sent me to my knees, just short of the runes. The dagger—laced with glint—pierced my lung and burned the right side of my chest every time I gasped for breath. Warmth trickled from the hole below my shoulder.

"If you move another muscle, I'll end you for good," the alchemedis hissed in my ear. "It doesn't take a crimson dagger to send your kind to the void. Anything sharp enough will do."

"That warning extends to you as well, Milla. If you do not comply, we will kill him." Delilah stood in front of the barrier, her hands clasped in front of her. "Remember this: we've spent quite a lot of time together. I know everything about you now. Your strengths, the extents of your power, your limitations"—her eyes glanced my way—"and your weaknesses."

Milla lifted her chin an inch. "Then you also know that without this barrier, I could turn you to dust. You can't touch me anymore. If you want my key, I'll have to give it to you willingly. And I will do so *if* you leave him alone."

Delilah smoothed a palm over the slick slant of her hair pulled high into a bun before nodding once. "A fair exchange."

Milla looked at me once more. I shook my head, encouraging her to keep fighting. Whatever the OIC wanted with her mark, it wasn't worth my life. Hells, I was a ticking time bomb anyway, thanks to a missing shadow.

"What do you want me to do?" she asked.

Delilah looked at the alchemedis still holding a blade to my throat. "Knock him out, first."

"Milla, *no*—"

I lurched forward, disregarding the dagger. But the woman behind me stuffed a rag soaked in something foul over my face. My body went limp, out of my control, only to plummet into darkness.

THE DARK DIDN'T CONSUME me fully. I still heard everything. Could vaguely witness the entire operation from the front-row seat. My hands and feet were bound behind a chair near the edge of the barrier. My remnant dull and quiet.

Milla's tortured screams haunted the haze of my delirium, clearing away the fog. I could only watch as the images they drew on her skin glowed a blazing orange as they bled and dripped dark blood down the sides of her arms and legs.

Delilah claimed they needed her awake for the procedure, but I think they just wanted her to hurt. She tried so hard not to show them how much pain they put her through, but in the end, she conceded the fight, writhing on all fours as strange science turned the ink on her body into something molten.

Thunder rolled overhead, drawing my attention briefly to the sky. Dark clouds drifted across the starlight, accumulating like an incoming storm. The night had darkened completely as the moonlight was snuffed out, illuminated only by flashes of dry lightning.

The first fall of rain hit the top of the barrier, rolling down the translucent slope.

"Alright, I think you've loosened it. Make the transfer." Delilah held out her arm.

"We should let the Arcane penetrate deeper, just to be sure it doesn't break—"

"Make the transfer!" she hissed.

The alchemedis sighed and drew a symbol across Delilah's forearm.

My fingers twitched, the sensation returning with every quickening pulse of my heart. Neither of the scientists paid me any mind. If she could hang on a bit longer, I could stop this. With the little control returning to my wrist, I gathered the cape covering my belt and slipped a dagger from the sheath near my hip, thankful they hadn't thought of taking my weapons.

The mark on Milla's spine glowed, similar to a symbol on Delilah's arm. I imagined Luther had gone through something similar in the experiments he spoke about. Delilah would take Milla's mark by taking her power as well, just as she had taken Luther's and bound it to the watchman.

"I'm going to open the boundary," Delilah said. "If you do anything to harm me, my assistant will make sure your lover suffers."

Milla didn't respond. Her form trembled, like it took all her strength and focus just to hold herself up.

Before she could open the boundary, the ropes binding my wrist snapped as I cut through the last knot. I emptied the contents of my pockets, rolled them behind the equipment to conceal the small, highly flammable orbs. A quick dash through the barrier, and I pulled Milla's trembling form into my chest, holding her steady as she lashed out in my arms.

"Milla, relax. It's *me.*" My voice tamed her fight, though her heart still hammered against her ribs. "I've got you."

"What are you doing?" she whispered. Icy fingers dug into my shoulders, slipping beneath the armor. "I told you not to cross the line!"

Delilah laughed. "You think you can protect her in there, Bender? You've made a foolish mistake."

I ignored her remark. Instead, pressed my lips near Milla's temple. "Cover your ears."

"*What*?"

I pulled her into my chest and shielded us both from the succession of explosions. Four of them detonated.

Only a quick scream rang in the air before the sounds of the explosion cut them off. Metal twisted within a fiery cloud of ash and charred debris, swirling outside the barrier that blocked out the bedlam. Milla dug her face into my neck, shielding her eyes from the flash of light, followed by a flurry of destruction.

Less than a minute had passed before a soft hiss was the only sound beyond the barrier, the burned remains of equipment and dead bodies settled across the ruined lab in a fine dust. Flickers of lingering flames burned the ash dredged across the floor, joined by the moon peeking behind the thunderous clouds, draping the debris in pale light.

A shiver rolled down Milla's arms. "How did you know the barrier would keep out the bombs?"

I tapped her chin, tilting it upward. The gold in her eyes filled with silver from the moonlight. "It kept the rain out. I figured—and hoped to hell—it would keep out the rest of the elements."

"Your faith always impressed me," she said with a nervous laugh. Her gaze fell back to me. "But now we're trapped in here together. I'm assuming you have a plan to escape?"

"More hopes, actually," I said. "Luther will come check on the tower when I don't show up at the meeting point. He'll see the smoke and come to help us."

"Luther is here as well?" Her eyes widened. "He came back to this place?"

"Of course he did. He was the first to volunteer, and as it happens, the only one who can control the stone thanks to Delilah's experiments. All the cousins are here except Esme, but she's worked tirelessly in her own way to bring you home."

She shook her head with a look of disbelief. Warm tears rolled from the corners of her eyes, meeting my thumb still cradling her face. "You all came for me? Why?"

Because I love you. Because they know I do.

I wanted to say the words I'd kept saved for the right time, but that moment wasn't here, not in a filthy lab where unspeakable acts most likely haunted her memories. I settled on, "Because you're an Attano now, princess. The house has been entirely too quiet without you."

She adjusted on my lap, wrapping her legs around my waist to sit more comfortably. The position made me ache for her, despite the situation, our surroundings, the hole in my back, my cock seemed to disregard the rest of the world when she was near. Her scent, the silky skin over her throat, those eyes that were my personal form of glint, rendering me powerless as they crossed me—this is what I'd burn the world to have and keep forever.

"Delilah told me everyone thought I was dead. She made me think no one was coming." Her forehead split as her brows furrowed. "Is what Felix said about Sera true, then?"

It wasn't the way I wished she would've learned about her friend's death, but I nodded anyway, unable to keep the truth from her. "When the train stopped, I found what I thought was you in an altercation with Felix on the roof. You said something to him, and he shot you through the stomach. I brought you home, buried you next to my family, all to find out after a few days that it wasn't you at all. It was Sera, wearing your skin."

Milla crumbled, her narrow shoulders sagged with the weight of her grief. "Why would she . . ." She shook her head. "This is all my fault. She shouldn't have ever been involved in all this. Her death was for nothing—"

"It was not," I snapped. She peered up at me, eyes glazed. "Sera made the whole city believe you were dead, including the Firenzes. Imagine how much worse things would have been if Felix believed you were alive. Sera's sacrifice gave us time we desperately needed to get you back. I don't consider that a waste."

"Someone betrayed Delilah, though. Felix said he knew she lied about keeping me." She swiped the tears brimming in her eyes. Taking my false hand, which was lifeless without my remnant, she held it between us, tucking it against her stomach. "How did you find out?"

"Aramis." His name wasn't what she expected by the twist of her expression. "Milla, there is a lot to catch you up on. Some things that are not my place to share with you. But once we get home, we'll tell you everything, alright?"

She gave a small nod in agreement. My right hand smoothed down the length of her thigh, hooking her around my hip. It was strange, realizing it had been nearly two months since I'd felt her body, and yet the time apart was like dust in the wind now that I had her back. Like a bad dream, nearly forgotten with the arrival of a new day.

Her torn tunic slipped down her shoulder, the only coverage she donned was a linen band around her breasts and similarly made undergarments. Chill bumps prickled her skin. I did what I could to wrap the thick material of the watchman's cape around her shoulders.

A smile flickered on her lips. "For what it's worth, I'm really glad you're here. I didn't think . . ." She swallowed hard. "I didn't think I'd ever see you again."

The pain of that truth filled her eyes, and the force of it nearly broke my heart. "There isn't a hell in the void that could keep me from you, Milla. I'd suffer for a lifetime to have another moment on your lips."

My honesty was rewarded with the tip of her chin, lifting her mouth to mine in a way that felt like an offering. "I think we have a moment to spare."

Without sparing another, I kissed her.

There was no gentleness left in my body, no mercy in my heart. I claimed her mouth like I was taking back every second. Milla returned the force of my kiss with equal parts passion and need, as if I was the air to her flame. The heat between us became a tangible fire, burning away every painful moment without her, burnishing it with a new purpose. Making way for a future.

Without breaking the seal of our lips, she slipped her arm around my neck, threaded her fingers into the length of my hair and pulled my face to hers, forbidding me to move away—like I'd dare try.

My hand traveled up her waist, down the slope of her backside, pressed her firm against my hips as her body writhed against the armor between us. I wanted to rip off the leather and metal, wanted to lay her down in this circle where nothing could touch us and fuck her like the first time. She'd let me have a taste of everything before it was all taken away, and the tease of knowing how good it could be, how it was supposed to be, had driven me into a mild madness waiting to experience it again.

I angled my face to deepen our kiss. Milla's lips parted in invitation, sucking my tongue into her mouth with a demand that dragged a moan through my chest. She pulled back, taking control of this wordless conversation, this fight for dominance between our tongues, and pinched my lip between her teeth.

"*Fuck*, I missed you," I said as she took a ragged breath.

A sweet whimper fluttered from her throat in reply as I stole whatever words she had with another thieving kiss. My hand snatched the indent of her waist, thumbs inching toward the underside of her—

"Should we come back later?"

Never had I been so frustrated and relieved to hear my cousin's voice. Milla gasped as she jolted back from my face, turning her gaze toward the intruder.

"Luther!" she shrieked.

He coughed once to clear his fluster at finding us in such a compromised position. But a smile spread across flushed cheeks, the coloring matching the red tint in his mustache.

His eyes narrowed on Milla as he dipped his chin. "Hello, boss."

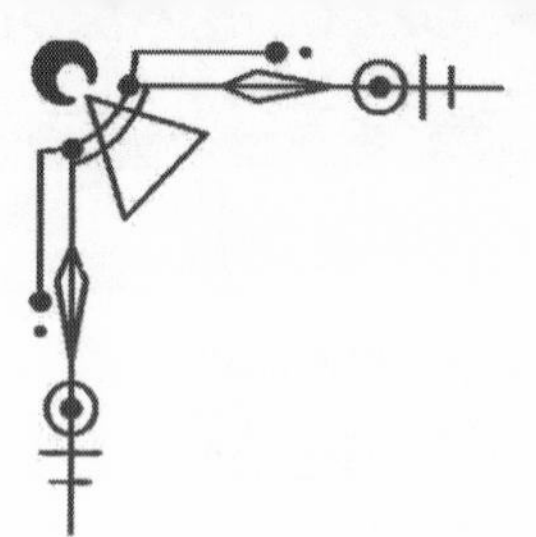
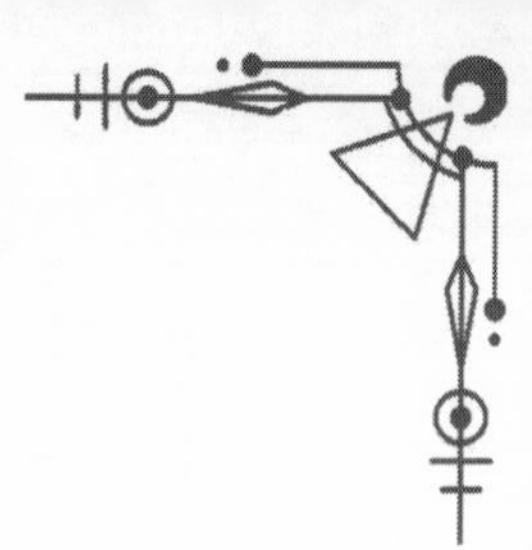

CHAPTER 15

CAMILLA

He came for me. They had all come for me.

I didn't let go of Nico once I had him, worried this was all a well-constructed dream that would disintegrate if I didn't hold on to the illusion strong enough. Though I dropped his hand for a fleeting few seconds to hug Luther's neck after he disrupted the barrier.

"Good to see you still causing chaos, boss," he muttered in my ear.

I laughed, but it broke apart. "Just like old times."

He slipped from my arms, still grinning. "The rest of the boys are downstairs, watching the doors. We released the prisoners and armed them each with the weapons from the guards we took down in the process. What's left of the Watch near the docks is being taken care of."

They'd started a riot from the sounds of it—and he had the nerve to call me on my chaos. I pulled my torn tunic higher over my shoulder, wishing I had something more durable to escape in.

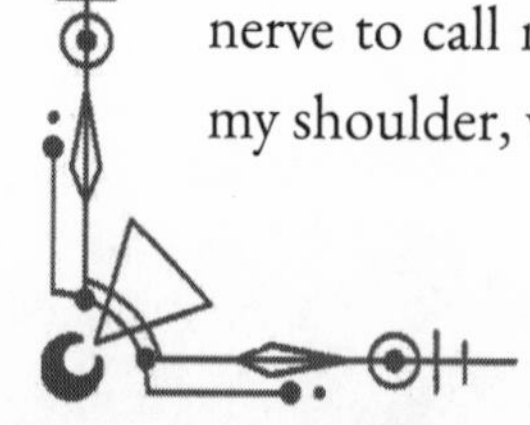

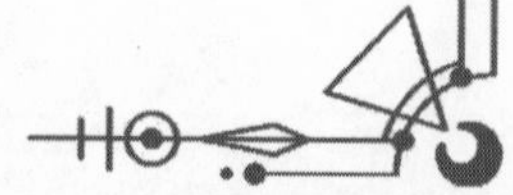

"Here," Nico said. As if reading my thoughts, he unlatched the shoulder gauntlets holding up his cape and hood. Making two incisions quickly with a dagger for my arms, he wrapped the thick material around my body like a robe, using a strip of my old tunic as a sash to hold it all together.

"This will work," I said, impressed.

Grey eyes swept over me before nodding in approval. Nico held out his hand for me to take, but a raspy groan tore my attention from his offering to the rubble behind us.

"Milla . . ."

I disregarded Nico's warning to inspect the sound. Swiping a glass shard from the floor for protection, I pulled back a twisted piece of metal and found the source of the suffering.

A charred body lay sprawled over a mound of debris. Bright red hair still clung in places to the singed flesh, and I held my breath to prevent choking on the scent of the burnt alchemist. Her breaths wheezed with every movement of her chest wall, but her eyes were wide on me, aware of everything going on around her.

"*Help.*"

My grip tightened on the glass until it cut into my palm. I wished it would have felt better to stand over her as she suffered. After months of torturing me, it should have been more rewarding than this. To watch her die. To know I'd leave this tower, and her bones would be lost in the remains of stone and forgotten tragedies now crumbling like her plans.

I should walk away. Let her die deliberately. Let the ash in her airways smother her slowly; let the deep burns make every final second one of pain and agony. It was no less than she deserved for what she did to me, the other prisoners, to Luther.

"Milla." Nico was behind me, taking the broken glass from my hand. "What do you want to do?"

"Give me your dagger."

He replaced the shard with a more practical tool for the job. I knelt near the alchemist. Pity didn't exist in my heart for her, no emotion attached to the moment. "This is more mercy than this tower has ever seen, but I will not become the monster you tried to make me. I will not let this place change who I am. I will not let you win."

The dagger slipped into her burnt flesh with little resistance, striking her heart, and the muscle squeezed around the knife, lurching once more, before giving out. The little light left in the alchemist's gaze flickered out. As quickly as the fall of a blade, my oppressor was dead.

"One down," Nico murmured. "A whole city to go."

I wiped my tears before he could see them. "Let's get out of here."

LUTHER COULD MOVE THE STONE. I had no idea how or where he learned the power to do so, but he quickly got us through the hall, removing any rubble that had fallen from the force of Nico's bombs. We emerged from the tower moments later just as the night air slammed into me with a wild breeze from the sea, forcing me to hold together my makeshift robe.

"Milla!"

So many familiar voices spoke my name, it was almost overwhelming. Gideon and Adler rushed to greet me, quickly adding their joy at seeing me alive and on my feet. Nico kept his right hand on the small of my back, urging us to keep going.

"Your remnant is still dulled?" I asked him.

He nodded curtly. "The glint here is stronger. I likely won't get it back for a while, so we need to get to the ship as quickly as possible."

I had no argument against making haste to leave. If I never saw this island again, it would still be too soon.

The yard was empty, though the distant sounds of gunshots carried in the east wind. Nico abandoned his touch on me to grab his own gun. Gideon looked back at me, offering one of his own weapons.

I held up my hands, which blackened from the prime of my remnant. "I'm good, Gideon. But thanks."

The cousins startled at the first impression of my power, while Nico's laugh was wicked with admiration.

He charged his weapon, sliding the round into place. "Is it wrong I'm hoping we run into trouble now?"

A small part of me hoped the same, if only for the opportunity to burn this place to ash. "Don't tempt me to find some, Nicolai. I'm not in the right mind to be merciful."

"She's stunning when she's homicidal, isn't she, cousins?"

I nudged him in the side with my elbow, though it was impossible not to catch the contagious grin he wore as I stole a glance at him. His face was thinner than I'd remembered. I noticed every new line that crafted the shadows around his eyes, a deeper darkness in his smoky gaze. His hair had grown and was left unstyled and unkept. A man so normally well-groomed, who cared about his appearance, and he'd abandoned his usual contemporary style for something more unbalanced. A manic result of his apathy, and yet that same stoic ambition lingered beneath the craze.

He was danger and darkness and deliverance, and he was every desire of my soul embodied.

Nico caught me staring and passed a hand through his dusty hair, smoothing it out. "I need a haircut, I know."

"That's not what I was thinking," I replied.

"Then what?"

I winked at him, glancing at Luther standing too close behind us. "I can't tell you just yet."

"*Hells*, here the fuck we go with these two," Luther muttered.

We made it through the empty yard and back into the main building with no resistance, but as soon as we came to the center hall leading to the front gate, trouble finally found us.

"I thought you cleared them." Nico spoke to Luther, sounding very displeased.

"We're still working on it," he clipped. A section of the wall moved to reveal a surge of guards. While Luther unloaded his gun on the group, Nico shoved us both into a room off the hall before we were caught in the return fire.

Alchemy beakers stood dormant on their burners, the pantry of ingredients lined one wall, and the familiar scent of sulfur had my eyes widening. We were in the alchemedis's room. A different lab than the one in the tower. Nico pulled me down into a crouch to hide from any stray bullets that might have ricocheted off the walls.

"Nico, there's too many of them for your cousins to take out themselves."

The floor rumbled—Luther must have made his own blockades in the hall with his power over the stone. In the dim light of the moon slipping through the skylight in the ceiling, his eyes shifted as he planned and plotted.

I snatched his arm, drawing his gaze back to me. "I have an idea, but I need to get out there, in the main room."

A muscle clenched in his jaw. "Impossible. As soon as they see you, they'll take you down."

"Then they better not see me." The table behind him held an assortment of beakers, but I knew well the stuff that counteracted their glint. The smell of it, the color, the way it burned at first touch. Looking through every drawer, I searched until I found the salve Delilah rubbed on my skin before each trial.

"Here." I uncapped the jar and spread a generous amount over two fingers. "Give me your arm."

He extended his right arm in my direction. "What is that?"

I spread the sticky balm over his forearm, grateful he'd lost the watchman's gloves.

"Give it a moment to absorb, but it will nullify the effects of the glint. Delilah and her team used it on me before they—" I swallowed. Now was not the time to unravel that thread of conversation.

Nico's brows furrowed, and I knew he'd pocketed the moment to pull out later.

His false hand flexed in the pale light. "So, what exactly is your plan?"

I smiled, rubbing together my stained black hands. "Turn off the lights and count to ten. I'll take it from there."

"Milla—"

The cousins stumbled inside the room, carrying Adler between them. A bright red stain soaked the front of his guard uniform. Nico cursed and ran to help them, propping his cousin in a nearby chair.

The bender groaned, doubling over to brace the site with his palm. "I'll be fine. Their aim is shit."

"And a good thing, or you'd be dead. Luther, put pressure on the site to slow the bleeding until we can see the haelen," Nico ordered. His head swiveled back to me. "You were saying?"

I nodded, feeling a little breathless at the sight of Adler's bloody front. If that bullet would have been an inch to the right, it would have gone straight through his heart. The Watch would be closing in now, blocking the hall so we couldn't escape. We needed to be quick.

"Let's go."

Before Nico stepped out of the room and into the hall, all the light in the building faded into darkness. Rarely did he use his remnant to control the light—rarely did he need to when the wind and time were powerful enough on their own. Concealed by the shadows, I snuck along the wall leading into the building's center, where the halls branched from the circular intersection.

Not a gun went off. The watchmen must have been worried they'd strike a comrade, and it worked in my favor, though I remained stealthily flush with the wall to avoid any wild ideas. Each breath from my lips was a countdown.

Seven, six, five . . .

I needed to make sure I was in position at the end of the hall before time ran out—before Nico lifted his remnant. A corner materialized beneath my fingers, and I rounded the edge, crossing the point of no return. Too far to turn back, too late to run.

Three, two, one . . .

Moonlight spilled through the glass ceiling. Gas lamps flickered alive once more, lining the room and adding to the illumination. I stood before the entrance of the hall, in front of my husband and his family—my family—with hands filled with dark power and the eyes of every guard locked on the black flames curling down my wrists.

They didn't raise their guns, didn't waste their bullets. The lot of them, over a dozen from a quick count, turned on polished boots and ran in the opposite direction.

They were *afraid* of me. Hells, it felt good to watch the fear flood their eyes, quicken their strides. Cowards couldn't face me now that I was no longer bound by drug or chain.

Recalling every agonizing memory from this place, I let the anger inundate my veins, become the fuel to my fire, the force behind my power. Marco Gallo, the prisoners they left to die on the side of the island, the games they played to test my remnant. My hands slammed into the ground, assaulting the hard stone that had trapped me all these months inside its cold, coarse fingers. I unleashed what I had always held so close, too afraid to let go completely in fear it might hurt someone innocent. But there was no innocence in this room, no reason to hold back any longer.

A single word from my heart commanded my remnant to do what it did best.

Destroy.

The air charged, filling with static. The glass dome shattered, raining large chunks of glass over the fleeing men. From where I stood, the fallen shards nipped at my bare skin.

The ground gave way, cracking into a thousand pieces before turning to black dust. Fire ate away the foundation beneath their retreat until nothing was left but a gaping hole leading to the cells below. The guards didn't make a few paces before they were each swallowed into the abyss, disappearing with the sounds of their screams as they descended toward an obscure bottom deep beneath the prison.

I stood too fast and swayed on my feet. An arm hooked my waist before I could topple into the hole after them.

"Careful, princess," Nico whispered too tenderly in my ear. "Too much, too fast, remember? Even Chaos has limits."

My hands balled into fists, fearful to touch him before regaining some sense of control over the furious temper still dancing with my pulse. It took his embrace and the soothing words in my ear to realize I was crying. My cheeks were wet, flooded with the expression of all my resentment for Hightower. What it did to me. What it did to all of us.

"I *hate* them." I slid the words through my teeth. "I hate them all."

Nico stroked my shoulder, holding me up against him. "I know, and the rest will pay for what they did to you, Milla. I vow it on my life."

I nodded mechanically, clutching his false hand over my racing heart when I could finally think straight again. Gideon and Adler came up behind us with Luther between them, eyes wide at the hole in the ground.

"*Seven hells,*" Gideon whispered. "Remind me not to piss you off, Milla."

"Gawk later," Nico snapped. "Get to the docks."

I took one wobbly step before Nico scooped me in his arms and carried me through the front doors, somehow still held together on their hinges. My head fell into the soft curve of his neck and remained there as we departed Hightower.

Never lifting to look back.

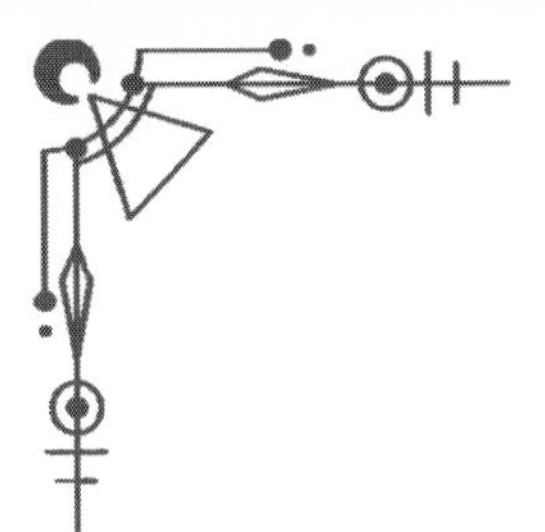
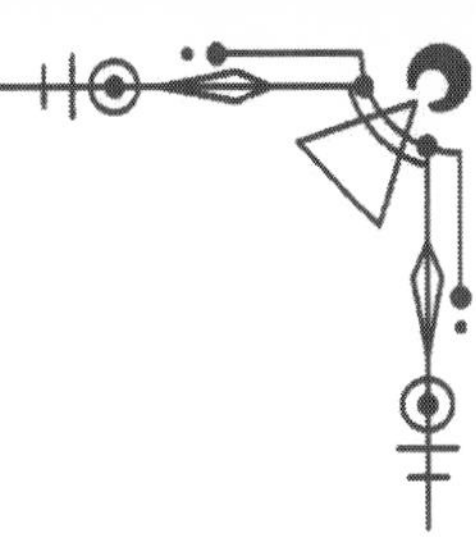

CHAPTER 16

CAMILLA

A ship waited in the distance at the end of a long pier jutting into the sea, far from the treacherous shoreline. Nico set me down on the grassy slope in front of the prison steps, scanning the scene before us. Dead guards lay prostrate across the lawn. Prisoners donning grey tunics, similar to my own, waited in quiet deliberation, lining the way to the docks. Between them, a man in a navy overcoat. Neither guard nor prisoner.

A Firenze.

Nico stormed toward the man on his knees.

"Where are the rest of you?" he shouted in that deep, demanding tone I'd only heard from him a few times.

The Firenze glared up at Nico and snarled. "Gone. They took one of the guard boats back up the Ada. You'll never get them now."

"They left you?"

"He was a distraction," one prisoner said. In his hand, a watchman's revolver. They all carried similar weapons stolen from the

guards. "Drew our attention away as he fled toward the ship while his associates stole a boat. The family and their men escaped. We figured we'd keep this one alive for you. A way to show our appreciation."

Nico crouched in front of the bleeding Firenze, who'd been struck several times in the face with a blunt force—the butt of the gun, perhaps. "We can't use him to negotiate anything. He's of no value to the Firenzes if they left him behind."

"Fuck you," the captive spat.

Nico shrugged. "Leave him here. If he tries to follow, shoot him in the knee." He stood, still staring down at the man. "No more easy deaths from now on."

Bone-chilling wind slipped beneath the fabric of my coverings and lifted the stringy hair hanging lifelessly over my shoulders. I didn't know if the shiver lashing through my skin was from the chill or the treacherous calm of Nico's voice. He was terrifying like this, supremacy seeping from every step, demanding the attention of every man in his presence. They were free because of him, and they each knew it, regarding him like he was a king among subjects. The Attanos hadn't just come for me—they'd come for us all.

The freed prisoners dragged their captive away, tying him to the stairwell handrail. If he kept up his thrashing, the crows circling above wouldn't consider him carrion just yet. They'd pick at the other dead bodies before they considered him.

"Milla." Nico's voice was gentle as he spoke. I turned from the Firenze, finding his hand outstretched to me.

"Felix knows I'm with you now," I whispered. "He'll go back to Lynchaven and tell the rest of his family." Sliding my palm into his, we walked together down the long pier where the steam ship floated on a restless sea.

"Let him. I'm not worried about the Firenzes."

"What will this mean for us going forward?"

"It means . . ." He sighed, gripping my palm tight. "It means we need to figure out why the alchemist was working for the OIC and why they need to open Oblivion. Fortunately, you still have the key they desired. If you're safe, they cannot proceed with whatever they have planned."

"But they'll come for me, eventually."

He nodded once. "They will."

"You know what this means, Nico."

He stopped just as we reached the ramp leading to the upper deck of the ship. I couldn't stay and put his entire family in danger. The OIC knew exactly where to find me once we returned to Lynchaven. We had the ship and now a window of opportunity.

Nico, however, seemed unconcerned with the prospect. "I promised I'd make the city safe for you, and I have to an extent. Let's go home and focus our efforts on the next demand. Give the city a fighting chance. If it goes to hell, I'll get you out. Deal?"

After all he'd done, how could I disagree?

I stood on my toes to reach the top of his head and combed my fingers through the length of wild, outgrown dark hair. "Only if you add a haircut into the terms of agreement."

His lips fought a smile, losing the battle. In a single second, he grabbed my curious arm and lifted me over his shoulder. He ascended the ramp, and I shrieked, clinging to him like a cat over water, staring over the slim ledge into choppy waters.

When we reached the top, he finally put me down, though his hand lingered around my waist.

I laughed and struck him softly against his chest. "I'm teasing, Attano. It's not like I have much room to talk concerning appearances."

"I don't know what you're talking about," he whispered,

dipping his head to my ear. "You're the most beautiful thing I've seen."

"You're full of shit." I canted my chin to kiss his jaw. "But I always liked that about you."

"I'm glad I still have a few redeeming qualities left for you, princess." His smile stretched and left me weak in the knees. How many times had that face haunted my empty days in Hightower? How often had I bartered anything to the universe to witness his cruel beauty again? Whatever debt required to be paid for having him returned to me, I'd have paid it.

His eyes shifted to something off to the side, his grin fading. "I forgot to mention, I have a surprise for you."

"If it's not a bath, a seven-hour nap, and a pair of pants, I don't want it."

"Not even if it's your own family?"

That voice . . . I knew it well, had been berated by it enough to know it belonged to my brother. Though it was easier to believe the Attanos would come all this way to find me. I had to turn and see the shocking truth for myself.

He stood at the opposite end of the ship, white-blonde hair whipping like a flame in the breeze, catching the first streaks of dawn.

My breath caught in my throat. "Aramis . . ."

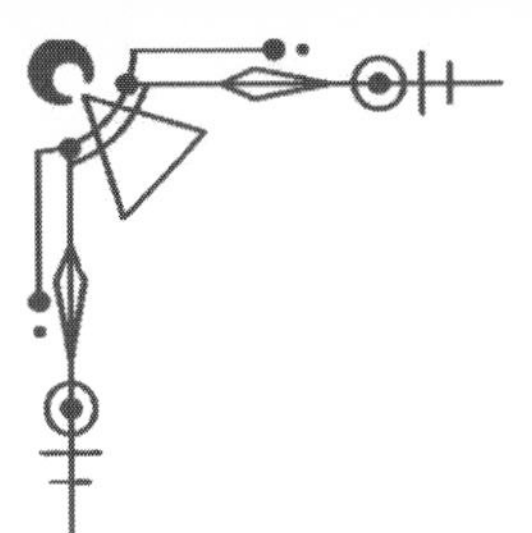
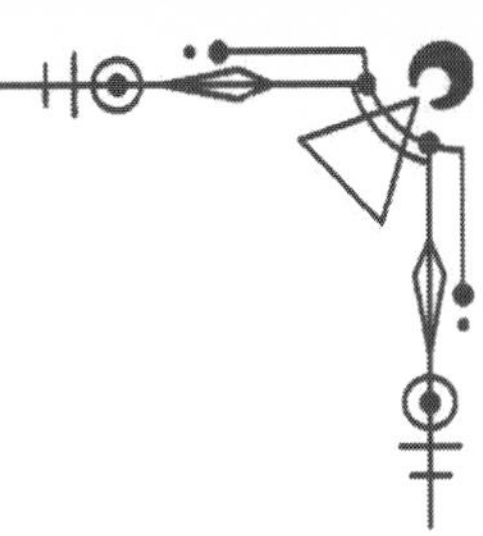

CHAPTER 17
NICOLAI

Milla slipped from my arms to run to her brother, disregarding me for the first time all night. I allowed it, but only because I knew how much it meant for him to be here. I wondered if this was the first time he'd ever shown up for her. The bastard didn't deserve an ounce of her appreciation, but I'd never tell her that.

I'd tried before, and it broke her heart to hear the truth.

"Wait!" The other one emerged from the scullery door. "I'm here too!"

Milla gasped as she saw the twin and broke from Aramis to embrace him. They talked about the trouble she'd caused, the shit they went through to find her, and then Milla's face sobered. Her eyes scanned the deck.

"Where's Jasper?"

I looked away, didn't want to see the look on her face when they broke the news.

"Aramis?"

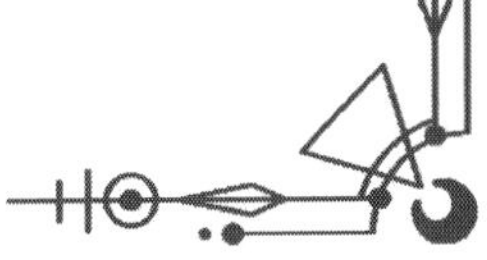

The crack in her voice drove me mad. The men we rescued began boarding the ship, my family coming to stand beside me.

"Jer, where is he? What's going on?" She shook. I could hear it in her words.

Turning to Luther, I said, "Get every prisoner below deck in the galley. Take this logbook and make sure everyone is accounted for. I'll see Milla and her family to the rooms."

He glanced at Milla and her brothers, a solemn look in his eyes. "On it, boss."

The cousins began filing the prisoners toward the stairwell leading below while I approached the Marcheses.

"Why are you looking at me like that? Did he not want to come? Is he hurt?" she asked, demanding something from her brothers besides silence. Aramis was paler than normal. His mouth worked but nothing came out.

"He's dead, Milla," I said, confirming what that look in her eye suspected.

She flinched like I had struck her across the face. "No . . ."

"The Grey Hands killed him like they killed Giles, by order of Felix Firenze."

The breath that rushed from her chest blew a white cloud in the chilly morning air. She drifted slowly to the edge of the ship, blindly feeling for the iron railing for support.

"Felix knew what I did," she whispered. "He knew I screwed them over so he couldn't take my train, and he punished me for it."

"You did the right thing," Aramis said. "If we would have filed that contract like I planned . . . shit would be much worse right now."

For once, I was grateful for something that came out of his mouth. Milla's fists blanched. She faced away from us, towards the hazy sunrise.

"Was there anyone else?" she asked, voice raw.

"Giles, Jasper, and Sera. Those were the only casualties that day."

Each name sagged her shoulders a little more until I was worried the wind itself would be enough to knock her down. "Come, Milla. Let's get inside before you freeze." I slipped a hand around her thin waist. She was so emaciated from her time in the prison, it felt as if she'd snap in half if I pulled too hard.

"We'll be there in a moment," her eldest brother said, and I was surprised by his tenderness. "Jer and I will go help start up. Once we're on course, we'll come join you."

"Wait!" She reached for him, grabbing her brother by the arm. "Before we leave, I need you to circle the island."

"Milla, we need to leave—"

"Please, Aramis," she implored him. "This is important. Just a quick trip around to make sure we aren't leaving anyone behind."

The Marchese looked at me with a quirked brow, but I shot him a look that ensured he did whatever the hells she asked. Milla finally let him go when he agreed.

With little strength left to resist, she followed my lead to the captain's cabin in the center of the deck. Unlike a classic ship where the sails would take up most of the deck, this boat ran on steam. Dark smoke billowed from the chimneys as the operators below prepared to depart. Aramis kept his staff slim and trustworthy, draining the family bank accounts to keep the men he trained for the ship's operation a wealthy secret.

Most of them were miners from northern towns seeking better opportunities than the dusty work below the mountains. There wasn't much I admired about the Marcheses, but this—that he'd solely developed this ship from the ground up based on old sketches of his father's plans. His love for Milla was spoken in his own unsaid language, through actions that were measurable and scored.

Yet I'd never heard him say the words aloud. Whether incapable or heartless or just stubborn, it was easier to put Aramis into a category and dismiss his silence. It wasn't as easy to dismiss my own.

The cabin was a one-bedroom suite with a bed built into the metal wall and a sitting area across from it. A bathroom door led to the lavatory, but Milla collapsed onto the mattress, pulling the thin coverlet around her body. Soon, the small room was filled with heat from the furnace and dull groans as the ship's engines started us off.

"There should be some clothes for you packed in the locker," I said. "We tried to prepare as much as we could."

"Thank you," she murmured.

Silence stiffened the air between us. It was the first time in months I felt the world stop. "Are you alright, Milla? I know this is a lot to take in at once."

"It's strange." She rolled to her side, facing me "They died months ago, and yet for me, it might as well have happened yesterday. The world has moved on. Life has continued, and yet I'm stuck in the past, forced to navigate this alone."

Joining her on the bed, I laid a hand on the bend of her knee as she tucked into herself. "When I came home, it had been years after my father committed suicide, but it was the first I learned of it. It felt similar to how you just described it, and I was completely isolated in my grief."

A hand slipped from her cocoon and grabbed my own. "How did you move on?"

"I didn't. I was angry for a very long time, Milla. Until I found a reason to be happy again. Once my purpose shifted from revenge to . . . someone else."

Her icy fingers threaded between mine. “Is this the part where you tell me revenge is never the answer?”

“That would be my uncle’s job, and I would hate to take the pleasure from him.” Her lips twitched in a smile. I continued, “We’ll take our vengeance, princess. No more forgotten names.”

“No easy deaths,” she repeated my own words back to me.

A knock sounded at the door. Luther announced himself before letting himself in. “Oh, sorry. Didn’t know you two were . . .” He cleared his throat.

“What’s wrong?” I asked, reading the discomfort stiffening his movements.

He licked his chapped lips. “We went over the roster like you asked, boss. Everyone is accounted for, except for two.”

“What do you mean? How are they not on the books?” If anything, I expected to have more names than bodies, not the other way around.

“We’ve set aside the two in the engine room for you to question. Did you know there’s no holding cells on a steam ship?”

“A design flaw if I ever heard one.” I turned to Milla, squeezing her hand. “I need to go check on this. Will you be alright until I get back?”

She frowned, seeming displeased with my plans. “I suppose. Go do your boss things.”

I felt even less inclined to leave her, but the situation piqued my interest. “Get some rest. You certainly won’t get much when we get home.”

“*Nico*!”

“I was talking about my aunts! They’ll never stop fussing over you when we get back. Get your mind out the gutter.”

She rolled her golden eyes and smirked. “Liar.”

Accurate, but it earned me another smile. Well worth the trouble. I stood and followed Luther out the cabin door.

"It's just going to get worse, isn't it?" he asked. "You two."

I barked a laugh as we descended the steps. "I sure hope so."

He sighed and shook his head. "Next time, I'm sending Gideon to interrupt you."

My hand clapped him on the back. "Wise, cousin."

SMOKE FILLED THE ENGINE ROOM, burning my eyes with the heavy haze. Engineers and boilermakers ran from their stations to create more steam under the direction of the watchkeepers, speeding the ship along. A heavy dusting of coal sullied their sweaty chests and faces. The workers ignored us as we wove between pumps, too focused on arduous work to care for the two descendants bound to steaming pipes.

Four of our men surrounded the pair, who seemed displeased to have found themselves in confinement moments after being freed.

"Who the hells are you?" The man spat. One look at him and I could tell he was a thief. Lithe frame, nimble fingers covering the tie of the ropes pinning his arms behind his back. One flick of his wrist and he'd be free. The only thing keeping him there was most likely his curiosity, and I had become an object of interest to him, the way his sharp eyes gave me a once-over.

"He's the man that decides if we toss you overboard, so mind yourself," my cousin said in introduction.

"My name is Nicolai Attano, and I just have a few questions to make sure you aren't dangerous to anyone on board." My name registered nothing obvious in his gaze. But his companion, a woman of similar build and appearance—a sister perhaps—shifted to mumble something in his ear.

"Let's not keep secrets," I said above the hissing sounds of the engine room. Her lips froze to take a long breath. Dark eyes lifted from my boots to my face.

"Did you say Attano?"

"I did."

She turned back to her companion. "What if he is the same one she spoke of? Remember what she shouted at the guard?"

"We can't risk it—"

"What choice do we have, Cal?"

I interrupted their banter. "I have a mentalus I could easily use to search your thoughts. Questioning you is a gesture of goodwill on my part, an effort to be polite, but I will use him if I must." I squatted in front of him. "I'll ask once: Who are you, and why were you sent to Hightower?"

The man fidgeted in his seat on the dirty floor. "My name is Callow. This is my sister, Vesper." He stole a glance at her, and she nodded. "We weren't sent to Hightower exactly. We were part of an expedition and landed on the island thinking it was part of the mainland, and because we are darkthieves, they locked us up since we wouldn't state our business."

"Where is the rest of your crew, then?"

He swallowed. "Dead. They tried to escape, but the Watch took down our ship. Everyone drowned."

"What do you mean expedition?" I asked. "Where did you come from?"

Vesper leaned forward this time. "We're from the Continent," she whispered, keeping her words from traveling outside our conversation. "And we came here for your wife."

The barrel of my gun buried itself in the center of Vesper's forehead. She froze, eyes wide as her companion cursed. My men followed my lead from the succession of guns clicking into place.

"If what happened at the prison wasn't demonstration enough, allow me to be very clear on how I handle people threatening to take my wife from me," I said. "Start clarifying why you want her so much, or I'll forget my manners."

She licked her lips as a tremble struck her jaw. "I didn't mean—I didn't mean we wanted to *take* her. *Giver and Greed* . . ."

"Then what do you want with her?"

"We need her help!" Callow blurted, his teeth clenched. "We're part of a resistance organization in the southern portion of the Continent. We know about her remnant—" He glanced up at a pair of engineers passing nearby. "And we have come to retrieve her before the Sons of Order find her."

I lowered my gun but kept my finger over the trigger. "How do you know about her remnant?"

"She told us," Vesper said. "We were with her in the tower."

"How do you know it exists at all?" I clarified. Knowing what Milla had wasn't revolutionary. Many knew of her strange remnant after she let it slip to protect us from the Watch. But if what they said was true, they weren't even from the Isle. They must have known some other way.

"Things are . . ." Vesper dropped her voice once more. "Different where we are from. We know the truth about Chaos."

"The last king is dying on the Continent. Soon," the other darkthief said. "The power over the last kingdom will be up for grabs. Descendants were suffering years ago when we left. Saints know what things are like now. Her power is the only thing the Sons of Order fear, and we came to find Chaos, in hopes of bringing the remnant back and saving our country."

There was still much they weren't sharing, but some of the rancor dispersed between us. A shadow bender was hardly a threat to my remnant, and on a ship coasting the edge of the Isle, they had nowhere to go. When we got to the harbor up north, it would be practical to keep them close by, however.

I stood and motioned for my men to release them. "How do you plan on getting back to the Continent if your ship was destroyed? How did you get across at all?"

"Very carefully," Vesper said, wincing. "It was a terrible trip. Most called it a suicide mission, but we made it after dropping half the cargo and lightening the ship during one of the bad storms. Unfortunately, we have no way back, and have lost all hope of seeing home again."

A smirk formed on my lips. "On my Isle, Darkthief, hope can be manufactured. Come, I'll bring you to see my wife."

"Wait," Callow said. "There's something else you should know, Mr. Attano."

"What?"

He licked his lips. "We had no idea Milla was the one we were looking for. Running into her in the tower was ordained by fate itself. Instead, we were given a contact in the main city. Someone to go to who would know where to find Chaos."

My brows pinched. "What was the name?"

Callow glanced at his companion hesitantly. "Rosa Bianchi."

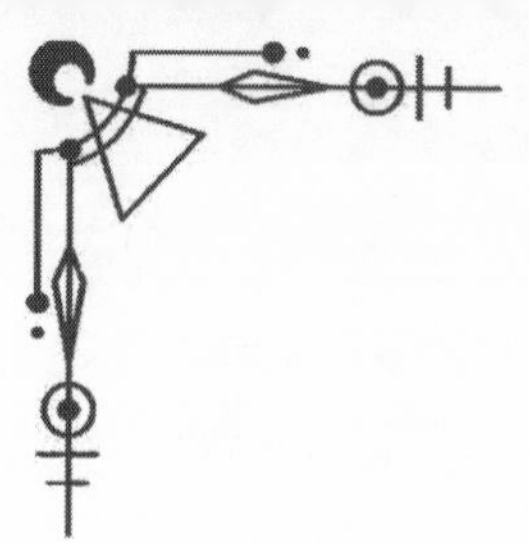
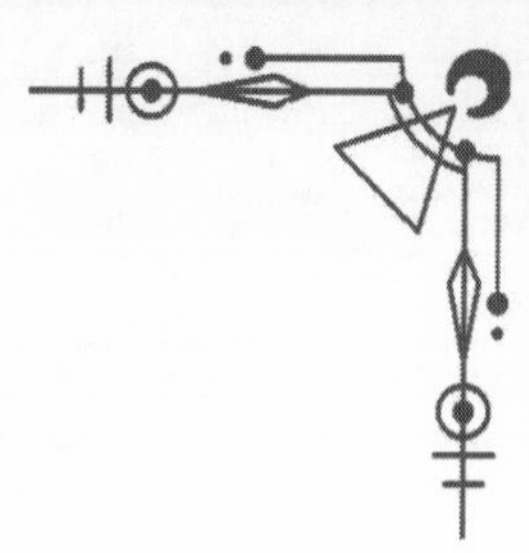

CHAPTER 18

CAMILLA

The sleep Nico demanded I chase never came close enough. I tossed and turned on the soft mattress, unable to adjust to the plush support. It was comfortable—*too* comfortable. After sleeping on the floor for two months, I'd forgotten what it was like to be embraced with warmth and quiet. The rare sunlight streaming through the cracks in the curtains wasn't exactly helping.

But I was used to sleepless nights by now. Rolling off the side of the bed, I found the bag of clothes in a locker by the bathroom door Nico had mentioned and grabbed an outfit that covered every inch of my skin. A pair of fitted trousers, a long-sleeved linen shirt, and a quilted vest to throw over it. I tossed a pair of leather boots, gloves, and a thick coat to the side if I felt like leaving the room later.

A flash of red caught my eye as the silky interior of the coat caught the kerosine light be the bed. A painful tightness squeezed around my heart, catching my breath. The color was just a shade of

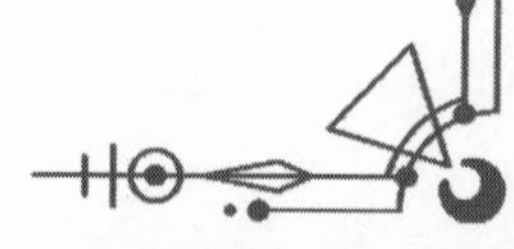

crimson to anyone else, but to me, it was a reminder that I had something before Hightower. Those memories were a part of me more than anything I experienced in the prison. I had something good, and I could have it again.

This skin had far more scars, but I was still the same underneath.

The bathroom was simple. A small shower stall with a toilet and sink. It was the first time I'd seen my reflection in months, as there were no mirrors in my cell, and I didn't know who stared back at me, this sickly version of myself.

My skin was sunken around my eyes, appearing bruised in the low light. Some of my hair had fallen out, and what was left was long, stringy waves that had lost their former luster. But the most obvious change was the shape of my body, which was once composed of dramatic curves and soft edges. Now, my breasts were flat, my stomach concave, even the fat filling my collarbones had disappeared, leaving all my bony prominences protruding.

Some of the bloody ink the alchemists used for the last trial had dried and flaked away, leaving thick burns in the shape of their symbols across my skin. I pressed a cool rag against the angry flesh on my shoulder, wincing at the sting. There were so many burns, I gave up trying to tend to them and left it for a haelen to heal later.

They would scar, but I'd let them. There was no forgetting what happened. No point erasing the evidence when it was already seared into my heart.

I turned from the mirror and dressed quickly, trying to forget my image. It was just a body.

Just a body.

I'd go back to the Attano residence and Nonna would fill me out in no time. There were more important things to worry about. People were dying—had died—for me to walk free from my captors. It seemed frivolous to be upset about something like a body. At least I still had the breath in my chest, the beat of my heart. Some weren't so fortunate to say that.

A knock sounded from the bedroom, followed by the slow creak of an opening door. Nico announced himself, mentioning he had guests.

"I'm in here!" I called to him.

"May I come in?" he asked through the crack of the bathroom door.

I sighed at the hairbrush in my hands. Now that I knew what I looked like, my knee-jerk reaction was to hide from the man who had once worshipped my appearance. How he still looked at me the way he did—like I hadn't changed at all—settled some nerves in my chest. "Of course."

He slipped inside, filling the space with his towering frame. With two fingers, he tipped my chin to look up at him. "What's wrong?"

"Nothing."

"Don't you lie to me."

"Why would you think something's wrong?"

He frowned. "I can tell when you've been crying." As if to make a point, he skimmed a patch of skin over my cheek, still cradling my chin. A cold tear smoothed out beneath his touch—one I hadn't realized I'd shed.

"It's not a big deal, really. I just . . . I saw myself for the first time and it was a bit startling."

His sigh made me feel like such a disappointment. The hand beneath my chin dipped down my neck, caressed the line of my shoulder. "Are you alright?"

I gave him a small nod, gaze falling to his chest. "It's ridiculous, being upset about it. I'm alive and free, and I should be grateful. Yet all I see is what they did to me."

A silence stretched between us, though his hand continued to stroke the unburned places of my skin. How he remembered where those were, I didn't know. My clothes now covered all signs of injury. "Do you know what I see when I look at you now?"

"If you say something about beauty, I'll call bullshit."

He laughed, and the sound was a balm to my grief. A finger traced my collarbone, sending shivers across my skin. "In the hollow places, the body mass you've lost when they deprived you of food, I see where your tenacity filled you with willpower. Every scar discoloring your skin was a battle fought and won, and a reminder of each time you called on your strength to fight back, to *live*."

A metallic hand wrapped around my thin waist, pulling me flush against his hips. "Your laugh is a song of victory, proving you faced their worst and not only survived, but came out with joy still in your heart. And that fucking smile, not to mention your eyes—the light still shining in your eyes—they are beacons to me, guiding me to my true home as they have since the first time I caught a glimpse of them."

I might have wept when his false hand rose and fell down my spine, stroking my insecurities down like he calmed a flame. "This body might feel and look different, Milla, but every change reminds me of how much you fought their cruelty. This body got you through Hightower, and for that reason, I will worship every sign of its resilience."

"You wouldn't if you knew what it was capable of," I murmured. Nico looked at me like I was an altar, but I was the fire from Oblivion, a flame from the deepest hell in the void.

"Is that why you asked Aramis for his glint?"

My eyes widened; he had somehow overheard on our way to

the cabin. He offered a soft smile. "The wind is always in my favor, Milla."

"You mean you were eavesdropping."

"My time with your brothers hasn't changed anything. I don't trust them," he said. "If you want to take a few tabs to help you rest, that's fine. But Milla, suppressing your gift will only make it more unmanageable in the end. You can't ignore who you are."

"I'm not ignoring it. I'm just not dealing with it right now." Someone coughed in the bedroom, dragging my attention from the bender. "You mentioned guests?"

"Some friends of yours from the tower."

"Friends?" The word threw me off enough to put a pause on my tears. Wiping my face, I tried to guess at who it could be. I made no friends in that place, only . . . "Wait, from the *tower*?"

He cracked open the door and beckoned me through. From the opening, two prisoners still wearing their grey uniforms sat in a pair of armchairs near the wall across from the bed. Their features were identical, with dark skin and eyes nearly black—even in the sunlight that peeked through the curtains.

"Vesper? Callow?" I asked. Their heads swiveled in my direction, the sound of my voice triggering them to stand.

"Milla?" the woman asked. Definitely her. I'd studied their voices for weeks when they were all I had left beyond the darkness of my cell. "*Saints*, I can't believe you survived the last trial. The guards said . . ." She shook her head.

"I figured out a way to get by the glint treatment." I crossed my arms as she examined me for the first time. "I see you met the husband I threatened on everyone."

"You did what?" Nico asked.

I smiled and leaned my weight into his side. "I might have thrown your name around to strike some leverage. It didn't work."

"That's why I said your name sounded familiar," Vesper said, looking at Nico.

I cleared my throat to bring her attention back to me. "Did you need something? After abandoning me in the tower, I didn't think I was of any use to you."

"Abandoned you? They claimed they were allies of yours," Nico growled.

I patted his arm to calm the inner beast yanking at his chain.

"Technically, we were neighbors, but they went silent when I told them my secret." My legs ached from standing for a brief time, courtesy of lying on my back for so long. Sitting on the bed, I beckoned for her to speak. "Tell me why you care so much about my remnant."

Vesper explained what she apparently had shared with Nico in the engine room, divulging how she crossed the sea with Callow in search of Chaos. When I mentioned my remnant was of the saint they were searching for, it startled them enough to render them silent, unsure if they could prod without risking giving up their own confidential information.

"You mentioned a name as well," Nico said beside me.

Vesper nodded. "We were told to find Rosa Bianchi, that she could lead us to Chaos."

"Bianchi . . . As in Sabina Bianchi? That must be a relative of hers. Perhaps she could help—"

"Perhaps she would help herself," he said dryly. "If the Bianchi family knows about Chaos, then Sabina has kept secrets. She'll be the first person we visit when we get back home, but we'll need to be cautious how much we share with her in return for information. A trade of interest is never perfectly balanced."

I nodded in agreement as the conversation went stale between us. It was Callow that broke it first. "Not to sound ungrateful, but is there food on this ship?"

"You can look in the barracks, but I doubt the last crew left anything. The train is waiting at the docks, where we have food and water and whiskey for everyone. The family haelen will also be available in a medical car to see to any injuries. Until then, you'll have to endure." Nico walked lazily toward the cabin door as if in hopes the pair would get the hint to leave. "It won't be more than a few hours. The steam ship can travel twice as fast as a sail ship."

"It would endure the storms as well." Vesper arched a brow.

"It would, if it needed to." He jutted his chin toward the door. "The crew deck is below. There should be a spare bed or two to claim while we travel. Keep our conversation between us, or I'll reconsider finding you a spot on the bottom of the sea floor."

"Come on, V." Callow pinched her shoulder. "I think Mr. Attano would like his wife back."

Vesper stole a glance my way, her cheeks flushing. She eventually nodded and followed her companion out of the cabin. Nico shut the door and locked it, releasing a long sigh that slumped his shoulders.

"You must be exhausted," I said.

He scrubbed his face with a hand and offered a mirthless smile. "The adrenaline is wearing off. I could use a few hours of sleep."

I reached for him, still sitting on the bed. "Come lay with me, *husband*."

His smile stretched enough to flash dimples in both cheeks. "Why must you say it like that?"

"Because everyone keeps calling me your wife like I don't have a name or a purpose beyond the title."

His hands slid into my outreached palms, connecting with cold metal and warm skin. “You can be called anything you like, Camilla, but your title will never change what you truly are to me.”

“And what is that?” I asked.

Bringing both of my hands to his lips, he kissed the spot they overlapped. “*Mine*.”

My heart shuddered inside the cage of my ribs. “Nico, I need to apologize.”

“For what?”

He slid onto the mattress, maintaining his touch. I rested beside him on the same pillow. “For not telling you about the marriage license. I told Giles to file it before the Salt Ball. I was worried my brother would try to screw you on our deal. He threatened to wed me to Felix behind your back—”

He gently stroked my forearm. “Milla, I know all of this. You saved my family from certain ruin, probably saved all Lynchaven in the process. But we have one problem with this union of ours.”

My brows furrowed together. “What do you mean?”

He sighed, stalling his reply. “A marriage is only legally binding until death deems each party separate again. When you died, it meant we were technically no longer bound. I’m not sure how it will work legally if you come back from the dead.”

Disappointment welled in my chest, and I blinked back the burn of tears. “So . . . I’m *technically* not your wife anymore.”

“Now, when have technicalities ever defined what we mean to each other? Do you want to be mine or not? It’s as simple as that.”

There was no question about it on my end. I had originally filed our marriage license to protect us both. But now? The time separating us had only deepened everything I felt for him, proved how far I’d fallen. When I was taken, it had followed a night I’d remember for the rest of my life, when we’d spoken words of commitment to each other.

And then those words were tested, leaving us hanging in this newfound place we'd just discovered. An area so new and yet so comfortable, it felt like returning home. I'd meant every word then, and I still meant them now, and I wanted to linger forever with him in this place we found.

His gaze darkened as he waited for my answer. Inside that smoky stare, my fire had found a kindred flame.

I smiled. "I'm yours, Nico."

I DIDN'T SLEEP, and instead listened to Nico's labored breath as he slept in my arms while we traveled north. The Isle had a single bay that ships once utilized as they came from the Continent when the storms weren't present over the Sea and forbidding passage.

A bang on the chamber door disturbed the quiet.

He startled awake, every muscle in his body went taut at attention, and his free hand reached for the gun he hadn't remembered he'd placed on the table before he crawled into bed. When he realized where he was, he relaxed, cursing under his breath as he scrubbed his tired face with his hand.

"Who the fuck is it?" he groaned.

"Luther. We need you downstairs."

"Why?"

"Take a look outside, lovebirds."

A shadow passed over the windows, cutting off the light that had been fighting to spill between the break in the curtains. Nico, sensing something strange as I did, stood from the bed to peer out the window. A lazy smile stretched across his sleepy face.

"Ahh," he said. "That's why."

"What is it?"

He pulled the curtain aside. When my eyes settled from the glare, I noticed the Iron Saint waited in the distance, steam rising in a cloudy pillar from the chimney.

"Welcome home, Milla."

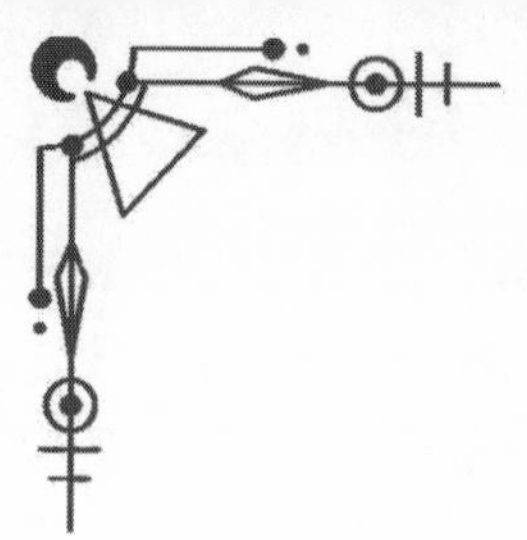
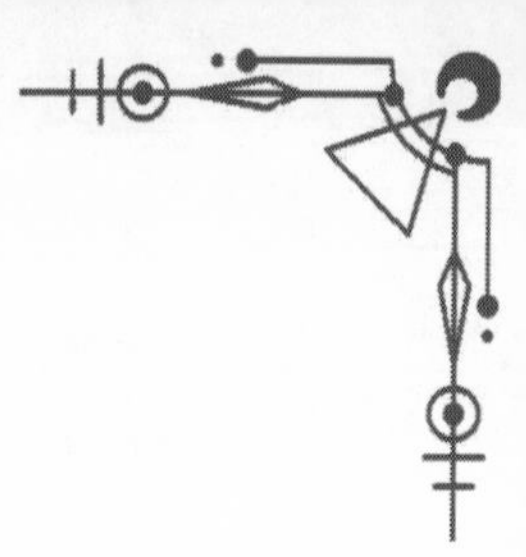

CHAPTER 19

NICOLAI

Camilla rode with her brothers in the refurbished suite in her family's former private car. I had the entire interior remodeled so it wouldn't be so familiar to her. Everything from the stain of the wood paneling to the color of the pillow stitching. It all was thrown out and remade, hopefully stripping away anything that would trigger the bloody memories that haunted Milla's quiet approach as she boarded the train.

She'd said nothing since we started the journey to Lynchaven. Hadn't refused my demands for her to see the haelen for her burns. Too docile for something not to be bothering her. But there was a time for everything, and prodding wouldn't be helpful while we were still on the object of all her self-reproach.

Regulus had remained near the Marchese family, trailing them like a shadow. I noticed he slipped out for a smoke when I checked on the family not long ago, just before I returned to the medic car to help with Adler.

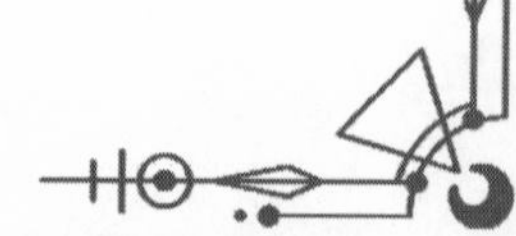

Luther remained with me, holding down our cousin as the haelen retrieved the bullet in his chest.

"Good thing his aim was shit, right?" I reminded him.

Adler gritted his teeth as Ruth pulled the lead out of his flesh. "Not feeling very appreciative at the moment, cousin."

I smiled at his misery. "Then I'll be grateful for you. Better a moment of hell than to face it permanently."

"Always the rational one."

I turned from the haelen's makeshift station in the sleeper car, where she had used a fold-out bed as her workspace. Luther stared out the window, his arms crossed.

"How are the rest of the liberated?"

"Mostly whole," he clipped. "Nothing ole' Ruth here couldn't seal or mend."

"Do *not* call me old, Luther Attano."

He swatted his hand in her direction. "Anyway, Marcus has scheduled us to stop at the station to drop off the family. The evacuees will be taken to the industrial park to stay at the old warehouse. Mother and the aunts have organized cots and food for the next few weeks until they can find permanent accommodations."

I nodded in confirmation. "While we travel, collect names of loved ones from each man and woman and we'll contact their families when we return to the city. I'll need to check on the tracks over the river as well—"

"You'll do no such thing, boss. You've got plenty of men and cousins to delegate these tasks." He patted my shoulder lightly, then squeezed it. "Do us all a favor and take a day off."

As nice as that sounded, shit still needed to be done. There would be no rest for any of us until the threats to our family were dealt with and eradicated for good. "The Nine will be looking to strike soon—"

"The Nine are powerless! We've got the upper hand—"

I shirked off his hand. "And if we lose sight of our goal for a moment, the advantage will slip right through our fingers. The bridge was only one point of access to the north side of the Isle, Luther. They could take that ship and everything we have if we do not continue what we set out to do."

Some of the victory filling his shoulders dwindled. "When does it end, Nico?"

After the planning and execution of Milla's rescue, I understood the wariness in his tone. Felt it deep in my bones. Worsening the ache was the unseen end point of it all.

"When we can rebuild the bridge."

I took his silence as a dismissal and started out the sleeper, opening the door to pass between the adjoined railcars.

The train jolted. Breaks screamed, and we shifted from full speed to a skidding stop. The jerk was so sudden; I was forced to brace myself on the nearby railing to prevent falling off the gangway connection.

Why the hells are we stopping?

We had stalled in the middle of a trestle, a bridge of steel latticework suspending the tracks over a dip in the landscape, ensuring a flat ride for the train between cresting hills. The tips of evergreens pierced the fog on either side.

I searched for a reason for our sudden stop. But without the ability to access the engine, we were stuck here.

Luther appeared in the doorway. "What the hells?"

"I don't know." An uncomfortable feeling curled in my stomach. We fell silent, waiting for some explanation to show itself.

"Do you hear that?"

In the quiet of the wilderness, the clank of metal on metal. Small at first, then near enough like it was coming closer. Luther and I watched the fog, waiting for the sound to actualize, when a black gloved hand reached over the top of the bridge, pulling up a masked face of a watchman.

Luther reacted before I did, pulling his gun to shoot the man in his face. The mask cracked but didn't concede to the bullet. He unleashed a round until the watchman slipped from the tracks and fell into the blanket of fog.

"Lock the doors," I shouted. "We're being attacked!"

I took off down the next railcar while Luther informed the ones following behind the sleepers, repeating the order to anyone who lingered about until I reached Milla's family's suite a few cars ahead. All three of the Marcheses stood, looking out the window to gain a hint of what was going on.

"Get down and cover the fucking window!" I hissed, pulling the curtains closed. "We've got watchmen crawling up the side of the bridge.

"How did they know the train was coming through here?" Milla's hazel eyes were wide on me, and she crossed her arms around her middle. "They couldn't have had enough time to organize an attack after Hightower."

"Good question, and one we'll answer later when time allows." I ripped up the aisle runner and pulled a section of boards free that had been glued together to form a lid.

"What's that?" Aramis asked.

I glared at him. What the hells did it look like? "A hidden bunk." Snapping at Milla, I said, "Get in and hide. I'll come for you when it's safe."

"It's happening," she whispered. Her breaths quickened. "I can't do this again, Nico."

"We've got a train full of remnants, princess. We'll be fine. But I'll bet money they're here to take you back, so I need you to hide."

I outstretched my hand, and she glanced instead at the covered window. "Please, Milla." I dared not say her name louder than a whisper.

She winced, but finally cooperated, lying on her back in the narrow compartment. A perfect fit, no longer nor deeper than the size of her form. Before I shut the lid, I leaned forward and placed a kiss to her forehead.

She sucked a shaky breath, but her voice was firm as she spoke. "Don't be a good man. Come back to me, Nico."

"Don't worry about that, princess." I placed a gun over the hollow part of her stomach. Her fingers wrapped around it. "There is no line I wouldn't cross to be with you. I'll be quick, I promise."

No sooner had I placed the lid back over the bunk than did the car creak. Someone was climbing to the top, evident by the rocking. Stealing a glance at the brothers, I found Jeremiah staring up at the ceiling. Aramis stood by the door.

"What are we to do?" Jeremiah asked in a terrified whisper. He was younger and had been guarded enough to be inexperienced with this kind of danger. Watching his twin die must have been an incomparable tragedy. A shock to his privilege.

The roof groaned where the guard stepped. I pointed my second revolver at the spot and shot three times, adding new holes to the ceiling. The gas lamps flickered as a solid weight hit the roof with a thud. The guard's dead body landed hard before slinking off the side, briefly tipping the car.

"Do that. Keep this car clear and lock the door behind me."

Jeremiah swallowed hard but nodded, reluctantly unsheathing the gun at his hip. Aramis wore a look I couldn't translate, nor did I spare him another second to try. There were three passenger cars that needed checking, and if the Watch found me in here, they'd know exactly where Milla hid.

I opened the door, finding a guard fiddling with the lock of the next car. He turned just in time to look down my barrel before the bullet sunk into his forehead. I shoved him to the side before his knees gave out, where he fell over the edge to be swallowed by mist.

The door to the sleeper was locked, and I banged twice. "Open up!"

Facing one guard was simple enough, but remaining out here was less than ideal. Crawling to the roof where I didn't know how many waited would be a death wish.

Thankfully, Gideon recognized my voice and let me in the medic car. Adler had Ruth under his arm on his good side, insisting she'd be alright. The haelen wasn't convinced by the way her wide eyes shifted to every window.

"Luther is with the passengers. They looking for Milla, you think?" Gideon asked.

"I doubt they're trying to hitch a ride."

Glass burst from a shattered window. Ruth screamed as Adler threw them both flat on the aisle. Bullets ripped through the car, though neither of my cousins had lifted their guns. My remnant roared in my bones, and I paused the time to get to the window, shoving the gunman in the face just as I released the second. He fell back with a scream.

But more took his place.

"Watch the suite!" I shouted at Gideon. "Stay low and make sure no one compromises the family car." The last thing I needed from this ordeal was another casualty in their family. And if I trusted Milla's life in anyone else's hands, it was my cousin's. There was little faith left as far as Aramis was concerned.

Screams erupted from cars behind us, and I ran toward the sound, exposing myself as I crossed the gangway to pound on the door for Luther. The platform lurched as a heavy weight landed behind me. Without time to raise my gun or my remnant, leather gloves wrapped my throat, pressing me into a hard chest to cut off my windpipe.

"Like a rat on the run," he hissed in my ear. I struggled against his hold, the squeeze of his arm tightening until I couldn't breathe. "But you've got nowhere to hide now, vermin. Where's the key?"

Blades slid from the fingers of my false hand, sinking into his forearm. The man cried out and stumbled back, releasing his grip enough so I broke free. I whirled around, arm pulled back to strike him. But as I went for his throat, he grabbed my metal hand by the wrist.

The glint from his glove must have affected the ability of my remnant to move my hand as he grasped it, and my fingers went dead and out of my control. The concept startled me.

He recoiled his opposite hand and landed a fist on the bridge of my nose.

Blinking back tears, I wiped away the beginning of a stream of blood pouring from my face and spat a mouthful at his feet. "Is that all you got?"

He lunged, and I was ready to catch him with my active arm, until he stopped dead in his tracks—quite literally. The watchman bled, though not from anything I had done. His eyes, his mouth, his nose, even the orifices of his ears spilled blood until he choked on his own fluid and doubled over. A pile of bones and flesh, his skin held a bluish tone as he bled out all over the metal platform.

"Get in, Mr. Attano!"

I turned to see a woman with pale hair and eyes so light they were almost clear. She reached out to me, beckoning me inside the car. A Blood remnant by the expression of her power. Not everyone who could control the stuff became a healer. Some had more disturbing ways to control it.

I gladly accepted her invitation, reapplying the blockade they'd constructed from a table and a few chairs ripped from their foundation in the floor once I was inside.

"The other Attano is in the next car," she said between panicked breaths. "Can you tell us what's happening?"

As if in answer, the car shook as the weight of several watchmen stood on the roof. The passengers fell quiet, becoming so still we could each hear the cock of their guns. With a wild burst of wind from my remnant, I shoved aside the crowd, parting them until they jammed against the walls. No time for them to react; gun shots tore through the ceiling, littering the floor with lead where the descendants once stood.

An ache throbbed a pulse through my bones at the quick rush of release of my magic, but the threat was far from dealt with. Remnants primed, the air prickling in the car, ready to fight back with whatever the saints had left to their descendants.

But the watchmen didn't fire again. Odd, since I assumed they were trying to kill us. Instead, metal pipes filled the gaps. The sound of the men above tinkering with a mechanism followed, and a hiss of something spilling through the pipes. The wind I controlled suddenly felt out of reach. A smell like sulfur touched the air.

Gas.

"Cover yourselves!" I shouted, doing the same by pulling my coat over the bottom half of my face, if only to filter whatever it was they pumped into the space we congregated. Passengers pulled blankets over their heads, giving the stock my aunts packed on the train an additional use. There was nowhere to run, couldn't even leave the car since we were suspended on a bridge.

Eventually, despite my best efforts, the magic in my bones was dulled with the bitter aftereffects of what could only be accomplished by glint.

"Not poison," I spat. "Just their usual shit."

A man pushed off the wall, glowering. "You say that like it's a good thing! We have nothing to defend ourselves now. No better than fish in a barrel—"

A loud bang came from the door, the one opposite of where I'd entered. It too was barricaded, but I beckoned towards a group of descendants with my good hand, silently ordering for them to clear it.

"If they wanted *you* dead, you would be," I told him. "Let them in. We'll see what they want."

Satisfied they no longer wanted to kill for killing's sake, the passengers moved away the chairs that bolstered the door. As soon as they finished, it burst open from the kick of a guard.

Four of them ushered inside. Black and silver body armor hugged their form, light for the climb they no doubt scaled to reach the bridge. Black masks concealed their faces, adding to their commanding presence, which was about as subtle as a damn steam train. Cloaks drifted toward the open door, but their hoods remained over their obscured identities.

The passenger car behind us had been searched, if the similarly broken door was any indication.

"We've searched your passengers, but she's not there." The leader of the group stepped toward me. I only needed one good hand to shoot a gun, but he had three more to avenge him if I lifted my arm. "Where is the key, Attano?"

"I don't have a key."

He took another step forward. The barrel of his shotgun lingered over the descendants still pressed against the wall. "There are a lot of fugitives on this train, Mr. Attano. Harboring criminals could get you in trouble for a long time. None of these men and women will ever be allowed to work in the city. They'll be hunted down until the Society detains them once more and returns them to Hightower."

I sucked my teeth as he talked. "You think I care about the law? Tell your new inspector, Neal fucking Caldwell, if he wants anyone in my Row, he'll have to come through me."

"Which is why we'll bargain with you this once," he hissed. "We'll pardon the crimes of your family, as well as everyone on this train."

Murmurs started amongst the descendants, humming like flies attracted to shit. Which was exactly what I thought about the integrity of this deal. "I'm assuming you will absolve us all our sins if I hand over the key."

"Exactly."

"Burn in Oblivion."

The men behind him assumed a more active position, holding their guns defensively. "We are leaving here with the key, Attano. Either give her to us, or we'll pry her from your cold, dead hand. There is an easy way and a more difficult one, and I think your people would like you to reconsider your choice."

From the yearn in their stares, his assessment was accurate. The way this guard tried to manipulate me into doing the right thing was amusing, spreading a slow smile across my face. My hand clenched at my side. "Unfortunately, I already promised someone I love I would not be a good man today. Don't bother appealing to my heart, watchman. I assure you, it's not in this car."

The room took a collective breath. They didn't understand why keeping Milla from them was so important, must have assumed I just thought with my cock like Regulus had mentioned —and they turned on me. One by one, their trusting looks had turned to sideways glares, but if the stragglers from the Continent were any indication, Milla's remnant was important to keep guarded from the city and the alchemist that ran it.

And—more simply put—Camilla was mine.

"Suit yourself," he said, sounding indifferent. He pointed his gun in my direction, and I braced myself for the weight of the lead.

"Nico, let me in!"

Milla's voice.

The guards forgot about the descendants altogether, lunging toward the barricade behind me. I threw myself at one of them, shouted at the men and women in the car to help me stop them. But I had lost their loyalty by choosing Milla over their lives, and they wouldn't forget anytime soon.

"Hold him down."

One of them pinned my active arm behind my back and shoved me to my knees. A second jammed his gun into my temple, threatening to finish me if I dared make another move. I gnashed my teeth as the other two guards moved the rubble from the door, clearing it free.

When I saw her standing on the other side, I shut my eyes, trying to will away her image.

She was still there when I looked again, aiming a gun at the first guard. "Tell your men to stand down, let the descendants go free, and I'll do whatever you want."

The watchman scoffed behind his mask. "At least you can see reason, unlike your husband."

"A man who wants everything is never good at negotiating." She lowered her weapon slightly, still avoiding my attention. Where the hells were her brothers? Why had Aramis let her out, hadn't talked her out of this?

And *what* was she wearing?

Her body was draped in men's clothes, with a large shirt sagging into pants pulled high over her hips and a belt cinched around her waist. Without further argument, she handed her weapon to the watchman, who allowed her to pass and come to me. With my arm still pinned behind my back and the barrel of the guard's gun still an inch from my temple, I couldn't return her embrace as she draped graceful arms around my neck.

"Milla, what are you doing?" I seethed. My anger was unfocused, not directed at her, but was lashing, nonetheless.

She brushed her lips over the shell of my ear. "Finishing what Sera started. Watch those blonde bastards."

My body went rigid. She pulled back to look at me, the brown in her eyes too muddy, not enough golden green. Her form kissed me hard then, a strange, aggressive approach that contrasted her usual softness.

"Not bad, Attano," Regulus said as he pretended to be Milla, wiping her bottom lip with a thumb.

How had he avoided the gas? Then I remembered, he went out for a smoke. He must have somehow avoided the whole thing entirely. My shock wore off enough to warn him. "You know what they'll do to you."

Regulus nodded, though I noticed a flinch tighten his jaw.

"That's enough," the leader of the watchmen spoke. "Get her down the ropes. We need to get out of these cursed Wilds before daylight runs out."

With that, the man holding the gun to my head snatched Regulus by the waist and threw Milla's form over his shoulder, winking at me before he walked them both out. "Should we glint her before we go?"

The guard shook his head. "All the cars were gassed. Don't

waste anymore until we get back to the city. The dose should hold her for a while."

The group left, calling to their comrades in the next car to clear out. I watched them go with Regulus in tow, knowing full well they'd kill him as soon as the next glint dose was due. He wouldn't be able to hide the identity for long, but he'd given us time to get the hells back to the Row, where we were all safe again.

As soon as they were gone, I bolted back to the Marchese family car, ignoring my cousin's shouts as he called for me.

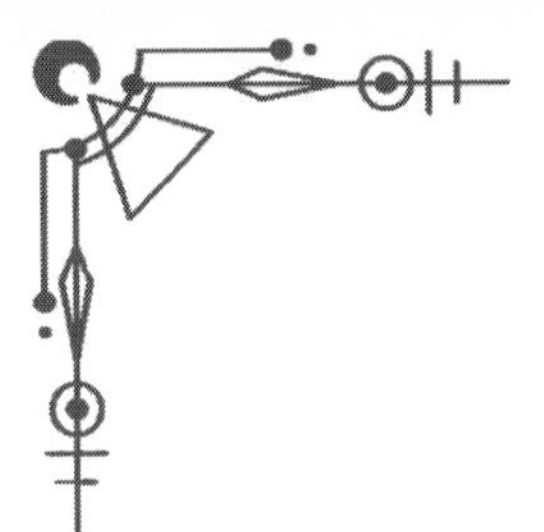
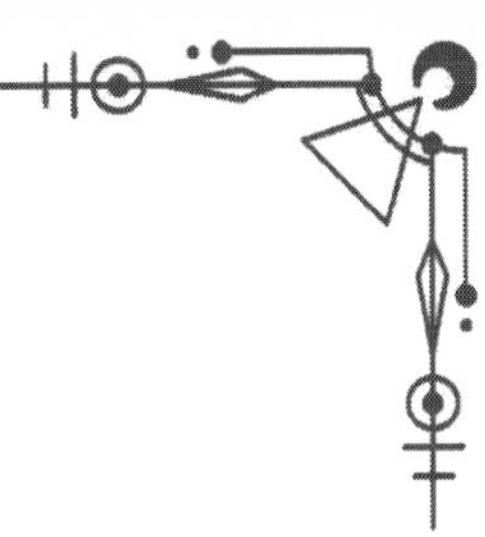

CHAPTER 20

CAMILLA

As soon as Nico closed the lid over the hidden compartment, the merciless darkness I had known for months returned like a bad dream—one I'd slept through on a hundred nights. It resumed with a vengeance, every bit as suffocating and restrictive. Yet this time, overwhelmingly isolating.

It felt as if all the air in the compartment slipped away. Like I had lain here for hours. The cold metal of the gun lost its sting, warmed by my body heat. A single hole was drilled through the rug and the wood, so that if I shifted my head, I could find a hint of fresh air or a slab of light.

My brothers bickered amongst themselves. Even with their voices unclear through the floor, I still tried to focus on their conversation to distract myself from my breath against the top of the compartment.

Something fell, hitting the floor hard. Their voices went quiet, and the silence exacerbated the anxious skip of my heart. Too much

time had passed, too much time to give trouble an opportunity. Power seeped into my veins, priming my hands in case I needed to break out. I peered through the hole where shadows stretched between the gas lamps.

Another voice joined the murmurs, though this one was different. Much deeper than either of my brothers'. Had a cousin come to help—Adler perhaps? He spoke in a similar timbre, possibly to compensate for being the youngest.

But another thud pulsed through the floor. No guns went off, but a scent tainted the little breath of air I could suck through the hole. A putrid smell.

It made the magic in my bones go quiet immediately.

Panic sank in, and it rose like a tide until I drowned, trapped beneath the swells of my rising distress with only a small hole as a lifeline. Then something slid over the peep hole briefly, and the rug was torn from its place on the floor.

This wasn't right. The mechanism Nico used to seal the lid was tinkered with. My thumb rolled back the safety on the pistol. Someone had found my hiding place.

A door opened and slammed, shots were fired, and a third weight slammed into the floor. Warmth dripped on my leg, soaking through the material of my pants until it clung to my skin. I hardly breathed as footsteps slowly traveled the length of the car, pausing for a beat before shutting the opposite door they came through.

I waited . . . and waited, but not a sound stirred in my family's suite. Wetness spread up my calf, drenching the left leg of my pants. What if Aramis bled out on top of me? Jeremiah? One of the Attanos?

The edges of the bunker closed in. Soon the narrow gap over my face wasn't enough, the race between my breath and my pulse outmatched anything else. I knocked tentatively on the lid, unable to handle it any longer.

"Hello?"

No answer. Not even the faintest shudder in the floor. I was alone—and trapped. Just like before. I was back in Hightower, where no one was coming for me.

My mind unraveled from there.

"Let me out!" I beat my palms against the lid to be heard by anyone nearby. But no one came, even after I shouted again and again, slapped the metal lining of the lid until my palms stung.

"Milla!" My name was a command, loud enough to cut through the layers between us—but not my nerves.

"*Let me out*!"

The resistance against my hands finally disappeared, and Nico pulled me out by my thrashing arms.

"It's alright, Milla," he said in an even voice. Slowly, as if taming the fight in my body with an invisible rope, his words reined me back.

I quickly scanned the room and found the evidence of all the noise: a bleeding watchman. My brothers were slumped on opposite ends of the car. It only numbered my questions. "Are they?"

"Just knocked out," he said.

I settled some. The shake of my nerves stilled until I could hold Nico's hand steady. He stroked my wrist with a thumb; his false hand hung limp at his side.

"What happened? Did they leave?"

He nodded. "Regulus pulled one of his shifting tricks and pretended to be you, so they'd leave us all alone."

"But that would mean—"

"He knew, Milla. He knows what will happen to him."

This car was cursed. It seemed every time I stepped on this

train, someone died in my place. My grip tightened around my upper arm, pinching it until the tangible pain distracted from some of the hurt in my chest. "Why would he do that? He doesn't even know me."

"With all respect, princess, I don't think he did it for you," Nico said. Any explanation died on his tongue as Luther approached us.

"Boss, I don't mean to interrupt, but we need to get the hells out of here."

"We'll get the haelen in here to look at the Marcheses," Nico barked back. "Even without her remnant, she might help rouse them."

He stood then, letting my hand slip from his own, and checked the cylinder of his revolver.

"Where are you going?" I asked.

"Going to have a little chat with our engineer, and make sure there's no further delays." He jerked his chin at his cousin. "Stay with Milla until I get back."

Glancing once more at my brothers still knocked out on the floor, he scowled and turned toward the gangway connection leading toward the engine.

"He's upset," I observed out loud. Looking at Luther, I asked, "Did something happen in the other cars with the descendants?"

Luther helped me up and into a chair and cleaned up the area, focusing first on the dead watchman. He sighed, taking in the size of him. "Unfortunately, boss, there were only a handful of people who knew we'd be taking the train back to Lynchaven with the rescued prisoners. All of whom Nico trusted. Most of whom are along for the ride. There wouldn't have been time for the Society goons at the island to drive home and organize this attack."

"It was planned from the beginning, then," I said.

He nodded, looking at me then with a grim expression. “Someone on this train is a snitch.” His wayward glance at my brothers sunk a stone in my stomach. “And Nico is going to figure out who, sooner or later.”

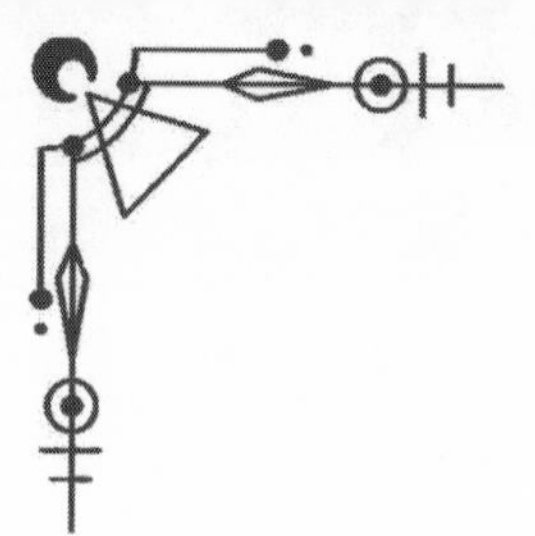
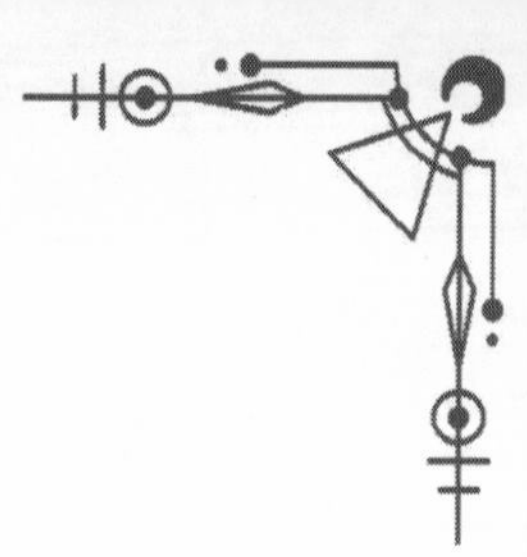

CHAPTER 21

NICOLAI

"How are you feeling?" I asked Milla as we turned down the isolated road leading to the Attano Estate. She had changed out of the bloody clothes the watchman ruined, opting for a pair of warm leggings and a crimson sweater that hung to her mid-thigh. She still wore my coat, claiming she'd never been tolerant of Lynchaven's winters.

She bit her bottom lip as she stared out a frosted window. "Just anxious to see everyone."

I squeezed the hand cupping her knee, thankful the carriage bench was wide enough to allow me to sit beside her. Her curls were pulled up into a neat updo on top of her head, allowing me a flattering view of her slender neck.

"Understandable, though there's nothing to be concerned about. They missed you very much, Milla. Nonna especially missed you in the kitchen. Hasn't let us forget how incompetent the rest of us are when it comes to a stove."

Her lips tipped in a smirk. "How is she?"

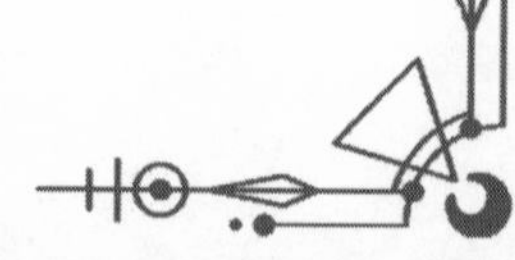

"Old."

"Nico, really," she said, smiling fully.

I sighed. "I think the years are starting to catch up to her. She's not as sprightly as she used to be. Hasn't fussed at me since the day you were taken, and I've given her plenty to raise hell over."

Her smile fell. "That's not good," she mumbled. "Maybe she's just . . . tired. I don't know. She can't be dying. Not yet."

"No, princess. Not yet. I'm sure she'll live to torment us for many years to come."

Milla only nodded hesitantly, letting her gaze fall back to the passing landscape outside the car. "You hired more guns." Not a question, but an observation, noting the men behind the iron fence returning her assessment.

"Not a damn squirrel will pass by unnoticed on the property. The house is completely impenetrable. You'll never have to question your safety here."

"What about the rest of the Row?"

Just thinking about her leaving the boundary of the property triggered my heart rate. But I couldn't lock her up forever, no matter how much I wished I could. "With the right escorts, the Row as well."

The carriage slowed as the asphalt turned to gravel. Milla sucked a long breath when she saw the house, not bothering to wipe the tears that slid down her flushed cheeks.

This. This moment made every sleepless night, every bullet to the back, every day full of plotting her rescue worth it. I grabbed her hand and kissed it, savoring the connection. "Welcome home, my love."

She blinked and glanced at me, as if surprised by something I'd said. But before I could dismiss the slip, the car parked near the east entrance, and my family quickly snatched her attention as they waited outside.

"I sent Gideon ahead to brief them," I explained. "I'll let you get out first. Esme looks like she's going to combust if she has to wait a second longer."

She placed a hand around my arm. "Nico, wait, I want to tell you something first."

"What is it?"

"I wanted to tell you that I'm . . ." Her lips wavered on a thought. "I'm so grateful to have you and your family, and not just because you saved me from Hightower. You saved me long before I ever knew I needed to be rescued."

My hand slipped up and down her thigh. "You didn't need anyone to save you, princess. Not then, and not now. But the Attanos will be here whenever you need to be reminded."

"Well," she drawled, "sometimes I can be very stubborn."

Understatement of the century, but I didn't tell her that. "No. You're just perfect, Milla."

The tip of her chin invited my lips to meet hers, and I crashed into them with a driving kiss. My hand slid up her thigh, wishing I had her alone already. When she kissed me like this, slipped her palm around my neck, it made me feel like the only man in the world. Her touch shattered reality with its all-consuming snatch, and nothing existed but her.

She crossed her right leg over her left just as my fingers slipped beneath the hem of her sweater, locking my wrist above the apex of her thighs. My grip dug into her leggings, wishing I could strip them off, feel the heat of her skin as it permeated through the material—

Three knocks banged loudly on the window.

"You can kiss her later, Nico! Open the door!" Esme shouted through the glass.

Milla laughed against my lips, about to move away until I kissed her harder, using my free hand to pull the blinds shut and block out my nosy cousin.

The sound of a door unlocking broke us both apart—fucking metal locks.

Esme's conniving face appeared in the carriage; a bright grin stretched across her cheeks. "Camilla! Don't make me bend this car out of shape just to get to you—"

My cousin didn't have time to finish her threat before Milla was out of her seat. By the time I made it out of the carriage myself, they were wrapped in an embrace so fierce, I might have lost my other hand if I tried to break them apart.

I hung back, watching from a distance as my aunts took their turn, one by one, welcoming Milla home where she belonged. The side driveway quickly became filled with murmurs of happy reunions and sniffles from their tears. My uncle, however, approached me first, leaning a little more than usual on his cane. Winter made his already terrible knees that much worse.

He said nothing at first, only threw an arm around me in an embrace I hadn't been expecting. He released me just as quickly, clearing his throat. "Gideon briefed us before heading back to the warehouse to help with the rescued prisoners. *Saints*, Nico. We're all so thankful it went so well."

"Not for Regulus," I murmured, who was most likely dead by now.

Solomon nodded slowly, as if remorseful. "It is unfortunate to hear about the shifter, but you couldn't have foreseen a betrayal so close. We'll figure the rest out, Nico."

I nodded sharply, though I didn't quite agree. I should have suspected something when the getaway went too smoothly.

"I've always made known my reservations, but I'm so damn proud of you, Nicolai. Your father—" He looked away toward where another carriage approached.

Adler drove the Marcheses back, stopping just long enough to let them out before he was peeling down the driveway, back to the industrial park to assist the rest of my cousins.

I ignored whatever else my uncle said. Instead, I focused on Aramis and his brother and how they looked at Milla with her new family—the odd resentment the scene planted in his pale gaze. He must have felt my glare, the way his eyes shifted to me then.

"Did you hear me?" Sol asked.

"I'm sorry." I shook my head. "You said something about the aunts?"

"Yes, after they finish saying hello, they're going to help the boys at the warehouse get everything settled. Fran can notify the families, since she knows practically everyone."

"Good plan. I've been ordered to take the night off, but we'll see how long that lasts."

My uncle scoffed before patting me on the shoulder. "Enjoy these moments, Nico. These days, they come few and far between. One day, you'll look back and wish you hadn't prioritized work over family." He pivoted on his better leg and started back toward the house.

"Where's Nonna?" Milla asked.

Fran tucked a fallen strand of golden-brown hair behind Milla's ear. "Upstairs. She isn't feeling well today, but she's still expecting you to visit as soon as possible."

Milla turned to me then, her hand extended to me. "Come with me?"

I'd have taken it no matter where she led me. To the end of the fucking realm, if that's where she was going, I'd follow. Perhaps Solomon and Luther were right. Maybe it was just as important to steal sweet moments with her when I could, just as much as constantly trying to fight for a future full of them.

Taking her hand in my false one, I leaned close to murmur in her ear, "Only if I get to take you to my room after."

She smiled without looking at me. "You have yourself a deal, Attano."

MY GRANDMOTHER gradually smothered any arousal heating my blood as she made us sit with her for the next three hours, Milla next to her in the much-too-large bed, as she listed off every shameful memory of mine since I was old enough to embarrass her.

"There was a time when Nico was an absolute menace to society," Nonna went on. "Poor child couldn't keep his hands to himself. He was a little thief everywhere we went. Stole a woman's pearls right off her face without her knowing, charmed her with that darling face to distract her. Gave them to his mother as a gift for her birthday. Do you remember what she told you, Nicky?"

I sighed. "That I was a very naughty child, and the Society was going to come take me away. I thought she'd been rather ungrateful."

Nonna looked at my wife, a devious gleam in her eye. "He barricaded himself in his room for three days. Scared him sick."

Milla bit her lip, trying to leash her laughter.

She rambled on, her memory sharp as a whip, about the time I got my "abnormally large for my age" head stuck between the bannisters of the west wing stairs. How I called my muscles "muffins" for a solid two years because of a lisp.

"When he was twelve, I caught him reading my dirty romance books in his room at night."

"You *knew*?" I asked.

Milla's brows nearly flew off her head.

"Of course I knew," she said with a wave of her hand. "You thought you were so sneaky, lurking around in my room like I wouldn't notice my missing books. Esme was too young for me to suspect her, though now, I wish I would have snuck a few onto her shelves."

"Nonna!" Esme said, exasperated.

"And you let me keep reading them?" I asked, absolutely mortified my grandmother had known what I read late at night in my room—and inadvertently encouraged it by not interfering.

She shrugged. "What? It was the safest way for a boy to learn about the birds and the bees. I figured your future wife would thank me for it." She looked at Milla. "Were my intuitions incorrect, Belladonna?"

"Don't answer that," I told her.

Nonna glared at me, but thankfully dropped the subject. At this point, I'd gladly welcome any reason to get out of this room. My silent pleading paid off when our butler, Grimm, knocked on Nonna's half-open bedroom door.

"What is it?" I asked.

"A message for you, Mr. Attano. Just arrived from the station."

I stood to take the note from his hand. "Thank the saints."

The envelope was unmarked. The note inside was little more than folded scrap paper, lacking a salutation to note the sender.

Meet over the river at dusk, where our worlds still cross. Come alone.

"What is it?" Milla asked, probably reading the concern in my expression.

"I've got to go down to the station." I looked at Nonna and the rest of my family. "As lovely walking down memory lane has been, I need to check on something. I'll see you all after dinner."

"I'll see you out," Milla said, taking her own excuse to leave. She kissed Nonna on a wrinkled cheek and muttered something about getting hungry. My grandmother, being the insensitive hag she was, encouraged Milla to go put some meat on her bones.

"Ignore her," I said as she joined me in the hall.

She shrugged, crossing her arms over her midsection. "She isn't wrong. I could use a full meal to get some strength back." Before I could pocket it, she grabbed the note from my hands and read it over. "What's this?"

"I suppose I'm about to find out."

"You're going to meet a stranger by yourself? What if it's a trap? What if this is from Felix?"

I snatched the paper from her hands and tapped the symbol in the corner, where an eagle was printed on the stationery. "This is from the High Overseer's office. I know because I've seen it on his desk. If he wants to meet with me, it could mean the OIC is ready for negotiations. I've been waiting for word from them."

The worry creasing her forehead smoothed, but her lips pursed doubtfully. "Still, I wish you'd bring someone to the viaduct if that's where the letter is requesting you meet." Her gaze fell from the note to the floor. "And I wish you weren't being taken away so soon after we just arrived."

I took both her hands in mine, smoothing a thumb across her fingers. "I'll make it up to you, I promise. I'm all yours tonight, princess."

"All mine," she repeated. *Saints*, the way she said it sent a shiver down my spine. "Maybe you can show me what you learned in those books of yours."

My laugh barked an echo through the house as we descended to the main level. "You're just jealous you had to read about trains while I was learning how to fuck—"

"Nico!"

"You know, you weren't complaining back at East End." Her cheeks turned a lovely shade of pink as we made it to the bottom of the stairs, and I stole a kiss before she could even return it. "See you tonight, then."

FOG SWIRLED OFF THE RIVER, hiding the last reaches of the sun to darken the dusk. I bent the little light that still hazed the sky to guide my steps over the train tracks running over the steel-made viaduct. It was the only connection between the Districts and the Row, one heavily guarded on our side and not commonly used for foot transportation. If the train came through, one would have nowhere to go except into the river, but there would be no train tonight.

A glaring light split through the fog from a kerosine lamp. I used my remnant to brush away the mist, getting a clearer image of the person I'd meet without getting too close. They must have felt my wind, for the figure turned to face me, pulling down her hood.

"Vanya?"

The Overseer's daughter set down her lamp on the ice already forming over the wooden slats of the tracks. I neared her slowly, as if approaching an enemy—unsure if that line had been drawn.

"You really fucked everything up this time, Nicolai."

My wind swept behind her, checking for any hidden figures in the failing light of the gloam, but we were alone. "I'm sure I've put your father in quite an uncomfortable position, but that's not my problem."

"It's going to be," she hissed.

I adjusted the lapels of my coat tighter around my chest. The temperature dropped with the sun. Flakes of fresh snow swirled in the air, just flurries now. Soon, though, they might be blinding. "What have you heard so far?"

"So far?" she asked, brows raising. "You mean there's more than the bloody bridge, the Hightower Heist, and the fact you somehow let it spill that my father was involved with helping you take down Gavriel?"

"Is that what they're calling it? The Hightower Heist?" I had to admit, it had a nice ring to it. If she didn't look so cross, I might have asked for a copy of the *Isle Inquirer* for that headline.

Her gloved hands opened and shut into fists. "Did you not hear me?" she seethed. "The Niners know about what happened. They know everything because you told Gavriel I fed you the wrong fucking names. They know we took down their people."

"Shit." I scrubbed my face. I hadn't thought of the long term when I spilled my plans to the previous inspector. "Have you or your father received any threats? What are the Niners going to do about it?"

"Nothing." She crossed her arms. Her gaze fell to my feet. "They're going to hold it over our heads for now. Make sure we don't interfere with their plans, or my father will be removed from office."

"But we made sure the Nine had little support left to influence the ballots," I said. "There's no merit to these threats—"

She looked me in the eye then. "Neal Caldwell has turned this city against you, Nicolai. After you blew up the bridge, he blamed you for segregating our kinds, he blamed descendants for thinking they were better than us. The natives here now think you're just trying to starve us out, take everything we have until there's nothing left so you can swoop in and steal it all from underneath us, just as your father and your family did with the Steelworks. Then the railway."

She took a step closer. "The people think you're coming for them now." Her voice was lower, a pitch gentler. "Once word spreads about Hightower . . ." She shook her head. "The Nine will have all the support they need. My father is powerless against them, and even if he refuses their demands, they'll just put someone else up that will comply. The people will call for his head if we support you."

I paced a short path down and up the length of the viaduct. War had always been a possibility, but so had peace. Neal Caldwell worked the system to ensure the Nine got what they'd wanted all along. They'd forced me to take matters into my own hands to protect the ones I loved, to protect the people they were trying to harm from the beginning, and painted me as a villain for it.

I paused my stride for a moment. "I'm sorry you and your father are dealing with this. You know I never meant for this to happen."

She sighed, a white cloud spilling from her lips in the frigid air. "That's why I'm meeting you and not retaliating. It was always a risk, being found out."

"Did they say anything specific about Hightower? Were you at the meeting with your father when he was briefed?"

"I was there," she said. "They only said you emancipated the very dangerous descendants there. That you were possibly making an army out of them."

So, nothing about Camilla. Perhaps I could help her situation. "Vanya, I need to tell you about why I went to Hightower."

"What?"

"I didn't just go to the prison to free the prisoners. Sure, I wanted to help them. But the real reason . . ." I stepped closer and dropped my voice, in case it carried on the harsh wind. "Is because they had my wife."

Her eyes widened. "Camilla? She's alive?"

"Yes." I nodded. "She has a very powerful remnant, something the Nine want to use and we cannot let them have. That's why I broke into Hightower. There is a game being played here that they've planned for a long time, and we're only on the brink of whatever is to come."

Vanya was silent for a minute, absorbing what I'd just told her. Her shocked expression bounced over the tracks as she pondered. "Why is her remnant so powerful?"

"Because it goes against what the OIC wants—*Order*." It was becoming clear that Chaos, the antithesis of Order, threatened what the Nine and the OIC had been after all along. "They think it is the key to something, though I'm not sure what yet. Do what you will with that information."

She nodded slowly, the focus in her eyes detaching. "If I hear anything about their plans for Camilla, I will send them down the pipeline. If they believe me to be ignorant, they'll most likely speak more freely in my presence."

Vanya was more than just the Overseer's daughter or the Head of Public Affairs. She was the city socialite. She had connections to every family, thanks to her father's obsessive need to please his voters. Something that could give us an advantage. "Just be careful. Have you heard anything about a captured descendant?"

She shook her head. "No, why?"

Disappointment filled my chest. "I suppose it doesn't matter now." *Hells*, what if they tortured him? What if they kept him alive for the proper time, to play with us later? Felix knew I didn't leave a man behind. I gave up that card when I dragged every descendant out of Hightower behind my wife.

"I'll keep an ear out, regardless," she said. "This is messy, Nicolai, but we'll fix it. You don't want your people to suffer any more than I'd wish for mine. As long as we work together, we can beat them, but you must be as honest as I am with you. Trust me."

I winced at the word. I'd trusted plenty when I was younger, and experience had broken all my faith in men, but she had proven time and time again to have pure intentions, and I needed an ally among my enemies. "You're the only one I trust across the river, Vanya. Stay out of trouble."

Her lips curled in a grin, which began to purple from the cold. "Keep your eyes on the river. The temperature is dropping, the water is already beginning to freeze over. The Society won't need a bridge with that kind of connection. If I were you, I'd keep my eyes on the embankments." She picked up her lamp and dipped her chin. "Send your wife my best."

She disappeared, shielded by the fog and the thickening snowfall.

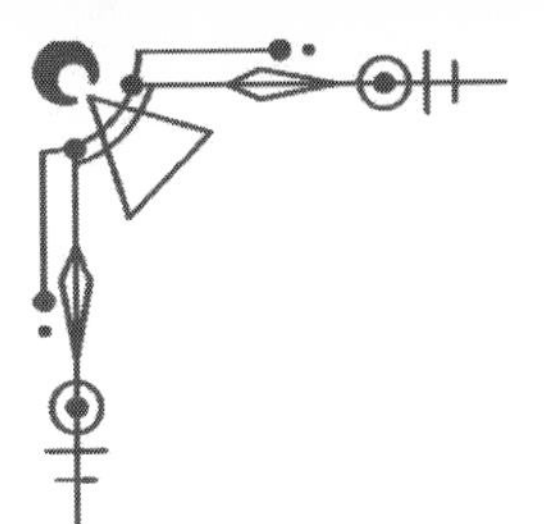
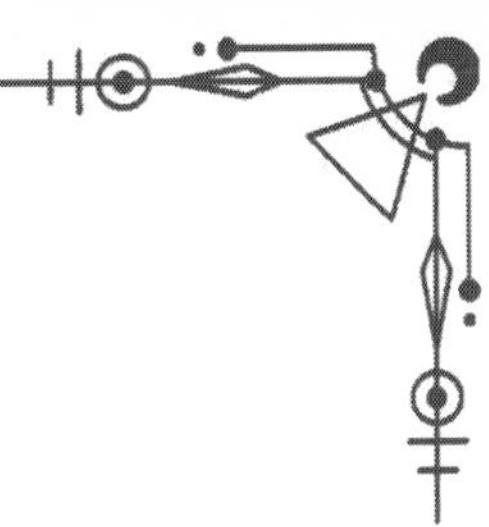

CHAPTER 22
CAMILLA

My brothers didn't come to the kitchen for dinner. Most of the family was gone, taking care of the rescued prisoners, so I helped myself to a roast Nonna had prepared ahead of time. With my stomach stretched full for the first time in months, I scanned the backyard for the guesthouse where Nico had boarded my brothers.

A two-story brick structure matching the architecture of the main building stood at the end of the garden, which wasn't much of a garden besides the elegant arrangement of dead flowers and brittle branches around a frozen fountain. Esme's garage was off to the side, the stables on the other, but the guesthouse was straight back, in the estate's shadow.

I figured if they hadn't bothered to come inside, they may have felt unwelcome. I'd been so wrapped up seeing the Attanos again, and stuck at Nonna's side, I hadn't had time to visit them properly —and without the shadow of my suspicious husband lurking behind.

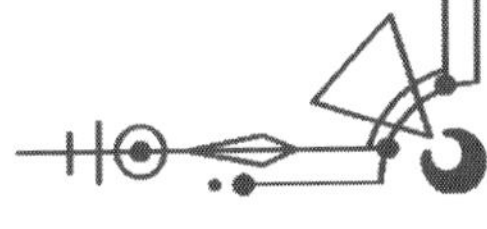

Grimm read my thoughts, and he brought me a coat to withstand the wind beginning to pick up strength. I worried for Nico being out in this weather, suspended over the river no less, then remembered who he was and what he controlled. He could shove the caller off the viaduct if they gave him any grief.

The yard was silent, the crunch of my steps over the slush of snow the only sound competing with the whistle of the hard wind. Light flickered behind the ice-covered windows on the first floor of the guesthouse, but as I approached, I noticed fresh prints mixing mud into the slush, leading around the front face of the building.

The footprints led me to a partially opened gate leading to a rear courtyard.

"Aramis?" I called out. His back was to me as he stared at something beneath a towering elm tree, hands in his coat pocket—and alone. Hearing his name, his shoulders jerked, and he looked back at me. "What are you doing out here?"

My answer came when I saw the tombstones. Pressed behind the rear courtyard of the guesthouse was the Attano family graveyard. Paulo Attano, Nonna's late husband. Nico's parents, his little sister, Anna, who, by the dates, had been killed at the small age of six. The last grave was a fresh one, the stone not yet marred by the elements.

My name was chiseled into marble.

Camilla Mercy Marchese-Attano
Beloved friend, sister, daughter, and wife.

The site of my grave marker hit me differently than I expected. A reminder of how near death lingered, how easy it was to be snatched in its grip, and how precious was the pulse in my veins. I wanted to be worthy of every title written beneath my name, so that the ones who called me such things would say them with pride. So such titles would mean something.

"The metal bender said she would make a plaque to replace the name," Aramis said in a voice dry of emotion. Though the tension in his neck told me he was anything but apathetic.

"Her name is Esme, and if she told you she'd do it, she will." I pressed into the side of his arm, shielding my face from the sting of the breeze. "I miss her too."

He was quiet for a while, letting that thought simmer between us. "We should have left this fucking city a long time ago."

"Maybe." Perhaps we'd still have Giles and Jasper and Sera. Then I'd never know what I'd have missed without Nicolai. There was no choice that didn't hold a great loss. "But where would it have led us? We know now that there is no running from this. Vesper and Callow only prove that the Continent is just as dangerous as this city."

"That's where Father told us to go," he clipped. "I will do as he asked, even if it's the last thing I do."

"To what end? Father isn't here now. He hasn't seen what's happened—"

"He foresaw this, Camilla!" He jerked from my touch, putting distance between us. "Why do you think he wanted us to leave? Why do you think he built the steam ship to get us across the sea? It is not safe for you here, nor anyone else who is trying to protect what you hold." He gestured to Sera's grave.

My eyes stung, holding back tears the icy breeze licked away before they could fall. "Don't you know how much I feel the blame for their deaths? *Saints*, I'd give anything not to be what I am."

He sighed, the glare in his eyes softened as he stood beside me again. "I know. Hells, if there was a way to trade places with you,

Camilla, I would. If there was a way to take this from you so you could have a regular life, I'd do it."

His admission stung a bit, even as he placed a comforting arm over my shoulders. "Have you been taking the glint?" I nodded. "Let me know when you need more. Marcus has been sliding me some on the side from the Districts. I've got plenty."

"What if I don't want to suppress my remnant all the time? Nico said—"

"Nico has had his entire life to practice using his remnant. You have no idea what you're capable of. Do you *want* to hurt someone?"

"Of course not, but—"

"Father fed that stuff to you for years before you got the familiar, you know. You missed a dose that day when you obliterated that creep on the train."

That . . . that was the first time I'd heard about getting glint without my knowing. "He drugged me?"

"He didn't want Chaos unleashed when you were in primary school. You could've taken out a classroom." When my nose scrunched, he dismissed the past with a wave of his hand. "Take the glint, Camilla. It's harmless. I'm just looking out for you, as Gio did."

Was that what he truly was doing? I couldn't quite see through my brother and all his layers. "Fine, but I don't want to do it forever. It doesn't feel . . . natural."

"Of course. Just for now. Until all this shit settles down." A shiver rolled through his shoulders. "Why don't we go inside? Jer was pouring drinks before I came out here. Care to have a round with your brothers like old times?"

Anything warm sounded pleasant and saints knew I could use a drink after everything. As we started towards the path leading back to the guesthouse vicinity, I asked, "Does Nico know you're in touch with Marcus?"

He scoffed. "Does Nico know what I ate for breakfast? What time I take my daily shit? Nico doesn't need to know everything, Camilla."

"He's just trying to keep us all safe, Aramis."

The arm over my shoulder tightened. "You regard him far better than he deserves."

My cheeks burned. That tone of his insinuating my question had rubbed a sore spot. "Funny, he once said the same thing about my regard for you."

He held the door open for me as we stepped inside. Jeremiah lingered in the kitchenette on the far side of the room, holding an empty glass over the sink as he stared out the small window overlooking the driveway. A small sitting area greeted the front door, swathed in the glow and comforting warmth of the hearth.

"We are your *family*," Aramis said, to continue the argument. "He has no right to question our intentions. We've cared for you a hells lot longer than he's even known you."

"Then I don't understand the constant animosity between you both." I shed my coat and threw it over a chair that had been a designated catch-all. Their bags from the trip were left strewn half-opened on the floor beside it. "You are my brother, and he is my husband. I love you both dearly. Why can't you just try to get along?"

"I have plenty of reasons not to like him, Camilla. Trust me when I say I've been on my best behavior for your sake only."

"I suppose I should be grateful then." I rolled my eyes and strode to the nearest couch, though something caught my eye in the depths of his belongings.

A red glow.

"Aramis . . ." I shuffled the stuff inside the carry-on bag to confirm my suspicions. "You still have the Niner blade?"

He had a drink in his hand and sipped it leisurely. "I've just been holding on to it. Where was I supposed to dispose of such a weapon? In the wastebin?"

"In the bloody Ada!" I snapped. "Nico's family was killed by Niner blades. If he sees this in your possession—"

"I tried to tell him," Jer said. "Bastard doesn't listen to anyone. Just like Father and twice as stubborn."

"Fuck off," Aramis muttered. His glare was severe as it crossed me. "I'll get rid of it, if it means that much to you."

His agreement was only a slight comfort. It should never have been on the property to begin with. "It does. Please see that you do."

AN HOUR LATER, a carriage rolled down the driveway, disturbing the gravel. I gently placed the crystal glass I held in the kitchenette sink. My brothers smoked and played cards to fill the time here, while I had been lost in my thoughts—my worry for my husband.

Peeking out the window facing the stable, I watched as he and the rest of his cousins unloaded from the carriage. My heart finally relaxed, seeing him on his own two feet, alive and hopefully without a bullet in him for once.

"Where's he been all night?" Aramis asked, noting the subject of my attention.

I grabbed the coat I had discarded on the leather chair. "Out. He received a strange note this evening, asking to meet someone on the viaduct. It sounded urgent."

"Who was the caller?"

"Don't know. I'm going to go see what it was all about. I'll talk to you in the morning."

Aramis grunted, exchanging a look with Jeremiah, who shrugged in response. "See you, then."

The winter night slammed into me as soon as I opened the door, the weather worsening two-fold during my visit. Pulling my coat tighter, I intersected Nico on his way down the driveway from the stables. Flurries of snow fell in thick sheets in the light stretching across the driveway from the house, collecting on his cap, the shoulders of his coat. He didn't even see me standing there at first, too focused on his thoughts.

"Milla?" he said, finally noticing me. "What are you doing out here?"

"You took too long. What else could I do but pace the snow?"

He pulled me close to his chest, placing a cold kiss on the top of my forehead. "Pace our room. It's much warmer in there."

"*Our* room?" I asked him.

His mouth hung open for a moment, as if he'd forgotten we hadn't lived across the hall from each other our entire marriage. "I might have made the decision to move you into my chambers properly."

"You might regret that, Attano," I said with a grin, recalling how tidy his room had been the day I intruded. "I don't clean."

"I don't care." His words whispered into my cheek as his lips grazed my skin. "I'll marry your mess. I'll take care of you, princess."

The heat of his tongue was searing as it contrasted the weather embracing my form against him, and I sunk into it, rolling my head back to give him better access to my throat. Letting him nip at the hinge of my jaw. Letting him tease all the ways he could take care of me.

"Get a room," Gideon teased as he passed. The other cousins murmured their agreement. Nico's smile stretched over the bend of my throat, and his hands slid lower, tracing the outline of my silhouette beneath my coat.

"Should we spare them?" he asked.

"Only if you tell me all about your evening." I dusted the ice off his shoulder. "Tell me, who wanted to get you alone so badly?"

His face returned to mine, brow to my brow. "Vanya Hartsong."

That name . . . It was familiar. And then it hit me all at once, knocking out all the heat in my body until I just felt cold again. That woman from Newport, the one I had eavesdropped on when I was curious about Nico's double life. "*That* Vanya."

"Yes, *that* Vanya." He grinned, apparently amused with the reaction her name triggered.

"Should I have been more worried?" I asked, slightly teasing. She was very beautiful from what I'd gathered during my first impression. Beautiful—and fond of my husband.

"Never. You don't have to compete for something that is already yours." He pushed me towards the side entrance. "Come inside and I'll explain everything."

I WAS STUNNED into a long silence after Nico explained Vanya and her father's role in taking down Gavriel. I'd almost forgotten not everyone in the Districts supported the Nine Crowns, though that had possibly changed in recent weeks thanks to the poisoning of Firenze propaganda—if *Vanya* had told him the truth.

"Do you believe her when she said she didn't hear anything about Regulus?" I asked.

Nico stared into the fire blazing in his bedroom hearth. "I've worked with Vanya for years. She had no idea about a captured descendant. Marcus also backs her claim. Says the Districts have been quiet at home."

"What the hells are they doing to him?" I chewed on my bottom lip as my imagination ran wild. "It tears me apart sitting here and doing nothing."

He took a long sip of his whiskey. "Regulus didn't want us to come for him. He made that explicitly clear."

"When have you ever listened to anyone, Nicolai?"

"When they mean it." He turned to look at me sitting next to him. "I hate the idea of leaving him behind as much as you do. It eats at me constantly, but he didn't want me to risk anyone coming after him. Hells, they're probably waiting for us to try."

"You risked it all for me," I pointed out.

"*You*," he said the word with a different weight in his voice. "You are different. You are my wife, Milla. There is nothing that would keep me from you, nothing I wouldn't sacrifice."

My hands stroked his chest, slipping beneath his shirt that he had halfway unbuttoned to relax for the evening. "Sometimes I wish I could be your old Milla. The one without a remnant threatening the lives of everyone we care about."

His false hand covered my own, disrupting my exploration. "I wouldn't change a thing about you."

"How can you say that?" I asked. "After all the hell it has caused us both?"

He shrugged, his stare falling to my neck. "Your remnant is

what makes you who you are. There's nothing good or bad about it. The only reason you resent your power is because how others have reacted to it, but that is not your fault, and it is not within your power to control how others see you—only how you see yourself."

I remained quiet, unable to think of a way to refute him.

"Remember what I told you that day when we were stuck on the train? It all still holds true. There is nothing bad about you, Camilla. That is the most certain truth I know in this life."

It was like he saw the very words I needed to hear and plucked them out of my head to feed my heart. He always knew, like the walls I had built around my insecurities were transparent to his attention. For the first time, I didn't mind being completely seen, not when my truths weren't used against me.

My hand slid lower down his chest, snapping buttons of his shirt one by one until it was completely undone. The cords of muscle lining the walls of his chest, the hard lines over his stomach, rose and fell in gradually building breaths—matching the rate of my own.

I shifted on the couch until I straddled his waist, sitting over him with my center pressed against his bare stomach. He moved quickly and found a new place for his drink, filling his hands with my thighs instead.

"Milla . . ." His tone was cautionary.

"Hmmm?" I hummed the question while my lips were busy kissing the side of his throat.

His legs widened, sinking me naturally over the hard ridge of his erection. "Just so we're clear, I didn't say any of that to get you in this position. Though, I am very pleased how it's turning out for me."

"Things always work out for you, don't they?"

"And not a cousin in sight to ruin it." He pressed me firmly against his hips, delivering a satisfying counterpressure to the ache between my legs. My fingers trailed from his hair to his broad shoulders. They skated over the scars of his left arm, slid down the smooth skin of his opposite, to remove his shirt completely.

His stare was intense as I drank in the sight of him beneath me, skimmed my fingertips over the smooth muscles of his chest as if to memorize for a sketch later. I got lost in the details of him.

"What's on your mind, Milla?" he said after a time, filling the heavy quiet.

So much. Too much. All my thoughts crowded near the door of my heart, waiting to be let out. More than anything, how much I wanted to lose myself in him. Forget the problems and pains of yesterday and drown the inner voice of my self-loathing with the sounds of his satisfaction.

To remember what it was like to be adored instead of feared. The healing his touch provided, one wanting stroke and longing look at a time.

"There were nights in Hightower where the dark was so complete, it drowned me. There were nights I clung to the clearest memories in my heart to remind myself of what was real and was a dream. Do you know what I thought about when I was in that cell, Nicolai?"

He grunted a sound of frustration. "What did you think about?"

"The night you became mine. I remember everything so clearly. The way you felt in my hands, your scent, the fullness of you inside me. But there was one thing I'd been deprived of before they took me from you." My hand slipped low, stroking him through his pants. "I never got to taste you."

The shadows lining his chest danced wide and short as his breath regulated. "Only if you're ready."

I lifted slightly on my knees, enough to slip my hand beneath my leggings and between my legs and gathered the evidence of my arousal. When I displayed it to him, he drew them into his mouth and licked my taste from my fingers.

"*Hells*, woman," he moaned.

I lowered myself between his legs, kneeling before him.

He grasped my chin briefly and swiped a thumb over my lip. "You're sure?"

"Completely sure." I unfastened his belt and his pants with trembling fingers, but the shakes weren't from fear. Not even from the worry of being inadequate at this—as inexperienced as I was. I knew I was safe with Nico. No, my fingers just couldn't work fast enough.

He lifted his hips so I could inch his pants lower, until his cock was on full display in front of my face, full and stiff and overwhelming. I didn't know how I'd fit him all in my mouth, only that I was ready to try, and other parts of me were vastly jealous of the opportunity. The sight of him so full of desire for me replaced the wetness I'd just swiped away. My back arched, and I rubbed my thighs together to find a measure of friction.

"Show me how you like it," I whispered and took his shaft in my hand. I pumped it once, lightly, skimming the soft skin with a feathery touch. My thumb rolled over his head, catching a bead of his arousal already spilling for me.

"*Harder*," he groaned and wrapped his hand over mine. His grip tightened, showing me the right amount of pressure, the right speed, the sensitive spot on the tip of his cock that made his body jerk and his breath shudder. "Fuck, Milla, right there. That's perfect."

He glistened with desire after several long strokes from my hand. I added another, creating a continuous caress from base to tip. Nico bucked into my hold, but I inched higher between his legs, so that my arms pinned his hips to the cushions, forbidding his help.

"Tell me what you want, husband."

"I want to be inside you."

Heat pooled in my belly, roared with a mutual desire to make that happen. His bed looked larger and more inviting than ever, but obstacles stood in the way. "Unfortunately, I haven't taken a single contraceptive since the first time we fucked, so you'll have to settle for my mouth."

A brief smirk twitched across his lips. "Your mouth will do, princess."

Smiling, I lowered my face to the crown of his shaft, rolling my tongue over the tip. The taste of him was like nothing I'd ever known before. Better than I could have imagined, brining my tongue with a tease of his release. His false hand slipped into my hair, and I knew then I had him exactly where I wanted him. A tangled mess of need and adoration. The strongest man I'd ever known, undone beneath me.

I loved it. Loved it so much, I craved more.

I was power hungry. Slipping my lips around his cock, my tongue darted down the underside of his shaft in the same technique as my hands. Nico's head fell back against the sloped edge of the couch, and his fingers pulled at my roots. A tension locked his body, like he held back the urge to thrash into my mouth.

Shifting some of my weight off his hips, I took him as deep as my mouth allowed, wincing at the fullness of him pressing into my throat. The gentlest push of his hand sent me deeper, pushing beyond a barrier I didn't know existed. He cursed every saint in the void, and I moaned to prevent the gag forming, communicating my encouragement.

He tested another thrust. Then another. Each time further than the last until his hips were off the seat, stretching my mouth until I was completely full of him. Nico watched as his cock disappeared between my lips. Smoky eyes swirled into black. His perfect lips parted to reveal gritted teeth. It was the last thing I saw until tears blurred my focus on him.

"Milla, you need to get off . . . I'm going to—"

A knock banged on the bedroom door.

"Who the hells is it?" he shouted at the visitor while I continued to work him like no one else existed.

"It's Luther. I wanted to know if you were coming—"

"*For fuck's sake*, Luther. Go away. Right now."

"Giver and Greed . . ."

"What's wrong?" Another voice that sounded like his uncle's joined Luther outside. Nico's cock slipped out of my mouth, my eyes wide.

"It got worse. It got so much *fucking* worse." Luther's voice trailed off, hopefully bringing his family with him.

Nico's breath was heavy and frustrated. I had to bite my lip from laughing. My hand stroked his cock until his attention was devoted to me once more. "You were saying?"

"I'm going . . . *Seven hells.*"

Grey eyes slammed shut, and he fought a moan as he released into my hand. Warm ropes of his release spilled into my fingers, coating my palms. There was so much of it, too much for my hands to contain. It spilled over his bare stomach that tightened with the force of his climax.

My hands continued to pump as he jerked in my grip, as his strained voice murmured my name. I only released him when he finished and caught his breath. The heat in his gaze smoldered the flames already catching fire in my center. Curious, I lifted two fingers to my lips and tasted the mess he left all over my hands, drawing another vulgar curse from him.

"*Saints*, Milla. Keep doing that and I'll have another problem for you to fix." He snatched his discarded shirt and wiped the excess off my chin before cleaning the rest. His hand remained fixed around my jaw, staring at me for a moment.

I caught my breath through swollen lips. "What?"

"You are so beautiful." Reaching behind me, he grabbed his glass and shot back the rest of his whiskey before tossing it back on the table. He jutted his chin toward the other side of the room. "Now get in bed, princess. It's my turn."

Another knock—this one much louder—sounded at the door. A flicker of irritation crossed his face.

"*What*?"

Gideon's voice spoke through the threshold this time. "Sorry to . . . urm. It's just my father is demanding a brief of what happened on the bridge. We tried to fill him in, but he wants it from you. Thought you'd rather me bother you instead of him."

"Meddlesome fucking family," Nico whispered.

I rose to my feet to stand between his knees. "Go talk to your uncle. I'm not going anywhere. In fact, I think I'll take a shower while I wait. I haven't had a good bath in so long."

"Fine." He met me toe to toe. I had to cant my head to look up at him as he pressed his still wet cock against the soft material of my shirt. "But don't you dare take care of yourself in there, princess. That's for me."

"Nico?" Gideon called out from the hall.

"I'm coming—I mean . . . *Fuck*. I'll be there in a moment!"

"Is Camilla coming too?"

I couldn't contain the bubble of laughter that burst from my lips. "Unfortunately, I am not."

"*Giver and Greed,*" Nico seethed, and his face reddened halfway to the door while he fixed his pants. But he looked back at me before he left, cracking a knowing smile.

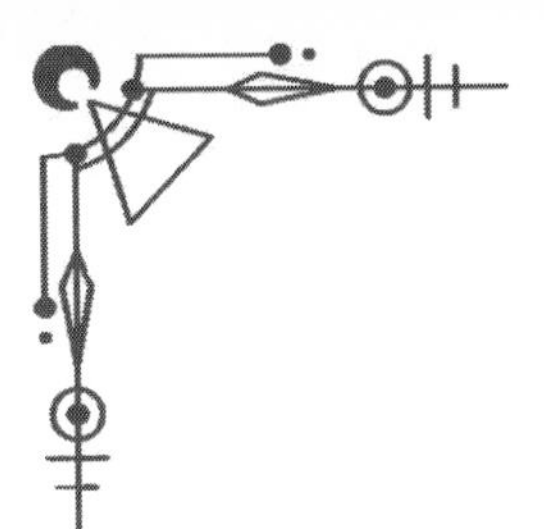
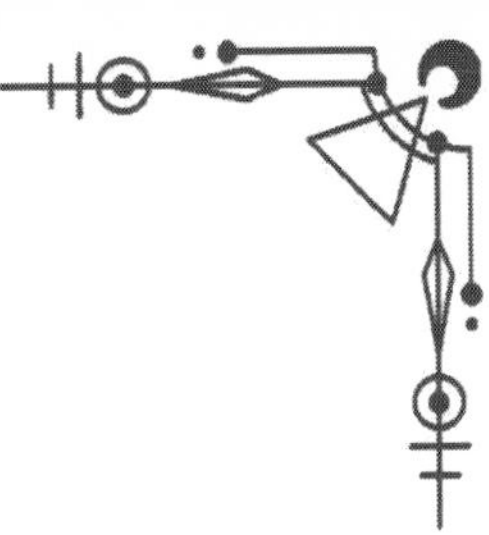

CHAPTER 23

NICOLAI

My knee bounced impatiently as Solomon went over every detail of what Vanya had informed me. Should I be listening to the words coming out of his mouth? Probably. But my room was a few floors above Sol's office, and I could hear the water groaning through the pipes in the wall. All I could think about was getting the hells out of here, so I'd catch Milla before she could put her clothes back on.

I sat with my heel propped on a knee in front of Sol's desk, desperately trying to hide the raging erection that was impossible to conceal thanks to the unforgiving cut of my pants. "Anything else you needed from me, Uncle?"

"Fran and the others say they will contact the families tomorrow morning. We'll also need to make a statement, something to send to the OIC, now that we have officially broken every law in the book."

"A little rebellion is healthy for society," I clipped. "I'll get it done."

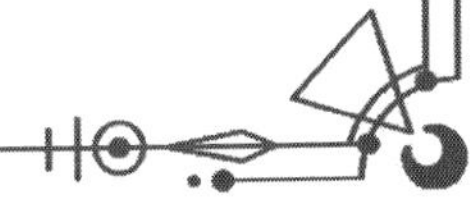

"Do you need anything from me?"

As much as I wanted to deny his help, I couldn't. There was plenty of work to be done. "I need to speak with Sabina. Two descendants we liberated from the prison that claimed they were looking for a woman named Rosa Bianchi. I have them set up in a monitored apartment on East End."

"Rosa Bianchi was her mother," he said. "She died several years ago. Why is that important?"

"Because they're from the Continent."

Sol stopped whatever he was writing and quietly placed the pen down. "The Continent? How did they—"

"Avoided the worst of the storms until they happened across the island prison, mistaking it as the mainland. Probably so desperate to get off the boat. How long did Nonna say the trip was?"

"A couple of weeks, but the ships weren't as efficient as they are now. It's hard to say."

I nodded, pocketing his estimation for later. A quiet stretched afterwards, and I stood from the chair.

"Now about Regulus . . ."

A weight threw me back in the seat. "What about him?"

"I hope you're not planning on trying to infiltrate the Watch to get him back. You know he's already dead or soon will be."

My hands clenched around the armrests. "No. I have no plans to rescue him."

He looked relieved, shutting his eyes briefly. "I wouldn't put it past you, Nico. So like your father in that way. A trait, I admit, I have tried and failed to purge from you."

"Why?" I asked, now glued to my chair. It was a question I'd wanted to know for years after sensing the dredge of his influence constantly tamping down my ambition.

Solomon licked his lips, looking at something he had written on his pad instead of my face. "Your father, before he went to the bridge that night, he'd said something very strange to me before he left, and in hindsight I should have taken him more seriously. He told me if by some miracle you got out of prison, that you wouldn't be the same boy who left this home. That you would come back dark and twisted, angry and vengeful. He begged me to not let you turn out like him."

"My father wasn't any of those things—"

"He didn't let you see how the attacks on your mother and sister affected him. And when he lost you—" Sol's voice broke, and his throat convulsed. "He knew he lost you because he was so obsessed with the past and making it right by making the Niners pay for what they did to his family. He had no hope left for himself, but he still had some spared for you."

He leaned forward on the desk, looking me in the eye. "I know you think I go out of my way to be hard on you, even more so than my own sons. But he made me promise to look after you, Nicolai, and I will not let my brother down again. I failed him, but I will not fail you."

My tone softened. "You never failed us, Uncle, and you don't have to worry about me anymore. I don't care about avenging the past. Camilla is my future, and our future is what I fight for. Nothing outside of her is a priority."

A smile flashed across his face. "Then you better marry her properly, Nicolai. None of this contract business. It's what your mother would have wanted."

"Don't bring my mother into this, Uncle." I rolled my eyes but smiled. The thought of Camilla in a long dress in front of the family, Nonna's ring on her finger as we spoke vows of forever, the formality of it all made my heart fill with air and soar in my chest.

"Milla deserves something grand, and I cannot give her that yet. Not with the world as it is."

"But soon?"

I stood, uncomfortable speaking with him of all people about it. I made plans for us on my own, but what Milla wanted was more important than anything. "Of course. If that's what she wants."

"Well, that will please your grandmother, so I appreciate it." He sighed. "But I've kept you long enough. I'm sure you're tired from the day's events. Get some rest." With that, he resumed his writing, and I could escape—what was left of my arousal completely wasted.

By the time I made it back to my—*our* room, Milla was fast asleep on top of the covers in the bed, wearing a silky emerald night shift completely impractical for the wintertime. Her wet hair was a dark knot on top of her head, her face soft from sleep. As tempted as I was, I didn't dare wake her. It was her first night in a real bed in months, and we'd gone through a lot just to be here tonight.

Unfastening my belt, I stripped down and slipped into bed beside her, pulling the heavy blankets over us both. She roused under the added weight of the sheets.

"Nico?" she murmured. "Are we still—"

"Go back to sleep, Milla. I'll have my way with you sooner or later."

She smiled without opening her eyes and buried her face in my chest. For the first time in months, I shut my eyes and sleep found me like a blessed reunion.

For the first time in months, I slept.

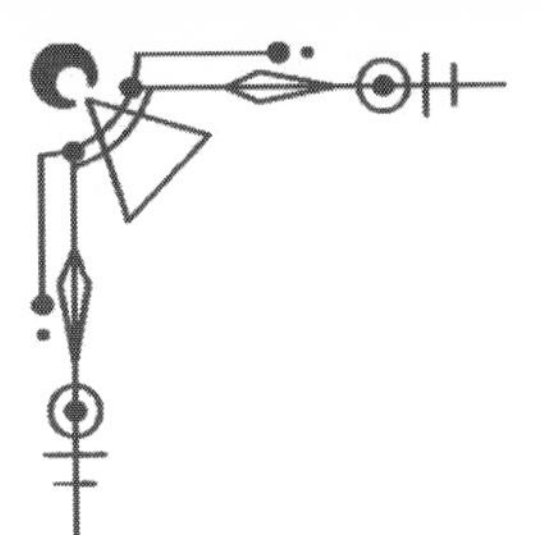
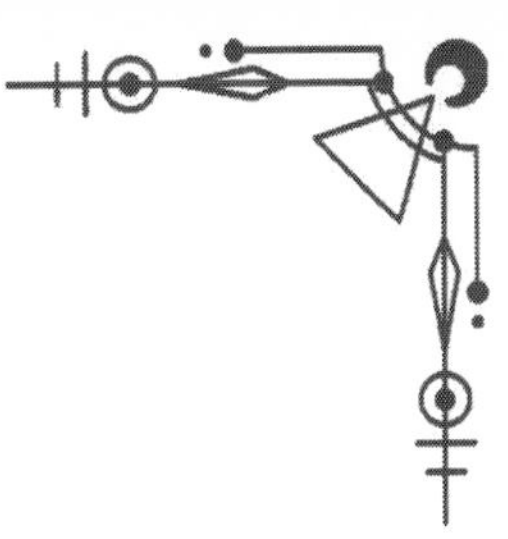

CHAPTER 24
NICOLAI

I had my way with Camilla, though not to the extent I'd desired.

Several days passed and I could count on one hand the number of times we left our room. Strange, how the city still functioned while I ignored the work that demanded my time, giving it to her instead. The world could have been on fire and neither of us would have been any wiser.

There was something I'd been putting off, however, and no matter how much I ignored it, I'd have to face her sooner or later.

It was late in the evening when I returned to Esme's garage. My false hand laid propped on a soft cloth on one of her workbenches. She didn't even look at me as I entered the shop.

"It's finished then?"

"Yes," she blurted. She stared at anything but my face. "Do you need me to show you the upgrades or—"

"*No*, no, that won't be necessary. I'll figure it out."

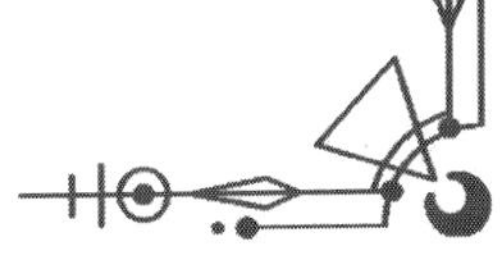

"Good."

Silence. Too much silence wrapped the room. I cleared my throat. "We will never speak about this ever again."

"I don't want to be speaking about it *now*."

Right, like this wasn't completely horrifying on my end, like I'd be here if my wife hadn't asked with those eyes that made me agree to her bidding. "Well, neither do I."

"Then go!"

"Fine! Milla says *thank you*."

Esme cringed. "Tell her, don't mention it. *Please*. Don't mention it. It's all my fault for offering in the first place." She pointed toward a pouch on the same desk. "Also, the bag is for Milla. Sera used to get her the contraceptives, but since she's gone . . . I took the liberty of contacting the haelen myself."

Next to my hand was a paper bag with medication inside. I cleared my throat of the discomfort settling there. "And I appreciate that."

She shook her head, continuing the finishing touches on the bike. The Marcheses had run it all afternoon as she fine-tuned the running gear. "I already have to babysit her brothers. I won't have any little Nico's running around and terrorizing me further. Saints help us . . ."

I couldn't hold back the laugh that caught us both off guard. "Definitely not. Thank you, Esme."

"Stop mentioning it."

I shook my head and quickly left the garage, attaching my hand without checking the upgrade she added and scrubbed the exchange from my memory.

The hour was late by the time I'd crawled into bed with my wife, who seemed to spend most of her time resting. She still hadn't mentioned anything about the prison, and although her bruises had faded and the burns had healed into pale scars, I noticed she avoided looking at herself in the bathroom mirrors.

I'd woken more than once to her thrashing in bed in a fever pitch, sweat soaking the sheets from vicious nightmares. She muttered names I'd never heard of, wept until the salt of her tears stained the pillows. Something happened on the island that she wasn't telling me, but until she let me in, there was nothing I could do but lay beside her as she fought her inner demons.

Tonight, however, she was at peace, and I hoped, for the sake of her exhausted mind, she'd remain so. Her body naturally curled against me as I settled onto the mattress.

It felt as if only minutes passed before we were both woken by a loud bang on the bedroom door.

"Nico!" My name was shouted from the hall. "Nico, get up! We need to get to Salt Street."

"What in hell? What's going on?" Milla untwined her limbs from mine.

The sun hadn't risen. It was early in the morning, and my body was reluctant to leave our bed, but the urgency in my cousin's voice sent a worrisome thrill straight down my spine.

"There's been shots at Sabina's," Luther said. "She sent a wearh calling for aid. Says the watchmen bastards snuck through the docks by her warehouses."

I rubbed my eyes awake. "Damn! We'll be downstairs in a minute. Have the horses ready."

I cursed as we both dressed. Milla rushed toward the large mahogany doors of the wardrobe, where I assumed she found the rest of her clothes when she searched for the shift. Meanwhile, I took to the closet and dressed quickly.

"No, no, no . . ." Milla mumbled to herself after I'd finished. "That can't be it!"

I tossed a coat over the clothes I'd thrown on to combat the frosty morning. "What's wrong?"

She was dressed similarly warm and in a similar style, with black leather boots pulled over a pair of tweed trousers. She wore an Attano-red coat over a loose white shirt and vest. Stuffed in the pocket of her coat were fur-lined gloves.

"What are you looking for?" I spoke again when she appeared not to hear me, too busy fumbling through the bag she'd brought from the ship.

"The glint! I thought I had enough to spare me until tomorrow, but I'm out. I need to go see Aramis—"

"Fuck that. You don't need that stuff, Milla."

Her eyes snapped to mine, an anxious energy in her stare. "Yes, I do. I can't let it slip, Nico. Not right now. The prison was different. But here? There are so many things that can go wrong."

"Milla." It took everything in me to swallow my frustration. "You either come with us or stay. There's no time to run to your brothers and get more glint."

"You don't understand." Her voice shook the words. "I *can't* control it. Something always goes wrong."

Only a few times had I seen Camilla truly afraid, and this time I could hear the fear in her voice. The dim light of the gas lamp reflected in the glaze over her eyes. But it was her hands, the way they shook even as she clasped them in front of her, that explained too much. I'd been negligent, assuming she'd made peace with her power from what I witnessed her do in Hightower. She wasn't confident in her ability at all, now that I really looked at her. She was afraid of her Chaos—afraid of herself.

I took both her trembling hands in my own and squeezed

them. "You took out three guards by yourself in the tower and a legion of them in the prison. Camilla, if that wasn't control, I don't know what is."

She shook her head. "I nearly crushed us all in the tower. We were fortunate the flames didn't spread too far, and they only worsen if I'm afraid. I don't want to use it unless I must, especially around my family."

"Would you rather stay here?"

A scoff left her lips. "After what happened last time? You're never facing a fight without me again."

I smiled. "You don't have to use magic to fight, Camilla. Your power isn't here." I held up her hands between us. "It's in that merciless soul of yours. I'll be beside you the whole time, and if you ever feel overwhelmed, we'll get the hell out. Alright?"

She nodded, the shaking in her fingers relaxing some. I held onto her hand to lead us out the door and down the stairs. "I'd rather you not use your remnant unless it's necessary, anyway. If the Watch was trying to sneak into the Row, you're most likely what they're looking for. Don't make it easy for them to find you."

She cleared her throat, keeping in step beside me. "I disagree. I don't think they're after me at all. If this was a direct attack, they're after Sabina for some reason."

When we reached the main floor, Luther tossed me my hunting rifle. Pistols shoved in a rush in my waistband, I propped the gun over my shoulder and held the side entrance door open for Milla to have a straight shot at the horses. The rest of the cousins and a few of our men mounted the remaining steeds, two of them pulling a carriage where Luther hopped on the back.

"What would they want from bleeders?" I asked aloud as I mounted the black beast behind her in the saddle.

"I guess we should ask Sabina." Milla took the reins in her

gloved hands and kicked the horse into a trot, leading our ragtag group down the gravel and toward the First Sector where the meat warehouses were located.

Indeed, we had a lot of questions to ask the Salt Queen. Hopefully, we'd all see the sunrise and get those answers.

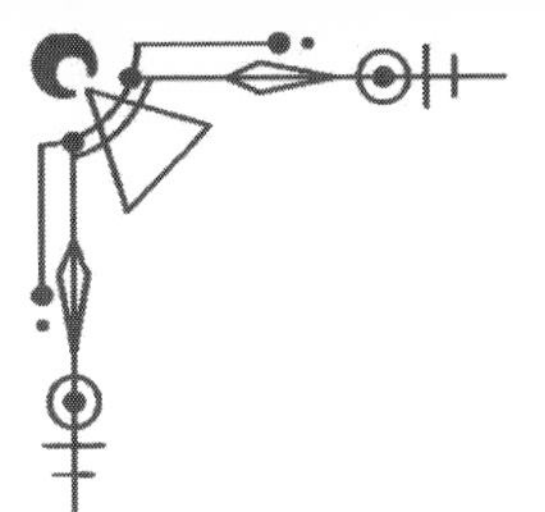
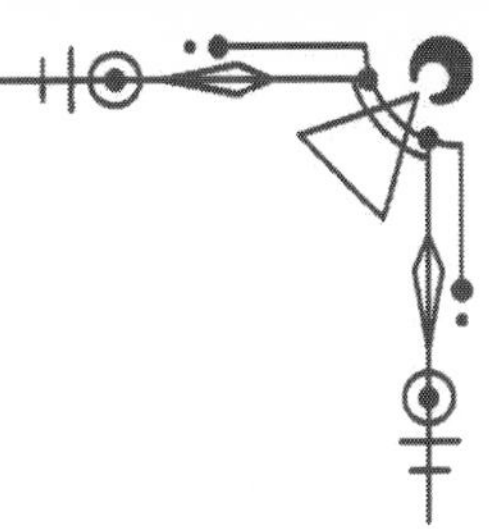

CHAPTER 25

CAMILLA

Fog and the clobbering noise of a fleet of horses filled the barren streets on the way to the First Sector. Every edge exposed to the chilly morning became slick from the icy vapor hanging heavy in the air, the dampness that seemed to pierce deepest and to the bone. Nico's arms wrapped around my waist, holding me steady as we led the way through the obscure morning, the visibility only clear enough to see to the next streetlamp.

Echoes of gunfire replaced the quiet. Lights flickered behind curtains, the sound waking people in their bedrooms, and I noticed the canvas covering the windows sway, allowing those inside to peek at us as we passed.

"People will worry now," Nico muttered in my ear. "*Hells*, if this is anything like I'm anticipating, we won't be able to keep the Row out of the fight any longer."

"One thing at a time, Nico. The Watch brought this to our streets, but this is our territory. This is our home, and we'll make sure all who live here never have to wake to gunshots ever again."

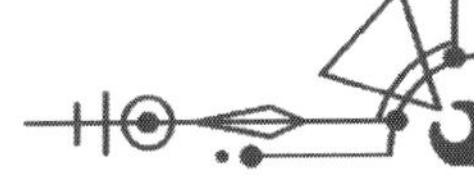

The false hand over my stomach pressed me back into his chest. "Spoken like a true Attano," he whispered roughly in my ear.

I scoffed. "I'm sure I'm missing a few choice words for that to be true."

"Hey, Adler," he called to the rider to the right of us. "What shall we tell the watchmen bastards when we see them?"

"*Fuck* off!" A chorus of voices answered with him.

Despite the fear coiling in my stomach, I laughed. "My point made."

The break in our melancholy march didn't last long as the scent of gunfire permeated the air.

We neared the First Sector.

Smoke mixed with the mist to conceal the source of the noises we heard throughout the city. The silence between gunshots was filled with screams of suffering and the crash of metal and glass as stray bullets hit buildings. Nico motioned for us to dismount and continue on foot when we were a few blocks from the sector.

"You can't see a damn thing," one man commented. Light from the streetlamps only reached so far, swallowed by the mist hovering over the cobblestones and wetting every step toward the warehouses. We passed the Meat Market, the open marketplace dark and quiet without its usual traffic.

"Who goes there?" a voice called from inside the gates in front of the market.

"Attano Benders," Nico answered.

A curse of relief preceded the appearance of several wearhs, who had watched from the entrance. "We've been stationed here in case the watchmen bring a squad to hit the markets. They've been hitting Sabina where it hurts. She thought they might come here next."

"How many?"

He sucked a cheek in thought before replying. "At least three squads, if the number of attacks means anything. They hit two warehouses and the tannery. Just storage and stock for now. It's hard to tell in the fog, but each group appears to be at least twenty in number."

Nico nodded, checking the chamber of his gun. "And the bleeders? Didn't think a few watchmen could overwhelm a group of natural hunters."

"These men are a different breed," he mumbled, as if hiding his words from the men behind him. "They have power their predecessors never practiced on us before. You'll see when you get in there, Bender. Do not underestimate what they can do."

"We know exactly what they're capable of." I spoke with the experience to match my confidence. "Where is Sabina? Nico and I can head to her first to see if she needs assistance."

"You can try," he answered, looking me up and down curiously. "Her manor is on the river, just behind the warehouses. Most of our wearhs took off to guard the road leading to her place."

Nico nodded to his cousins, who split the remaining men into factions and sped off toward the remaining warehouses. "Have they tried to contact you? Any terms or negotiations?"

The bleeder shook his head wearily. "Not that I'm aware of. We woke up to gunfire and strange magic rolling through the earth. Most of us with wearh senses could feel a strange sensation in the air. A scent we didn't recognize."

"Sulfur?" I asked. When the bleeder nodded, I looked at Nico. "Arcane magic, like the kind they used in the tower."

He sighed, his breath a ghostly white cloud from his lips. "We carve our way to Sabina's. Her warehouses have taken hits, but we need the Madame more than her stocks. Bring the chest."

Two of the hired benders went back to the carriage and pulled something out of the back. A rectangular chest with large locks over the opening. Whatever was inside it being apparently cumbersome from the way it took two men to carry it behind the group.

"Stay close, Milla." Nico positioned himself on my left side, opposite my shooting hand. But I had no plans to separate from him when my power was fully available. Even now, I felt it buzz inside my bones, aching to be released. Like it was angry to have been silenced it for so long and was now waiting for the opportunity to snap its vengeful bite.

I swallowed down the swarm in my chest and followed Nico into the mist.

THE GROUND SHOOK from the sounds of shots and falling brick as bullets exploded against the buildings. Nico shoved me behind a wall of crates, motioning for the men to scatter and lie low to avoid the crossfire.

"I'm going to scout out their numbers. Luther," he called behind him, "toss me some silvers."

Luther reached in the chest they'd pried open and did as he was told, throwing Nico a handful of metallic orbs.

"Bombs?" I asked.

He nodded quickly. "Freshly made from the steelworks. I'll be right back. You won't even know I'm gone."

I reached for him to avoid getting caught in the time suspension of his remnant, but my fingers caught air. One moment he was in front of me, the next he wasn't.

It wasn't right.

If he had scouted successfully and returned, he'd have restarted the time and it would have been as he said, like he'd never even left. But looking around, Nico was nowhere to be found; instead, he was still somewhere inside the mist that was concealing the sounds of close-range fighting.

"Luther!"

"Shit," he said, realizing the same.

My hands shook around my gun. "Gideon, can you blow away some of this fog?" He could bend the air, a bender ability commonly found in their family. It was some of the only coverage we had, but every second I couldn't see Nico sent my heart racing a beat faster.

Without question, he did as I asked, stirring a great breeze from the west. Salt and the metallic sting marking spilled blood carried on the icy wind from the river. Gideon was careful to only reveal sections at a time, like pulling back a blanket to reveal patches of ruined stock and destroyed commodities. The two warehouses near the river were in such a way to aid in the transportation via the Ada, but the Society must have destroyed the loading docks.

They tore everything apart that belonged to Sabina.

Three bleeders were pinned against a half-standing brick wall, metal rods shoved through their chests. Dark stains bled into bowls beneath their hanging feet, collecting the blood dripping down their laced boots.

"Seven hells." My voice faltered.

Without thinking, I ran to the bodies of two men and a female wearh that had been left stuck, suspended on the remains of the warehouse. Luther caught me before I could get to them.

"Milla, they aren't getting any deader. We got to clear out the rest of the Society so we can deal with them properly," he spoke in my ear.

"Let go of me!" I snapped, though not for the reason he probably assumed. My hands were already black, somehow my gun was still intact in my shooting hand. But one slip could destroy the man behind me. Could take out the entire sector. The remnant in my bones was stronger than ever, fueled by rest, food, and the need to binge on the power I'd kept starved.

Thankfully, he conceded without a word, releasing me just as a concession of bombs went off just ahead, trembling the earth. Luther beckoned to follow him, and I ran with my back arched low to the ground, sneaking past the four-story warehouse until we reached the next block.

There, in the cross section of the three depots, was the source of the sounds haunting the rest of the Row. Bleeders ducked behind overturned carriages, waiting to use their teeth and talons and supernatural speed once the officers on the riverside of the battlefield reloaded.

A hiss prompted our attention, just to the right of where we crouched. A bleeder glared up at us, baring her blood-covered teeth, blood that once belonged to the Society member lying dead beneath her. His head fell to the side, revealing teeth marks where the woman fed from him.

She gave us a once-over then fled.

I grimaced at the drained man. "Do they really have to do that?"

"It gives their remnant a boost," he explained. "Feeding off a body, even in just small amounts, can give them energy for hours. Though it's unpleasant for the rest of us."

I agreed, quietly taking in a detail of the guard I hadn't noticed at first, distracted by his throat. Written across his skin where the gaps in his uniform provided a glimpse were arcane symbols. Like the ones Delilah wrote on me. They flickered a milky blue glow until fading into plain black lines.

Approaching his body wearily in the alley, I pulled up his sleeve, avoiding the gloves that were oddly bloody at the fingertips. He wore the same armor the watchman donned in the tower, and I recalled easily how the laced leather burned.

The symbols differed from the ones Delilah branded on me. I pulled up my sleeve, comparing the barely there scar that blended with the paleness of my forearm. But the slight ridges marring the soft skin were enough to prove our marks were different. The ones on this man were of a different purpose.

"Milla!" Luther whisper-shouted. "They have Nico."

A WATCHMAN HAD Nico at gunpoint in the center of the road feeding the warehouses. He was surrounded, at the end of too many barrels, though not a flinch of fear showed on his face. I was unnerved enough for both of us.

"Why isn't he doing anything?" Luther murmured. The fighting ceased, clear the Society had the leverage they needed to prevent further retaliation from the Blood remnants. Nico was still as stone, molded from the steel funding his empire. He fisted one hand, his false one hanging limp.

"He can't," I whispered.

It hit me then, why the dead man had the blood of a bleeder staining his fingers. He'd used them to draw.

I looked behind us, scanning the area of where he was attacked. My search caught on a symbol glowing faintly across the red brick of the warehouse building. The rune was unfamiliar—a different kind of spell. A quick assessment of the street confirmed the other warehouses were similarly marked. They'd formed a barrier around the place—which meant Nico was under the effects of some kind of arcane science.

"Do you remember the barrier from the tower?" I asked him. "I think this is something similar. Look at the wall."

Luther followed the finger I used to point at the symbol, and his eyes widened. "We need to destroy it." He darted to the image, trying to rub away the bloody rune. He cursed when it barely smudged the image. "The blood has already stained the brick. Can you use your . . ."

"No, absolutely not."

He crossed the alley to crouch beside me once more. "Camilla, this is important. If they've shut off the magic somehow, we'll never stand a chance at pushing them out of the Row."

He spoke as if I didn't already know the stakes, like I didn't *want* to help. "Luther, you don't understand. The fog is too thick. I can barely see where my fire would spread and there's too many people around—"

Luther was shaking his head. "Don't lie to me, boss. I've seen you wield your remnant. You did it once, you can do it again."

"That was one time," I hissed. Hells, everyone had so much faith in me, but they didn't know the truth. Luther, of all descendants, should have known the tricks Delilah played on her subjects.

My blood boiled despite my heart's reluctance. The war inside me nearly tore me apart until I finally snapped. "I *killed* people in Hightower, Luther. You saw a glimpse of control, but it's never been so . . . so . . ."

"Predictable?" he asked.

I nodded, losing the rest of my words.

He glanced toward the end of the alley, where gunfire and shouting filled the street. "Grief, fear, regret, those memories that resurface every day, they are not something you'll ever be able to control. But that wall you keep putting up to protect yourself from experiencing them isn't keeping anything out, Camilla. It's just holding all those painful feelings inside."

He grabbed my hands. "I know what Delilah was like, boss. She dug you a hole so dark and deep and without a single foothold to climb yourself out. But your family is here to pull you out, no matter how many times you fall back in. You just got to reach out, alright? You can do this."

A warm tear rolled down my cheek, and I shook my head to clear the rest brimming in my eyes. "Alright, fine. Just stay back, please. Just in case."

"On it, Milla. I'm going to put eyes on Nico."

He disappeared down the way we came, assumingly to find another side street that fed into the center. My remnant rose and fell like waves lapping at a cliffside, slamming hard into my conscious one moment before retreating in the next. I stepped away from the edge of the building, letting it smooth out again, though the tide of power in my veins surged high and remained steady.

Tentatively, I placed my inky hands against the wall. Luther's words eased some of the reluctance holding me back. Whatever it took to get Nico out of the line of the Society's guns, I'd risk exposing myself, what I held down, and hope to hell it wouldn't backfire.

A disorienting quake rolled through the alley and more bombs exploded on the edges of the street. Silver smoke billowed and filled the air with a noxious smell. The coordination of the sudden, jarring shake and the smother of smoke over every sense, I lost focus on the control of my remnant as it slipped into the brick unsolicited.

Dark flames flashed from my hands spread in every direction, eating away the surface of the wall as it devoured the symbol and consumed everything around it, pulsing, cresting from fear. The smoke combined with the fog blocked out the sight of anything further than an arm's reach away, concealing my fire.

I shoved myself off the crumbling wall, swallowing smoke as I took a breath and inhaled the fumes of chemical vapors filling the air. The warehouse groaned amid the sound of gunfire and shouts. The crack of brick, splitting glass, and snap of wood framing sent me stumbling back.

A patch of wall visible in the streetlight, fighting to filter through the smoke, was obliterated into blinding dust. The roof caved in and sent a blast of air through the missing part of the wall, brushing my face.

Shouts, shots, screams of dying watchmen and wearhs combined then with the deafening sound of the falling building. I scrambled away, debris hitting the back of my head and coat, and the ground rumbled hard enough to knock my strides unsteady.

By the time I reached the place they had Nico, he was gone. I looked around, searching the smoke, but only flashes of faces appeared before vanishing into the thick fog once more.

A mask of obsidian found me first, turned its obscured front to me. The guard lifted his gun, but before he could pull the trigger, my hand darted out between us defensively—an involuntary reaction I'd picked up from my time in the prison.

He was consumed in the next moment, no more than red mist across the cobblestones, though his mask and gloves fell to the ground untouched.

"Chaos!"

My title was shouted behind me. I turned to find another sprinting in my direction. This one was closer, not giving me time to react before he wrapped my shoulders in a tight embrace, pinning my arms down. Gloved hands burnt the skin over my throat.

The pain of his touch was agonizing, and I would have screamed if he hadn't been choking my airway. My arms were locked at my side, and I was hardly a match for him physically. My fingers reached, skimming the handle of my revolver, still sheathed in my waistband.

I rested the barrel against the curve of my waist and shot until he fell limp to the ground, next to the remains of his fellow watchmen.

But more were coming. He'd alerted them of my presence. Keeping my gun close, I tried to backtrack my way to the warehouse. Bleeders rushed past, some of their figures no more than a blur, confirming I had broken whatever arcane circle that had once surrounded the area. Yet still, no Attanos appeared in the haze.

The wind stirred once more, though this time, the force of the gust could only be compared to that of a violent thunderstorm. Where Gideon's had been a gentle breeze, this was a gale, slamming through the street to clear the remainder of smoke and fog and nearly knocking me back in the process.

I couldn't even walk against it and instead was forced to get low and shield my eyes from the haze of dust carried in its wake.

An icy spark chilled my cheeks, spilling through the cracks of my fingers. This was no unintentional wind—this was Nicolai. Only he could conjure a force this powerful and simultaneously leave behind the faintest electric touch of his remnant across my skin.

Once it settled, I lowered my arms to look around, taking in the remains of storehouses, the bodies of both sides littered across the pavement, the stains bleeding across the grey ground and coloring it red.

But not all of them were dead.

A watchman scrambled to attention a mere ten feet in front of me. Black cape with sigil of an eagle flapped in the scraps of the waning breeze. I vaguely heard my name being shouted behind him, but that mask soaked up my attention, preventing me from looking anywhere else.

This one was different. I could feel something from this man, an energy pulsing in the space between us.

"Camilla," he spoke my name like a slur.

I gripped my hand around the handle of my gun, which was pointed in the wrong direction. Wouldn't matter if it was. This one's armor was twice as thick as his comrades'. Not an inch of skin, no weak point, was revealed in the solid black attire. The watchman did not reach for his weapon. Instead, he reached for my mind.

With a power I didn't understand how he possessed, he took control of my body—and *made* me kneel.

My hand relaxed, letting the weapon fall to the ground. Footsteps came behind me, closing in—and yet I could do nothing. Completely overtaken by this man and his remnant—magic from a guard that made little sense. Only twice had I felt this way, when Sera had bound me with her power, when her father manipulated my body, but this was a guard. He couldn't be a descendant—the Watch would never let one of them into their ranks.

The men behind us fired off their guns at whoever was trying to come to my aid.

"Stand down!" I shouted, hoping they'd listen to my orders. By the rapid fire continuing to press on, they didn't.

Then the whirr of a machine cut over the guns. I turned my head in time to see a bike emerge from the edge of the fog beginning to creep down the alley between warehouses. A fast bike—a white plume rising from an engine I could only assume was powered by steam.

The rider pointed a gun in my direction, and I could only stare wide-eyed and frozen in place by the watchman's magic as he fired —and shot me in the leg.

As the bullet tore through my flesh, the pain lost the compulsion over my body and I fell to the pavement, weak and compromised. It seared through me, sinking into the thick part of my thigh and spreading a white-hot agony through the rest of my body.

The watchmen scattered as more shots pinged their armor. All four of them fell, one by one, as the rider took them out successively. The one with magic must have realized he lost his backup, because he retreated toward the docks with the flap of his cloak.

Wind sliced through the area once more, this time in a purposeful direction, lifting the bike off course and tossing the rider into a nearby wall. Their head slammed into a brick wall, body falling limp against the ground.

When I looked toward the docks, the watchman and the rest of his legion were gone.

"Milla!" My name shook in Nico's voice. I sat up slowly to find him running toward me. The tan skin of his face splattered with blood, though none of it seemed to be his own. He took in the gunshot wound on my outer thigh before stripping off his coat, using his teeth to tear at his sleeve while his false hand was still immobile. He held the scrap to the bleeding wound.

"The haelens are on their way." Panic laced his words, his touch trembled. "Sabina's house has been cleared. We'll take you there to be seen first. Can you stand?"

Without letting me answer, he shook his head, dismissing his own question. He looked over at his cousins. "Help me carry her. I can't . . ." He grimaced and shook his head.

I placed a hand around his bare forearm. "It's alright, Nico. I don't think the bullet hit anything important. It's not even bleeding that bad." Trying to scoot to sit closer to him, the movement aggravated the lead still embedded in my muscle. I winced. "Hurts like a bitch, though."

His eyes darkened as they settled over the place where blood soaked through my pants. He shifted his attention to where a group had gathered around the fallen rider. "Take off his helmet!" he commanded. "I want to see who did this. I want to know who shot my wife."

Nico stood and started toward them once Gideon came beside me. The bleeders set the rider on his feet, who had apparently regained consciousness.

"I want to look him in the eyes as I strangle the life from his chest for—" He stopped dead in his tracks.

I gasped, disbelieving my own eyes. My voice came out as a shaken whisper.

"Aramis?"

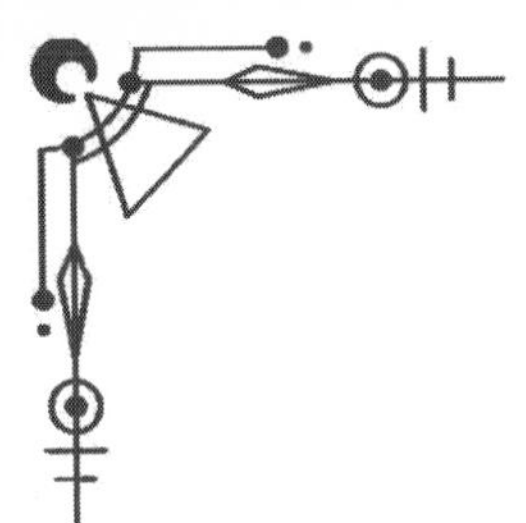
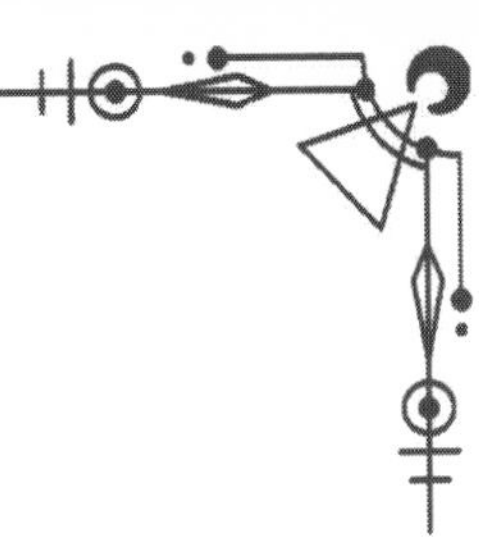

CHAPTER 26

NICOLAI

There was no mistaking that white-blonde head anywhere as the bleeders ripped off his helmet, nor that infamous Marchese glare he shared with his sister as he snarled at me. All my suspicions, my gut instincts, had led me right. There was something wrong with Aramis, and I'd given him the opportunity to hurt my family—my wife—when I gave him the keys to my guesthouse.

If it had been anyone else, they'd be floating to the void by now. But I couldn't kill the bastard with Milla watching.

I settled on punching him in his face.

"*Nico*!"

His nose gave away beneath my knuckles, giving a delicious crunch and certainly breaking it, while providing enough whiplash from the strike to send him flying back a few feet.

"*Fuck*!" He held his face and lashed on the ground. "What the hells was that for?"

"What was it for?" I asked, incredulous. "*What was it for*?"

Milla called my name once more, but I was caught in a delirious fury, and Gideon was holding her back. Her blood was still warm across my palm, and I clenched my fist, letting it fill the gaps between my fingers. My false hand hung useless at my side, but my punch had dealt enough damage that I didn't need it.

He stood quickly, wiping his face with his sleeve. "I was saving my sister from a watchman who clearly had a remnant. Which is a hells lot more than I can say about you, your family, or any of these so-called powerful descendants."

"How did you know he had a remnant?" I asked. "You just got here!"

He spat a mouthful of blood across the pavement, wincing. "Have you forgotten who you've had me contact in the Districts? She's mentioned things about the Watch and their implementations in the Society."

"Then why haven't you told me any of this? If you knew the Society had stolen our remnants somehow, why did you say nothing?"

"My apologies, I'll request a meeting with you next time." Blood flicked from his lips with every harsh syllable. "Perhaps you won't leave Camilla's family behind next time you put her in danger."

Selfish prick.

"Watch it, Marchese," Luther spoke lazily behind me. "We're her family too now."

Aramis glared at him and scoffed. "I did what I had to do to protect Camilla. My bullets are always laced with glint, and I'll provide her with a dose if a remnant ever tries to threaten my sister again."

"She doesn't need that shit," I spoke through my teeth.

He cocked a brow. "Oh? And you know everything, do you?"

He gestured to the mountain of rubble behind me. "Did your bombs do this? Or did my sister lose control of that thing inside her and wipe away an entire building and everything in it?" Aramis shook his head. "You're just like our father. Only cared about making her happy at the expense of the rest of us."

If that made me similar to Giovanni Marchese, then so be it. "Am I?" I said, feigning interest. "Perhaps that's why Milla calls me Daddy every night."

Disgust twisted his face. "You son of a—"

He returned the blow I'd given him, and I ducked out of the way just in time, catching his arm on the follow through and twisting it behind his back. "Don't embarrass yourself. These Blood descendants already think poorly enough of the Marchese line."

"Burn in every hell," he spat, just before I released him.

"Enough!" Luther shouted. The tone startled me enough to turn around and discover Gideon and another man we hired at Milla's side, helping her mount a horse they'd brought down. "Your wife needs to see a haelen. We've been told there's a few posted at Sabina's manor just a few blocks from here."

My heart softened watching her struggle to get on the steed, her cheeks wet with tears and her jaw locked. The venom in my veins only worsened for her brother.

Forgetting him for the time being, I reoriented my priorities. "I want every healer in the city down here this morning. No one goes without treatment. Get statements of what the bleeders witnessed from the Society. I want anything out of the ordinary that they saw this morning in an official report. Sabina will have to take care of notifying the families and organizing the clean-up, as this is her ground."

Luther fell into step beside me. "Anything else you need me to take care of, boss?"

"Yes," I said quietly, approaching Milla's horse. "Get those two prisoners we spoke to in the engine room. Vesper and Callow. Bring them to Sabina's."

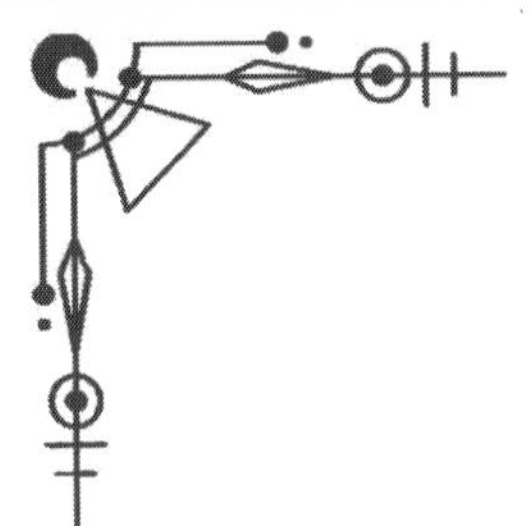
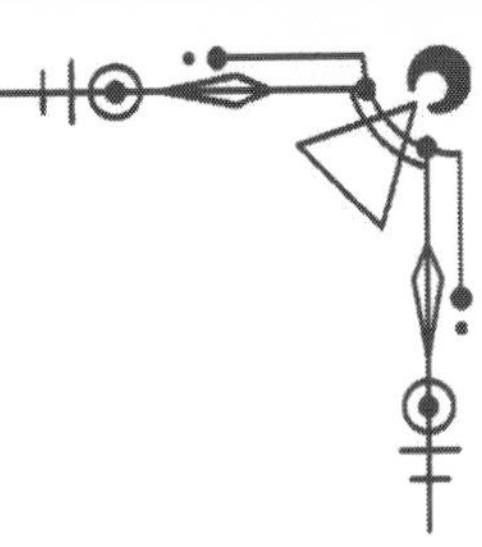

CHAPTER 27
CAMILLA

Nico swirled two metal fingers around the hole in my pants where the bullet had struck. I sat draped over his lap, sharing a leather armchair while we waited for Sabina in her parlor. The healer remnant extracted the bullet quickly and healed the wound like it had never happened, though the glint lacing the lead remained steady in my blood.

Vesper and Callow sat on a dark green velvet couch with a tufted backing. The room was a similar style to the grand homes of Lynchaven, though Sabina's decorum was more . . . rustic. Silken skins of animals lined the hardwood floors, contrasting with the elegant gold accents of the lighting fixtures and wallpaper that reminded me of a forest from its design. With the mounted head of beasts lining the walls, it was impossible to look anywhere in the room without something dead staring back.

My brother stood near a window, draped in the grey glow from the overcast morning—and ignoring us all. The healen had set his nose right again and sealed the fractures in his cheekbones from

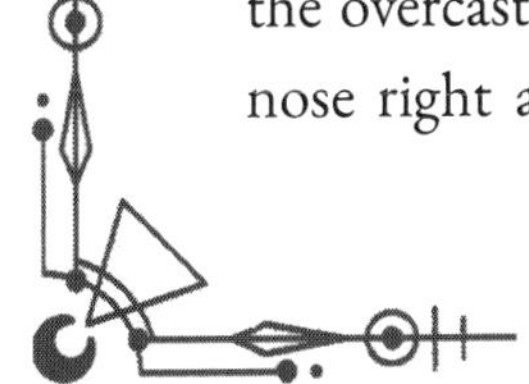
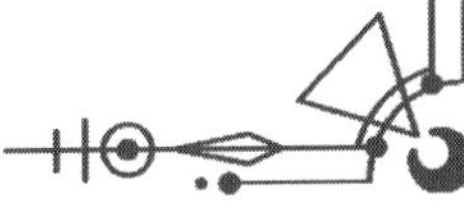

Nico's blow, but blood still stained the front of his white shirt. He'd dressed in an obvious hurry, as we all had, and I wondered if Esme had given him permission to use her bike. He might face worse than a punch to the nose if he did so without it.

"What happened today?" I asked Nico. "When you left to scout, why couldn't you get back to me?"

He sighed a long breath. "As soon as I crossed a boundary of some kind, my remnant stopped working. It wasn't like glint. I still had my power, but I couldn't use it. Almost like the kind of stuff they use in the homes in the Districts to keep out descendants and our magic. They were sure to drug me when they caught me. I think they wanted to use me to draw you out."

I shifted in the seat to sit up straighter, and his hand fell between my knees. "Well, it nearly worked. That watchman, though. He was different. Do you think he's a descendant?" Nico shook his head, quickly dismissing the idea.

I bit my lip. "There's no other explanation for what I felt. The power he wielded was too much like a Mirth remnant. Not even Delilah used magic like that in the tower."

"It sounds like your watchman has learned how to control the Arcane," Vesper said, crossing her legs to lounge back on the couch.

My interest piqued at the word. "Delilah mentioned the arcane frequently," I said. "Is that something they use on the Continent as well?"

She nodded. "It's a bit complex. The Academy controls most of the knowledge concerning the science behind it, but the Arcane is a way for—as you call them—natives to manipulate magic without a remnant."

"Without a remnant?" Nico's brows raised. "How could one use magic without access to a remnant?"

Vesper bit the inside of her cheek like she debated how to answer him.

Callow leaned forward, propping his arms on his knees with a thoughtful expression on his face. He finally said, "On the Continent, the Academies control the source of the Arcane. It acts like the fuel to their power. They use Siphons to hold an ancient kind of magic that was given to the world by Giver. The Arcane draws from the Siphon. So where the Siphon is power, the Arcane is the code that tells it what to do."

When Chaos sent her armies to fight against the natural order of the world, the saints had fractured themselves to distribute their power to their Remni, and every descendant alive was the product of that sacrifice. Giver and Greed, the two-faced saint, had given them something as well, apparently.

"I'm not sure I'm following," Nico murmured.

"The Arcane is the language of life," Aramis said. We all looked at him in mild surprise, but his stare remained on the view of the river. "There are three studies of the Arcane: Matter, Mind, and Myth. Everything in this life, the matter, has a code that keeps it in order. There are laws of nature, certainties in the way an object reacts with the world based on its code."

He pushed off the window, taking a sheathed blade from his pocket. "For example, if I drop this, it will fall to the ground. That is law, a measurable truth, an action, and a predictable reaction. But"—he pulled the blade from its sheath, revealing the bright blue glow from a dip of glint—"if you rewrite the law, combine it with something else that outsets the previous limitations, you have created something entirely new, and yet it still has order because it is measurable and predictable."

He pointed the knife at us all. "Order despises divine magic. It breaks the very laws the Creator made the world with. Normally, light shrinks the darkness, but as a darkthief, you can do the opposite with your remnant. The Attanos can move wind where there is no breeze, impossible things that go against nature itself."

Aramis tucked the knife back in his pocket. "There are alchemists, like the Firenzes, who have taken their studies beyond the laws of this world and have sought to use them to understand and control the divine. The goal is to provide order to what is undefined, a way to regulate remnants, give them restraints and laws. Because nothing, even the remnants that seem to defy the law, exists without a code. If the Creator made it, which he did the saints, then the Arcane exists as a fundamental form in each power of every descendant."

This was what Delilah had been doing all along. Her life's work, as she called it, studying the Arcane and the codes of existence. Those symbols she used as weapons, like magic when I first experienced them, were nothing more than the manipulation of the laws using science—manipulating with the Arcane.

"What the watchman performed," Vesper said, "confirms that your Society has learned how to not only use the Arcane, but how to use it against you. Though, I'm not sure what they're using as a Siphon. Not when the Academy holds the source of all arcanist energy on the Continent."

"Blood," I said. "They drew markings with the blood of the wearhs. Delilah mentioned the source of a bleeder's remnant was in their blood. Perhaps they're using that as well to source their arcane spells."

Aramis crinkled his nose and shook his head. "They might use blood, but there's something else here. Something not as difficult to distribute."

"But why?" I asked them. "What's the goal of all this?"

"Control," Nico muttered the word. "If they can figure out

how to industrialize this power, they can manipulate everyone. Gavriel said it best when he explained how much he despised remnants for taking his family's empire. This is about control and money. Always has been."

"I was going to say Order," Aramis muttered. He paced up the length of the parlor, stepping between the bands of silver daylight.

I suddenly saw my brother from a different perspective, viewing a stranger where he stood instead. He'd never shown this much interest in the business of alchemists or their science. Nico seemed to sense something off as I did, sitting up from his leisure posture, his grip around my knee tightened.

"So you learned all this from our contact, did you?" he asked my brother in that sleazy voice, suggesting he thought otherwise.

Aramis shrugged a shoulder. "We used to be close to the Firenzes. I pieced together what I knew and what I learned from Narcissa. Why do you think I was desperate to get Camilla out of the city? I knew they were brewing trouble."

If Nico was unsatisfied with that reply, he said nothing. Though I could practically hear the wheels beginning to turn in his head, that beautiful mind of his conjuring his own theories and a hundred different possibilities they could spurn—never one to be surprised.

"Then my key, as they call it, is it a code as well?"

Aramis nodded slowly, as if unsure. "I would assume. If it indeed is a key to Oblivion, then taking it from you using the Arcane would allow them to use it."

"But why?" I asked. "Why would they want to open Oblivion?"

"Perhaps it holds something they want." Sabina spoke from the archway of the parlor, leaning against the thick wood frame like she had been listening for a while. She pushed off to cross the room, standing in front of the large hearth that dominated the sitting area. A smile stretched across her face as she noticed me. "Good to see you again, Camilla."

The bleeder queen didn't seem surprised I was sitting here, not like the wearhs who supported her. I had felt their stares, the weight of their whispers as we rode to her riverside mansion, and I'd been thankful the watchmen hadn't infiltrated Salt Street far enough to hit Sabina's home.

Her long silver-white hair was pulled up into a braided bun on the top of her head, away from the hood of a thin coat that hid the rest of her curvy figure down to her leather boots. A fur belt tied at the narrowest part of her waist. She appeared to have just arrived from being out, the bloodstains still fresh on the black fabric of her coat.

She glanced around the room. "And who are the rest of you?"

Nico gestured with his chin. "Aramis Marchese. Milla's family." My brother only nodded in greeting, clearly displeased with his introduction.

"Another Marchese back from the dead." She looked him over. "*Saints*, you're the spitting image of your father."

"You knew my father?" Aramis cocked his head.

She scoffed. "Unfortunately." Her stare fell to the couch. "And these two?"

Callow and Vesper stood slowly, stating their names. "They are the reason I was keen to set up a visit with you, Madame," Nico explained when Sabina was obviously confused about their presence, her smile wavering. "Are we alone?"

"At the moment. My staff is busy doing damage control." She sighed, her gaze flicking to the windows for a second. I thought I saw a flash of emotion on the frigid woman before she set her face again. "No one's around to hear anything. So get to the point. I have a lot to do today."

"Of course." Nico shifted, gently sliding me from his lap to stand. While I resettled in the wide seat, he stood behind it, bracing his hands on the backing. "But these two benders have traveled a very long way to speak with you. Or, more specifically, your mother."

That surprised the bleeder. "My mother? She's dead. Has been for years."

"As Nico said," Vesper spoke quickly, "we aren't exactly from around here. We traveled to Lynchaven on behalf of a resistance organization, and our leaders told us to find Rosa Bianchi so we could complete our mission."

Sabina looked at me, swallowing hard. It was the only time I'd ever seen her even slightly unsettled. "Where did you say you're from?"

Vesper glanced at Callow, who nodded. "We're from the Continent."

The bleeder took a step back, like she'd been struck. I sat straighter in the chair, sensing a new tension in the room. "What the hells are you doing here?"

"We were sent to find Chaos." Vesper looked at me then. "But we found her Remni instead. We were hoping you knew more about Chaos, if your mother spoke of them—"

"Stop." Sabina spoke the word like an order, clipped and precise. "Stop talking."

"This is poor timing," Nico said. "We'll come back another time when you have less to worry about, Sabina."

"You'll sit the fuck down and wait for me to think, Attano," she snapped back. Aramis chuckled quietly, earning him a glare from my husband.

"Camilla," she said. "You must understand something first, before I indulge these two with some unsolicited information. And I think . . . I think it was obvious to us both from the moment I tasted your blood, when I tasted the fire of Oblivion, I knew what you were, and I denied it." Sabina appeared visibly frazzled now. I'd never seen her so beside herself, so out of control of her emotions. "For that, I must apologize."

The apology unsettled me. "Sabina, what are you talking about?"

She didn't reply at first, instead pulled off her coat and draped it over a nearby chair. She braced her hands on the back of the seat. "Rosa Bianchi brought Chaos to this Isle when we fled the revolution building on the Continent. If you recall from our previous conversations, I was just a girl then myself."

It was like I had swallowed a stone, and every word from Sabina sunk it deeper down my throat. "Then you knew Chaos as well," I said. The saint who gave me her remnant.

She nodded. "Yes, Camilla. I knew your mother."

"WHAT DO YOU MEAN, you knew her?" I asked as Nico handed me a drink. After the revelation Sabina had dropped in my lap, I found it difficult to sit. The bender made himself useful in the only way he could: by helping himself to the bar cart.

The sun had barely risen over the river, but I took a sip anyway, wincing at the burn. Nico's usual blend of tobacco dispersed in the air as he lit a new cigarillo, and I let it fill my lungs, let it loosen and soothe the knot in my chest.

"We found her on the ship. She claimed she was an orphan of

the times. My mother, being the kind of woman she was, refused to let the child out of her sight for the next twelve years. She was . . ." Sabina sucked in a long breath. "She was my best friend. We grew up together. Close as sisters, honestly. By all rights, I could be your aunt."

"Then why keep this from me? Why didn't you say anything that day when you claimed you knew?"

"Because it was impossible for you to be hers! No matter all the similarities between you nor the taste of your blood." Her gaze shot to me, pinning me in place with its weight. "I *saw* Nadine leave. I brought her to the damn ship myself. I begged her to stay, but she had . . ."

"She had what?" I snapped. Saints forbid she got emotional on me now—that she pretended to care.

"She had a *baby*," Sabine whispered. Her shoulders fell slightly. Nico offered her a glass of brandy as well. She nodded her thanks to him and held it close to her waist. "Nadine fell head over heels for that Marchese creature. I didn't see what was so great about him to risk her life and the rest of the realm, but here you are."

She threw back the entire shot like it was water. "I just don't understand," she said. "She disappeared on me after she married Gio. I thought he kept her locked away, but then I realized she was trying to hide her pregnancy."

"Why, though?" I asked. "What put us in danger in the first place?"

Sabina's crimson eyes narrowed. "I wasn't the only one who found out she was a saint in mortal form. There's a longer story behind what I'm telling you now, Camilla. And I will share it if you ask me, but for the sake of time, I must be brief." She pointed a finger at me. "Someone she foolishly trusted as much as she trusted me betrayed your mother."

"Was her name Delilah?" I asked. Judging by the way Sabina straightened, the name triggered a memory. I recalled the alchemist's words when I'd asked her if she killed my mother.

I did something worse.

There were few things worse than death, like losing a life while your heart still beat, having friends like family and true love just to have it ripped away.

"Tell me that bitch isn't still alive," she hissed.

"She's dead," I said, then took a small sip of amber liquor. "I drove a knife through her, just to be sure."

"Good." Sabina shut her eyes briefly. "But yes, Delilah the alchemist, distant family of the Firenzes and psycho scientist herself, tried to take advantage of Nadine. Gio got her a ticket out, though. Just to keep her safe. One good thing he did, I suppose." Her focus left me, staring down a thought. "Something must have gone wrong if you're still here. I watched her get on that damn boat."

Silence settled into the conversation, letting us all take a moment to think about the implications of Sabina's confession. If my mother was Chaos and she was last seen alive trying to leave the Isle, then perhaps she was still out there somewhere.

The hope bloomed and died just as quickly in my heart. If my mother was still alive, surely she'd try to get back to me. If I was important enough to take when she left, wouldn't it have been just as important to find me if we were separated? Unless . . .

"What if Nadine isn't really my mother? What if, like the saints before, she just gifted me a piece of her power? Perhaps I'm just her Remni, not her daughter."

Sabina shook her head before I could finish. "You are Nadine's child. I'm disappointed in myself that I didn't see it as soon as you approached me in the Salt Exchange. Being a Marchese with that hair and those wild eyes . . . *hells*."

It didn't feel like enough, being identified by someone who knew her. But when I looked at my brother, who picked at his nails with a knife as he listened, the differences in our features were damning. "Then how do I have the power of a saint? I've never heard of the divines having children before."

Sabina took a long breath before she explained. "Chaos, as I'm sure you remember from our biased books, came from the Creator's soul. The other saints came from his hands, his mind, his body, and his heart. Those things can be broken, and the remnants inherited. But a soul cannot be split. Chaos couldn't break herself apart to defend herself like the others—"

"That's why she made the demons." Aramis spoke up then, flipping the blade around his finger.

Sabina squinted at him. "Yes, she made the demons to fight against the divine armies, but that is a history lesson for another day." She placed her empty glass on the wood table between us, looking at me. "Chaos couldn't fragment herself, so she multiplied. Nadine was afraid of what was happening on the Isle. She demanded to return to the Continent, insisting it was safer—bigger. That she had allies there now."

"She did, and she does," Vesper spoke as she stood, squaring her shoulders as she looked at me. "Many of us know the truth about the First War and we are ready to stand against the Orders. As long as Chaos exists, as long as she lives, there is hope for us. Order cannot exist if Chaos does."

A bubble of laughter floated from my chest. "What could I do?" I gestured to the window. "Look at what happens when I fight back! I took out an entire warehouse because I couldn't control my fire—"

"You did what?" Sabina asked with new interest sharpening her voice.

I dismissed her with a wave of my hand. "What about my power gives anyone hope? It's not like other remnants that can be controlled. There's something volatile about its nature. It unravels everything it touches—"

"Nadine had the same fire, Camilla," the bleeder said. "She kept it similarly hidden for years, but I saw it work when she needed it to. It destroys, but it can also create. If you only knew what you were capable of . . ." Sabina glanced toward the archway as if worried someone would overhear. "The OIC wants you, Camilla. Thank the saints Nico got you out of that prison before they could use you. Because your power in the hands of the ones who want control over us all. Well, the rest of us wouldn't stand a chance."

My hands gripped the crystal glass firmly, swirling the last sip of brandy in thought. This was too much to take in at once. Between Aramis and his understanding of the Arcane, Sabina and my mother, my *mother* being a shitting saint . . .

"We need to find out what is in Oblivion," I murmured. "If we are to stop whatever the OIC has planned, we need to know what they want."

"And how will we do that?" Nico asked. He'd been quietly listening the entire time, pacing behind the sitting area.

The answer, I found, was surprisingly simple and difficult all at once. "The book. Delilah had a book that Chaos herself wrote. Everything she knew about me, she learned from that book."

"And where is this book?" Sabina asked.

I flinched. "Felix has it."

"Well, since your brother is so close with the Firenzes," Nico spoke as if he weren't standing there, "perhaps he can figure out a way to get the damn thing from him."

To my surprise, Aramis didn't fight him on it. Instead, he shrugged. "Give me a few days to contact Narcissa and work something out. I'll try to learn what I can."

A loud knock interrupted our scheming. Sabina cleared her throat of whatever emotion lingered from her outburst and started toward the archway. "That'll be for me." She snapped at Nico. "Attano, walk with me upstairs for a moment. We need to discuss matters for the rest of the Row."

Nico snuffed out his cigarillo in a nearby ashtray. "I'll be right back," he said, then placed a kiss on my temple. "The cousins are out front if you wish to go home."

"I'll wait for you," I told him. He seemed to hear all the words I didn't say, for he squeezed my shoulder, replying in his own nonverbal way that everything was going to be alright. That he was with me in this mess. There was so much communicated in that single touch that I nearly broke from the overwhelming flood of them all.

"Attano!"

"*Seven hells*," he murmured. "I'll be back."

Their footsteps disappeared out of the receiving room door. Vesper had a strange look on her face. "Milla, can I ask you something strange?"

I almost laughed. Because what could be more bizarre than the previous conversation? "What is it?"

"Your husband," she drawled. "What happened to his shadow?"

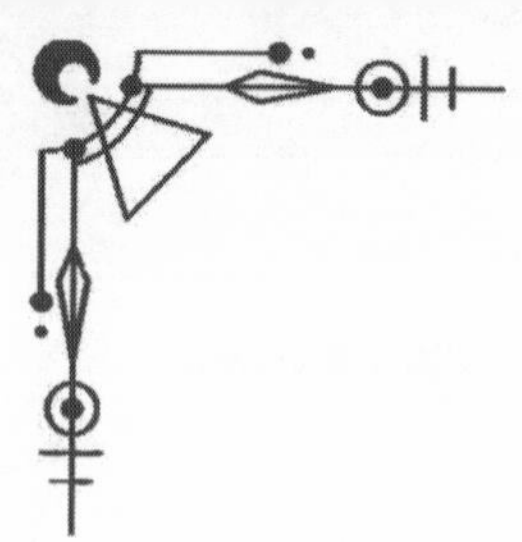
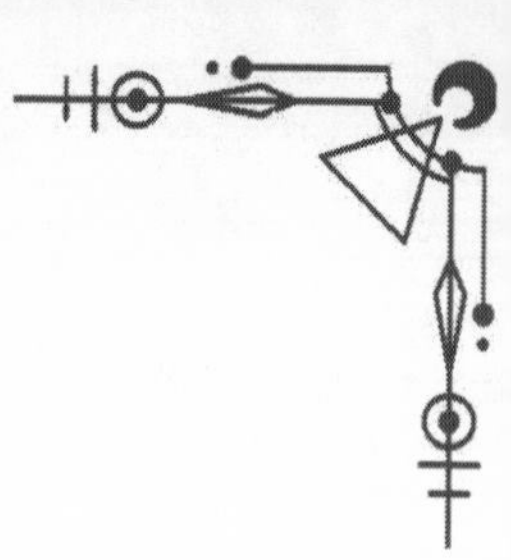

CHAPTER 28

NICOLAI

Sabina took me to an upper floor, to a room on the corner of the raised house that had both a view of the river and the smoke from the warehouse fires still burning. The morning had nulled the bite of winter's freeze, clearing some of the fog heavy over the river with its arrival, though the Districts were still concealed on the other side.

Two women discussed the day's schedule with Sabina, and I waited for her to explain why she dragged me up here. They reviewed the clean-up and the meetings to account for the stock along with the projected loss from the hits, adding insult to injury with every bullet on the list.

"For hell's sake," Sabina snapped, "just get out. I'll deal with this later."

"But Madame—"

"*Get out*," her boss hissed. I flinched for her. "Tell Vincent to handle things until I'm ready for my next appointment."

Her assistants gave small bows before scurrying out of the

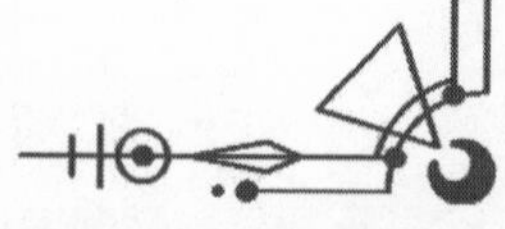

room, glancing at me before they left. We stood in silence for a moment once they were gone, letting the dust of the day's disturbances settle some.

"We should have foreseen this," she said at last. She faced the floor-to-ceiling windows, staring out over the burning remains of her sector.

"I didn't think they'd be so bold," I admitted. Certainly not here, anyway. The viaduct, the Row's station, my factories, all places I would have bet the Society would have attacked before Sabina's warehouses.

"You know why they came after me, don't you?" She faced me at last. The morning glare outlined her figure like a silver halo.

"You supply the Row with ninety percent of our goods. The meat from the Wilds, the tannery for clothes and leather products, we're lucky they didn't hit the Salt Exchange, or we'd be screwed."

"All good reasons, yes. Though not the one I was thinking about."

I crossed my arms, unsure of what I'd missed. "What then?"

"The deal you have with Desmond, or have you forgotten now that your wife is home?"

I cursed, releasing a long sigh. "Of course I haven't forgotten. But what does my deal with him have to do with you?"

"I'm the middleman!" she shouted. "I've been his contractor in Lynchaven, for *both* sides. The Society has been watching me for years; they just never had proof to charge me. But now—" She threw her hands up, gesturing widely. "Now we're at war. Now they don't care about laws or innocent lives."

"How would they know about my deal with York?" The Society bastards had busted the party that night, but I'd left none alive to share my face.

"The Demon Dealer has been looking for someone to move

that shit for six weeks. Word must have gotten back to the Watch somehow. The stock, however, remains a mystery. Only that it comes from the Lowlands and is apparently very valuable."

I couldn't think of anything profitable enough to risk this amount of headache in the south. Not that it mattered. My very life depended on getting this job done and done fast. "What's the timeline?"

"The drop is next week. I'll send you coordinates where the buyer wants you to load. Until then, we need to prepare the Row properly."

I nodded, looking out to where smoke was clearing thanks to the morning breeze. "We can distribute weapons to the business strip along the river, but the bombs stay with my men. And my men stay by my wife. I'll not risk someone blowing themselves up because they don't know how to work an explosive safely."

Sabina chuckled darkly. "That's probably wise. I'll send Vincent to your offices to discuss the distribution. For now, I need to deal with my sector."

"I understand. If you need anything else, don't hesitate to call on the Attanos."

"Thank you, Nicolai." A pause. "For everything." She said the last bit in a softer tone, one I'd never heard from the bleeder before.

I turned to leave but suffered one last thought. "You did all this for her, didn't you? Helping me so much to get Milla back. It wasn't because we were allies. It's because of her mother."

The bleeder queen lowered herself into a chair, eyes drifting to the furthest window, where the view was consumed by the rough waters of the Ada. "To everyone, Chaos was a saint, a monster who tried to break the world. To me, she was my closest friend. Sometimes my only friend, and I loved her more than I loved anyone else in this life, save for my own miserable mother." Sabina's dark gaze rested on me then. "I owe it to Nadine to look after her daughter in her place, but trust me when I say she would have been grateful for you as well."

The admission shifted something in my chest. Something heavy I didn't know had rested there. "Thank you, Sabina. That means a lot, coming from someone who knew her."

"You love Camilla," she said then, completely off topic.

I couldn't deny it. Didn't want to. "I do."

"Have you told her?"

"Not in those words exactly."

Sabina rolled her eyes. "Men. You have all the courage to bust into a high security prison and rescue your woman, but saints forbid you say a four-letter word." She scoffed and waved me off. "Get out of my sight before I drag you downstairs and compel you to tell the girl the truth."

Honestly, it wouldn't be her worst idea.

By the time I made it down the ebony-stained stairwell leading to the lowest level, Luther was running up to me from the entryway.

"Boss! It wasn't my fault, I swear it."

Gideon was behind him, scrubbing his face with a hand. "It's completely your fault, Luther."

"What's wrong?" I asked, looking around for Milla. I started towards the parlor when Gideon held up a hand, insisting it was pointless.

"She isn't there. She went home with Adler and Aramis."

An uneasy sensation curled beneath my ribs. I asked Luther once more, sliding each word through my teeth. "*What. Happened.*"

He winced. "I got you in trouble."

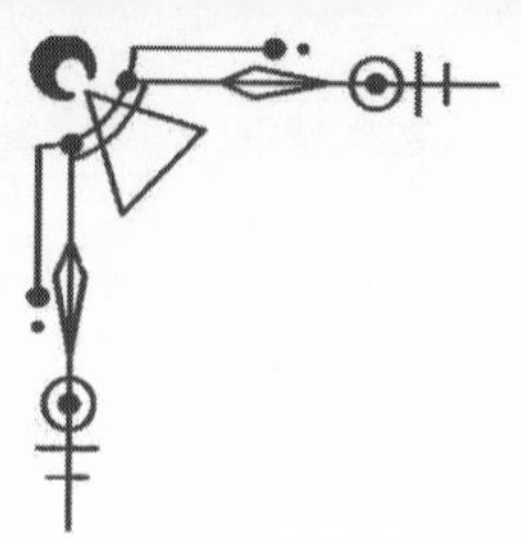
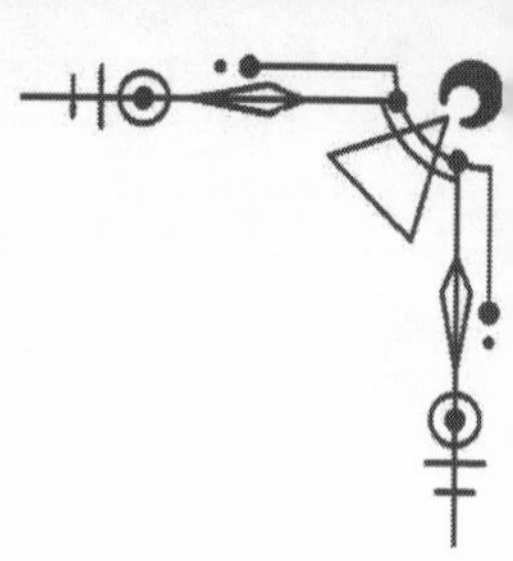

CHAPTER 29
CAMILLA

His shadow.

He gave up his fucking shadow—and hadn't even told me. Vesper and Callow had explained the implications of someone taking a shadow, that it had to be willingly taken off a person, that it could be used to control or even kill them if needed. And someone who called themselves the Demon Dealer—according to Luther's story—had Nicolai's shadow.

The idea terrified me so much, I couldn't sit there any longer. I was sick over the situation—angry he hadn't told me when we discussed the details on how he established a portal to break into Hightower. He had the chance, and he avoided the truth. What else had happened over these six weeks that he was keeping from me?

"I wish you were here to tell me I'm overreacting."

I spoke to the tombstone glazed in ice, where I sat cross-legged in front of the marker, twirling a dead rose from the garden

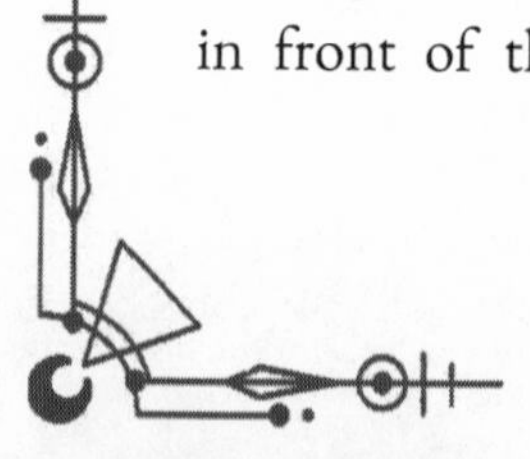

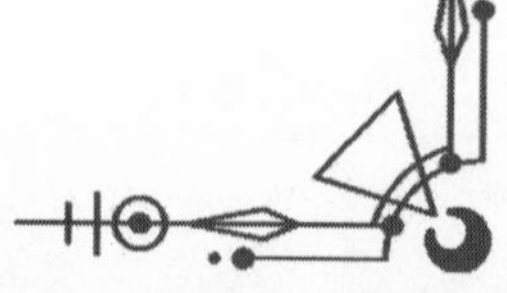

between my fingers. The frost tipping the blades of grass melted, seeping into the thick material of my pants.

True to her word, Esme had faceted a metal plate over my name, replacing it with Sera's. At my request, she'd also scribed the name of her father as well, though his body had dissipated in the breeze. At least he'd be remembered whenever someone read the face of his daughter's grave.

I'd killed Marco Gallo with my own hands. A single touch. Somehow that was supposed to spark hope in a world that didn't need my help destroying good and perfect things.

"I'd know exactly what you'd say, though." A smile teased my lips. "You'd tell me I need to be patient. That Nico's intentions are pure, if not a little misguided sometimes. You'd tell me not to worry about Aramis, that he only wanted what was best for me, and I'd actually believe you because you were always right in the end. Even about that stupid dress."

It was like she was still here, still in my head and whispering the words I needed to hear with her remnant. My smile fell. "I'm sorry for everything."

"Are you talking to yourself?"

I turned to find my youngest brother standing near the gate to the family graveyard, wrapped in a thick coat with his hood pulled low over his head. His boots crunched in the frozen grass as he came to sit beside me, settling with a grunt of discomfort.

"What are you doing out here?" I asked him.

"Trying to figure out what the hells you're doing out here."

I scoffed. "Just talking to myself, I suppose."

He didn't reply right away, allowing the quiet to build between us. I couldn't recall the last time we'd had a conversation. We'd always relied on the family glue, Giles, to be our human buffer.

He gestured toward the dead flower between my fingers. "It's not easy losing a best friend. Even after Jasper died, I kept turning to the right to tell him something. It took weeks for my body to realize he wasn't there anymore. Sometimes I still look for him when the silence stretches too long."

I reached my free hand to link my arm around his, leaning into his warmth. "You were always together. I think this might be the first time we've spoken alone."

"Yeah, probably." He forced a chuckle. "It's awful, knowing I'll never have him around. Having a twin is like . . . sharing a soul. I feel like I'm only walking around with half of myself, and I'm just left to be incomplete the rest of my life."

The hurt in his voice cleaved me in half, a timbre that bruised my heart. "I miss him. I wish we'd spent more time together before."

"I think we're all a little to blame for taking each other for granted, and I'm sorry for that."

"Me too."

He shifted in his seat. "And I'm sorry I didn't join Aramis today. I don't . . . I don't like fighting. I'm not that kind of person, and I never was. Father despised that about me."

It made me feel sorry for him, knowing he believed that. "I don't expect you to fight battles that aren't yours, Jer. I don't even know why Aramis was there today."

He rolled his eyes, as if he'd tried to figure out the same. "When he heard Nico took you to the docks, he freaked out. He's worried about you, Camilla. Your power is . . ." His lips thinned.

"Terrible. I know."

"That's not what I was going to say," he said, to my surprise.

"You don't think so?"

He shook his head. "You're my sister. Nothing about you is terrible."

I twirled the thorny, dried-up stem between my fingers in thought. "But this power has become my whole identity—and I can't even control it. How can something so unpredictable be trusted?"

Several seconds passed. A strong breeze roused the frozen branches of the looming trees behind the graveyard, causing the ice dripping from their limbs to clink in the wind. He said, "I don't really have any experience with magic or power, but don't descendants control their remnant, not the other way around? Maybe you just need to trust yourself."

I looked at him then, really looked at him for the first time in what might have been years. For so long, after our father's death, we'd competed against one another as if he were still alive. Still seeking his approval beyond the grave. We had lost so much, with Giles and Jasper, our friends that had replaced the family we never had. Now it was just us, and having the world meant very little when the ones we fought to share it with were no longer here.

"Milla?"

Nico's voice called me from the gate. His hand rested on the wrought iron post, wearing an unsure look on his face. His cheeks were pink from the cold, like he'd ridden here quickly without cover from the elements. "Can we talk?"

Jeremiah stood first, helping me up after. My legs had nearly gone numb from sitting in the position for so long. The back of my pants were wet and cold and stuck to my skin uncomfortably. Eager to shed the morning and the rest of my soiled clothes, I followed Nico up to the main house, but not before whispering my gratitude to a brother I wrongly once believed cared far less than he did.

As soon as we entered the house, a decadent smell invited us to the kitchens. Nonna was baking cinnamon buns, and my stomach growled at the memory of the sticky sweetness glazing the spiced rolls. I stopped Nico before he could ascend the side stairwell leading to our floor.

"I might be more inclined to tolerate you with a stomach full of Nonna's buns."

He did his best not to grin. "Your stomach will curse you later. Do you know what she puts in those?"

"Two rolls won't hurt. Not as much as a bullet to the leg, and I've already done that today. Please?"

He rolled his eyes, a smile breaking his lips. "Go change into something dry. I'll bring them up. Nonna will have a fuss if you walk in there looking like you pissed yourself."

I returned his smirk, even if I was still cross with him. "You spoil me, Attano."

"You're already spoiled, princess."

He waited to speak until I finished. My stomach stretched from the overindulgence, vowing to pay me back later from the brief experience of cinnamon buns. The bread practically melted in my mouth, complimenting the hot coffee Nico brought with them.

"Nonna can bully me as much as she wants as long as she keeps making those." I put my plate on the coffee table and rested on a pillow, curling my knees into my chest to brace the cramps already triggering from the eggs in the batter I was unfortunately still allergic to.

Nico arched a brow at me. "You sure you feel alright?"

"Never better." I licked the cinnamon glaze off my fingers, one by one, just to prove a point. A lie—but a point.

He watched me hungrily, looking at me like I had looked at the pastry. "Do you mind if I speak, then? If you're quite done."

I waved a sticky hand in invitation. "Grovel away, Attano."

He sighed, shaking his head. "I wanted to apologize for not telling you about the shadow business. Honestly, with everything going on, it has fallen down my list of priorities. But I do have a plan to finish our bargain."

"Using the train, I assume?"

He nodded. "We'll send it down empty. I have a contact through your family that's going to ship a load of sand to me across the river for some industrial purposes. Completely legitimate. The Watch shouldn't give it a second look. Whatever the stock this buyer needs me to ship, I'll bury it in the cars."

It was a good plan, but not without risk. The Watch could investigate if they wanted to, which meant we'd have to be very careful not to draw their attention. "It might work. Hopefully, Marcus will agree to it."

"He already has."

I took a steadying breath, feeling better about his prospects. The Watch trusted Marcus. He'd been our engineer countless times, frequently filling roles wherever we needed him. If he operated the controls, they'd let him through the south side of the city.

"Don't ever do something like that again," I said. All the icy fear thawed away from the sweet rolls had returned. Nico's life was under constant threat without his shadow, and I couldn't live with the idea.

His lips flattened. "Respectfully, Milla, I'll do whatever I must to keep you safe. He could've asked me to hand him my entire fortune, and I would have given him the Row on top of it to get you back."

His admission left me breathless. "Why, Nico?"

He stood from his lounge in the chair and crossed the small space between us. I sat straighter as he knelt before me, my hands dropping the pillow as he reached for them, pressing one over the space above his heart, where I knew beneath the black fabric of his shirt was a symbol of three interwoven circles.

"For three days—three entire days out of my life—I believed you were dead. I watched you get shot, watched the light leave your golden eyes, carried your stiff body five miles back to the train station in utter shock that you were gone. It broke me in a way I don't think I'll ever fully recover from. Those images haunt me to this day, like a bad dream I can't shake.

"So, when I learned you were alive, I vowed to do everything and anything to get you back. Because I don't want to live another day without you, Milla. I buried you once. I wouldn't survive doing it again."

That tombstone with my name had once been his reality. For three days. I couldn't imagine how gutted I'd be if the roles were reversed. Three days might as well have been an eternity. "You're stronger than you think, Nicolai."

"But you are my greatest weakness."

I didn't want to talk about death or dying or losing the other. Those threats always surrounded us like a dark fog. But he was here, and so was I, and we were whole and alive and wasting seconds wondering *what if* when we could take advantage of the time we still had.

I claimed his mouth with a fierce pressure, desperately needing to replace that haunted look in his eyes with their previous hunger. He made the shift seamlessly, slipping adept hands down the length of my arms to embrace me against his hard chest, guiding my legs to wrap around his waist.

"Do you have anything planned today?" I asked between kisses.

He groaned, digging his fingers down the curve of my ass to grip my legs. I arched my back, rubbing my center against him as he broke our kiss, assumingly assessing how to remove whatever fabric was between us. "My schedule is suddenly wide, *wide* open."

My head tipped back in offering as his mouth moved to my neck, placing sweet, gentle kisses along the column of my throat. "Then what is that envelope on the table?"

"Nothing."

"*Nico*."

He growled in frustration. "Fine. It's a summons to meet with one of Sabina's assistants this morning. But it can wait—"

"Nico." I laughed and gently pushed him away. "You can't ignore that."

His fingers squeezed my thighs. "Watch me." But I kept my hand braced against his chest, which displeased him greatly. "*Milla*."

"*Nico*. Let me get dressed and I'll ride with you down there."

The grip was nearly bruising now. "How much longer must I wait to have you?"

I thought about it. We'd been together for an entire week now and yet still hadn't been able to reconnect in such a way. There was no excuse now except for time. Esme got me the contraceptives I needed, and I wanted him just as much, though my desire wasn't as rock solid between us as his was currently.

"How long is the ride to your office?"

He shrugged, running his tongue between his teeth. "Fifteen minutes."

A wicked smile spread across my cheeks. “That’s plenty of time to show me your new upgrades.”

Grey eyes widened.

“I’ll get the carriage ready.” Nico stood so quickly I nearly fell over at the loss of him. He lingered in the doorway, a feral look in his eyes. “Be quick about it. That meeting is very important.”

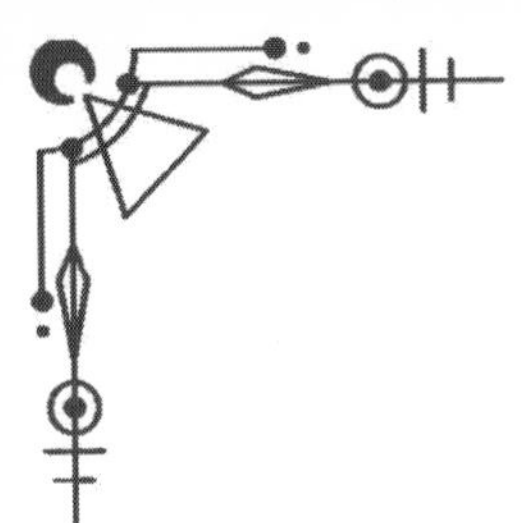
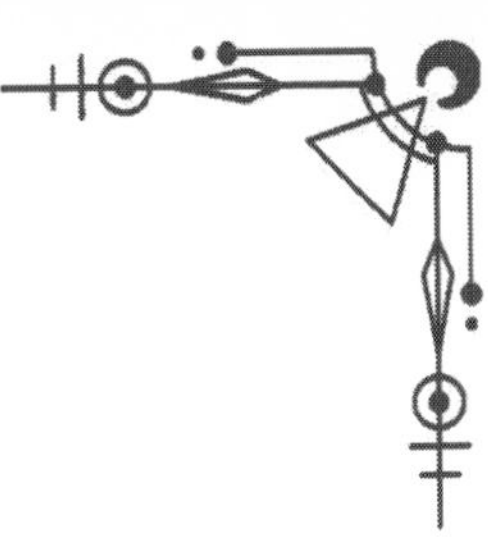

CHAPTER 30

CAMILLA

Luther met me in the hallway first, just outside the side entrance. He had changed himself, into his usual black tweed suit and silver vest, dressed for the day's business. "You headed to the office, Milla?"

"I am."

"Mind if I hitch a ride? I can just hang on the back. Won't take no space up at all."

"Sure. Why not?" I shrugged. "Oh, and Luther?"

"Yes, boss?"

I licked my lips, making sure Nico was out of hearing range. "Please keep what I told you between us for now. I'm going to tell Nico about Hightower, I'm just . . . not there yet."

He winked at me, extending his arm for me to take. "I understand. Just know he'd never look at you differently, Milla."

That wasn't a fear of mine to begin with. No, when I brought this truth to Nico, I wanted to be sure I'd forgiven myself first before I sought it elsewhere.

Nico waited inside the carriage when the footman opened the door for me, unaware his cousin was joining us. As soon as Grimm shut the door behind me, Nico helped me out of my coat.

"You wore my favorite dress, I see," he murmured into my bare shoulder.

"Aren't they all your favorite?"

"True. But you wore this one to my pub, and it drives me especially crazy." As if to prove his point, he slid his false hand up the top of my thigh, and my eyes fluttered as cold metal brushed the heat of my arousal.

"Fuck, Milla."

"What?"

"You're not wearing anything underneath?"

"I never wear underwear with a silk dress. You'd see the lines."

He paused his perusal. "Do you mean that every time we've been together, and you've worn that, you weren't wearing anything?"

"Nope."

"The night we met?"

"Not a thing."

"*Seven hells*," he groaned. The car moved, and he shifted to sit on the floor between my legs, placing both hands on either side of my thighs. "Ignorance is truly bliss. You're going to torture me with this look for the rest of my life."

Nico slowly gathered the silk higher up my legs, eyes locked on my center until the hem of my dress was above my hips. He cursed again before shouting our driver's name. "Bellamy?"

The grate above my head slid to the side. "Yes, sir?"

"Take the scenic route to the office."

"Oh. Well, alright—"

I shut the grate before she could inquire about Nico's choice.

My husband grinned at me with a darkened gaze full of wicked intention. "I want to take my time with you, princess. Is that alright?"

My throat was dry from the hungry breaths building in my chest. I could only nod and brace myself for his wrath, parting my knees for him.

"Very good," he murmured and pushed my legs wide. I gasped, pressing a hand against the wall of the carriage. "Hells, you're beautiful."

Shitting saints . . . I ached for him, my pulse throbbing across a tender place, and he wouldn't shut the hells up. "You talk too much."

"Do you not like my voice, Milla?"

"Not right now," I breathed out.

His laugh blew a cool breath across the sensitive skin along my inner thigh. Without warning, his hands slipped beneath the bend of my knee and tugged me forward, so that I sat on the very edge of the bench with my legs draped over his arms.

Nico stroked my clit with a metal thumb, making slow, lazy circles around my center. I could only whimper as the beginnings of euphoria filled my hips. My back arched, giving him a better angle, trying to roll my waist to the rhythm of his hand.

His opposite hand clamped down around my hip bone, stilling me. "I don't need your help, Milla. You'll stay fucking still until I'm done with you, alright?"

There he was—the Nicolai Attano I married in my family's courtyard. Arrogant, demanding, in charge. Thankfully, now it was finally working in my favor. I nodded a silent consent and tried to relax against the back of the bench.

"That's my girl." His head dipped then, and he finally shut up long enough to kiss me in the most intimate of ways. His tongue swirled my center, trailing his finger. The contrasting warmth of his mouth and the incessant stroke of his false hand drew a cry from my chest. The hand on my hip tightened, keeping me pinned to the seat as he worked his tongue deeper.

I bit my lip to keep from making any more noise, but my breaths became too desperate not to gasp for air, to feed the flames rising between my legs where that devious tongue reminded me of the language of pleasure, how good my body could feel in the right hands. In *his* hands.

He broke away for a moment, but his false hand continued to work. "Don't you dare silence those pretty sounds for my sake, Milla. Let the city hear you if you want to be heard. Remind them all that I serve you. There's no one else I'd get on my knees for, princess."

Something changed then, the sensation between my legs. A vibration from his false fingers that stimulated so many points of pleasure, my legs jerked before falling weak. "What the hells is that?"

"My upgrade, as you called it."

Seven hells and shitting saints, he could vibrate them now? The look on my face must have been astonished because he smiled. "That's not all."

"*Fuck me.*"

"Patience, my love. We'll get there, but I think you're wet enough I can show you the best part."

I watched helplessly as he licked my arousal from the forefinger of his false hand. The configuration of the tubes shifted then, rearranging before my eyes, and coming together again to combine his first and middle finger, creating a very thick, very penetrating shape.

He rubbed the length of it along my center before positioning the tip at my entrance. "Do you want this, Milla?"

"Yes," I breathed out. Couldn't do more than breathe. The filthy sounds he made between my legs were thankfully covered by the road noise. Metallic knuckles rolled over a point that sent shivers across every inch of my skin. Now lubricated with my arousal, they slipped between my center—and I was ready for him. So ready to be filled, and if not with his cock, then with his hand.

He slipped himself in, barely an inch, before the carriage swerved hard to avoid something in the road. We hit a bump during correction that knocked me out of my seat and into Nico's lap. He caught me, hands around my waist, my dress still pulled high over my hips.

"Alright?" he asked.

"Perfect."

His lips claimed mine again and again, no space to be found between us. Sandalwood cologne and cigarillo smoke lingered on his skin as I stole small gasps of air. I tasted myself on his tongue as he swept my mouth. With every kiss, another piece of his affection fell into the place where it belonged, stored in my heart to keep forever.

"Turn around." His voice was a throaty growl. "Place your hands on the bench."

The arms around my waist loosened enough to allow me to brace against the leather seat. Nico's right hand slipped the strap of my dress down my shoulder. A rough hand dipped beneath the fabric, cupping my breast. His callous palm ran over the sensitive peak, squeezed, pinched, and I couldn't help the moan that flew from my parted lips.

"Perfect," he said in my ear. "So fucking pretty, those sounds you make."

My back arched again, seeking his heat behind me. He thrust his hips slowly, pressing his hard cock along the curve of my ass while his false hand returned to my center. I spread my legs wider, kneeling in front of him in the small carriage while he worked every part of me.

"I'll ask again, do you want this?" His false hand slipped around my hip and caressed the slope leading to my entrance.

I nodded, letting my head fall into the curve of his neck. "Yes, please."

He groaned in approval. "So polite. I'll fuck those manners out of you."

Finally, his fingers plunged inside me, filling me nearly as much as I recalled his cock had and hitting a place that sent my head thrashing back into the curve of his shoulder, my fingers slipped from the leather seat and clutched his arm, feeling the corded muscle roll with every stroke and knead over my body.

"I got you, Milla. Relax."

He took control, still holding me against him, still working my breast, still grinding his cock against my ass. I was just about to fall over the edge, the pressure in my hips too much to hold back any longer, when his thumb joined the combination of sensations.

Light vibrations circled my clit as he plunged his false fingers deeper into my center. I was powerless to the climax that rushed through me so hard, my eyes slammed shut and my breath shuddered. I rode his hand, seeking every last swell of pleasure he offered until my form trembled against him, like I had shattered instead. And every piece left of me belonged to him.

His false hand slipped out of me, but he held my waist steady until my breathing caught up with my racing heart. The tension in my muscles relaxed some, melting against his chest behind me.

"Your turn?" I asked, only half teasing.

He kissed my temple. "As much as I'd love to see those pretty lips around my cock, Milla, our driver has already circled the office twice. We should move this inside, shall we?"

I agreed reluctantly, letting Nico help me put my coat back on and smooth out the wrinkles he made in my dress. I didn't know how he knew we'd been circling. Our heavy breaths had fogged the windows behind the shades.

Bellamy knocked—very loudly—twice before swinging the door open wide. We were parked in front of a four-story red brick building in the center of the Row. Nico had moved his offices to be separate from the smokestacks at the steel foundries, if only to acknowledge all the other business the Attanos had going for them outside of the steelworks.

"Where's Luther?" I asked her, noticing the cousin no longer hung on the back.

"Luther?" Nico asked.

"He jumped off about halfway here." Bellamy cleared her throat. "He said something about needing the exercise."

Nico's grey gaze was wide on me when I looked at him again. "You didn't tell me my cousin was hitching a ride."

I shrugged and took the arm he extended to me. "I wasn't letting him get in my way again."

Nico laughed, and it echoed through the quiet street we parked on. "This isn't over," he whispered the promise against the shell of my ear.

I smoothed my hair back, hoping it wasn't as disheveled as I felt. "I'm holding you to that, Attano."

NICO WROTE up a contract to prepare for Vincent's visit, letting me proofread the final document. He did so deliberately, taking great care to think on each word before taking the pen to paper.

I smiled as I watched him. Broad shoulders leaned over a massive oak desk. A strand of dark hair fell over his face, between his brows. His style had fallen from the waxy hold as the remainder of his pomade stuck between my fingers.

He wore spectacles that made him look even more sophisticated in his suit, claiming they helped him focus. I thought they suited him.

I took the time to survey his office. Much could be assumed about a man from what he took to work with him, and I enjoyed learning Nico bit by bit. I knew him better than anyone else, knew exactly what he'd say or how he'd react before he did so, had heard countless childhood stories to never be intimidated by him again, and yet—he was like picking up a book I've read a hundred times. There was always something new to be discovered between the lines, a detail I might have missed before.

His office was neatly organized, as I expected. A map of the Row hung on an exposed brick wall. The Attanos' land was outlined in red, neighboring the First Sector, where Sabina's territory was pushed into a crevice of the map. Some of Nico's sections were marked red—certain streets blotted out entirely.

"What . . ." I shut my mouth promptly before I distracted him.

"The homes and businesses on our payroll."

"*Saints* . . ." I murmured. How the hells did they afford to keep so many on good terms with the family? My own had done the same when we were in similar power. Sometimes, a copper or two was the only way to keep lips sealed and eyes looking the other way. One street blacked out was East End. I reached for the place on the map, smiling at the small dot that had become one of my most substantial memories.

"Picking out your next home?" he asked. I turned to find him watching me.

I scoffed. "Nonna would never let us move out."

"Would you want to, though? Say everything goes back to normal and we can move on after this. Would you like to start our own lives together?"

I hadn't even allowed myself to think about it, with the way things were. It seemed impossible for anything to go back to normal after so much bad had happened, but the option was tempting to dream about. "I suppose it would be nice to get some privacy. I love your family, Nico, but they're everywhere."

As if to note his location, Luther whistled as he passed down the hall. Nico smiled again, glancing at the closed door as if understanding my point.

"I guess I don't notice it as much, since I've been around them all my life. It's normal for me."

"And that's sweet," I admitted. "I'm just . . . not used to being looked after quite so much."

He stood from his chair and slipped behind me, holding my waist to turn me toward the map. "Close your eyes."

My eyes shut as I leaned against him while he guided my arm in front of me. "Point to a spot."

My finger landed blindly on a point, and when I opened my eyes, I found it to be in the Second Sector, not far from the Attano Estate.

"Hmmm," Nico murmured. "That looks like the Green Village. Not a bad spot."

"A spot for what?"

"To build our house, of course."

I laughed. "You're going to build us a house? Nonna will start a riot."

"Nonna can visit when she damn well pleases, but if you want a home of your own, Milla, I'll give it to you." He rested his chin on the top of my head. "The yards are a good size. You could get yourself a dog or something."

"I'm allergic to pets."

"Of course you are."

I bit my lip to stifle a laugh. "It sounds like you're planning to keep me forever, Attano."

His hands slipped from my waist, drifting lower. "I've got lots of plans for you. They all end in forever."

The word sobered the smile across my face. We'd never talked about forever, hadn't had the chance to look past the trouble of tomorrow. Making plans felt facetious when there was so much that could change, that we could lose in a second, but Nico had always been quite the planner.

Maybe, despite the unknowns, I could hope for forever with him as well.

"When is your meeting set to start?"

I felt him turn his head to look at a nearby wall clock. "Twenty minutes."

Pushing his hands lower until they rested beneath my hips, I said, "There's no one else here at the office today, I noticed."

"Just the security at the front and Luther. But I don't think he'll be bothering us."

I slipped from his fingers to stand behind his desk, bracing my hands on the glossy varnish. The desk was wide and came up to my hip, which might be a little uncomfortable, but I'd manage. "Have you ever fucked on this?"

The question visibly startled him, the way his brow rose. "I . . . No. Never."

"Think we have time?" I slipped one of the straps of my dress off my shoulder. Then the other. I untied the corset-like string that fitted the top around my ribcage, loosening it until the dress fell from my body. I stood in front of him wearing nothing but a bralette and heels.

He stalked towards me, unbuckling his belt. Grey eyes hard as steel took in every detail of my body in the gas light. He'd shed his coat when we walked in, showing off a black shirt beneath a grey tweed vest. A silver coat chain hung from the middle button to his pocket. Everything about his dress claimed he was classy and refined, but that look in his eyes bested the most savage of hunters.

Sometimes, when I looked in the mirror and saw what the prison had done to me, I resented what stared back. But when I saw my reflection in his eyes, I could only feel beautiful.

"I'll make time." With a rush of wind, the contract, his pen, anything loose, blew off the top of the desk. He freed his belt from his pants with a single pull. "Sit," he ordered.

I sat.

Nico stepped between my legs and kissed me hard. My arms fell around his neck, pressed my chest against his until there wasn't an inch to be found between our bodies. My hips bucked against him, seeking the friction of his hard erection pressing back against his pants.

His mouth trailed lower, nipping at the hollow of my throat, while his false hand cupped the back of my neck as his opposite slipped between us, undoing his pants to free himself. Guiding the tip of his shaft, he rubbed it along my clit through the wetness that hadn't stopped gathering there since we got in the car.

He groaned against my skin, rubbing himself along my center

as warmth spread once more through my hips. My head fell back, falling into his caress. "Saints, Nico. That feels good."

He only responded by entangling his fingers in my curls and gently pulling my head back further, arching my chest with the position. His free hand left his cock to pull down the bralette, to give his mouth freedom to suck and nip at my breast.

My moans grew sharper, building with every sensation he added to flame the fire burning in my blood. Pressure coiled between my legs; an emptiness that longed to be filled. I bucked my hips to run my center along his length as his tongue swirled around my nipple and teeth grazed the surrounding skin.

He whispered curses I couldn't hear beyond the breath panting between my lips, the pulse roaring in my ears. Finally, gently, he lowered me to the top of the desk, running his hand down the valley of my chest to where I opened for him.

"Fucking stunning like this. I'll never get any work done again with this memory locked away."

A knock. A *fucking* knock sounded at his door.

"Mr. Attano?"

Nico slid his tongue between his teeth. He then motioned for me to be quiet and positioned himself at my entrance.

"What is it?" he called out, just before plunging his cock into me.

I gasped, but Nico clamped a hand around my mouth. Looming above me, he thrust his hips in as deep as he could stretch me, filling me with a surge of pleasure before drawing out again.

"Your appointment is here. A Mr. Abernathy on behalf of Sabina Bianchi."

Nico gritted his teeth. His eyes squeezed shut as he tried to control the raspy edge in his voice. "I'm almost there—done. Tell him I'll be with him in a moment."

"He said he's in quite a rush, Mr. Attano."

My eyes fluttered from the waves of pleasure pulsing through me with every slam of his hips into mine. The hand still covering my mouth filtered the filthy sounds leaving my lips.

"Look at me," Nico said tenderly.

I tried to force my eyes open, to look through the haze of satisfaction, to stare up at him as he pounded into me over and over. Each thrust more merciless than the last.

"Sir, I can't see you . . ." the man at the door said.

Nico covered a groan with a cough. "I don't give a damn if he's in a rush. Give him a drink and tell him to—*fucking saints . . .*"

"You want me to tell him to . . . *fuck the saints*?"

"*No*," Nico seethed. He was getting close, if the tightening grip around my mouth was any indication. I wrapped my legs around his waist, arched my back to give him deeper access. "Tell him . . . I'm finishing the contract and will be . . . *right there* . . . in a moment."

My whimper slipped through his fingers, and Michael had to have heard it, because he finally left to tell Vincent Abernathy whatever the hells it took to give us some time.

I smiled against his palm, guided him by the wrist to slip his hand lower until it circled my throat. I almost lost myself feeling that cold hand pinch my airway. Without warning, he took the air from my chest and left me breathless.

"I told you to be quiet." He paused his thrusts. "I don't want that bleeder knowing what I'm doing to you. Is that clear?"

I nodded because I couldn't speak.

He didn't give me my breath back, not yet. Instead, he slammed back into me even harder, until every inch of him was seated inside me. My burning chest tried to scream as bullets of pleasure rippled through my core and tore me apart. Tears blurred my vision on him, my lips opened to take a breath he didn't allow me yet.

He pushed and pushed until I fell over the edge, body writhing with an electric euphoria as my climax squeezed around his cock. Watching me, he let me take a blessed breath, the rush of satiating air only elevating the pleasure to another level I'd never reached before. Not by myself.

He kissed me as he shattered, and I swallowed his moans with the sweep of my tongue, claiming them for myself. He jerked against my hips, spilling into me as his hands gripped my waist with a bruising hold.

After the waves of our joined climax settled into more tolerable undulations, he broke from my mouth, inching back to look at me. An adoration there I'd never seen anyone else offer me before.

"Worth it all."

"What?" I asked.

"You. You were worth everything."

Everything that had happened. All the trials and difficulties we've faced. We—us, together—were worth fighting every damn day for. To one day have our forever.

I'd never fallen in love before. But then again, I'd never felt like this, either. Like this thing between us was writing itself into my soul. I wondered if this was what forever felt like.

"I should get dressed," I whispered. "Before our visitor barges in here and gets an eyeful."

"I really don't feel like killing anyone right now, so that would be for the best." He sighed as he slipped out of me. "Let me clean you up at least."

He tucked himself back in his pants and found a clean napkin from the wet bar to clean off the mess he made down my legs before helping me back into my dress. I smoothed down my hair as he retied the laces cinching the fabric around my chest.

"Have a seat. You deserve the chair." He kissed my shoulder before bending to pick up the contract he'd tossed to the floor.

As soon as I lowered into the leather office chair, another knock rapped against the door. This one much louder and demanding in its intent. Nico rushed to the door and unlocked it, swinging it wide to reveal a red-faced bleeder holding a box.

"Ah," Nico said casually. "Mr. Abernathy. You're very early, to my inconvenience."

He pushed the box into Nico's stomach. "Trouble always seems to come when you least expect it, Mr. Attano. For the sake of the Row, you'll want to make time to open this."

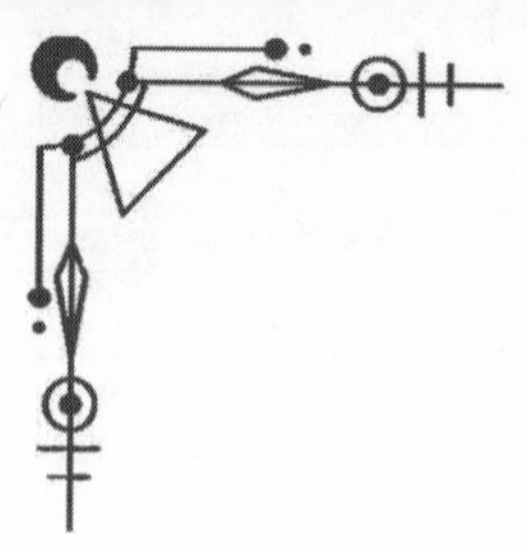
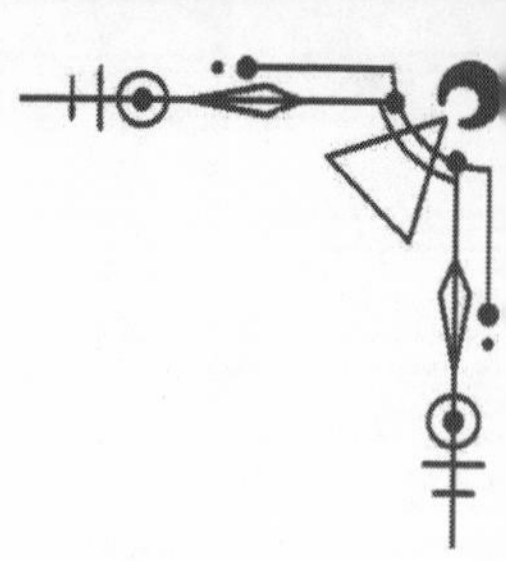

CHAPTER 31

NICOLAI

Vincent dropped the wooden box as soon as my hands wrapped around it and stalked to a chair pushed in front of the desk. His breaths were heavy, like he'd just ran clear across the Row to get here. My chest still heaved for different reasons. He glanced at Milla, giving her no more than a nod.

"Address my wife properly," I snapped as I dropped the box on my desk. I didn't care if we were no longer legally married. Milla was mine until she turned me away. And no one, no matter the dire situation we might face, would treat her as anything less than what she was.

She sat with her legs crossed in that chair and her graceful arms draped over the armrest. Her hair had already returned its luster from her time in Hightower, falling in golden-brown loops over her shoulder. Forget princess, she looked like a damn queen. And I'd just fucked her across this desk five minutes ago.

"Good morning, Mrs. Attano."

"Morning, Vincent, and please, call me Camilla." She gave me a

look, addressing me silently to relax. "Did something happen?"

He nodded as my fingers pressed against the polished wood, reaching for the air inside to assess its contents. I worried if the Watch had left something behind, it could be rigged, but my remnant showed nothing as sinister as my first assumption. Paper rustled inside. A slight resistance of an object that had the distinguishable shape of a pocket watch.

"We found this during the clean-up," Vincent explained. "Thought it was just something from one of the offices in the warehouses, but it was too clean. Like someone had just left it there."

"Have you opened it?" I asked.

He shook his head. "Sabina wanted you to check it out first."

The bleeder queen was well acquainted with the unique abilities of all kinds of remnants. She knew as a bender I could sense the shape of the air inside something concealed and decipher if it was a threat or not. In the past, she'd requested the help of my men who had a similar ability, controlling the wind.

Unconcerned, I unlocked the brass clasps and opened the box. Inside, I found exactly what I'd felt with my remnant. A gold watch was placed on top of a stack of papers. Setting the jewelry aside, I went first to the folded parchment.

Milla took the watch to inspect it while I read the note, written with fine penmanship.

"What does it say?" Milla asked.

"It's a warning. They're going to kill Regulus tonight," I told her. "It says if I can find him before the time runs out, I can take him back to the Row with no repercussions. No backlash. The Watch will stand down until then. After, if we are still on their side, they'll assume our business is hostile and will respond to the threat of our trespassing accordingly."

A knot formed in my throat. I barely knew the Mirth remnant, and yet I still felt responsible for what would happen to him, for leaving him behind. They were playing me as my uncle claimed they would. I couldn't look the other way if I tried. The OIC had sent a challenge, but I had to wonder . . . *Why?*

I read the bottom line out loud to her. "*What time is it?*"

With the flick of her finger, she opened the gilded covering and read the clock face. "The needles point to nine o'clock."

"It's nearly noon already." The bleeder pointed out. "Do you plan on playing their game?"

"Of course he does," Milla murmured. A small sigh left her. "The problem is, will the OIC play by their rules? Will they let you through the Districts without retaliating?"

My last conversation with Regulus in the carriage replayed itself in my head. He'd accused me of only caring about my family, that my choices had inadvertently affected countless others, including his own people. He'd called me selfish, and I had owned that title, knowing it was the only way I'd get Milla back.

But was it for Milla now that I did nothing? Or was it my fear to face the other side of the river without the security of my Row behind me? This man had sacrificed himself for all of us. Had proven he had twice the brawn than I could claim. If the OIC was giving us an opportunity to take him back, perhaps we owed it to him to at least try.

No. We couldn't leave him. Not when a door of opportunity had cracked open.

"If we do this," I said, "there are no rules. We do what it takes to find Regulus and bring him back."

"He could be anywhere," Vincent said with his hands gesturing wide. "You only have until nine if the watch indicates his final hour."

"And we're only allowed after dark," I mentioned. One of the few rules I'd left out on the initial reading. Along with, "They've also stated we are to stay out of the residential areas. Business strips only."

"That narrows it down," Milla said. "The only place for business would be the Capital Grounds. Though even then, there are a hundred businesses with a hundred basements and just as many stockrooms. There truly is no telling where they've hidden him."

She turned the watch over in hand, thinking. But we could keep guessing until the sun went down. Meanwhile, I needed to prepare for the evening. There'd been no rule specifying how many men I could take with me, only that we were to be gone when time ran out. I'd need guns with me to search the Grounds, guns to watch the train, and hells knew my wife wouldn't let me do this alone. I'd need the family around her, people she trusted in case she lost control of her remnant.

"We can speculate later," I said, sharper than intended. Just thinking about letting her near the Districts pulled the leash on my temper taut. "I need to get home and meet with the family. We'll need to notify Marcus as well that we'll need him after hours. Your brother will need to prepare the train."

Pocketing the note, I reached for our coats. Vincent stood and muttered something about seeing himself out. Milla watched me light my cigarillo as she grabbed her coat.

"I'm coming, you know."

Deep breath.

"I know," was all I managed to say.

She smiled, and it somehow lit up all the darkness haunting my soul. "The safest place for me is by your side, Nicolai."

"Not if they keep using me as bait to get to you," I clipped. "We could very well be walking into a trap. They want to take you back, Camilla. This morning was evidence of that enough."

"Then I won't leave the train, but I will not stay across the river, too far to help you should something go seriously wrong. Besides," she crossed her arms, "I know the Grounds better than anyone. You need my expertise."

I wanted to say I needed her alive above all else and out of the hands of the Firenze who seemed interested in her in more way than one, but I'd learned to pick my battles with the spoiled little heiress. She'd sneak on the train if I forbade her. Better to take her bargain and at least know she was contained and guarded.

"You don't leave the train," I repeated her words.

"You have my word."

If that's all she would give me, I'd have to take it. Slipping her hand around my arm, I led us out the office, asking Luther to gather the family at home. They'd be easier to brief all at once.

"I need to make a stop on the way home," I told them.

"Where to?" Bellamy asked as we reached the carriage, still parked in front of the offices.

"The old industrial park." Milla shot me a look, but I beckoned her inside the car before I explained. Some things were better left to speak for themselves.

AMONG ALL THE businesses and homes on our payroll, there was one street gang that had grown despite our influence, making their own name in the Row. A group of young men that had banded together in the skeleton of the old foundries that had moved when the Row was given to descendants and the natives moved south.

Milla was understandably confused as we pulled up to the

long-abandoned park still standing on the edge of town. I helped her out as we came to a stop.

"What are we doing here, Nico?"

Instead of answering right away, I whistled a particular pattern and waited.

Moments later, the buildings groaned. Metal shifted and scraped; concealed entryways formed as makeshift walls rolled out the way. My gaze lifted to the roofs, to the guns aimed at the road. They lowered when they realized it was me.

"Mr. Attano." A young man appeared from the gap in the building, with a dozen of his cadre following behind him. Each wore a gold handkerchief somewhere on their person. Some in the faded jackets they wore over a worn-out suits, others in their back pockets or in a band around their caps.

"It's good to see you, sir," the leader of them greeted us as they flooded the broken road.

"Rook." I shook the hand he offered to me, though his green eyes were no longer looking my way, but to the woman perched at my side. Letting go of his hand, I placed it on the small of her back. "This is my wife, Camilla."

"Rook Canary, leader of the Canary Boys, at your service, ma'am." He bowed slightly, taking her hand in his to kiss it gently. "It's a great pleasure to meet you."

Camilla smiled. "The pleasure is all my mine, Mr. Rook."

I could have sworn the tips of his ears turned pink.

"Easy, boy," I said with a smile, to insist my threat was light. "Where's Finn?"

Rook looked around at his boys. "Don't know. Must be out spending all that money you paid him for the Hightower job. You're welcome, by the way. Would you like to come inside while you wait for him?"

"We're actually not here for a visit. I need information, and in exchange, I'll have some jobs for your boys to do in the Row. Pays well."

"They always do." Rook smiled and rubbed his hands together. The skin around his nails was peeling, dry as bone from the cold and laborious work.

"A few months ago, I asked you for information that would give me leverage over a deal I was working against the Firenzes." I glanced at Milla and found her brow raised in a silent question. I nodded to confirm her suspicion. "You told me you knew they were experimenting on children in the Wet District and gave me evidence and first-hand accounts."

Some of the swagger in his shoulders faltered. "Look, sir, none of us are proud of selling ourselves to the alchemists, but we had to survive—"

"I'm not judging you, Rook, and I understand. I promise, I've done far worse for money even when I didn't need it. I just need to know why the Firenzes were experimenting on descendants?"

At first, I'd just assumed it was glint stuff, but if they had discovered a way to create a Siphon like Vesper had described, if they were manufacturing remnants, then perhaps Rook and his crew had been involved in something far more sinister than I ever imagined. Perhaps that was why Lavern backed off so quickly that day I wed Milla in her courtyard.

Rook sucked his teeth and ran a hand over the stubble covering his jaw. "They made us use our remnants in different ways to study the spectrum of our gifts. They'd take blood samples sometimes, plug us up to these machines that made odd ticking sounds, nothing painful or invasive. Then they'd pay us and send us back across the river. They'd pay us for referrals as well."

"Was the Society ever involved?"

"All the time. It was one reason I felt safe doing it, knowing a member of the law was there."

I cursed to myself silently.

"Do you remember what kind of remnants you sent them, Rook?" Milla asked.

"All of them," he replied.

His answer was a punch to the gut. Hells knew what they had discovered by taking advantage of mere children. The ones who didn't have families to ask questions, the ones desperate for coppers. I'd done bad things, things that kept me awake at night, but this was a different kind of evil.

I reached in my coat for a cigarillo. "Thank you, and as promised, I'll be in touch with a job for your boys. I've got weapons I need distributed to the river businesses. Can you handle it?"

He tipped his cap at me. "Just tell us when and where. You know where to find us."

I nodded and murmured a farewell to the rest of his boys who had been listening. Rook treated Milla with a parting kiss on her hand. Making a show of my sigh, I walked back to the carriage to open the door for her.

"If he ever does you wrong, Mrs. Attano, you know where to find *me*."

"*Rook*!"

A mischievous smirk flashed my way before he retreated to the safety of his home. Milla grinned, amused by my irritation.

She laughed. "He's quite brave. I'll give him that."

"Sometimes idiocy disguises itself as courage." Noting her wide smile, I asked, "Should I be worried, princess?"

She shrugged. "It's good to know I have options."

Spoiled little heiress.

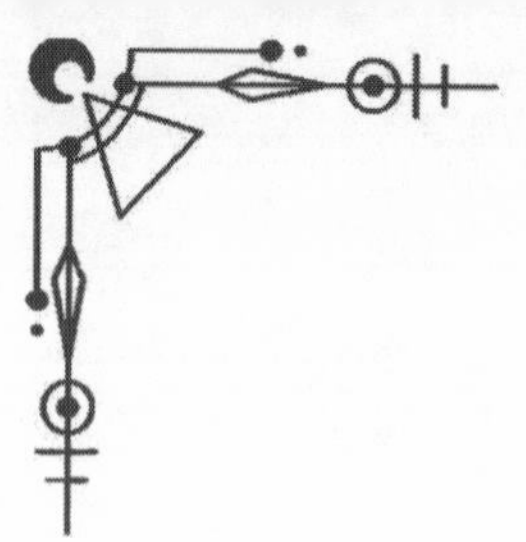
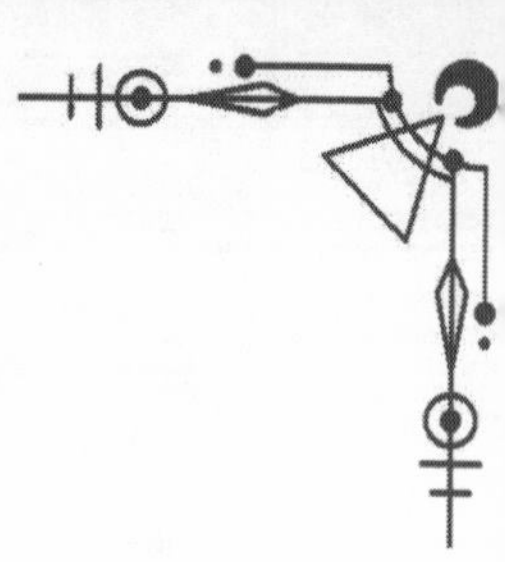

CHAPTER 32

NICOLAI

We waited at the station with twenty hired benders and my cousins. Aramis was in the engine car with Marcus, helping him shovel coal into the boiler to get the train running. They'd drive the Iron Saint through the city to the runaround track, where Marcus would assist him in turning the train around and waiting down at the Main Station, keeping the locomotive hot for a quick getaway if needed.

Her brother had kept his distance from me, opting out of taking the carriage with us. Instead, Esme let him borrow the bike again, and I wondered if he had somehow gained pity from her, especially considering the damage he'd caused the last time.

"Alright." I paced in front of our crew as the sun dipped behind the brick walls of the Industrial Station, assuming their attention. "We're to make this job fucking quick. I want fifteen men guarding the train while it's stopped. Five will come with me to the Grounds. Adler and Gideon will stay with Camilla. Luther comes with me."

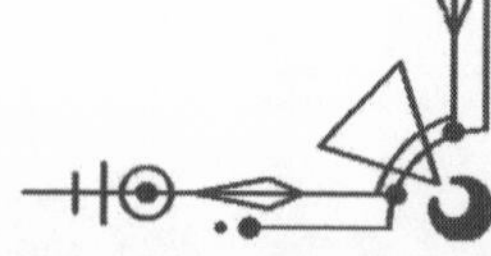

As they nodded along, I looked at my wife, who stood still at the edge of the platform, watching me pace. "There is nothing," I said to the group, "*nothing* more important than protecting her. We'll do our best to find and rescue Regulus, but the priority is Camilla. And if anything happens to her, I'll leave all your sorry asses across the river for the Watch to deal with. Is that clear?"

A murmur of *yessirs* softened some of the tension coiled in my chest. They were probably wondering why I bothered letting her come along in the first place if she was so valuable. I'd wondered the same at least a hundred times since she expressed her adamancy in tagging along.

"I can protect myself, Attano. You forget what I can do."

I nearly rolled my eyes. She'd choose to be confident in her gifts now in front of my men, but if the time came, I worried if she'd maintain that composure. Instead of questioning her, I stood at her side.

Slipping my hands around her waist, my gloves grazed the soft leather of the fitted vest she wore over a long-sleeved black shirt. Those bewitching hands of hers were concealed beneath similarly made gloves that laced up her forearms. She was a gentle stunner in a silk dress and a lethal beauty in black leather, with all her curves on display as the material clung to her form.

"I haven't forgotten, Milla. Neither has Felix Firenze."

Her chin lifted an inch. She pointed to the steaming locomotive. "My train." She cocked her head toward my cousins. "My family." Her hand drifted to my chest. "My husband." She gripped my tie and yanked me closer. "And my choice. If I can protect the things I love most in this world, I will not hide just because I am afraid of what might take them away."

There was absolutely no arguing with that, and she smiled knowingly. That little smirk that made me foolish.

Fuck. I was so in love with her—and I think she just confessed . . . she loved me, too.

"Boss," Luther said behind me. "We should head out to make the most of the moonlight."

I nodded and forced myself to step back. If I wanted to make this quick tonight, I'd need to push her out of my thoughts and focus on the job. "Stay on the train," I whispered.

She stood on her toes to place a grazing kiss on my lips. "Don't give me a reason to leave."

"Deal."

"*Cousin*," Luther called again. He was stressed, and rightly so.

I gave her one last look before turning to board the car behind hers. She'd stay in the suite while the rest of us boarded the single passenger car pulling behind it. Only two cars besides the tender box. It wouldn't take long for the engine to get moving without the added weight of its usual load.

"Nico, wait!" Milla called before I stepped off the loading deck. She handed me the pocket watch from the box. "I've been thinking about the first place you should look. There's a name etched onto this watch, Fielder. I know him. He's the clock tower master." She clicked the top of the watch, and the back popped off. "I was messing with the needles and realized I couldn't move them. When I looked in the back, the cogs were missing, but there was something else." She handed it back for me to see for myself.

A key.

The watch wasn't a watch at all, but a holder for a small brass key.

"When the note asked for the time, I think that was a clue, not a question. Fielder is known to be a remnant sympathizer. He was married to a descendant before she died a few years ago. I hope this doesn't mean he's joined his lover because of his loyalties."

"Brilliant, Milla." I took the key from her and kissed her knuckles. "Thank you. We'll go there first."

"Be careful." Her smile was a brief flicker before she turned and boarded the other car.

We reached the Main Station at exactly nightfall. The streetlamps hadn't been lit, cloaking the streets to the Grounds in a murky darkness. Moonlight spilled through the shapes of wispy clouds, illuminating the cobbles in patchy spots. Our boots were silent against the stone, passing blocks of homes that had turned off their lights. The Districts had gone dark, no doubt alerted of our presence tonight.

I bent the moonlight to shine over the street, thickening the shadows behind the wrought iron fence line separating the apartments lining the roads. My eyes fell on the abandoned carriages parked in front of the homes, watching for any surprises. If the OIC had trained the people here to hate us, the Society wasn't the only threat we needed to be wary of.

"I fucking hate this," Luther whispered behind me. "Let's get this done and get the hells out of here."

The clock tower chimed seven times. We had two hours, but the journey on foot to the Grounds had eaten away at least fifteen minutes. Transferring Regulus—if we found him—would take twice the time if he was hurt. In actuality, we had far less time than the bell gave us credit.

The clock tower stood at the point of a triangular strip of government buildings. The rest of the markets and storefronts surrounding the shape, with the point opening wide to the riverwalk. In a way, the clock tower overlooked the River Ada, while the rest of the Grounds stood in its shadow. The moon pierced a clock-face we couldn't see from the rear of the marketplace.

The last time I'd been here, I'd escorted Milla to the House of Records. The same building that stood in front of me now. Who would have thought her past would have been as important as it is now? The breadcrumbs she had followed led to so much more than either of us could have fathomed.

"Eyes on the roofs," I whispered, taking the street that wove to the right of the House of Records. Either way would have led us to the tower, but the shadows angled toward the right side, and if we were ambushed, we'd have no cover besides the cloak of darkness.

But so far, the note had been truthful. Not a single guard roamed the streets, nor did I see a flicker of movement in the windows or on the roofs of the adjacent businesses. The center was completely barren. Eerily quiet—unnaturally so.

Sounds of the restless currents of the Ada met us as we reached the tower. A pair of arching, mahogany doors built into the stony structure composing the tower made the entrance at the base, with brass handles gleaming in the silver light.

They were locked, but as Milla suspected, Fielder's key was exactly what we needed. This had to be the place they kept Regulus. But a clock, of all places? It wasn't the strangest fact of the evening, but it made my questions multiply far faster than I could solve them.

All six of us took a collective breath as we entered. It was pitch-black, but one of the men found a kerosine lamp and started a small flame. Even with the small reach of light, it was evident where the path led us next.

Up.

"*Shitting Saints*." Luther grumbled his displeasure at the stairwell stretching higher than the light could reveal and sighed before ascending the first step. "Next time, I'm staying with Milla."

We'd already eaten away thirty minutes, realized by the deep vibrations humming down the throat of the tower as the bells rang once more. A chorus of something sharper—more pressing—joined them.

I passed Luther on the stairs, taking the steps two at a time, because hidden behind the solemn chime of the clock bells was a song I had sung once before myself. One I knew from memory.

The scream of a suffering man.

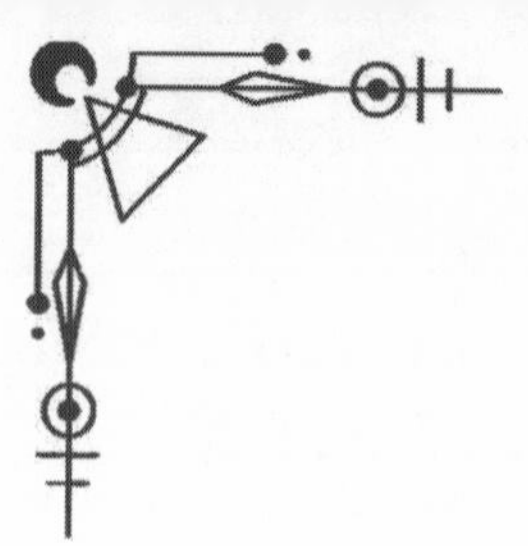
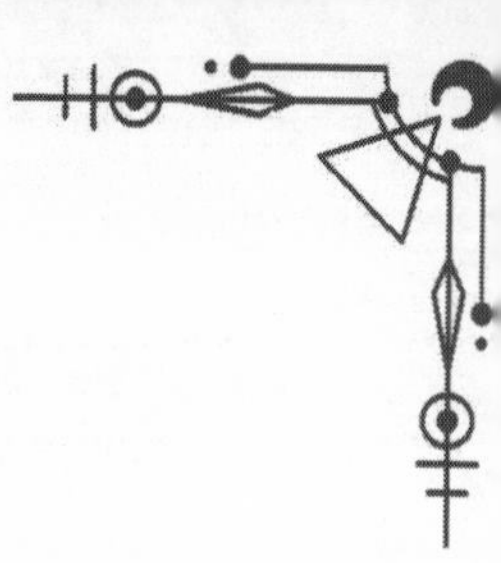

CHAPTER 33
CAMILLA

As soon as Nico and his men stepped off the passenger car, Aramis and Marcus went to work. Using a few of the Attano Benders, they separated the tender car from the one I hid inside with Adler and Gideon. My brother and our usual driver would drive the engine to the roundhouse, where a turntable would redirect the train to head back to the Row. Only two cars could fit on the round platform—the engine and the tender—so we had to wait until they came back for us to reconnect.

We sat in silence and shrouded in darkness, too worried to show a flame in the windows and reveal our presence. The men in our car had let themselves out to guard it with the rest, the number of them enough of an excuse for the requirement of two passenger cars instead of one and to distract from the idea anyone else—like myself—would still be inside.

The city was so quiet, we could hear the chime of the clock tower all the way in the Main Station from the Grounds. The first sound noted the hour just as Nico left. Then, thirty minutes later,

the song of Lynchaven sung from the belfry. The three of us sat on the floor of the train car; neither of us had moved between the hour chime and the half-hour mark.

Gideon nudged my laced boot with the toe of his own, seated across from me. "You going to take that tab your brother sneaked you?"

My fist curled in my pocket around the pill. How he'd noticed Aramis slipping it inside my hand before we boarded was lost to me. My brother had expressed his worries of leaving my remnant *unguarded* in a situation like tonight, where discretion was imperative. No matter how much I practiced keeping it down, the power simmering in my veins seemed to flood every instinct when we came face-to-face with danger.

I shook my head. "No. We might need a little Chaos tonight if Nico doesn't get back in time. I can't risk being powerless." I promised I'd protect this train, and I intended to keep my word—even if it risked the safety of the Districts. Even if it meant exposing myself.

Gideon nodded. "Glad to hear it. We need you, Milla." It was difficult to make out his face in the spare bits of moonlight sneaking through the breaks in the blinds covering the windows, but there was a relief in his voice as he spoke.

Warmth spread across my chest at his admittance. It felt good to be needed outside of my family name for once. "I kept it just in case I can't control it. I'd hate to hurt anyone nearby."

"Of course." His voice quieted a level. "I wouldn't judge you if you took it now, Milla. Just want you to be comfortable."

"Thanks, Gideon."

Though I had a remnant like the descendants of the Row, I'd always consider the Districts my home. I'd grown up here, knew most of the working men and women in the Wet District. They were friends and clients, people that were neither evil nor malicious despite the government representing their interest.

The Order of Inner Courts spoke for this city, governed this Isle, but a river dividing our worlds didn't make us enemies. And I hoped, when the time came—and it would come—they would have the courage to stand up for what was right. That what happened on the Continent would never happen here because they knew the truth and wouldn't let manipulative men in high seats tell them what to believe and how to think.

Until that reckoning hour, however, I'd protect them any way I could, starting with keeping the fight away from those who rested in this restless city.

"Gideon?" I whispered in the dark. "Don't tell Aramis I didn't take it. Or tell Nico that he offered it to begin with." We were all skating over thin ice after Sabina's.

A long exhale left him. "He's my boss. I won't lie if my cousin asks me, Milla, but I won't bring it up."

I scoffed. "Fair enough."

After what felt like an eternity, the car moved. A sharp wind whipped through the car as the benders remnants pushed the railcar up the tracks to connect with the engine once more, which was now facing the opposite direction. A groan of metal rubbing metal rumbled through the floor as they attached it to the tender.

"That went smoothly," Adler said quietly beside me. He stood to stretch, peering out a window to assess the progress.

"Perhaps the OIC was honest in their intentions for once," I said.

The brothers shook their heads.

"Doubtful," Adler said. "They're waiting for something. Don't lower your guard until we're back across the river."

I gazed out the sliver of space he'd made between the curtain and the window, watching as the Attanos' men surrounded the car. Each held shotguns against their chests, scanning the area with sharp eyes.

The door to the gangway connection opened and shut quickly as Aramis stepped inside. His clothes clung to his form with the sweat from working the engine. Despite the freezing night, he was flushed from the effort. He gestured to the cousins. "Alright, I did my job. Time for you two to get out there."

"Thought you were helping Marcus drive?" Gideon asked.

"Marcus has been doing this longer than I have been alive. He doesn't need help," Aramis clipped.

"Nico told us to stay with Milla—"

"I'll be with her. You are of better use with the men actually protecting the car."

They glanced at each other, communicating some wordless exchange.

"No," Adler said.

Aramis rolled his eyes. "Suit yourselves." He started unbuttoning his shirt then, ripping it off his chest to toss over an empty chair. "We still got the extra whiskey in the desk?" he asked me.

I shrugged and moved out of his way so he could search the drawers, eventually finding what he needed. He took a shot straight from the bottle before placing it on top of the desk.

"You shouldn't be drinking," I said.

"And you shouldn't be here, but when has a Marchese ever been reasonable?"

Unable to argue against his point, I crossed the length of the car to sit near the back—away from him. On the wall nearby was a clock, and I dreaded every lonely second as the hands ticked closer toward the ninth hour.

"Where are they?" I murmured. It shouldn't have taken this

long if I had been right about the location. Hells if I was wrong—or if Nico had gotten in some sort of trouble on the way there—we'd wouldn't know until it was far too late.

My mind filled with every awful scenario until my head ached.

"He'll come back, Milla." Gideon came to stand beside me, his voice soft and assuring. His hand gripped my shoulder. "Nico always finds a way. You can count on him."

His smile had always been infectious—his faith, however, was not.

The door to the connection opened once more. A bender who'd been guarding the car. "We got trouble. Watchmen, a good legion of them, blocking the way back to the Row."

"Wondering when they'd show," Adler grumbled. "Did they say what they want?"

He nodded. "They say cars must be searched when they enter and leave the Districts. Said Mr. Attano was informed of these new parameters weeks ago."

Gideon stood in the aisle. "Not passenger cars. That's for freight cars and they know it."

The man shrugged. "Just passing along their—"

A bullet ripped through his neck. He wobbled slightly, his eyes going wide as he realized in that half second before death claimed him what had happened—and collapsed across the gangway.

I gasped, and the whole place erupted afterwards.

Gunshots went off with a fury outside, and we fell to the floor to avoid the shattered glass as stray bullets struck the windows and the walls of the train. Gideon darted to the back door of the car, guarding it since it was open and exposed while Adler crawled his way to the other.

The Watch had most likely asked our man to send a message to figure out which car was still in use. I cursed the simplicity of their tactics while ripping off my gloves.

"*Camilla*," Aramis growled and glanced at my hands, already primed from the reaction of my racing heart.

"I can do this, Aramis," I hissed. "Let me out and I'll finish them all." I *could* do it. I'd practiced controlling the ebb and flow of fire from my fingers, knew how to shape it into objects of annihilation. Fire was always unpredictable and dangerous, and I wasn't perfect—no, far from as good as I should be. The look in Aramis's eyes insisted he'd doubted I could contain it, but if I could save even one of our men at the risk of exposing what I was while possibly taking out half the station, it would be worth it.

"Not even as a last resort," he growled.

I rolled my eyes. The entire point of me being here was to be a last resort. What about that had he not understood?

Living with him for the last twenty-one years had trained me for this. He'd never believe in me. There was nothing I could do that would prove to him I was capable—nor was it my responsibility. I'd learned to have my mind long ago, and when it came to my remnant, I'd have to learn to have faith in myself again. Even if he didn't.

A line of bullets aimed at the hinges pelted the door behind us. Gideon moved aside to avoid being grazed, but the door fell open to reveal a pair of watchmen. They reached inside and snatched him before he could retaliate. Gideon screamed out as they touched the bare skin of his throat with their gloves.

"Gideon!" I rose to my knees to lunge after them.

My brother pulled me back down. "You'll not risk yourself for a fucking Attano!"

My glare bore into him. He had no authority over me anymore, though he didn't seem to realize that either. "I *am* an Attano."

My brother's gripped tightened, but I jerked out of his hold and darted toward the empty doorway in the back of the car. Adler was too busy guarding the front, shooting and dodging incoming bullets.

Gunsmoke curled in the night air, but no one lingered behind the car as I peered out, searching for Gideon. Flashes from their guns briefly illuminated the haze, like dry lightning in a cloud.

Stay in the car.

I muttered a silent apology to Nico and climbed down to the tracks, but I couldn't sit by and let the guards take Gideon. Considering how they treated descendants? We'd be right back here in a few weeks, playing another game of risk and wagers.

Pulling my revolver from its sheath and my hood over my head, I remained low, crossing over the tracks to swiftly find cover behind a parked railcar. Moonlight cut beams of silver over the yard as passing clouds drifted across the star-filled sky. Already, small flames twisted between my fingers. But they didn't do any harm—not until I told them to.

A force of wind slapped my form as the benders used their remnants to fight back. Their windstorm turned up dust between the gravel, worsening the visibility. Sparks bit at my cheek as lead bullets skimmed the aluminum wall of the railcar. There seemed to be no line to define sides. I waited until the bullets paused, for the watchmen to reload, before running to another car parked idle on the tracks. Gideon and his attackers were still nowhere to be found.

Someone shouted an order to withdraw. Footsteps charged toward my location, disturbing the gravel between the tracks. With no further cover, I went to the railcar door and pulled—finding it locked.

I let my fire spill from my fingertips, corroding the lock, drawing back the flames as I practiced before so it wouldn't take out the entire door as well. With the men nearly upon me, I quickly slipped inside the empty car and crouched between two rows of leather seats, keeping my head below the window. Their voices carried through the thin glass.

"Not here . . . Came alone."

"Is he done?"

"Hold out a few more minutes."

"*Giver and Greed.*"

Their words were clipped and sparse, dimming as they walked quickly past the car. A quick peek over the edge of the window and I was alone once more.

"Where are you, Gideon?" I murmured, my words fogging the glass. Moving to the other side, I scanned the darkened marshaling yard for any sign of the cousin. Dead men from both sides scattered the empty tracks, but none of them resembled Gideon. My heart broke for them, anyway, knowing Nico would have to notify every single one of their families. Such an unnecessary way to die.

The car rocked as the wind from the remaining benders picked up, a strength joining them that hadn't been there before. The windows rattled, and I covered my head just in time as every single one of them imploded from the gale.

I didn't know which of the Attanos had that kind of strength—only experienced with Nico's. But this breeze didn't feel like his, a kind I'd know anywhere. The yard went still then; the dust stirred from the gust settled some to clear the view. I stood slowly, inching toward the door with my gun still in hand.

He appeared from a haze of dust.

Gideon limped down the tracks. His face bloody, his clothes shredded and falling off his body. He winced as his right foot took a step. I jumped out of the side of the car and ran to help him.

"Gideon, are you alright?" I asked. He blinked several times at me, as if not believing his eyes.

"I'm nearly drained," he groaned. "I need to get back . . . You shouldn't be out here."

Behind him, the flash of a gun drew my attention. The silver barrel caught the moonlight. But before the watchman pulled the trigger, I shoved Gideon to the side with my shoulder and fired first.

He dropped, and the last gun went quiet in the yard.

"Thanks," Gideon gasped out from the ground. I pulled him up and threw his arm around my shoulders to assist him back to the train.

"Was that you who created that gust?" I asked.

He nodded. "I had three men on top of me, took turns beating me to a bloody pulp. One of them stabbed me three times in the side—"

"Hells, Gideon!"

"I'll be fine. It wasn't deep. He was going for nine. Heard him counting down. Before the glint from his blade could take effect, I used all the power I had left to push them off. I think I might have sent them flying for a few blocks."

I sighed. "Good."

The train came into view just as we rounded a parked car. Steam billowed from the chimney as Marcus tended the boiler and kept the engine hot. The watchmen had all but disappeared, and I couldn't help but wonder—what was the point of this? Why attack just to retreat a few minutes later?

The distant chime of the clock tower informed me it had been much longer than a few minutes. My adrenaline distorted the perception of time, making it difficult to think past the next second.

Adler saw us coming and jumped out of the private car to assist me. Taking Gideon's full weight, I slipped out from under his arm and was about to board after them . . . until something caught my eye down the tracks.

A watchman crawled from *under* the train, his pale cheeks sullied with black. He glanced around, a pistol in his hand, when he caught me watching him.

"Stop!" I said, my gun pointed at him. "What are you doing?"

He froze, eyes wide. Dressed in a similar fashion to the rest of the Watch with a black uniform, he didn't wear a cape or a mask. This one was of no rank or importance. They'd left him behind.

On top of that, he was soaking wet.

"Tell me what is going on, and I'll let you live," I told him, keeping the tone of my voice as calm as I could.

His jaw clenched while his chest rose and fell with quick breaths. The grip on his gun adjusted.

"Don't even think about it," a man hissed behind him. One of the hired benders appeared from the haze that hadn't quite cleared yet, his own weapon aimed at the trespasser.

"We can read your thoughts," I lied. There wasn't a remnant that could do such a thing in our group, but he didn't have to know that. "We can take your thoughts, or you can give them freely—and walk away tonight. The choice is yours."

Before either the bender or I could react, the man pointed his gun to his temple, and shot himself.

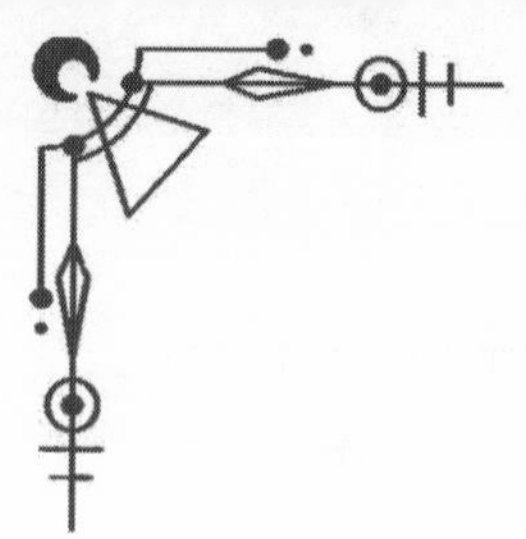
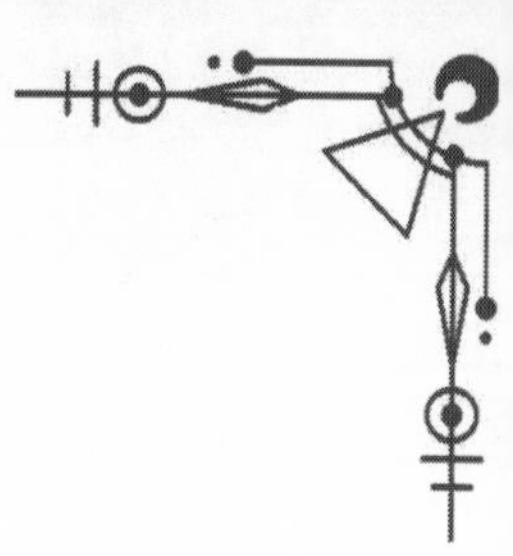

CHAPTER 34

NICOLAI

My chest burned from the labor of ascending at least ten flights of stairs at a running pace. Behind me, Luther was in worse shape. His gangly frame hunched over as he grabbed at the handrail for aid, every step an effort. At last, we came to a door at the top of the stairs, the first platform before another set of steps.

Using the key on yet another locked door, we came to a hallway that wrapped around the four sides of the tower. On one side was a solid inner wall, on the other, the opal glassed face of the clock. A mechanism stretched between the two walls, turning the long hands around the numbered circle.

The silhouette of a man was pinned on the outside.

"Regulus!" I beat the glass behind him. He appeared to be suspended by the wrists, hanging from the frame.

At the sound of my voice, his body jolted.

"He's alive," I spoke more out of surprise. "How do we get on the outside? There must be some kind of maintenance ledge . . ."

Way ahead of me, Luther scanned the outer wall, the space between only big enough for one man to fit through at a time. He slid a bolt from a built-in exit designed to look like it was part of the wall. "Here." He stood back to let me through the small crawl space.

Peering out, I stared into a grate. A narrow outcrop ran beneath the massive clock face, no more than a few strips of metal separating the long fall to the ground below.

Luther cleared his throat. "I'd do a lot of things for you, Nico, but you couldn't make me walk across that."

"Appreciate it, cousin," I replied. Gritting my teeth, I pulled off my coat to prevent the wind catching it like a sail and slipped outside before I could think about the possibility of becoming part of the pavement.

One hand flat against the clock face, I sidestepped along the tower, trying my best to ignore the frigid wind breathing beneath my clothes. *Fuck*, it was cold. Especially up here, where the elements were unrestrained.

"Nico, wait!" Regulus called out. "Stop the clock!"

"What?"

"I'm going to fall!" he shrieked, looking up at his hands. I followed his gaze, where the hour hand was nearly at the ninth number. The minute hand ticked slowly behind it, but the shorter, sharpened hand of the hour skimmed the rope tying Regulus to the steel framework composing the clock.

If I moved him, it might be enough to snap the fraying rope. Just the wind swaying his body along the sharp edge of the hand was enough to begin the process.

"There's a room just up the stairs," he said quickly, "with cogs and wires. They took me there. Stop the clock first, maybe try to wind it back so the hand won't rub against the rope. Then go up to the observation deck and pull me up."

"Shout if it gets worse, Regulus. I'll have a man out here to try to catch you, just in case."

"Just stop the fucking clock, Attano!"

I ducked back inside and ordered two benders to stand on the ledge and wait. The group was reluctant to volunteer, so I selected two men and reminded all of them who paid their salaries. They slipped outside with no further motivation.

Meanwhile, the rest of us pressed down the narrow hall and back to the stairs, heading to the next floor where the clock room was located. There was an entire floor dedicated to the workings of the hands. A large table of gear trains held various cogs that turned at a steady pace.

"How the hells does this work?"

Luther nudged something on the floor behind the other side of the table. "He might have been able to help."

Around the mechanism lay a dead man in a pool of his own blood. A knife jutted out his back. With a mane of grey hair and wrinkled skin, I figured this might be the owner of the watch in my pocket. Fielder, Milla had called him. A remnant sympathizer. Could he have tried to help Regulus and got in trouble for it?

I looked back to the task at hand. "Just destroy it all."

"No, wait," a voice wheezed. The old man's eyes fluttered.

"Fielder?" I crouched beside him.

"You could speed it up if you . . . hit the wrong . . . cog. There is . . . a balance." He forced the words out in shaky breaths. "As long as the pendulum swings . . . the clock will sing."

"How do I wind it back?"

"The lever." He pointed a shaky finger toward a mechanism that propelled from a gear train. "Each turn is a minute." He hacked a mouthful of blood across the unfinished pavers. When he fell quiet, the sound of the clock—the tick-tock beat counting down the seconds to Regulus's demise—was suddenly all I could hear.

"Keep him warm, Luther," I whispered, tossing him my coat. There was nothing to do for the man but make him comfortable on the doorstep of death.

I studied the back of the mechanism more closely. A metal wheel spun within the arms of an escapement, attached to a string tied to a pendulum that must have swung beneath the floor we stood upon. Shaped like a star, the wheel caught on the sides of the arms as the pendulum pushed them open one at a time, side to side.

I shot the string connecting the wheel to the weight, leaving the rest intact. There was no more ticking, no movement of the cogs. The entire clock went still.

Regulus shouted something incoherent outside.

I snapped at the nearest man. "Wind it back as far as you can and don't stop until we've got him down. The rest of you, get to the top!"

We weren't far from the hour's completion, but it would hopefully give the rope enough slack against the hour hand for us to pull him up without it snapping as well. The stairs led to a ladder, and my cousin and I climbed one at a time up to the belfry, where a deck wrapped around five copper bells of various sizes.

A banister surrounded the area. We both dashed to the side where Regulus hung from the iron baluster, gradually giving the rope some resistance to pull him up. The Mirth remnant cried out as we moved him, inch by inch.

"It's splitting!" he shrieked. I peered over the edge, swallowed back bile when I saw the drop from the height of the deck, and realized he was right. The rope frayed where the hour hand had rubbed against it.

"This might feel strange at first, but trust me," I called out to him.

He whimpered, completely helpless to my demands. I gathered the wind from my remnant and pushed him sideways, so he swung across the clock face like a human pendulum.

"Are you out of your *fucking* mind, Attano?" Regulus's shrill voice echoed over the entire city.

"Stay here in case the rope unties from the banister," I told Luther, ignoring the screaming shifter. "The momentum puts less strain on the rope, Regulus. At least . . . *I think.*" I muttered the last part to myself. Science had never been my strongest subject, but I could at least use the force of the wind to support the weight of him as he swung from side to side. Thank the saints no one was out here to witness this. I could only imagine how this looked from the ground.

Regulus swung to the right, nearly hitting the side of the steel framework. I pushed a rush of wind to send his momentum in the opposite direction. Leaping over the handrail, my right hand clung to the banister, and my false hand reached to catch him.

He reached the crest, and I sent a final gust to push him a little higher and grabbed him by the wrist. Securely wrapping his forearm, I clutched the banister as he dropped, bracing myself for the full weight of him as it yanked on my arm.

Regulus cried out from the jolt, but I gritted my teeth and held us both against the clock until Luther and the other men reached us, assisting me in pulling him over the edge. We both collapsed across the deck. My arm, fingers, and face were numb from the winter wind fighting against my control of the air.

As I collected my breath and gradually stood to my feet again, they freed the Mirth remnant's wrist from the rope bindings. Regulus crawled on trembling arms off to the side to dry heave. His entire body shook like a struck cord. From the cold, from the fear, from whatever the Society had done to him—the cause wasn't as important as fixing it.

"No time to waste," I barked. "We need to get back to the train."

"He can barely walk—"

"Then carry him!" We might have stopped the clock, but our time here was still running out. The gunshots in the distance did nothing to ease my worries.

I led the group back down the ladder while Luther went on a rampage between the bells, striking them with the handle of his gun and composing a chaotic victory song that sung over the Districts, no doubt letting the city know we'd taken back one of our own. If anything, it would at least alert the rest of our group we were done here.

My boot caught on the limp body of Fielder as I crossed the clock room, having been distracted by the pressing problems of the night. My fingers were too numb to find a pulse, but if he wasn't dead yet, he was about to be.

"You can't do anything for him, boss," Luther said when he finally joined us.

Obviously, but I couldn't just leave him here. Not after he helped us. Not when he was most likely punished for having a heart that cared for both sides of this wretched city.

For those reasons alone, I wrapped the old man in my coat and lifted him over a shoulder and started the long descent down the clock tower.

LIGHTS STRETCHED across the streets as we quickly made our way back to the Main Station. Still carrying the old man with no idea where to leave him, I felt the eyes of the natives behind their windows follow us back to the train. They didn't hide this time, watching boldly as we carried two injured men down the main street leading to the station.

My steps slowed, yet my breathing quickened. The dead weight on my shoulder dragged me down considerably, even with Luther's help.

"You got to leave him, Nico," he muttered. "He's a dead man. He doesn't care where his body is found."

"It's . . . *principle.*" I spat out.

He breathed a curse. We were still several blocks from the station and undoubtedly out of time. But just as I was about to give up, something stirred in the street before us.

The men behind me dropped Regulus to grab their guns as natives appeared in the street. His body hit the cobblestones, and he protested the drop with a groan. I merely lifted my free hand in surrender, insisting we wanted no trouble.

"We're just trying to leave," I called out.

To my surprise, they lifted their hands in return. Free of weapons. I motioned for my men to stand down.

A woman stood in the center of the street. Long grey hair braided over a shoulder lifted in the wind as she pulled her coat around her. "Leave Fielder with us," she whispered. The night was so still, she didn't have to speak very loud for her voice to carry.

I nodded and slowly laid the man's body down in the street.

Two men behind her approached to take him, quickly taking him inside one of the apartments lining the street.

"He advocated for your kind," she said. "They took him a few nights ago. He lived right there." She pointed with her chin to the adjacent flat.

Luther sighed. "Boss . . ."

"Right," I said. "Well, he was bleeding out by the time we got to him. Just wanted to make sure his body was found and taken care of."

"Thank you," she said before tossing something in the air. It landed at my feet.

Keys.

"You can take our carriage the rest of the way. We'll risk the Watch in exchange for your kindness." Her head canted, looking at Regulus struggling to sit up.

"Thank you," I said, before darting to the only car with horses ready to ride. This was a mercy we never saw coming, and Regulus whispered a prayer of thanks to the lost deities of the realm as the men pushed him inside the carriage.

Just as we set off, the steam train's horn whistled twice.

A warning of its departure.

Ordering Regulus to hold on tight inside, I set the horses into a charge.

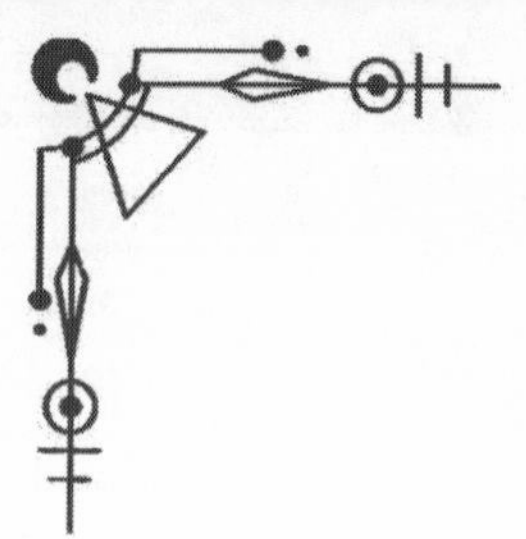
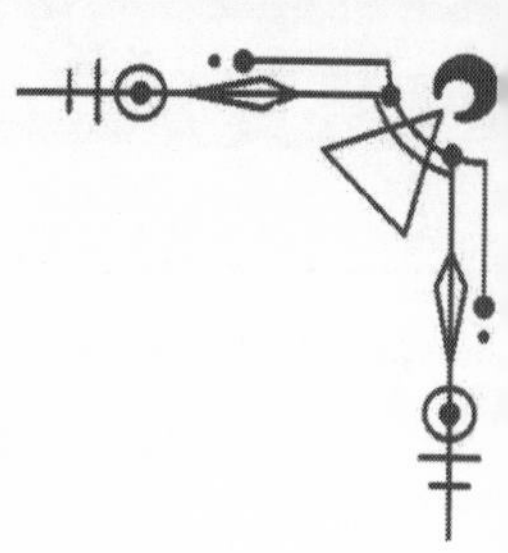

CHAPTER 35
CAMILLA

Why was he underneath the train?

The question bothered me even as one of Nico's men escorted me back into the private car, which was at the caboose now, thanks to the shift in direction. Adler brought Gideon to the passenger car where medical supplies were stored to treat his superficial injuries.

My focus remained on the platform, however, waiting for Nico and the group to appear at any moment. I thought I'd heard the bells of the tower, but the night had been silent since, and I didn't quite know what to make of it.

Through the windowpanes—now empty of glass thanks to the crossfire—my silent pleas were answered.

Nico appeared in front of his men, Luther at his side. His face flashed with concern as he assessed the train, the bullet holes branding the cars. All the tension in his gaze melted when he met mine. I blinked, and he was gone, appearing at my side—inside of the car.

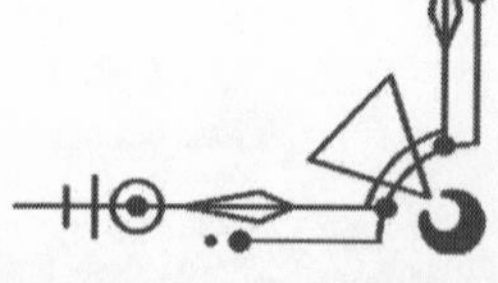

I jumped, my nerves still on edge. He didn't use his time bending skill often, and it always startled me when he did. His arms wrapped around my waist in a desperate embrace, and I forgot the rest of my worries as my hands connected with his neck, assuring myself he was safe at last.

We had done it.

"Finally," Aramis hissed behind me. "At least we can leave now."

"You got him?" I asked. "Regulus."

Nico nodded as his head burrowed into the bend of my shoulder. He was cold all over, like he'd been exposed to the winter weather all night, though for once, he had no holes in his chest. The blood on his shirt belonged to someone else.

"We heard gunshots," he said. "Is everyone alright?"

"We lost some men, Nico. Adler did his best to collect the bodies."

He released me and stepped away, glancing at the men moving a limping Mirth remnant to the car in front of us. "Guess we'll be adding more families to the payroll, then." He mouthed a curse as his focus went distant. "Fuck. Aright, I'll go signal Marcus then. He kept his head low?"

I scoffed. "The engine is the safest place to hide from bullets. He's fine, if the steam from the chimney is a sign."

"Good. Stay in here. The other car looked like a mess."

He opened the door leading to the platform to wave at our driver. As the train moved again, he jumped back into the passenger car, most likely to check on his cousins. Aramis went to the gangway door, as if guarding it.

While I brushed shards of broken glass off a chair, I kept my eyes and ears trained on the marshaling yard in case the Watch returned. But the smoke was clearing now. The moonlight illuminated all the empty spaces between the lines of tracks, and there was no one in sight.

As we picked up speed, Aramis paced near the door.

"Are you okay, brother?" I asked him. He was acting strangely —stranger than normal, anyway.

"I'm fine." He cleared his throat. "Do you hear that?"

"What—" But he cut me off with a finger to his lips, demanding I listen. A rattling sound, like something on the train was loose. The train horn wailed on repeat without pause.

I stood then. The air in the room was churning with the speed of the train. We were coming up to the viaduct. There was no need to go this fast. Leaning out of the window to look ahead, I saw the peaks of the steel framework of the bridge coming up.

I ducked back inside, my jaw quivering from the cold. "Why aren't we slowing for the bridge?" The Industrial Station wasn't far from the viaduct. If we wanted to stop there, we were going much too fast already.

Something wasn't right. I headed toward the door to investigate further, but my brother blocked the way ahead. "Aramis, let me through."

He didn't move. The rhythmic chug of the axel around the wheels shifted in pitch as we crossed the viaduct, gaining instead of slowing.

"Aramis!" I made to slip past him, but he stepped in my path. "What are you doing? I need to get to Nico. I need to go check on our driver!"

"There's no time." He pushed me, forcing me back a few steps. "We need to uncouple before it picks up too much speed."

With that, he turned and opened the gangway door and slammed it shut behind him. I lunged for the handle, which he had locked somehow, and was about to let my dark fire burn my way through the door when a screeching sound betrayed his idea. By the time I'd summoned enough power to destroy the door between us, Aramis had already pulled the cut lever, separating us from the rest of the train.

We'd made it across the bridge, the station in sight in the distance. But the Iron Saint barreled on into the night, with everyone I loved still on board.

And no working brakes to stop it.

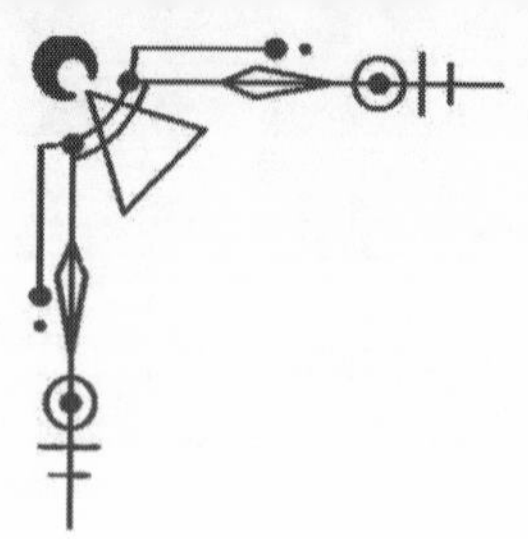
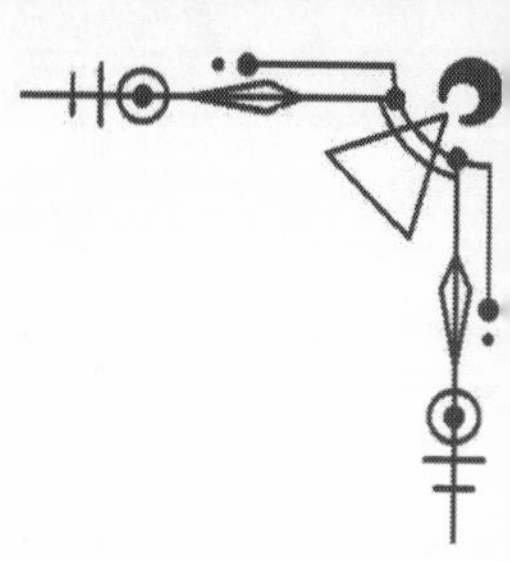

CHAPTER 36

NICOLAI

Everyone settled once we crossed the viaduct. The men laid Regulus on a bench. His arms had gone out of socket from being suspended from the tower for so long, and the Mirth remnant was too weak to stand or sit upright by himself.

"We'll take you to the haelens right away, Regulus," I told him as he grimaced in pain. "I'm going to go tell Aramis to bring Camilla home so I can take you myself."

"Don't you dare leave her with him. Didn't you—*fuck*." He sucked a breath as someone hit his arm. "Didn't you listen to my warning? I told you not to trust the blonde bastards."

"What did you mean by that?" I asked. "Why?"

He sighed deeply, resting his eyes to retrieve the memory. "When I went out for a smoke that day, I heard the watchman climbing the ropes, so I hid on top of the tender and waited." He shifted in his seat. "I listened and watched, and either the Marcheses forgot to lock the car, or they let the watchman inside, because he walked straight into that bloody car."

"They're not that stupid to forget," I said. My cousin had vouched for Aramis herself, reminding me he was more intelligent than I first assumed.

He nodded. "Either way, I went to help them. Found them both knocked out—not shot—on opposite ends of the room. The guard was messing with something on the floor."

"That's where Milla was hiding. You think it was a set up?" I asked him.

"Well, it was real convenient he knew exactly where to look and the brothers came out without a scratch. But I didn't ask questions. I shot the man and went to find you. It wasn't hard to assume what they wanted."

"Why would the Marcheses help me rescue their sister if they planned on merely giving her back to the Watch? It doesn't make sense." Nothing about Aramis added up. He cared for Milla, that much was obvious from the brief time I'd spent with him, and yet his actions had contradicted that affection time and time again.

A loud bang from the rear ceased all conversation in the car.

That sound . . . a sharp clash of metal on metal. There was nothing in the world I could have compared it to, and when a sound was misplaced like this one, it meant nothing good. Nor did the direction it came from.

"Camilla . . ."

I lunged down the aisle to reach the door, to find my worst assumption on the other side.

"*Nico*!"

Milla stood in the doorway of the last car, shrinking as we were separated, as the train she was no longer connected to traveled further down the tracks. I hadn't noticed how fast we were going, being caught up in Regulus's story, but when we passed the station, I knew something was very wrong.

"What's happening?" Gideon asked behind me, a tremor in his voice.

I only cursed and darted back through the car to the opposite end, climbing over the tender to get to the engine where Marcus fiddled with the controls. His nimble frame slipped along the narrow passage along the boiler to check the various gauges attached to the metal pipes.

"Marcus, what the hells?" I shouted.

He jumped, eyes wide a moment before he continued with his work. "They busted the tank! The brakes are shot!"

"What do you mean the brakes—"

"There's no water!" he shrieked.

I'd never seen him like this, so terrified. And if an expert on steam trains was afraid, I'd be wise to be as well.

"Explain quickly," I ordered.

He wiped his sweaty face and slipped down the engine to face me. The fire in the boiler was glowing a bright orange against the darkness as we traveled toward the Wilds, through uninhabited lands.

"The boiler heats the water to make steam. That's what powers the train, the brakes, all of it. But somehow, we have no water left, so I can't control anything. Hells, I know we checked it before. I don't understand how this happened!"

My brain tried to come up with a solution, but I knew nothing of these metal beasts. Steam trains were like a living organism, too many parts working together in a science so impossible it could have been magic.

"I have a cousin who can control the heat," I said. "What if he cooled things off?"

Marcus shook his head, tears dripping from the corners of his eye. "The pressure is too high already. The copper stripping has gone soft . . ." he muttered more incoherent ramblings. "The damage was done before I realized what happened. I'm afraid we're about to blow, Mr. Attano, and there's nothing to do about it."

"Get in the passenger car, Marcus," I barked. If there was nothing he could do, no sense standing right next to the volatile engine.

As soon as we hopped over the tender, I asked him to help with the coupling, separating it as Aramis had done.

"Impossible . . ." he said.

My jaw locked, grinding my teeth together. "What now?"

"It's jammed! The cut lever is—"

I pushed him back and tried to pull the same switch, but it was no use. Even my false hand didn't have the strength to push it open.

"This was fucking planned," I growled, anger replacing any useless drop of fear in my heart. Marcus would never let the water get that low. He'd run this train for days and weeks on end. He knew too much to make such a mistake.

Strange how Aramis could break himself and Milla off before he had to deal with this.

"We need to jump." I barked the order as soon as I entered the car. The bruised and beaten cadre of benders stared back at me.

"We're traveling at over sixty miles an hour," Marcus said. "We'll die if we jump."

"We'll die if we stay!"

"How many times must I *probably* die today?" Regulus groaned.

I opened my mouth to tell them all to shut up and take a leap of faith, but something was approaching behind us. A small thing with a thin trail of steam pouring from its small engine.

Esme's bike. But it was not my cousin on the back, driving the damn thing.

It was my wife.

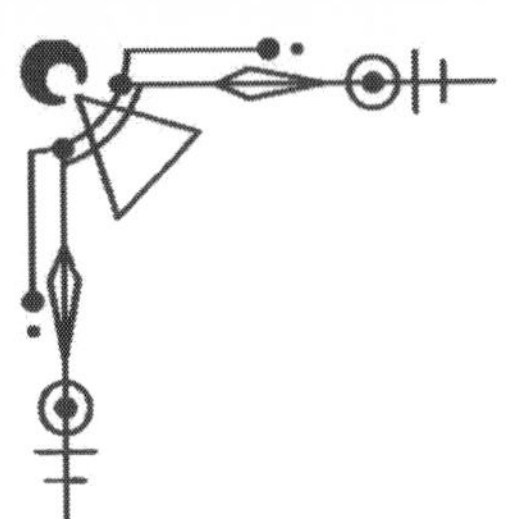
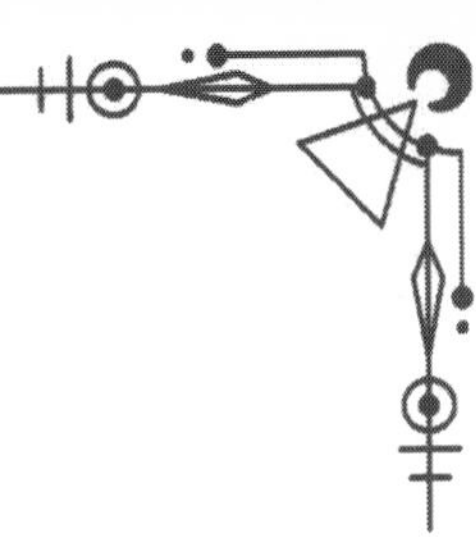

CHAPTER 37
CAMILLA

Aramis's arguments were an echo lost in the wind by the time he realized what I was doing. He thought he had me cornered, that I wouldn't go straight to the steam-powered bike he had parked on the platform. He assumed Esme hadn't showed me how to work it, that I was useless just like all the other times he'd assumed my choice.

Good thing he didn't know me well enough.

I switched between gears to gain speed, not quite as seamlessly as we'd practiced, but I neared the train all the same. Thankfully, it wasn't operating at full speed—most likely because there wasn't any steam to power it further.

Harsh winter wind burned my cheeks. I blinked furiously to clear my vision of tears as I followed the guide of the engine light down the side of the tracks, nearly missing Nico when he filled the doorway.

"Milla! Back off!"

What was it with the men in my life constantly telling me to

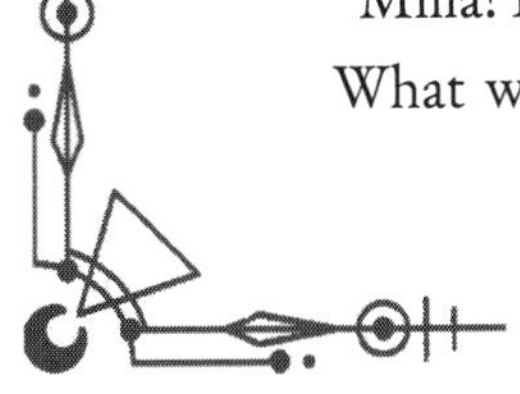

stay away? I gripped the handlebars and edged closer, and I could have sworn I saw him mouth a few choice curses.

"What's wrong?" I shouted above the wind, the whirr of the engine, the power of the train.

"The boiler is going to blow!"

Right. If that man had leaked out the water, then the boiler was probably moments away from exploding. I'd never seen or heard of it happening in my time, only that it had once before many years ago and the consequences were devastating.

"Detach!" I shouted.

"The rod is jammed!"

I was the one who cursed then. Kicking the bike into another gear, I passed the passenger car and focused on the coupler merging the tender and the car. Keeping one hand on the handlebar, power seeped my veins to burn away the glove over my right hand. Dark fire coiled in my palm, and I lashed out towards the coupler like I was snapping a whip.

As expected, Oblivion's fire slashed it right in two.

My front tire hit something slick—a patch of ice—jerking the handlebar from my grasp. The force of the swerve flung me off the seat, and I could only brace myself for impact as I flipped, landing sprawled in the snow.

The landing was jolting, but beyond the aches of the initial collision, I didn't feel anything too broken to be concerned about just yet. Thankfully, the beginnings of a snowfall now crept over the north side of the city, and the fresh snow had cushioned the impact.

The whiplash still jarred me enough to weigh down my movements. Lifting my head from the blanket of frost, the last thing I saw was the Iron Saint continuing down the tracks, a serene picture with the moonlight draping the snowy wood behind it. A runaway train spitting its last plumes.

It exploded a heartbeat later.

My eyes squeezed shut, blinded by the intensity of the blast. Heat washed over me as I lay flat against the ground, my front cased in ice while fire breathed down my back. The worst was the noise, the tumultuous grind of metal as it twisted and snapped and groaned as the engine was obliterated.

Only when the flare of heat settled and the Wilds went quiet did I allow myself to look up again. There was nothing left of the train besides the running gear, specifically the drivers and the wheels. The rest had been melted or tossed deep into the forests bordering the tracks where flames nipped at dormant pines.

Just like that, it was gone. The object of all my motivations, the source of all the discourse in my life, the reluctant responsibility I had inherited—was gone. Though the law had not recognized I was alive yet and though the company was no longer mine, the tears still fell as I watched something my family had poured their lives into be destroyed. The efforts of generations of Marcheses, all erased in a single moment.

"Camilla!" Nico shouted.

Gradually, my arms and legs pushed off the cold earth to prove to him I was fine. Banged up and winded—but fine.

He appeared in front of me with wild eyes that tamed some after running their assessment over me. "Anything broken? Can you stand?"

He helped me up, and I winced as a sharp pain shot through my knee and hip. "I'll live."

"Seven hells." He pulled me into his chest. "I thought you snapped your neck for a moment."

"It's gone, Nico." I despised how my body trembled in his

arms, betraying the hurt in my heart that was far worse than anything in my bones.

"I'm so sorry, Milla. This is all my fault. I'll . . ."

He'll fix it, that was what he wanted to say. It's what he always said when I was upset, but trains like ours couldn't be built in a day, not even with a metal bender like Esme to assist the process. It was a complex machine, converging various specialties. I doubted even with his influence in this city he could accomplish what needed to be done to fix this.

He knew it too from the way he shut his mouth and swallowed the words he so badly wanted to assure me with.

"I'm sorry," he whispered.

"This isn't your fault. This was . . . this was sabotage."

Footsteps crunched in the snow, approaching us. The cousins split from the group that had gathered outside the passenger car I'd separated, everyone appearing accounted for and alive at first glance.

"I'm going to go put out the fires before they get out of hand," Adler said.

Nico nodded, finally releasing me from the cage of his arms. "How is everyone?" he asked.

"No worse than before," Luther answered, "but Regulus needs a haelen. Some of the men have already left to retrieve horses."

"Good," was all Nico said. He was quiet as he looked back at the isolated fires burning the trees as Adler used his remnant to cease the flames. Wordless, he walked back to the bike I'd flipped off and straddled the seat, testing the controls to make sure it was still functional.

"Gideon, I'll expect you to make sure everyone gets home and taken care of. Make sure our haelens see them, not the hospital's."

He looked back at me with an expectant look. "Come on, Milla. There's someone we need to talk to."

I SAT behind him on the bike, my arms wrapping his waist. It would have been more intimate had my husband not been so quiet —a kind of silence that only accompanied his most violent of tempers.

"Think of the positives, Nico. We got Regulus back. We did what we set out to do—"

His head snapped to the side to speak against the wind. "And now the train is destroyed, Milla! Do you know how many people rely on the Iron Saint? The companies I'll have to break ties with? The job I was supposed to—"

His mouth slammed shut, and he looked back at the approaching city. Saints, I had nearly forgotten about his deal with the black-market man. He was supposed to move cargo next week. How the hells would we accomplish it now? The freight train was up north and wasn't set to come back down until the parts were delivered. Parts that wouldn't be delivered now. With the Wilds being impassable on foot, we'd never get them there in time.

Yet the question remained. How would we get his shadow back without it? My throat closed with a hard swallow. "We will find a way," I told him, though I didn't even convince myself.

"Did you see something?" Nico asked. "You mentioned sabotage. Did you notice anything to make you believe that?"

The tracks curved as we entered the barren edge of the industrial zone leading to the station.

"Yes," I admitted. "I saw a watchman crawl from under the

train, but . . ." I bit my lip. Was this my fault? Should I have not questioned him more, or at least investigated? My head fell against the curve of his back, angry at my negligence. We'd been in such a rush, I hadn't thought to check the engine.

"I'm not accusing you, Milla. I just want to know who did this." He shifted gears, slowing down the bike, so it was easier to speak. "Clearly, they were just using Regulus to get us across the river. It gave them time to destroy what gives the Row the advantage. Could have even destroyed us as well."

"We knew this was a risk, Nico. Now we have to deal with the consequences."

"I'll deal with them alright," he murmured, his gaze fixed on the Row.

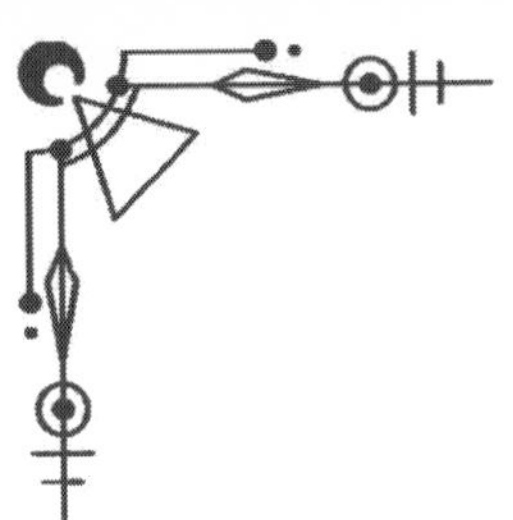
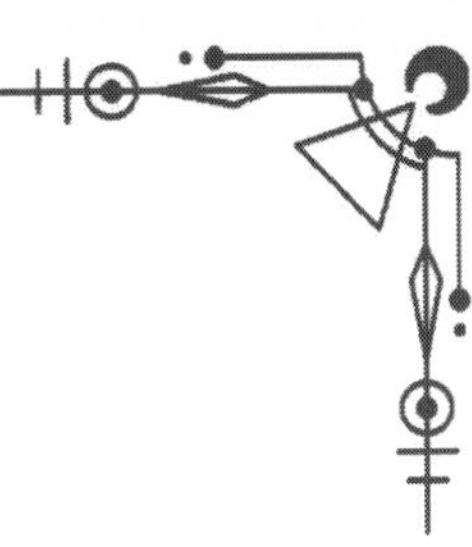

CHAPTER 38
NICOLAI

It was the dead of night by the time we pulled up to the estate. The windows were dark besides a pair on the main level; most likely my uncle and aunt who'd stayed up to make sure we came home. But thoughts of my family quickly dissolved when I saw the bastard waiting for us.

Aramis was crossing the yard as soon as we pulled up, his strides long and face furious. Jeremiah maintained a few paces behind him as he followed.

"What were you thinking, Camilla?" he shouted at his sister as I knocked down the kickstand. "What is the point in trying to protect you when you rush headfirst into danger?"

"Don't you fucking talk to her like that," I seethed, swinging off the bike after her. "She saved no less than twenty-five men tonight, no thanks to you!"

"And if something happened to her?" Aramis asked. "Would it have been worth it?"

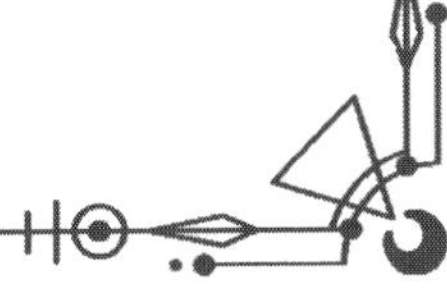

"Well, if we're asking stupid questions," I spat as my vision filtered red, "I have a few for you, Marchese."

"*Nico* . . ." Milla said, a warning as my body took a defensive posture.

Aramis rolled his eyes. "What now, Attano?"

Damn the bastard, I wanted to strangle the condescension from him right there and then. "Why weren't you helping Marcus with the engine?"

He scoffed. "I didn't need to."

"*Or* did you know something would be wrong with the boiler, and if you were there, you would have no reason not to catch the issue." Milla placed a hand on my shoulder, trying to talk me down again, but I shirked off her touch and took a step closer.

The back door opened then, light spilling from the entrance. Solomon came out in his sleepwear, limping without the support of his cane. "What's going on out here?"

"Tell him, Aramis." I shoved my finger in his face, felt the spit lining my lips as I barked the words. "Tell him how you knew there would be something wrong with the train, which is why you positioned yourself in the car with your sister and left the rest of us to burn!"

"You think I had something to do with tonight?" He shoved my hand away while he took a step back to distance himself. "You fucked up. Someone out there is playing you, and it isn't me, Attano, but *saints*, I wish it was." Pale eyes looked me up and down, his top lip curling. "You should be thanking me for being there for my sister. Hells, she'd probably be dead—or worse—because you wanted to save one fucking descendant and risk her life by exposing her in the process."

Before I knew what I was doing, my gun was in my hand and pointed in his face.

"*Nico, stop!*" Milla's scream was hysterical, a shout I'd never heard from her before. "Think about this! Think about what you're doing."

But I had thought about this. This man—this blonde-haired, insolent Marchese—had been the source of every wrong thing in my life. The reason I'd been sent to prison, the reason my father had died, the reason Milla had been taken in the first place. Every time I planned something he was in on, it fell apart—and my family was put at risk.

Saints, I had thought about this for a long time. So often had I dreamed of this opportunity that it felt as if I were looking down on myself, watching with my family at the door.

Aramis didn't flinch, only raised his chin an inch. "I'll never apologize for keeping Camilla safe. You want to shoot me because I couldn't care less if you and your men burn, Attano? Then do it, because it's true."

"Aramis, for the love of the Creator, just *shut up*."

The order didn't come from my wife, but from the other Marchese. The one who'd been watching in the shadow of his brother since the day he set foot on my property. Jeremiah didn't look at me directly, his focus remaining on the ground near my feet. Though his voice was steady, his chest filled and collapsed as burst of cloudy breath streamed from his lips in the chilled air.

"Nico, whatever Aramis has done, spare him."

"Why should I?" I asked him.

He lifted his gaze to mine then. "Because he's our family, and while he might act like an idiot, he's not a traitor."

Esme had emerged from her garage, where she frequently slept. Fran had followed her husband, lingering in the doorway with a look I couldn't discern on her face. They all stared at me. Silent. Waiting for my decision.

"Nico, if you do this," Milla whispered, "if you do this, I promise you will lose me forever."

Was that something I could live with if it ensured our safety? My vengeance? His death would satisfy the thirst in my bones for atonement, charging my motivations as villainous at best. It would ensure I'd cut off a poisonous limb from the family tree. But losing Milla wasn't worth vengeance. I'd paid that price once, and it nearly killed us both.

I lowered the gun, and she gasped like she'd been holding her breath.

Not taking my eyes off Aramis, I sheathed the pistol. "Since you don't care about my family or returning the same protection they have offered you the last three months, get the fuck out of my guesthouse. If I see you in the morning, I'll have my men—the ones you would let die—toss you on your miserable ass back across the river."

He said nothing, only maintained his glare as I turned from the Marchese sons and stalked back to the bike. Milla rushed over to stand in front of it, hands braced on the handlebars as if to block my way.

"Where are you going?" she asked. Wet lines trailed down her cheeks. She wanted to talk—I felt her questions in the way she looked at me. But my anger was a thrashing beast inside of me, and I'd only make things worse if I stayed.

"I need some space to think."

"About what?"

"*Everything*, Camilla."

As soon as I said it, she released the bike. "I see."

I had no idea what she was thinking, but from the flinch in her withdrawal I knew my answer had hurt her all the same. I sighed, trying to tame the violence in my voice. "I'll be home soon. I promise."

I pushed away, backing up a few feet before hitting the engine into action, leaving her in the middle of the driveway as I sped back toward the Row.

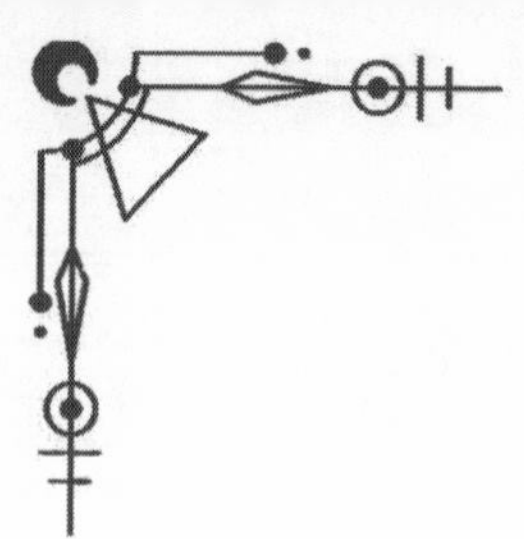
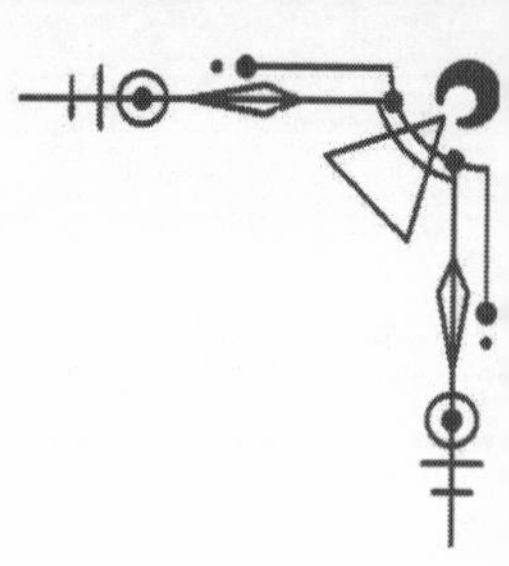

CHAPTER 39

CAMILLA

"Where the hells are we to go?"

Aramis cursed my husband as he packed his few belongings. Jeremiah gathered his things much slower, more reluctantly.

I watched them both from the hallway on the upper floor of the guesthouse, trying to rebuild the fragile bridge that once stood between my families. I told him, "Let me speak with Nico before you go. We still need you to help us get the book back from Felix. You're the only one out of all of us who knows so much about the alchemists."

"Why would I help your bastard husband?" he spat as he shut his suitcase.

Leaning against the doorframe, I winced. "Because you'd be helping me."

His shoulders tensed. "Every time I try to help you, Camilla, you reject it. You tell me how I don't know what I'm doing, or you

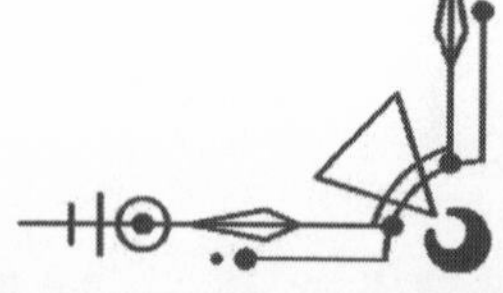

run off to save the day despite all my efforts." He shook his head. "You don't actually want my help."

"Not when your help puts everyone else at risk! How can you turn on the people that have taken you in?"

He spun around, facing me with icy fury in his blue eyes. "My entire life, I have watched over you, Camilla. When Father died, I was the one who bore the responsibly of your secrets. I was the one he expected to protect you from the evils in this world, not because you have a remnant but because you are my *sister*. I have sacrificed everything I have truly wanted to make sure nothing happens to you. Friends, jobs, lovers . . ." He swallowed hard. "I denied myself them all to be here for you."

Some of the ice around my heart began to thaw. I'd assumed he was just a boring person, never wanting to do anything or be anyone other than a Marchese son. Perhaps I hadn't realized just how much he'd given up to remain by my side. Did he regret it now that Sera and our family were all gone? Had I been worth all the missed opportunities?

My eyes burned, but I blinked back the guilty tears his admission collected.

"I never asked you to give up your dreams for me."

"You didn't have to. It was my choice. Father had little faith in me as his eldest son to take on the business. He thought I was too impulsive. When he caught me with the Nine Crowns, I lost his faith for good." He smoothed a hand along his neck, rubbing in the lingering dirt from working in the engine. "I thought I could keep the family together, but I've just been proving him right every step I take."

"Then stop walking alone." I pushed off the doorframe to approach him. "We're all on the same side, Aramis. You can't win a war without allies. Nico—"

"Nico can't see beyond his damn Row," Aramis growled, his irritation returning. "He might call you his wife, but has he promised to protect you for the rest of his life? Does he put you above his family? Has even told you that he loves you?"

"He doesn't have to say any of those things . . ." I tried to speak with affirmation, but the truth came out weak. Aramis saw through my façade, anyway.

"The difference between your husband and your brother, Camilla, is that I will do whatever it takes to protect you, even if you hate me for it."

"What the hells does that mean?" I asked.

My skin prickled from the thoughts he left unsaid, shaking my question off with the wave of his hand. "We're just going in circles. What's important is that you're safe now. I had news before your deranged bender husband decided to kick us both off the property."

He'd dropped the subject too quickly to be casual, but I let it go for now. The news he mentioned tempted my curiosity, a bait wisely offered and snatched. "Let me talk to him before you leave. I'll deal with it." I crossed my arms and approached the doorway. "What news did you receive?"

He lifted something from his bedside table, unfolding last week's newspaper to show me the headline. "There's a ball next week at the Overseer's mansion. Everyone in the Districts will be invited, as well as the natives in the surrounding area that contribute to the Isle's political agenda, and I've heard from the courtesan who spies on the commanders that while everyone is at the masquerade, there will be meetings behind the scenes."

"What kind of meetings?" I asked.

"The kind that will make sure the Nine isn't just an underground operation, but an entire movement. A nation." He sat on the bed with a sigh. "The Marcheses were once part of the Nine. It wasn't just me and Giles who joined, but our grandparents as well. Did you know that?"

The conversation pulled me into the room to sit beside him on the bed. "I had an idea when you flashed the Niner blade and called it an heirloom." My eyes darted to his suitcase, wondering if he'd gotten rid of it when I asked—and doubtful. "Why did we leave?"

"Because Father wouldn't support a group that was actively working against his favorite daughter, would he?" Aramis shook his head. "After the Attano murders, Gio panicked. He took you straight to the alchemedis when you let your power slip on that train hand. He didn't want the Nine to find out about you. I didn't realize why then, but when I inherited the estate in his will . . ."

"You learned about my remnant."

He nodded. "I've known for a while but kept it to myself. It was safer, the fewer people that knew. Giles and I stayed as nonactive members in the Nine to keep tabs with the group, and the connections they provided were too good to pass up. We would've gone broke a lot sooner without the help of the Nine."

My shoulders slumped. It seemed an impossible task to go against them if that was the case. "If they're so powerful and well-integrated with the city, how are we to take them down?"

He shrugged like it was simple. "We go for the Firenzes. They're the ones with the formulas and the Arcane laws. We just need an opportunity to get inside the Wet District."

My body and mind were tired. It had been a long day preparing for an equally rough night. But the bruises over my ribs were a nagging reminder that our enemies weren't taking their time any longer. They weren't playing defense anymore. If we wanted to run them out of the city, we'd need to get ahead of them again.

"You said this ball is hosted by the High Overseer?" I asked Aramis.

"Yes. Well, his social board, I'm assuming."

A social board I had a hunch was led by none other than the socialite herself—the Overseer's daughter. "Vanya Hartsong," I said the thought out loud. "Vanya will be the one planning the party, which means we have an opportunity with her."

Aramis stood to stretch. "And how will Vanya Hartsong help us?"

I smiled. "What if the Overseer's mansion can no longer host the soiree? What if . . . I don't know . . . there's a rat infestation or the plumbing backs up. What if something happens and the Firenzes, the Niners themselves, hosted the party?"

He stared at me with a skeptical look on his face. "How would that help?"

"There will be hundreds of people there. Plenty of distraction to get inside their walls and look for Delilah's book and little time to place intensive security measures. We'll just need to get them to volunteer or—"

"They'll do it," he said, the decided tone in his voice catching me off guard. "I'll . . . I'll contact Narcissa. She's good friends with the Firenzes. And the Hathoways. And the Caldwells . . ."

"Yes, I'm sure she's very well-connected with all the rich men in the Districts," I blurted.

Jeremiah lingered just outside the door, listening while puffing on a cigarillo. "Don't mind me. Just want to know if I should be packing or not."

"Not yet," I told him, trying to assure him with a smile that wilted on my lips. I took the opportunity to see myself out. "Anyway, I'm going to head back to the main house, just in case Nico comes back soon. We have . . . a lot to talk about."

Aramis scoffed. "Yes. You do."

Ignoring him, I made it to the hall before letting one last question turn me back. "Can I ask you something?"

He gestured around himself as if to say he had nowhere else to be.

I licked my lips, unsure how to articulate the unsettled feeling in my stomach. "Can we trust you, Aramis?"

He blinked twice, as if taking the time to process his answer. He stood then and braced a hand on the open door. "You can trust me, Camilla. Everything we do"—his eyes darted to Jeremiah—"is for you. Never forget that."

He shut the door before I could inquire further.

NICO DIDN'T COME HOME like he promised.

I tossed and turned in our bed, finding it difficult to fall asleep without the weight of him nearby. I'd spent so many nights on the prison floor alone, cold, and in the dark, that his company had become a distraction from the memories that liked to surface when I shut my eyes at night.

And when I was alone—like tonight—I relived every moment in the cell and the trials. Thoughts of all the things I should've done differently nagged at the boundary of my dreams until my eyes were wide-open and staring at the canopy draping above the bed.

My stomach burned, and I shoved off the covers when rest became futile and ventured downstairs for a snack.

There I found an old woman, hunching over the counter and kneading a large mound of fresh dough. "Nonna?"

She glanced up at me, her constant frown evening out some pleasantly. “Belladonna, what are you doing up so early?”

“I could ask you the same.” But she only raised a brow, insisting I give her a real answer. I shrugged and sat on a barstool across from her. “I couldn’t sleep. Nico left last night and hasn’t come back.”

She nodded knowingly. “He’ll be home soon. I heard what happened last night. Best to let tempers cool down before moving forward.”

“Do you think we can?” I asked. “Move forward. He held a gun to my brother’s face.”

Nonna clicked her tongue. “And he should *not* have done that. I am not excusing my grandson’s actions, but Nicolai does not raise his weapon or his remnant without cause. I am curious to find out what pushed him to such a decision.”

My fingers drew circles in the flour dusting the counter. “He doesn’t trust my brother. That about sums it up.”

She paused her kneading. “Is he wrong in that?”

“Yes,” I said at first, but the word tasted like a white lie—one aimed at myself more than Nonna. “Maybe. No. *I don’t know.*” Resting my head on the cradle of my arms, I let the tears I’d held back slip free, no longer strong enough to keep them back, a crack in a pipe that burst from too much pressure.

Something had bothered me since the explosion. Nico said the coupler was jammed, but my brother was the one that put the cars together. Why was our car fine and theirs not? Because *if* he was working against the Attanos his actions were even more sinister in their potential motivations.

There were so many damning coincidences in the past few weeks that pointed to him being associated with the Firenzes. Like how a single guard had incapacitated them both on the train when we were stuck on the bridge. How he knew exactly how to protect me when the watchman used his power in the Salt District. His sheer understanding of the Arcane. There were so many incriminatory signs that Aramis wasn't being entirely honest with me—*hells,* he'd never been completely transparent a day in his life.

But there were truths to him I couldn't ignore, either. Felix had killed Sera. Why would he help the man that shot his—as he called her—*lover*? Aramis was family, one of the last blood relatives I had left in this world, besides Jeremiah.

He'd promised I could trust him—and I *had* to believe it. Any alternative to these truths would break my heart beyond repair, and I had been conditioned to give him the benefit of the doubt. So dominant was that instinct, the choice was made innately by default.

A bony hand smoothed the tension knotting my shoulders as I tried to swallow a guttural sob. "Stop your tears, Belladonna. It will all be fine. Do you think this is the first time an Attano has threatened to shoot an in-law?"

I lifted my head slightly to look at her. "It's not?"

She cackled and went back to her work. "Hells, no. My mother nearly shot my husband when he told her he was taking me across the Narrow Sea. Do you think my family thought it was wise to leave everything behind for an Attano with not a reole to his name? We're all here, aren't we? Well, besides Paolo, saints rest his soul. He died of a big heart, though, not a bullet."

She rolled the dough flat and spread a generous amount of butter across the sticky surface. "I have not had the displeasure of speaking with your brother on a personal level. However, Esme tells me he's a smart man. From what I've gathered, your brother and Nicky are very much alike, and perhaps that's why they butt heads so much. If you want peace between them, they need to be fighting on the same team. Find some common ground."

I scoffed. "What could Nico and Aramis possibly have in common?"

She glanced at me. "You."

"I'm not enough, Nonna." I never had been. That much was clear from the way things were falling apart.

Without warning, she grabbed a handful of flour and tossed it across the counter at me, flinging it in my eyes. The powder burned until more tears cleared my eyes, made me choke as I inhaled the stuff I disturbed trying to dust it out of my hair.

"Speak kinder about yourself." She continued to lecture me above the sounds of my coughing. "The things we whisper to the shadows have a tendency to come true." Without missing another beat, she sprinkled cinnamon sugar across the butter. "Now, if you're quite done crying and moping, make yourself useful and start on the glaze."

"Cinnamon buns?" I said, hopeful.

Her lips fought a smile. "There's no bitter heart a little sugar can't sweeten up. Bad days call for indulging."

Nonna taught me the recipe as we finished up prepping the rolls, and I was given a brief reprieve from my family trouble and the world's problems knocking at my door.

"Mrs. Attano?"

Both Nonna and I turned around to see Grimm, Nico's steward, standing in the kitchen doorway.

He glanced at Nonna briefly before settling onto me. "Sorry to disturb you, miss. A message just came for Mr. Attano. He told me you could take his calls when he was gone, if you wish."

I dusted off my hands on the apron I'd thrown around my waist. "I'll take it for him. Thank you, Grimm. Don't you ever sleep?"

He smiled politely. "I sleep when Mr. Attano sleeps."

I scoffed, understanding all too well. "Take the night off from Mr. Attano, Grimm. I'll look after things from here."

He bowed slightly, shoulders falling an inch. "Don't hesitate to call on me if you need anything."

I debated on what to do with the message after Grimm disappeared down the darkened hall. On one hand, it could be very important. Something Nico would need to respond to quickly. On the other, he might get upset if I opened something addressed explicitly to him. Weighing the consequences of both, I opened the letter.

It was a call for a meeting on the viaduct. Immediately. The sigil of an eagle was pressed into the stationary, making it obvious who'd sent this across the river, having seen this paper before.

"Business calling?" Nonna asked.

Business, indeed. I tossed the note into the fire heating the stove, destroying it, before running to the back door to grab my coat and gun of choice.

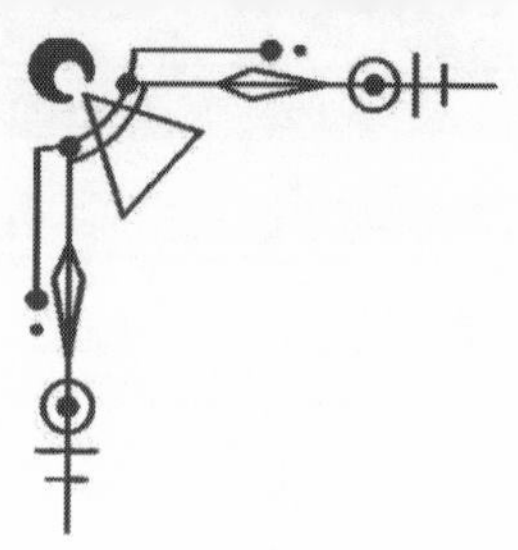
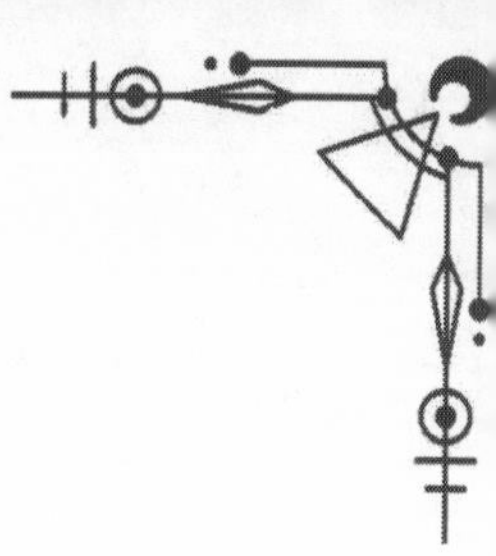

CHAPTER 40

CAMILLA

The wind had finally taken a break from its usual beating. Moonlight glared over the frozen river, and a thick plane of glass covered the torrential flow beneath. While the tracks were wide and sturdy, able to hold a multi-ton steam engine, it only took one false step to send one over the edge.

Vanya didn't bother hiding her reaction when she saw me coming.

"Oh—Camilla. I . . . wasn't expecting you."

I stopped far enough to ensure I was not a threat, but close enough we could speak without shouting. "I know."

Her mouth hung open for at least another second before shutting again. She was exactly as I'd remembered—her lithe figure cloaked in a navy fur coat. Though her black hair was shorter, ending near her chin. The cut only exaggerated her graceful neck and beautiful face.

"Is everything alright?" she asked. "Nico usually—"

"Whatever you need to say to him, you can say to me."

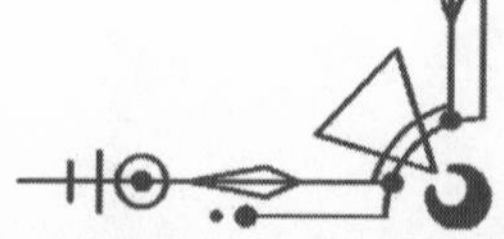

She winced at the harsh edge of my tone. "I only wished to find out what happened last night. Rumor has spread through the city that the Attanos were lurking the streets, looking for something while there was a shootout at the station."

"Like you don't know already." I nearly laughed. "You mean to tell me that your father, the High Overseer, the man who is over the inspector himself, wasn't aware that the Watch held a descendant hostage in order to bait the Attanos across the river?"

Her confusion only triggered my irritation.

I sucked a long breath to tame my freshened temper. "Don't act so surprised, Vanya. My train is destroyed. This city's way of life is now at risk because the men in power prioritize control over compassion. Nico put your father where he is now, and he has done *nothing* with his position!"

"Our cabinet is overrun, Camilla," she hissed. "Nico did a fine job of pissing off the leadership of the Isle when he declared war—"

I shook my head. "He declared *change*. That is not the same."

Her eyes shut briefly, and she released a long breath that fogged in front of her lips. "It is the same to those who see change as the enemy, who see it as the opposite of progress."

"Do you know what the Nine has planned next?" I asked her point-blank.

Vanya blinked several times before replying. "Let me make this clear, Camilla. The Niners do not trust me or my father. They have threatened my life in very unspecific terms, and the High Overseer will do their bidding if it keeps me safe. We did not bargain for the people here to turn to the Niners in support, but after Nicolai was framed for killing you and your family, for spreading his family's monopoly, we became severely outnumbered."

"So why are you here, Vanya?" I asked. "Why did you want to meet with my husband if you are of no help to him?"

"Because I am supporting his cause in other, quieter ways—how women frequently launch their campaigns. Wars are not only fought in the cabinet rooms and the battlefield. Sometimes they are fought over tea. Sometimes movements are started at birthday parties and social dances. Sometimes, Camilla, ideas are spread in the quiet whispers of sisterhoods."

She took a step forward, her chin raised slightly. "If you think I am sitting idle across the river because a few big men pointed their guns in my face and told me to be quiet, you forget who gave Nicolai the names to kill. He might have done the deed, but I was the bullet in his gun. You underestimate me? Good. That means the Niners do as well. And when they realize I fooled them all again, it will be far too late."

A thrill rolled a shiver down my spine, and a smile crept across my lips. "I knew there was something I liked about you, Vanya."

She smirked. "Tell me what you need, and I'll see it done."

Inhaling a long breath, my gaze fell where the sunrise was peaking over the horizon. She'd need to leave soon if she wanted to remain under the cloak of night. "You're hosting the gala next week, correct?"

"Yes, but—"

"Don't," I said simply. "Make up a reason for the Overseer's mansion to be an inhospitable venue for the party and instead, throw the responsibility on the Firenzes. They've hosted events before. They love showing off to potential investors. Get the party moved and we'll take the rest from there."

"Do you need inside their wares?" she asked.

I shrugged, not eager to give her too much to work with. "They have something that could be dangerous to the descendants. Secret codes. Science able to control magic. If we don't stop them now, we might not get another chance."

"What makes you so sure they'll have the event?" she asked. "Why would they care? The Firenzes would let the party be canceled before they'd let anyone inside their home."

Dawn crept closer. I took a step back to wrap up the conversation. "I have it on good terms that they have very important meetings scheduled. If they're important enough, they won't want to miss them."

She glanced at the horizon and bit her lip before nodding. "I can sabotage my party, I suppose. I'll bring it up at the next meeting and ask Firenze specifically. Hopefully, he'll be too flattered to be suspicious."

Having said all I needed, I nodded once. "Send word when you can. I'll inform Nico of our plans." I turned my back on her.

"I hope you aren't upset with him, Camilla, that he meets with me in secret."

My steps paused, turning half a step to look at her. "You were never a secret between us, Vanya. I'm not upset with him."

She offered a tight smile. "Upset with me then? I can tell you are uncomfortable. He must have told you."

"Told me what?"

"I . . ." She tucked her hair behind her ear nervously. "I proposed to him."

That wasn't what I'd expected her to say at all. Her confession shocked me, must have shown on my face from the way her face morphed. "*Weeks* after your funeral, I offered to peacefully unite our sides through a marriage. He refused, of course."

I scoffed. "Because I was still alive."

"No. He told me it was because I wasn't *you.* I understand what he meant now." She paused to let her words sink in. "There is nothing that man wouldn't do for you, Camilla. You are truly the center of his world." Pulling her hood over her head, she sighed. "I suppose I'll see you in a few days, then. Don't forget your mask."

Vanya winked, then turned on the small heel of her boot to walk quietly back down the viaduct to her side of the city as I returned to mine, feeling the weight of the night lift some with the approach of a new day.

There was nothing Nico wouldn't do for me—that was a truth everyone in this city was coming to understand.

And that terrified me above all else.

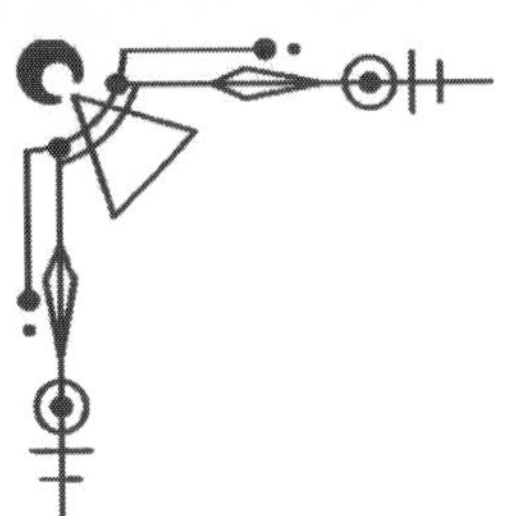
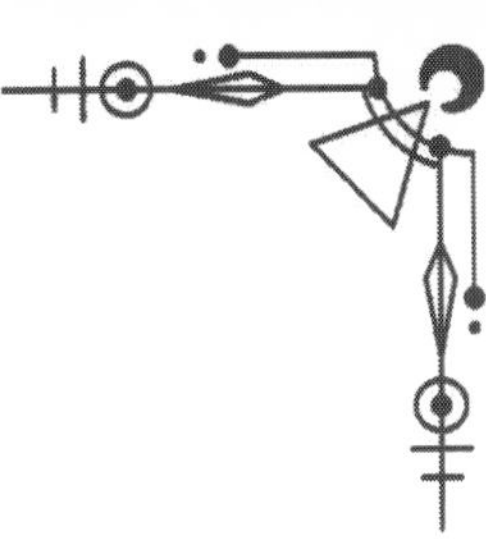

CHAPTER 41
NICOLAI

I could count on one hand all the things I regretted in my life. Threatening Aramis Marchese was not one of them.

Don't trust the blonde bastards.

Regulus's warning was a poison I knowingly drank from. I knew I couldn't prove it, knew it would be bad for me in the end, but I just couldn't stop indulging myself. After the warehouse attacks, combined with the activities of the night and all I'd learned of past betrayals, there was no doubt in my mind that the Marchese sons hid dangerously dark secrets.

There was just one problem with believing he was a traitor: Aramis would never give his sister to the Niners. For hell's sake, he tried to flee across the sea to the Continent just to protect her. Why would he help them? And had Regulus assumed one too many falsehoods about the scene he walked in on that day on the train? My disdain for him—and him for me—didn't necessarily mean he'd betray his sister.

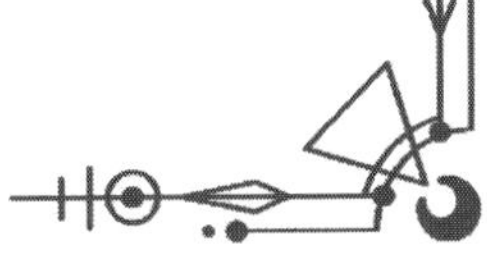

When things didn't add up, it usually meant I was missing a key part of the equation.

I'd been driving around the city for hours, trying to find it, but my thoughts kept running in circles. By the time I'd returned home, it was nearly dawn. My shirt was damp and clung to my chest from driving too fast down the backstreets of the Row. Only once the adrenaline from my anger subsided, and the inevitable weight of my consequences came crashing down in its place, did I feel the sting of the freezing morning.

The lights of the guesthouse were still on, which meant Aramis and Jeremiah hadn't heeded my warning. Typical. I'm sure Milla had something to do with their refusal to leave.

Nonna was finishing up her baking in the kitchen as I entered, keenly aware I was still wearing the shirt the clock master, Fielder, had bled all over a couple hours ago. She looked me up and down, the crease over her brow deepening.

"You stop right there, Nicolai Roman Attano. I don't need the blood of your enemies staining the marble."

I held my hands up in surrender. "I'm just here for the cinnamon buns."

She wrestled a smile back. "In trouble with your wife again?"

"That's not the only reason. I like cinnamon—" She interrupted my lame excuse with a frown. "Yes, alright. She's very cross with me. I need your comfort food to help me win her back. There must be some kind of magic in the filling."

"You won't win this one back with food, Nicolai," she said dryly. "But all the same, I'll give you a plate to bring up. Can't have you ruining the only marriage my grandchildren have successfully manufactured."

"You are a saint, Nonna," I told her.

She scoffed, setting the plate in front of me. I took a roll while I waited. "Don't look so smug. Your wife isn't even home."

My heart skipped. "What do you mean? Where is she?"

"Oh good," a sweet voice chimed behind me. I whirled to find the heiress herself, summoned by her name. "I was hoping they'd be done by the time I got back." She hung her coat on a hook, and I noticed a revolver tucked into the waistband of her pants. Apparently, she'd gone somewhere that required protection.

"Milla, where—"

"And my husband is home at last," she said with a bright smile. The sight of it and how she regarded me was so shocking, almost unnerving—until she pulled me down by the neck and kissed me hard enough to knock the wind from my chest.

Nonna muttered something in the old language that I couldn't discern between approval or disgust. Milla pulled away but kept one hand locked around my neck. Her opposite reached for the bun in my hand, snatching it from my fingers.

"Milla, where did you go?" I was able to get the whole question out this time, now that her mouth was busy with the pastry.

"Business," she said around a mouthful, then swallowed the rest. "Come upstairs and I'll fill you in. Thanks for breakfast, Nonna."

I grabbed the rest of the sweet rolls Nonna had set out for us. My grandmother pressed her lips together, shaking her head in disbelief. I motioned to the plate and shrugged. "Told you. *Magic.*"

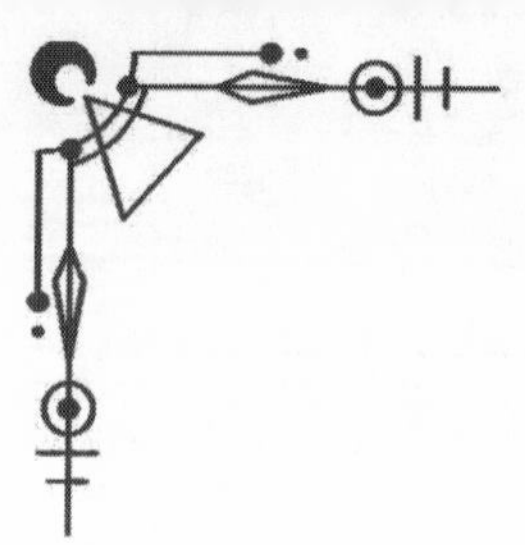
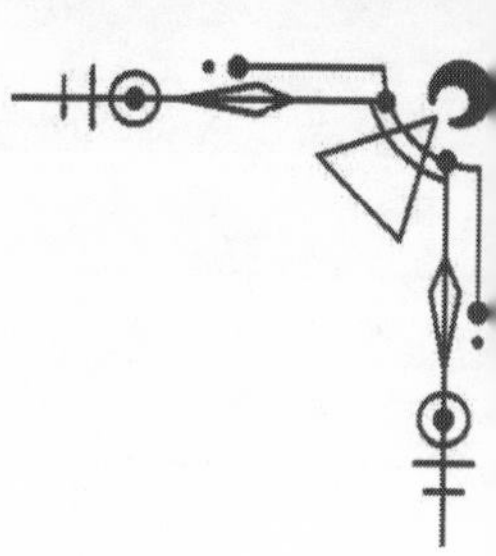

CHAPTER 42
NICOLAI

Milla was stripping out of her warm clothes in the closet when I finally made it upstairs after her. I waited for her to change, lingering outside of the closet. Milla propped her foot up on an ottoman in the center of the space and unlaced her boots. She'd gradually found a way to shove more of her things in here, and soon my tweed suits had been overrun with silks and softer fabrics. Blacks and silvers were now overrun with jewel tones and beaded skirts.

"Where did you go?" I asked once more.

She pulled off a boot and cast it aside near the other, where they both laid in an informal spot near the rows of heels she hoarded like a prized collection. I tried to hide my wince at the mess she made.

Don't make things worse for yourself, Nico. You nearly shot her brother.

"Where were *you*, husband?"

I released a long breath. "I just went for a drive to clear my head. Is that so wrong?"

"Yes," she clipped. Some of the sugar must have leveled out in her bloodstream because the glare she served me now proved her former frustrations had returned. "The Row isn't safe for us to be out on our own. Anything could have happened to you, and we would have never known! You made me worry."

I cocked a brow. "Yet, you went out as well?"

"I took a few men with me." She shrugged. "And I was armed. Besides, I knew exactly who I was meeting with."

She was smiling now, and that bothered me. "Who did you meet, Camilla?"

"Your friend, Vanya. She sent a note to meet with her immediately, but you were not here to receive it. So, I went in your place."

Camilla had met with Vanya. Arguably the two smartest women in Lynchaven had a private meeting—and hells knew what they had discussed. Vanya most likely wanted more information about last night before word got out, if only to control the rumors in her social circle, but Milla was too pleased with herself for that to have been the only thing they talked about.

"How did it go?" I only asked.

"Good."

I stood there, waiting for her to continue. "And?"

"And I might have figured out how to get Delilah's book from the Firenzes. We'll need the appropriate attire, however." She started browsing her gowns, flipping through the hangers.

"What kind of dress code are we talking about?" She couldn't mean the masquerade. The place would be crawling with watchmen.

She pulled out a beaded, floor-length gown with nude netting around the arms and shoulders. "I'd say it will be quite formal, though I don't expect an invitation to give us a proper notice."

"*Camilla.*"

She sighed, putting the dress back, before turning to me. "The party will be moved to the Wet District. We'll infiltrate the Firenzes' warehouses while the party is going on. And no, I don't know where to look for the book on their property, but Aramis has been there several times. He's negotiated with them before, so he knows the layout of the land. He's going to help us, and you will *not* kick him out."

She was further out of her mind than I thought. The party . . . sneaking around the Wet District, taking advice from her brother? "I will *never* work with Aramis ever again, Milla." I turned and started towards the bathroom, eager to rip this foul shirt from my skin and walk away from this conversation.

My wife followed me, as expected. I grabbed a towel and turned the water on in the shower to warm up while I undressed.

"I know how things looked last night, Nico—" The rest of her thought disappeared as I dropped my pants and began fumbling with the mechanism holding my false arm to the end of my residual limb.

"Then why would you even ask me to work with him, Camilla?" She was plucking the nerve that had already been aggravated earlier this morning. I didn't want to fight anymore, but I sure as hells wasn't conceding either.

The shower was near scalding as I stepped beneath the spray, letting it hit the broad of my back and loosen the muscles tightening further with every roll of my wife's eyes. She stood in front of me, on the opposite side of the glass. Her arms were still crossed and wearing a glower that cut through the steam.

"We *need* his insight!"

I lathered the soap, like this was just another normal conversation married couples spoke over their daily baths. "We need to get rid of him. Every time he's involved, things go wrong. Tell me you haven't noticed the same." When she said nothing, I made my decision. "You want us to walk straight into the headquarters of our enemy based on knowledge he feeds us. Nothing in that sentence makes a lick of sense!"

"But we still need the book!"

That cord she plucked finally snapped. The soap fell from my grasp, and I bracketed my hands against the wet glass, staring down at her. "Not as much as I need you, Camilla! I will not risk losing you for a fucking diary!"

She flinched, realizing the source of my discordance. The fear behind my hesitance.

"I wasn't asking you for permission," she whispered. "I'm doing this *for* you."

I shoved off the glass and turned away. "How is any of this for me?"

"Because while this party is going on, we'll have the men moving the railcars."

"The cars?"

There was a pause before she continued, nothing but the falling water to fill the silence. Her voice echoed through the bathroom. "Without the trains, there's only one other option to safely and quietly get them through the Districts. We'll have to push them."

"Push them?" I asked, unsure if I heard anything she had said correctly. "You *are* aware we have no idea what kind of stock we'll be transporting."

"It doesn't matter. Even I could push a fully loaded car by myself . . . once I got it moving. The cars will be stored in the stockyards outside the South Gate of the city where all the cargo is checked. We'll have to get past the gate, but once the cars are in the city, we can push them along."

I shut my eyes and let the water pour down my front, letting the blood and sweat of the night disappear down the drain. Steam filled my chest as I inhaled deeply, settling the frustration burning in my heart. "I don't know, Milla . . ."

The shower door squeaked on its hinges, and I opened my eyes to see Milla, fucking *naked*, slipping into the shower with me. She'd undressed silently as I simmered.

"Think about it," she said, interrupting the stream of the water as she neared me. Gentle hands slid up my chest, hooked around my neck.

"We have a few days to work out the kinks," she continued, though her voice dropped into a softer sound. "But I will not lose you to some stupid black-market dealer. We're getting the book *and* your shadow back." She swallowed hard and inhaled a long breath of steam. "Besides, it's the only way I can keep you both."

"Camilla—"

"Save your breath." She stopped me with the shake of her head. "I know you're not sorry for what you did. I know you hate Aramis, and I don't expect you two to ever get along. But I won't choose between you or my brothers. My circle has shrunken small enough. I need you all alive, because I am too selfish to give any of you up."

My hand, which had been rubbing circles around the small of her spine, drifted into tempting territory. A thousand curses flooded my head when her ass filled my palm. "You want the fucking book, princess? I'll get it for you. I'll do anything you ask, Milla. You already know that."

"I do," she whispered, "and that's become my biggest fear."

She threaded her fingers into my hair and pulled me down to meet her lips, where I understood that fear she shared with equal severity. I kissed her like I'd never kiss her again, letting the frustration of the night and all that had gone wrong unleash like a wrath upon our intimacy. Her tongue was laced with cinnamon and sugar. The shape of her pressed against me as she rocked her lubricated body over my hardened cock.

I broke from her lips, staring at the place our hips rolled together. "*Hells*, Milla."

"Should we . . ." She pulled back, biting her bottom lip. "I mean, would it be easier for you if we—"

"Finished this in the bed?" I asked. When she nodded, I couldn't hold back my smile. "Don't worry about me, my love. I can fuck you with one hand."

To prove a point, I lifted her with my right arm, and she wrapped her legs around my waist instinctively as I shoved her back against the nearest glass wall. Hot water continued to spray from the shower head, our heavy breaths contributing to the clouds of steam rolling around our writhing forms.

I balanced her hips on top of mine, using my freed hand to squeeze the swell of her breast and my tongue to tease the other. Her head fell limp against the glass wall, panting my name as I sucked at her sensitive skin and licked away the sting of where my teeth grazed. Her fingers were still entwined in my hair, the heat of her center slid along my length as she sought more.

"You'll still have me after everything?" I lifted my hips to guide the tip of my cock near her entrance. "You still want me, Milla?"

She relaxed her legs, slipping lower as if to steal back control. "Forever, Nico."

That one little word could send me to my knees, but we'd get to that position later.

My hand braced on her hip; I adjusted the angle between us to plunge inside her. The trifecta of her gasp, the way she tightened a little around my cock, and the rapid rise and fall of her chest as warm water dripped down the valley of her breasts almost made me spill right there and then.

Milla leaned back against the glass, her lower back arching to sink me deeper, to let me hit that spot that made her sing sweet sounds that she was making now. Every inch of her was perfect, like we were made to fit together, and of all the times I'd been inside her, this might have been the best. Every time was better than the last, and I constantly craved the next kiss, the next touch, the next fuck.

"*Hells*, I'm almost there," I said after thrusting into her so hard, I thought I'd send her through the glass. Thankfully, the wall held steady.

Her eyes fluttered shut. Nails dug into the crest of my shoulders, and she whispered something about being close as well. Her sighs of bliss echoed through the bathroom. She squeezed around my cock, and I chased her climax, falling over the edge with her a moment later.

I released so hard, I had to let go of her hip to brace my hand against the glass. Milla continued to roll her hips, drawing out my pleasure as I shattered piece by piece. She stroked my neck with a feathery touch, whispered her praises into my ear as I rode the remaining aftershocks of our climax and caught my breath at last.

When the haze of desire finally cleared, I slipped out of her. She untangled her legs from around my waist and leaned against the glass, pinned against me.

"Just because that was incredible, doesn't mean you won the previous discussion." I could barely finish the sentence before taking another deep breath of air.

She smiled. "Of course not. We'd have more sex if it were that easy."

Despite the weight of the world still heavy on my back, I laughed. "Spoiled little heiress."

THE SUNRISE WAS SPILLING through the cracks in the curtains by the time we finally tumbled out of the bathroom. Milla threw on a slip while I found some pants and finally climbed in bed for the first time since yesterday morning. She brought the cinnamon buns to the bedside table and sat against the headboard as I stared up at her. My eyes were heavy, and my body exhausted, but I couldn't look away.

"That was a first for me," she said as she grabbed a roll. "I think I like shower sex."

That was very good news for me. "It was a first for me as well."

Her brows kissed. "Really? I expected Nicolai Attano to be more adventurous in his past."

I scoffed, pushing up to lean beside her. "Just because I enjoyed my newfound freedom as a young man doesn't mean I don't still have firsts as well."

Her lips stretched into a small grin. "What else, then? What firsts of yours belong to me?"

She curled into my left side with her pastry in her hand, her head on my shoulder. And I wished I could stay here forever. I'd been waiting so long to tell her everything.

Waiting for this moment exactly.

"You were my first dance."

"Impossible! You were so smooth."

"My first dance that *wasn't* with my Nonna or aunts," I clarified. "Or my mother. The women of my family made sure their sons grew to be proper gentlemen."

She nearly choked as she swallowed a mouthful. "Gentlemen. *Right*. At least when the lights are on. I hope I'm your first wife, as well."

"The one and only."

Her smile fell half an inch. "Would you have accepted Vanya's proposal had I truly been dead?"

Hells . . . Vanya and her inclination for gossip. I straightened uncomfortably against the headboard. "No, I wouldn't have ever married her. There was no one before you, Milla. There never will be again."

She scoffed. "How can you say that? I wasn't your first, Nico."

"You were the first that meant something," I told her. "You were the first to truly have me. And—" My breath rushed out of my chest, stealing the words I so badly wanted to say. I'd never said them to anyone besides my family, and even then, it was different. They were a love forged from blood and kin. Milla was a love that stemmed and grew and bloomed from my very soul. One with roots that tangled into everything I was.

She sensed my nerves and shifted to straddle my waist, gazing into my eyes. "And what? Tell me, *my love*."

My smart woman. She already knew.

I dug my fingers into her hips, seeking her soft edges. "And this is the first time I've ever fallen in love, and I know with absolute certainty it will be my last."

Milla sucked in a breath. Her lips didn't break a smile, and her eyes didn't betray a single emotion until a thin tear rolled down the edge of her cheek.

"You love me, Attano?" she said, voice cracking.

I felt myself smile. "I do. I love you Camilla Mercy Marchese-Attano. I can't even remember a time now that I didn't love you. Even when you hated me, I realize now I was always so incredibly enthralled by you." My eyes caught on the cinnamon bun discarded on top of the bedsheet. "Even when you get crumbs in my sheets."

A smile collected the tears running down her cheeks, and she laughed. "I love you too, Nicolai. Tyrannical tidiness and all."

There was a long pause, the both of us too satisfied in the moment to break it. Milla fell against my chest, where our hearts beat against each other in quiet correspondence.

"Will you do me a favor?" she asked.

"Anything."

She looked up at me, resting her chin on my chest. "Tell me you love me every day. Don't miss a single morning."

My fingers combed through her wet hair. "I'll tell you every day, until our last sunrise. And even then, when we cross the veil, I'll whisper it through the void until my voice fills Oblivion. I love you, Camilla."

Her smile softened. "Perfect."

She returned her head to my chest and traced the interwoven circles marked over my heart. My eyes fluttered shut at last, having left nothing unsaid between us.

Never had getting my shadow back become more important—now that I had a thousand mornings ahead of me to spend just like this.

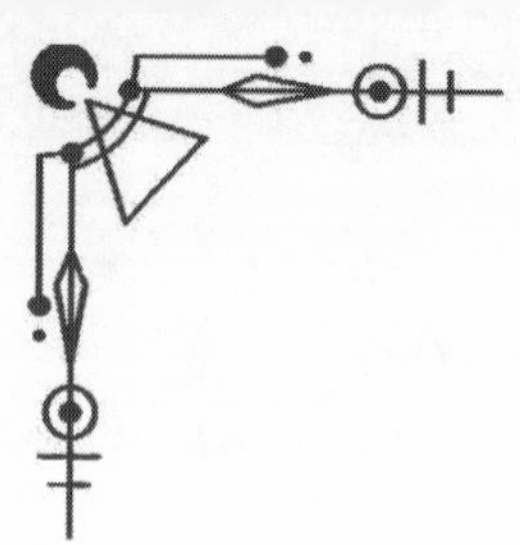
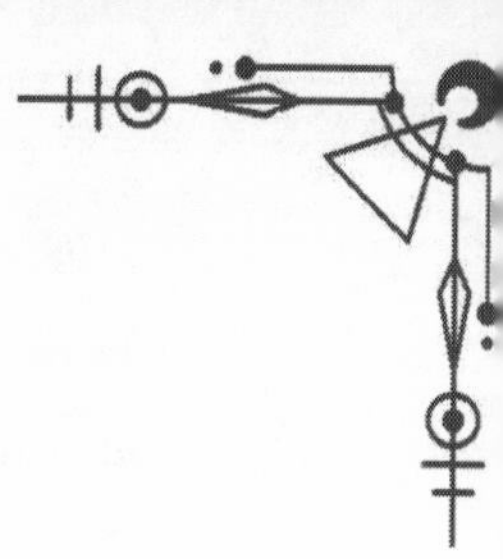

CHAPTER 43
CAMILLA

Two days passed before we received any word from Vanya, and that time was an eternity when the world was soaking in oil, one rogue spark away from going up in flame and smoke.

Marcus had quit. He'd taped his letter of resignation to the office door at the station; obviously he had decided before he left the Row a final time after the train explosion.

The news from the papers were no longer passed from the Districts, and the whispers of our enemies went silent. Meanwhile, Nico was gearing up for the final push in our war against the Firenzes. He'd spread his makeshift militia across the riverwalk, arming the businesses there with men and guns to defend the Row should our plans to retrieve the book and the railcars fail.

A seamstress arrived to measure us for the event, though it felt more like being fitted for armor. She took my measurements and sketched out a design that would hide my weapons, layering just enough fabric to conceal a pistol or two if I desired.

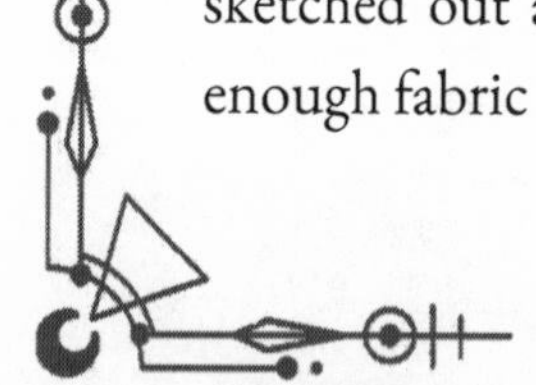

Sera would've approved of the design and intricate lace detail of the neckline, though she'd probably think it to be too modest for my personality. She was all I could think about as the tailor tacked and pinned her fabrics against my form. I could hear her now, saying everyone would be too distracted by the movement of the dress to give my face a second glance—and she'd be right.

The Attanos' seamstress was kind, but she wasn't as reassuring. Not like my friend had been when I needed it most, and it watered the guilty seed I'd kept buried inside my heart.

"Your mask," the tailor's voice broke through my thoughts, "will you be needing me to design you one as well?"

"No, that won't be necessary." Esme had that covered. She had been eager to feel useful and started crafting us custom, bulletproof masks that molded to each of our faces.

The tailor finished up my measurements just as Nico entered our bedroom, more tense than usual. The air around him was thick with cigarillo smoke. "You already have my measurements, correct Isla?"

The tailor listed off a few numbers from memory, and Nico nodded in affirmation. His gaze fell to a stack of papers in his hand.

"Still no news today?" I asked.

He shook his head. "I need to visit Sabina this morning and organize the drop-off for the dealer. I'm choosing to remain optimistic about our plans. Has your brother finished the sketches of the Firenzes' property?"

I jutted my chin towards the small desk pushed in the corner of the room next to the window. On top was a map Aramis had hand drawn at my husband's request—though I, of course, did *not* mention that to my brother.

"He marked the areas that were restricted to the public in red. There's a lab on the east side of the property. You need to have your darkthieves scout the area to see how many guards they have patrolling that repository. I'd think they'd keep their research near their experiments."

He scanned the map, sucking the inside of his cheek in thought. "It's a good place to start as any. I'll point them there. May I?" He folded the map and gestured to the inner pocket of his coat, as if to take it.

"Go ahead, I've already memorized it." He tucked away the map as I ran over the plan I'd rehearsed in my head. "The ball, I assume, will be held in the main house and the back courtyard. They can't hold the entire town inside, so they'll be outdoors as well, despite the cold. Aramis also said the courtesans were contacted to work the party, so we'll have the advantage of them distracting some of the very important guests."

"Any way we can narrow down who those might be?" he asked.

I nodded, stepping off the stool the tailor had been using. She saw herself out as we plotted. "The eagle pins should give them away. All the Niners wear them like patriots."

"I'm sure they'll be spreading all their Niner ideology to whoever will listen," he murmured. "We get them away, and then what? How will we get to the lab without arousing suspicion?"

I licked my lips, not entirely sure. "I had a small idea, but you won't like it."

"That seems to be the theme of the night," he sighed. "Go on with it."

I smiled. "We'll have to split up. It will be impossible for us to both monitor the car situation and look for the book. While you stay in the main room, Aramis will pose as one of the watchmen and escort me to the warehouse. We'll remain inconspicuous, but if by some chance we get caught, they'll be less likely to question us if he's bringing a potential investor to the lab."

It was a wonder my husband's teeth didn't shatter from how hard he clenched his jaw.

"And what then?" he clipped.

My lips twitched, though there was nothing funny about the matter. "Luther will spike the traditional celebratory toast that starts the night with some of Nonna's Vex Veritas. With the untamed egos that will be at the party, the place will be a mess in no time."

Nico's jaw loosened enough that it actually dropped. "Are you insinuating we make everyone sick with their own lies?"

I shrugged, pretending it wasn't my favorite part of the plan. "I'm quite tired of liars, and I think it's time the Firenzes and their friends be called out for the tales they spin."

He laughed. It was the first time I'd heard the sound in days. "Honestly, Milla, the only problem I have with that part of the plan is that I didn't think of it first. About us splitting up though—"

"Here we go," I sighed.

"It's not smart. Why can't we go as a random couple from the Lowlands attending the ball on behalf of our Overseer?"

"Because the Overseer of the Lowlands will most likely be attending," I told him. "Aramis informed me the guest list is stacked—"

"Has he seen it?"

"Apparently, Narcissa has heard lots of rumors from her staff."

He crossed his arms, squinting at me.

I shrugged and strode to the window. "You need to worry about getting the railcars through the city. We need people we can trust. People that can follow directions. It's dangerous, moving cars on the tracks at night. They're utterly soundless, and if you aren't paying attention, you can get run over or impaled by the coupler."

A memory surfaced of the last time a man had been at the wrong place at the wrong time while working on the tracks. He didn't even hear the car being moved behind him, nor did he know what hit him when a multi-ton car rammed into his back—until it was too late. I'd never wash that sight of when we found him out of my head as long as I lived.

"We'll time each car. I've already set up communications between the streets and the party."

Communications? "You mean, you'll have runners going between the party and the cars, keeping you updated?"

"Indeed."

I groaned, realizing exactly who he had in mind. "You are not using the Canary Boys!"

He returned one of my nonchalant shrugs. "They're the only ones who've been in the Firenzes' warehouses and the main house. They know the layouts, and they can sneak around easily. I can't deny their help now, Milla."

"They're kids—"

"The youngest I've employed is eighteen. They aren't kids, and if we want to make sure what is happening now doesn't happen again, we need to include the next generation." He crossed the room and placed his hands on my shoulders. "We can plan everything out, princess, but you know most of this is going to require thinking on our feet."

"Will you be recruiting Regulus as well?" I asked. His healing progress had been slow, but we still had a few more days until the gala if he wished to join us.

"I asked, but he respectfully declined. I have another Mirth remnant waiting on standby. One I trust."

My lips stretched an inch. I could imagine the colorful

response Regulus probably gave Nico when asked if he wanted to help again. I couldn't say I blamed him. "Did he say anything about the Society that could help us?"

"They apparently left him alone once they realized he was useless to them. His remnant is only dangerous to those he can deceive. They knew who he was, so he couldn't trick them anymore. They tried to get more information out of him about you, but he didn't know anything to give into their methods of torture."

I scoffed. "So they used him instead." My gaze fell to the inner courtyard formed from the wings of the estate. Nico's bedroom overlooked the convergence of the sprawling arms of the house, where four brick walls enclosed a garden in which Nonna kept her herbs and a few vegetables that could withstand the freezing winter.

"Is that . . ." My attention caught on something lying behind one of the raised garden beds. "*Seven hells*, is that Nonna?"

Nico's grip tightened around my shoulders when he noticed it as well. A red slipper jutted out from behind one of the wooden borders, as if someone were lying down beside it.

"*Fuck*," he whispered and lunged toward the bedroom door. I followed him out, maintaining his hurried pace. "Find Fran! She's most likely in the study."

I took the steps two at a time, left in his dust as he ran to the garden. The study he spoke of was near the parlor on the first floor, and as Nico suspected, the aunts were exactly where he said they would be. Huddled over their coffee and discussing the latest financial pitfalls the destruction of the train had created, they startled as I burst into the room without knocking.

"Something's wrong with Nonna!" I blurted.

Fran was the first to react. "What happened? Where is she?"

The shock was already wearing off, making room for the icy claws of panic. "I don't know, we saw her in the courtyard from the window upstairs—she must have collapsed. Nico went to help her and told me to inform you."

The eldest aunt took a deep breath as if to compose herself. "Ianthe, call for the haelens. Lucinda, gather the family just in case. Milla, come with me."

"In case of what?" I asked her.

She didn't reply, only placed a hand on the small of my back to usher us both toward the inner courtyard. "Fran," I spoke again, though my voice slightly trembled this time. "In case of what?"

"In case this doesn't end well, Milla."

It hadn't hit me until she said those words that a bad ending was an option. Normally, the people in my circle usually died from bullets or backstabs. Never had someone I loved died in their garden. Old age had never been a threat when no one lived long enough to face it.

"I'm in here!" Nico called out from a room off the hall as we neared the end of the wing. He must have heard the slap of our flats echoing through the quiet house as we approached. We found them in a guest room, Nonna resting on the bed as Nico tucked the covers around her still body.

"Her pulse is thready," he said as he worked. "I don't know how long she's been out there, but she's freezing. We need Adler—"

"Lucinda is gathering everyone," Fran replied while nearing the bed. She placed a hand on Nonna's forehead and instantly withdrew, cursing to herself. I took one step toward the empty hearth before Nico started the gas and tossed in a few dry logs.

"Can I help?" I asked him, despising how useless I felt in the moment.

His jaw worked and his eyebrows slammed down over hard eyes. But there was nothing he could order—nothing he could fix. "I . . . I don't know."

The room quickly heated with the help of the fire in the hearth. Adler and the rest of the cousins arrived moments later, pulled from their beds by the state of their dress. The bender with control over heat stood at the end of the bed, staring down at his grandmother, who was drained of color, who stood with her foot through the doorway of death.

"I shouldn't do this without the guidance of the haelens," Adler said. "If I raise her temperature too quickly or too much, it could do more harm than good."

"We don't know when the haelens will get here," Fran said. "Her breaths are spacing further apart; her pulse is slowing . . . Adler, I think we should risk it if it means getting her warm again. She can't last much longer like this—"

"Alright." He sighed, and his shoulders fell an inch, as if carrying the tangible weight of his Nonna's life. "Alright, I'll try."

"That's all we ask, darling," Fran whispered.

The heat bender slipped hands beneath the covers to touch Nonna's skin. The fire flickered in the hearth as a cold draft snuck between us. I hadn't much experience around Adler's remnant, though I could deduce he was taking the warmth from the hearth and giving it back to Nonna, raising her body temperature as slowly as he could.

In similar timing, the toning of her skin warmed. Just seeing the pink in her cheeks loosened a worry knotted in my chest. Fran kept pressing Nonna's skin with the back of her hand, nodding once she was satisfied with her temperature.

"That should help until the haelen's arrive." Fran pulled a low stool to the bedside and sat next to the seemingly asleep woman. "I wonder what happened to have made her collapsed. Why was she outside in the first place?"

"I think she slipped on some ice while looking over her garden," Nico said. "The snow from yesterday most likely melted in the afternoon and refroze last night. Milla saw her from the upstairs window, but we do not know how long she was lying there before she was found."

"This couldn't have happened at a worse time," Solomon muttered to himself as he entered the narrow room, pushing past his children to reach the bed. He assessed his mother while chewing the inside of his cheek.

"Why do you say that?" Adler asked.

"Magrahel."

A knowing groan passed between the cousins, as if he had made a morbid discovery. I leaned into Nico and asked, "What does that mean?"

"The veil between our realm and the void is thinnest during Magrahel. As you know, the void is composed of shadows, the same ones we receive at birth and lose in death. During Magrahel, the shadows try to return to the void since the barrier is more permeated, but the soul holds on—unless it's too weak to do so."

"The soul is like a tether, keeping our shadows in the living realm?" I asked him.

He nodded slowly. "A soul can let go of their shadow at any moment, from any cause of death. But for those who are particularly weak, like Nonna's currently, it's difficult for the soul to keep the darkness of the void assigned to the body."

I wanted to inquire more about the process, but there was a tremor in his voice I didn't recognize. To someone who didn't know him as well, they might assume he appeared stoic and strong, but I knew Nicolai as well as I knew myself. Perhaps even more so given the current circumstances—I still felt unsure looking in the mirror. That crease in his forehead only came out when he was worried. The swirl of his thumb over the back of my hand told me he was seeking comfort, and I'd bet if he hadn't left his cigarillos upstairs in his rush, he'd be burning one right now.

Esme had always chastised him about being the favorite grandchild, but I believed Nonna had inadvertently filled the space his parents left when they died, and she'd played that role of a matriarch in his life—even if he was too old to require it. And now he was watching her die.

Ruth, a haelen I recognized, knocked on the doorframe to announce her arrival. The family snapped out of their silent spell and shifted to the edges of the room to give her space to work. Fran stood from the bedside and came beside me.

"Is there anything we can do about Magrahel?" I asked her.

Fran offered a solemn smile. "We surround her with the things that keep the soul strong, Milla. Love and family, laughter and music, the things that bring her joy in life will nurture her soul and help her remain with us a long as possible." She glanced sideways at the sleeping woman. "If that's what she wants, of course."

Nico tugged on my arm. "We should give the healer some space." He looked at his aunt. "Let us know if Ruth makes any progress."

"You're leaving?" Solomon asked.

"I have to," Nico replied, already pulling me toward the hall.

"But she needs you, Nico. How can you keep working when your family needs you to be *here*?"

"Sol . . ." Fran spoke between them, a warning in her voice.

"No, Fran. This is important. She could slip away at any moment, and he still prioritizes business over his own family!"

"It's not a choice I make lightly. Nor would I expect you to understand, Uncle." Nico paused in the doorway, hand braced on the frame.

"Then help me, Nico," Solomon pleaded with him. "What is going on with you? The book can be found another day. My mother cannot wait until you have time for her!"

"If I don't do this, I won't have any time to give her at all." He tugged me into the hall, releasing my hand on the way to pull out a pocket watch attached to the chain on his vest. He cursed and tucked it back in its pouch and tore his false hand through his hair.

When we were far enough down the hall, I stopped him. "Why don't you just tell your uncle about your shadow? He would understand!"

"Doubtful," Nico spat, turning away.

"Nico, wait!"

"I've got to go, Milla!"

"Sabina can wait a few minutes," I told him, knowing full well the bleeder queen would disagree if she were present. "Look at me!"

He stopped, shoulders slumped, and slowly—reluctantly—spun to face me. "I can't do this right now. I can't . . . be *here*." He shook his head, fighting some invisible emotion.

Taking a few steps to stand in front of him, I slipped my palm around his jaw. "This is the second time you've run away in the past few days. Tell me, what's going on?"

His eyes drifted shut for a moment, letting a section of his wall down to let me through. "The more I try, the more I lose."

"What does that mean?"

He sighed and pulled me down the hall where a bench was

pressed near a snow-covered window. "How can I ask them to abandon Nonna on Magrahel when she needs her family more than ever? What if I make the wrong call and she dies because we weren't there? Or if I lose the opportunity to get the book and my shadow back—" He made an exasperated sound as he turned his gaze toward the view of the garden.

"You are afraid, Nico."

He neither agreed nor denied my claim. I grabbed his hands and squeezed them. "You are not any less the capable, brilliant man I know because you are fearful of losing everything you worked for. But fear can only be beaten with faith. You cannot do this all alone, Nico."

"You're spending too much time around Sol," he mumbled.

I smiled. "You once said I was your greatest weakness, but I don't think that's true. I think your inability to trust makes you vulnerable. If you aren't careful, it will lead to your downfall."

"This isn't a very good pep talk, Milla." He tried to jerk out of my grasp, but I held steady.

"Good thing I'm not trying to make you feel better." I stood on my toes to place a kiss on his lips. "You know what needs to be done; you're just too afraid to do it because of who it would require help from."

"I don't trust them," he whispered.

"Then trust me," I pleaded. "Trust my judgement."

A crease formed between his brows as he fell deep in thought, most likely trying to find an alternative. But the look in his eyes was resigned. "I do, even if it goes against my own."

My smile softened. "Good. Now go figure out the drop with Sabina and get back to your Nonna. I'm sure she'll want her favorite grandchild around, and you need to spend as much time with her until tomorrow night. I'll handle the other details."

"Yes, boss," he said with the bow of his head. "Keep an eye on her for me."

"I will."

I watched him disappear down the hall toward the side drive before I headed toward the rear yard in search of my brothers. I hoped Aramis had packed his finest suit—he was going to need it.

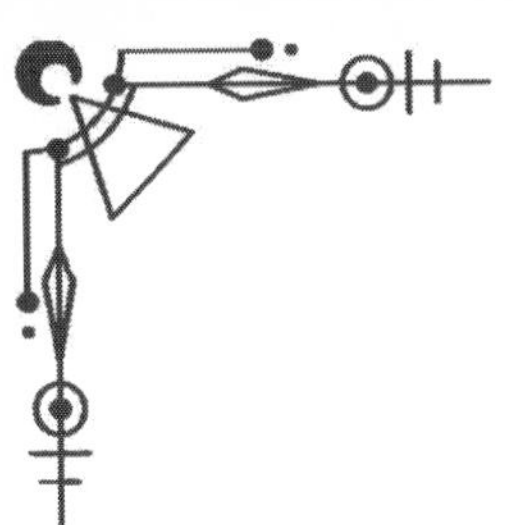
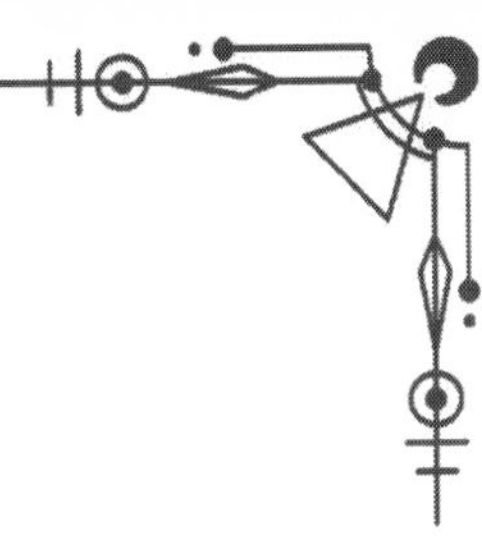

CHAPTER 44
CAMILLA

It snowed the night the veil between this world and the void thinned into a permeable barrier. White flurries dusted the tracks of the viaduct leading to the Districts. The Ada was frozen over, glimmering in the pale moonlight that shone in the cloudless night sky.

Nico held my arm as we crossed, worried my dangerous choice in footwear would send me over the edge of the bridge. "I told you not to wear those shoes," he murmured beside me.

"Well, I couldn't pair my evening dress with leather boots, Nicolai." Though, trying to balance my steps across the frozen stone and mortar composing the bridge was a skill set all by itself.

His breath clouded in front of his lips as he scoffed. Nico wore a classic black suit with a steel-grey tie tucked behind a satin vest with the OIC pin he'd been gifted from the Overseer attached to the lapel of his jacket to make his look more convincing. He hadn't put on his mask yet. We'd do that in the carriages, ones we would take separately so no one would associate the two of us together.

"All things considered," he whispered, "you look stunning. Though, I still believe you look better in Attano red."

"Your opinion is greatly biased." My cheeks were frozen stiff as I smiled.

The family tailor had designed my dress with long sleeves that started off the shoulder, tightly fitted around the bodice but with a forgiving material that allowed me to breath. With a skirt that was equally light and flexible, she added a high slit in case I needed to get away quickly. The garment was made to charm yet maintained a practical function.

It was the shade of green she chose, however, that made me feel the most comfortable I'd ever felt in a gown. A deep emerald lace with delicate jewels sewn throughout, the tiny crystals winked in the moonlight as we crossed the viaduct.

The color had been a personal request. It felt right to return to the Districts wearing my old armor.

"Nonna asked about you, Milla. She woke up not long after you left to get ready."

"That's a good sign, right? She hasn't been coherent since the fall."

Nico shrugged with the jerk of his broad shoulders. "I suppose it's better than being loopy all the time. I feel better knowing the cousins are with her, though I know they're very displeased to stay behind."

I peered over my shoulder at Luther, who took a swig from his flask before tucking it inside his coat. "All but one, anyway."

"I'll never shake Luther. He's my right-hand man—or I guess I should say my left." He wiggled his metal fingers concealed beneath his glove against my forearm, chuckling at the terrible joke.

"Glad you're in good spirits going into this," I said. "He has the Veritas?"

"Ready to go."

"And the benders you hired to push the cars?"

Nico stiffened. "Left this morning to take the bridge in Anghor to approach the South Gate from the low road. The Boys are scattered along the tracks through the city, and they'll send word when the cars are through. They scouted the route this morning, but most of the Watch is patrolling the Wet District, so they should be fine."

What he pointedly left out was the mention of Aramis cutting a deal with Narcissa to make sure the guards posted in the common areas were busy or somewhat distracted. A little copper could make anyone turn their head in this city, and Nico didn't ask questions when my brother asked for a small allowance to send Narcissa's way.

"Right." I sighed. "All that's left now is our part."

"How are you feeling?" he asked, just as we made it to the end of the bridge.

The small heel of my flat stepped off the solid bridge and sunk into a grassy knoll descending to a padded dirt path leading toward the Wet District. Three carriages, courtesy of Narcissa herself, were parked and ready.

"Spiteful," I answered him. The thought of returning all the pain the Nine and their supporters had caused us burned any hesitation away in my heart. I had my power inside my bones, my husband at my side, and my family behind me. There was nothing Felix could do to stop us from taking back this city.

"I was asking about your remnant, but I'm glad you're choosing malice tonight." He winked.

My hands balled into fists. Despite the testing and training, the various times I had proven to myself I could control it, my power still sat unsettled inside me. Like it was being held over a flame to boil. Whether it was my own nerves or the thinning veil that brought us closer to Oblivion, it took focus to keep it from crawling through my veins.

But I didn't want to worry Nicolai, so instead I told him, "It's fine."

He came to a halt before the cars, caressing my gloved hand in his own. "Show them all your malice, princess. You are a daughter of Chaos, and you have nothing and no one to hide from anymore. Trust yourself. Trust your fire." He kissed my knuckles before taking a deliberate step back, my fingers slipping from his touch. "I love you."

"I love you too," I whispered, too fearful to say them any louder in case the shadows listened as Nonna once warned. Life had a way of giving me everything I treasured most, but the darkness found its own cruel way of taking it back. He loaded the first car with Luther and Finn, who had already slipped on their obsidian masks nearly identical to Nico's.

With a glossy black veneer constructing a blank expression, the design was simple yet coincidentally disturbing. Nico had styled his hair differently, hiding his signature fade with an outgrown style that had to be combed back at the sides. Even the eyes of his mask concealed any recognizable feature of his face—including the intimidating steel-grey stare which had become well-known on this side of the city. Esme applied a thin, metallic coating to the glass on the outside, so Nico could see out, but no one could see through. *Snooping glass*, as she called it.

I hadn't required the same glass on my own, as my eyes were a more mundane color. But with the mask covering every inch of my face, it would be impossible to pick me out of a crowd—especially when I was still supposed to be dead.

"Let's go." Aramis sighed and held the door open for me. He

was dressed in a plain suit—an old one, but his measurements must not have changed much since the last time he was fitted. Not since Sera . . .

I shook her face out of my thoughts before she lingered too long. I needed a clear head to think straight tonight, and not one biased with a heavy heart and guilty conscience.

The seats in Narcissa's carriage were stiff and appeared hardly used. My brother sat across from me, his mask in his hands, staring at the metal in his palms while he brooded. Jeremiah sat beside me on the bench, a bit reluctant to be dragged along, but with the absence of the cousins, I wanted another number on our side.

"I'm only to keep watch, correct?" he asked.

"Unless something goes wrong. Then we might need you," I replied.

Aramis flipped his mask once between two fingers. "You'll be on the balcony with one of Narcissa's girls, watching the floor. Nico has that mentalus with him—"

"Finn," I said.

He shrugged like it hardly mattered. "Yes, Finn. He'll be monitoring your thoughts, so you can alarm him if you see anything suspicious. Be careful what you're thinking about up there with the courtesan."

"Like I care about courtesans." He slumped against the slope of the seat backing. The carriage had started down the pebbled path, shifting as we hit the beginnings of the cobblestone roads. "I don't understand why you brought me along. Anyone could be a lookout. I'm shit with a gun."

I patted his bouncing knee in an attempt to distract him from his nerves. "You have your own talents, Jer. But most importantly, you're a Marchese. There's no one else I trust more to be watching over us."

Aramis grunted across from me. I studied him before he put on his mask. He hadn't said a word all night, had hardly spoken the days before besides the mentioning of his workings with Narcissa. Without the train and Marcus going back and forth to communicate, we could not coordinate anything further than our original plans for Magrahel.

Thankfully, the carriages still arrived on time and in place, which meant the rest of our deals should be similarly arranged.

"No pushing your glint on me tonight, brother?"

Aramis looked at me then, peering up through his pale lashes before settling them back on the mask between his fingers. "Not tonight."

My gut sensed something was wrong, unsettled by the lack of pushback.

"The party started an hour ago," he said before I could ask him why he was being so lenient tonight. "So the events of the night are well underway by now. Most of the guests will have arrived, and the drinks have begun to flow. Jer, you'll wait at the foot of the stairwell for the escort."

"And what about us? How are you going to change into your disguise?" I asked.

"Narcissa should have planted a watchman's uniform in one of the servant's lockers down by the kitchens. I'll change quickly to make it look like I'm escorting you to the lab at the Firenzes' request."

It felt too simple. There were bound to be problems we weren't planning for—weren't prepared for. "And you're sure the book will be in the lab? What if Felix keeps it in an office—or even his private quarters?"

Aramis was shaking his head before I even finished. "No. I've seen Felix with his important work before. He keeps all his references and research in a small office in the lab itself. We don't have time to search the main house. Our energies are better spent investigating the most probable location."

I sucked in a breath and peeked out the window to gauge how much longer the ride would last. Ten minutes with my family and I was already desperate for some space. Thankfully, they fell silent the rest of the way. Aramis and Jeremiah applied their masks while I made sure the thin chains clasping mine to my head were secure and in place. The last thing I needed was a surprise unmasking in front of a room of Niners and their supporters.

The carriage came to a stop over a gravel driveway, and I took a calming breath as the lights from the Firenze estate slipped into the dark carriage.

"Everything is going to be fine," Aramis whispered just as the driver opened the door to let us out. My brothers got out first, assisting me after. I grabbed both their waiting hands, clinging to them even after I was steady and walking up the front steps to the group of guards standing at the entryway.

The home was stunning, even more immaculate than the rumors had painted: a three-story structure with thick ivy growing between rows of windows brimming golden light from the gas lamps inside. Music hummed through the brick, and my pulse picked up to the jovial beat.

Nico and his own men were already inside by the time we reached the front doors, swallowed by the party lights and sounds. The watchmen stationed at the entrance each wore the formless mask and black and silver capes. Their posture was informal—a casual slouch tipped the guard's shoulders as we approached.

Aramis wordlessly handed him an invitation—though I had no idea where he'd swiped one. "The Ingolia Family from Inverstead," the watchman muttered. His brow cocked. "I didn't know we had a patron family that far south."

"Word spread fast across the Isle when the bridge was destroyed," Aramis spoke in a low voice. "And we could no longer ignore the threat growing in the heart of our country. We've come to officially join the ranks of the patrons before us."

The guard was quiet for a moment, flipping the invitation over in his hand. Finally, he nodded to the watchman standing idle to the side. "Search them."

My breath hitched as a man came behind me, and I had to fight the knee-jerk reaction to shrink from the gloved hands that reached for my frame. Thankfully, my satin gloves were pulled high up my arm, and he only searched the places covered with fabric, avoiding my bare skin.

My brother stepped toward us. "Now, I don't know how you men do it here in Lynchaven, but down in Inverstead we don't touch a lady down there without permission," he said lightheartedly as the guard patted my skirts. "It's downright indecent."

I would have rolled my eyes had the man behind me not cleared his throat uncomfortably. "I meant no disrespect, sir. It's only—"

"You're worried a small woman might be harboring weapons of destruction underneath all those layers of brocade? That's a very convenient notion, if you ask me." Jeremiah joined the conversation as the other guards finished searching them.

The watchman patted around my hips cautiously, as if my brothers had convinced him he truly was being indecent by doing his job. The air shifted as he stepped back and returned to his post next to the rest of the Watch, not even bothering to move aside my skirts.

"Gentlemen," I said, faking a warm laugh and offered the group a delicate wave with my fingers, flustering him further if the bob of his helmet was any indication. The mask made it difficult to read people, which was simultaneously beneficial and problematic in my position. It was difficult to anticipate one's intentions when I couldn't see their eyes.

Without waiting for the guards to change their minds, my brothers and I were swept into the dull roar of a hundred more patron families, the lights of a grand party, and the music that swelled from the heart of the gathering.

Nico and his men were nowhere to be found, and I searched for them in the sea of taffeta skirts and feathered masks, even as Aramis dragged me into an empty hall that extended from the main foyer.

He rounded a corner at the end of the hall where a narrow staircase wrapped the inner wall. Brushing my skirts aside, I removed the pistols attached to the sheaths around my thighs and handed them both the weapons I'd kept hidden until we got past security, grateful to be rid of the bulky guns so I could walk normally again.

They shoved them quickly in their waistbands before anyone joined us in the quiet corridor, concealing the hilt with their jackets. Aramis nodded toward the stairs. "Wait there, Jer. She should be along to retrieve you soon."

Jeremiah grumbled his excitement at the opportunity. I wanted to remind him he had the preferred job out of anyone tonight, but Aramis was already pulling me by the arm back to the party. The navy and olive designs on the wallpaper were a mere blur as we rushed past. I only had time to look back at my younger brother and whisper the words, "Be careful."

"Take care of yourselves," he replied quietly.

The empty expression of his mask was the last thing I saw as we turned the corner once more.

"Where are the servants' quarters?" I asked.

"In the back, near the kitchens. Just use your nose."

"Will it not be strange that we're lurking around in the halls while everyone else is in the main room?"

Another hall intersected our path; this one I understood ran along the right side of the home. According to Aramis's sketch of the place, the Firenzes' manor was essentially formed by a right and left wing with a large entertaining area in the center. The second and third floors had corridors running north and south to the main room where the party was held, where one could look down over the gathering from the comfort of several sitting areas. The Firenzes that lived here had rooms on various floors, spaced out from each other. Not even Aramis could narrow down the purpose of every room—all thirty-odd something of them.

The savory smell of broiled meat, heady spice, and baked breads led us to the left, heading back toward the main area. Couples gathered on the sides of the hall, escaping the noise of the party to talk in private exchanges. The staff, noted by the starch white shirts and white gloves donning their uniform, wove between the groups, disappearing through a pair of swinging doors. Aramis hadn't marked this area on his map.

"I'll be right back," he muttered. "Don't talk to anyone while I'm gone."

Before I could argue, he slipped behind a servant and disappeared through the kitchen entrance. My brother seemed confident enough that he knew where he was going, so I paced up the hall to busy myself, eager to gain a glimpse of the party despite the risk of drawing someone's attention.

"Excuse me, miss!"

I swerved just in time to dodge a tray of empty champagne flutes. The server dashed around my left side as I dodged him to make room for his wide tray. It was chaos, watching the staff leave with full trays and return with empty ones, a continuous cycle to fuel the debauchery.

Velvet curtains framed the archway leading into the main room, and despite my disdain for the family who owned this frivolous display of wealth they called a home, I couldn't help the way my eyes widened behind my mask, taking it all in.

Four crystal-dripped chandeliers hung from each corner of the ceiling, reflecting their flickering candlelight against the tin ceiling tiles and enhancing the warm bronze of their beveled faces. My gaze fell to the wrought iron banisters lining the upper levels, where my brother would watch from a safe distance.

A ten-piece band was playing against the far wall, yet no one danced. Instead, they socialized, shouting over the music and the blaring horns that only provided a backdrop for the party. Still, I searched for Nico, his cousin, and the young mentalus that followed them.

Like an ardent breath against my cheek, a gentle breeze stroked the left side of my jaw, guiding my head slightly toward a group standing near the wall of windows overlooking the back of the Firenze property. Nico stood with Finn and Luther at a table, pretending to drink and smoke, if the contents of the table were any indication.

A slight pressure pressed my temples inward. Finn must have been reading my thoughts in case I needed to tell them something. I let him know my satisfaction at finding them safely past the first hurdle in our plan.

He lingered in my head too long, and I figured, if I had to wait here, I might as well enjoy myself.

My focus went to Nico, an idea flickering in my imagination as I smiled behind my mask and delighted in the way Finn's posture went completely rigid. The band of pressure around my head disappeared immediately.

Someone interrupted my fun. Vanya was making her rounds among the guests and finally made her way to Nico's table. Her mask only partially hid her face, unlike the one covering my own, and her dress was a lighter shade of platinum that reminded me of molten silver melting from her waist as she moved.

There was something missing, however. The hosts of the night were nowhere to be found. In fact, I hadn't seen a single Firenze among the crowds, and I wondered if they were already upstairs in their elusive meetings Aramis had mentioned.

Some of my nerves dissolved, seeing Nico with one of our allies. I nodded in his direction and turned to walk back down the hall where I had left my brother—running straight into the hard chest of a man in a navy suit.

"My apologies, miss," the man said. "Is there something I can help you with?"

That voice. It had haunted me enough to draw a bad taste in my mouth, a nervous flutter in my heart. My gaze lifted from his tie to his face, and I nearly gasped at the smug smile exposed from his half-mask.

Felix Firenze.

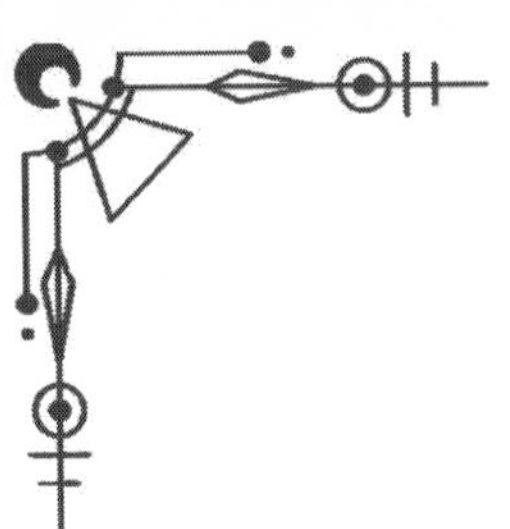
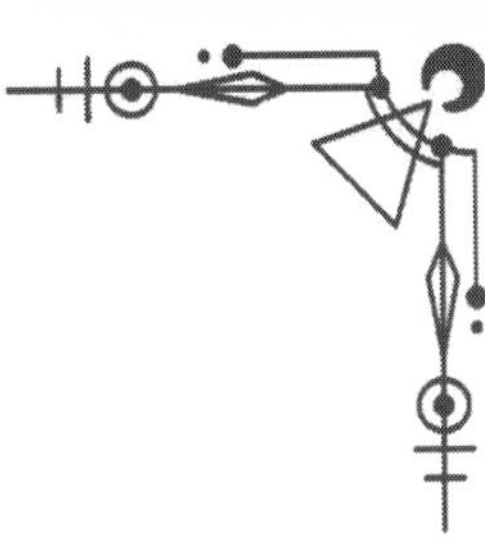

CHAPTER 45
NICOLAI

This night was feeling like a bad dream I couldn't wake from. The one-way glasses in front of my eyes were private spectacles, allowing me to stare at anyone I wished without their knowing. Their eyes were shameless anyway, watching us as we entered, as if they could smell our remnants wafting off us like reeking street dogs wandering into their party.

I supposed we carried an air about us unknowingly, because Finn assured me there were no suspicious thoughts spurning from our late arrival. We let a staff member show us to a high-top table on the far side of the room, giving us a clear view of the entire floor, and before we made our next move, I waited until Milla's brother perched himself near the balcony on the second floor. His escort offered him a cigarillo, which he accepted quickly.

Luther finally joined us. "There are watchmen at every exit. The western stairwell is guarded as well, only letting in a few men on an approved list. I'd bet they're hosting their meetings up there."

"It'd be a shame if they lost their list."

He handed me a folded piece of paper. "I thought the same."

I took it and slipped the list inside my suit jacket for later. How he snuck it off them so quietly was anyone's guess.

It was difficult to eavesdrop on the conversations surrounding us, even more so with this fucking mask that made it hard to breathe so close to my face. More than once did I catch Finn rubbing his temples like he was getting a headache from it all.

"Hanging in there?" I murmured, bending to speak near his ear.

"Is it obvious I don't do well in crowds?" His shoulders lifted with a forced laugh. "I'll be alright. Just need to focus on someone to drown out the rest. Some thoughts are more intrusive than others."

I understood that better than he knew. Scanning the floor, my gaze caught on an archway I'd noticed the servants using as they filtered in and out of the party. A woman stood there in a deep green dress and a silver mask, her hair loosely curled and twisted in an updo to show off her slender neck and scarred shoulders.

Milla had been hesitant to reveal them, insisting a modern lady in the Districts didn't have such marred skin. I thought it was worth the risk of reminding them all of her resilience.

"She's looking for you," Finn said beside me.

So she was. I reached out with my remnant and barely skimmed her face to turn in our direction. Her shoulders relaxed some as she noticed us.

"She's relieved we made it past the guards," he translated her thoughts.

I scoffed. "Likewise. Anything else?"

He paused. "She thinks you look very handsome tonight. She likes your mask and—" Finn stiffened beside me.

"And?" I asked.

"I . . . don't think I can say it out loud."

"*Shitting saints*, don't you fucking dare." Luther groaned, shaking his head as if he could guess.

"That's not very professional of you, Finn," I teased. "I hired you for a job, and you're not being completely transparent."

He cleared his throat. "Fine. She imagined you wearing your mask while you were on top of her in *bed*. A fantasy I could have gone the rest of my life *not* seeing. Happy?"

A slow smile spread across my face despite the situation as Luther whispered a string of curses. I patted Finn lightly on the shoulder. "Very much."

"Fantasies? What a stimulating topic of conversation." A woman appeared in front of our table with her silver gown and black feathered mask, blocking the view of my diabolical wife.

Vanya.

"Was wondering when you'd show," she murmured. "Where's the rest of you?"

I placed my forearms on the table to lean forward, shortening the distance our words had to travel. "I have an ill family member the cousins needed to stay with. Magrahel is notorious for stealing the sick and weak from their tether to this world."

"My condolences," she replied. "But I wasn't talking about your cousins."

She was looking for Milla. I wondered if the two had struck up an unexpected friendship the other day when they met in secret. "She's here, looking for the book."

She made a strange sound in reply, and her dark eyes swept over the two men standing beside me. "What do you need help with?"

"I want to know what they're discussing upstairs." Removing

the note Luther snatched, I unfolded it and showed her the names. "Anyone you recognize?"

Her mouth pulled down in a frown. "Felix mentioned something about important guests, but I've been in enough meetings the last month for my skin to crawl at the mention of attending another. These are the Isle's richest families; each come from a different Third. Most of them should be upstairs already, but I think I saw a Blavatsky chasing a few skirts in the study. Perhaps you could fill in for him. He's far too drunk to be of any worth to the Firenzes upstairs."

The thought of getting into that meeting had my pulse racing. It was risky but too good to pass up. "I'll need someone to keep him busy."

She pursed her lips. "You'll owe me for this."

I smirked. "Just add it to my tab, Vanya."

She offered me the ribbon hanging from the eagle pin on her dress, a type of pass that was given to the important guests she mentioned, to slip by the watchmen.

"I'll need that back, so don't make me regret this," she said and slipped away toward the front entrance of the main room.

"Wings on the roof," Luther murmured under his breath.

My eyes lifted to the third floor, where a young man stood clad in a simple all-black suit that was clearly not made for the standards of this society. A gold handkerchief peeked from his vest pocket. One of the Canary Boys already had news to report.

"Finn?"

He paused, reading the young man waiting in the shadows. "The first car is halfway through. The second is on the way. Routes have been clear so far."

I nodded, and the runner disappeared once more, far more acquainted with this house than any of us. Everything was going smoothly. Our enemies were ignorant of our infestation—and hopefully would remain so until it was far too late.

"I'm going upstairs. Keep an eye on things, cousin."

Luther nodded once, and I slipped away, carrying the cigarillo that had been left burning at the table. It wasn't my usual blend, but it gave my false hand something to fixate on before I throttled the first Firenze I crossed. It also prevented anyone from grabbing that hand and feeling the solid metal beneath the glove, which would be difficult to explain myself out of.

A single guard stood at the end of a staircase as I rounded a corner in the hall branching from the main room. He rolled his head, stretching his neck as if he'd been posted there far too long with far too little entertainment. I adjusted the lapels of my jacket to show off the pin and ribbon as I approached the guard, who held a hand up before I could pass.

"Name?"

"Blavatsky," I said curtly, hoping I'd pronounced it correctly.

The watchman reached in his back pocket, cocking his head when something he was looking for must have been missing. He began patting his person, muttering to himself as he searched for something I knew to be missing.

His list.

"Is there a problem, sir?" I asked him. "Should I go get another officer?"

"No, no, no," he blurted. "That won't be necessary. Blavatsky, you said? Go on ahead. Second floor to the left."

The stairs led to a loft, splitting the space between two rooms. Velvet couches and leather ottomans furnished the floor while a hearth blazed heat and light across the sitting area. To the left, where the guard below had directed, a pair of doors with a golden wood grain were shut with another guard in front of them.

Noticing me, he stepped to the side and opened one of them to let me through.

I glanced across the house, towards the opposite railing where Milla's brother lounged on a stool. He was watching me, his mask level with mine. I shirked off his attention before anyone noticed our connection and entered the private meeting.

Conversations fell silent as I took the only empty chair at the end of a long table with eight others; Lavern Firenze sat the head on the opposite side. Each attendee was the designated figurehead of their family or business. Each wore their mask to conceal their own identities for various reasons—possibly from each other.

The door shut and locked behind me, committing me to my decision. But I smiled behind the metal pretense; they had no idea what they had just allowed into this room. In a house full of rats, I was the snake from the garden they should've killed when they had the chance.

LAVERN STARTED the meeting with a lengthy speech, and I thought the shadows might take him before he had the chance to finish, the way he struggled to speak. His barrel chest would inhale a massive gulp of air between talking points and struggle to get out all his words. I might have felt pity for him had he not been a piece of shit.

"Firstly, thank you all for coming to our city this evening. The pride and concern you show for your country does not go unnoticed."

There were murmurs of acknowledgement from the table.

"Some of you are familiar with the history of our foundation," he went on, "but we have a few new families I'd like to brief. Our roots date back fifty years, when the first descendants came to this Isle and we were forced to make room for their kind. My grandfather, Dante Firenze, was High Overseer at the time."

He coughed into a handkerchief before pulling his fist against his chest. "Seeing as we couldn't send them back, he saw an opportunity to use the remnants to speed up production in the factories and keep our hands clean. He wisely separated our kinds to protect the natives of the Isle, and we profited off their gifts until they cheated the system and took our land and businesses out from beneath us."

My eyes rolled behind the snooping glass.

Lavern sighed and looked down at the bloody cloth in his hand. "What he didn't foresee was their ambition, and how families like the Bianchis and the Attanos would slowly take our city—and soon our Isle—out of our control." He tucked it inside his pocket and leaned on his cane. "But some of us did foresee this, which is why we founded the Nine. Three families from the Upper Knotch of the Isle, three from the Mez, and three from the Lowlands. Each with substantial wealth and influence over their Thirds. Not just to keep an eye on the descendants, but to make sure those who held our ideals remained in power."

It was a history lesson I'd heard from my father following the horrid acts committed against my family. He'd tried to explain to me why someone would do something so wicked, defining the true motivations of the Nine that sought to keep us under their thumb in a single word: *fear*.

They were afraid of us. Afraid they would lose their positions because our magic seemingly gave us more power, even when we had earned our place in this city just as any of their predecessors had. The Firenzes couldn't allow an outsider—a descendant—to do better. Be better. I was thankful for the mask now, if only to hide my glare I fixed on the old man.

"But no longer will the descendants have the advantage," he said with a small smile. "Thanks to the funding from your families, we can continue to lay the foundation the OIC has provided. We can establish Order once more."

That wasn't the first time someone from his side had thrown that word around. My skin prickled as a shift in the room had the other members straightening in their seats. Lavern motioned to a guard near the doors, who opened them to let in another speaker.

Neal fucking Caldwell.

"I'd like to welcome the head of the Watch, Neal Caldwell. I'll give you the floor, Inspector."

"My appreciation, Lavern," he said with a bob of his head. He wore a simple mask that covered the left side of his face, hiding nothing about his identity. Like he desired the attention the new title gave him. "But first, let's have a toast, shall we?"

Behind him, two staff members entered with trays of flutes filled with a bubbly drink. They served each of us, placing a drink on a square napkin in front of each attendant. Neal stood where Lavern once had, raising his glass. The room followed his lead, and I lifted my own to fulfill the role I played.

"I raise a toast to the new families joining the cause, and may the ones they replaced rest eternally in the void. To the Marcheses and the Clemontes who could not be here today, but without whom, thanks to their groundwork, this night would not be possible. To Order, and to a new future!"

"To Order," the rest of the room chanted before tipping their glasses to the lips of their masks to consume a long sip. I faked the act, faked a swallow, and replaced the spiked drink back on the table.

Neal's smile was even more irritating with the newfound confidence he must have gathered over the past few weeks. He set down his own glass. "I know many of you have been very concerned about the Hightower Heist and the implications of its destruction, but the research obtained at the facility—and the mines—has been recovered and we have not only replicated the Head Alchemist's results, but we have expanded upon them."

"And what about the descendant we had hostage following the Heist?" The man beside me spoke out of turn, interrupting the inspector. "Did you not give him back to the Attano Benders?"

"We organized his retrieval so that the Iron Saint would be parked at the Main Station, and thus allowing us to impair the locomotive. Our sources have confirmed the train is destroyed beyond repair. The Attanos no longer have that advantage and have been severely weakened."

The group murmured their delight over the fact, but I got hung up on two words. *Our sources*. Who the hells was feeding the OIC information about us? And was it the same one who got us stuck on the bridge that day Regulus was taken? The one who jammed the coupler that night we were *severely weakened*?

"Furthermore," he continued, "we have something now that we didn't have before when the descendants came to the Isle half a century ago."

"And what is that?" a deep voice asked. I recognized it—might have been that Halloway character that threatened me the last time I was here.

Neal smirked. "We have the Arcane."

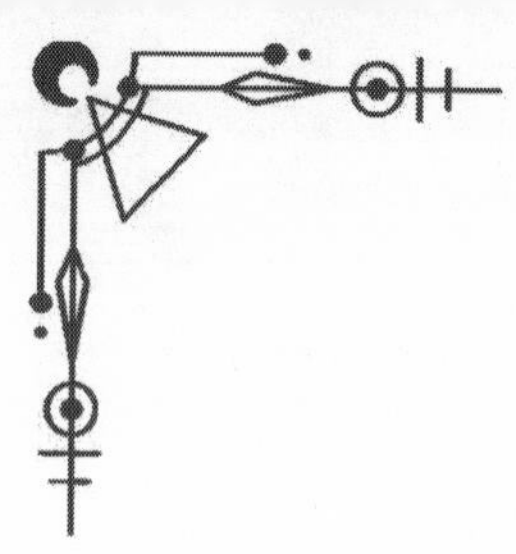
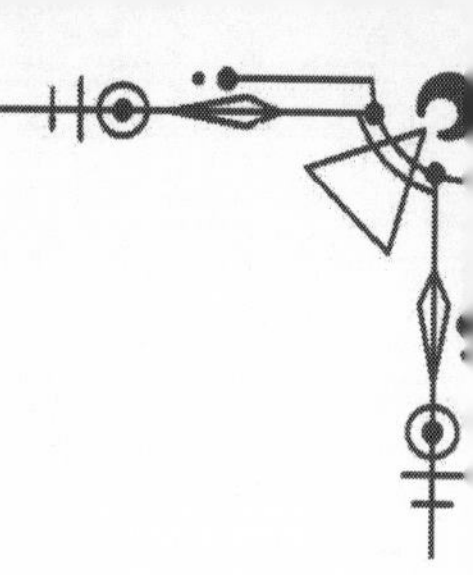

CHAPTER 46

CAMILLA

I had just thoughtlessly run into the man who was single-handedly responsible for hunting down my family, murdering my best friend, and destroying my train. Gauging the easy smile he wore as he stared down my dress, I knew he had no idea who I was.

To my right, a servant passed with a tray full of used dishes, cutlery gleaming in the light from the gas lamps. How easy it would be to grab a knife from a plate and shove it into his throat. Let him bleed out all over the pearly starched collar that dug into his thick neck.

I took a steady breath instead. His time would come if I stayed patient.

"Are you looking for something? Perhaps you'd like to go somewhere quieter?" he spoke again when I didn't reply to his previous question. But I had to take a second to compose myself—to still the tremble in my voice.

Think, Camilla. I needed a good enough lie to get out of here

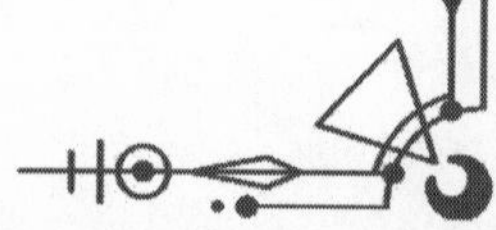

fast before he recognized the scars on my skin, which were far too numerous for a woman of my supposed position.

"How kind of you to ask," I said in a pitch higher than my usual tone. "It's actually the funniest thing. You see, I left my engagement ring on one of the plates the servants took, not realizing I had done so when they cleared the table. I was just heading to the kitchens to see if they found my ring before it was lost forever."

The mention of a betrothed must have soured some of his excitement, for his eyes finally found my face. I lowered my chin to look instead at my hands, rubbing at the spot on my finger where a ring should have been.

He sighed and took a small step back. "I can . . . go check with the kitchen?"

I shook my head. "No, that won't be necessary. I already have a guard searching for me. I'd hate to waste your time, Mr. Firenze."

His lips thinned as his smile stretched, and I suppressed a shiver, recalling how I had nearly married that oily grin. "What did you say your name was?"

"My name is Ingolia. Jules Ingolia. It was lovely to meet you." I gave him a mock curtsey and walked away. He held up his hand just before I could get around him, skimming the space above my navel.

"I hope you find what you are looking for, Jules."

The way he said the words made me feel like there was something more to them. Or perhaps it was just the arrogance in his raised chin, the disdain I held for him in my heart that disfigured the way he looked down at me like a bird toying with a mouse.

Without another word, he finally lowered his hand and left me standing there in the hall, my pulse racing from the strange interaction.

"There you are. *Hells*, I told you not to move! Where have you been?" My brother's gravelly voice snapped me out of a trance. He was wearing a full watchman's uniform. The obsidian helmet covered his head, while silver shoulder gauntlets and the black cape draping behind his back fit him well enough to look like it was tailored just for him. Narcissa chose her victims well.

He glanced behind me, eyes flicking over the strangers behind us. "Never mind, we need to get moving. It's getting late."

I nodded numbly, letting his irritation with me roll off my back like rain on a window. "Lead the way."

He turned on his heel and ventured back down the hall from the direction we originally came, though this time, we passed the main hall stretching down the right wing and kept going straight. He brought us to a side entrance concealed by the turn of another corner, where rows of overcoats and women's cloaks hung neatly on a bar beside a side exit. These didn't belong to the guests but to the occupants of the home, obvious by the sectioning of certain styles and sizes.

Aramis pulled one off the rack and handed it to me. "Here. The lab is on the river, and the wind will freeze you solid. We'll go through the greenhouse to stay out of the weather."

"You're nervous," I said, noting the slight shake in his voice. Aramis never showed his nerves. He'd always kept his emotions submerged in a frozen pool, which is why it surprised me so much that he had been drawn to Sera—someone who could see right through the ice.

"Let's just get this over with." He sighed, not looking back at me as we left the sounds of the voracious party with the shut of a slim door.

The night was obscenely quiet. I expected more guards to be posted out here where a driveway looped around the side of the house and connected a private road I assumed led to stables, greenhouses, and hopefully the lab where the Firenzes kept their research.

We kept to the side of the road shrouded in darkness without a lantern to light the way, and I pulled the edges of the coat tight around my shoulders. A pleasant perfume lingered in the warm wool, a scent I had owned myself when I lived in the Districts. An uplifting scent of orange, citrus, and blooming florals. Perhaps that was why it smelled so familiar.

Aramis glanced behind us every few minutes, but it was so still out here, we'd hear an approaching horse or footfalls before it was too late. Winter had stripped the trees of their leaves, glazing them in frost and lacing a canopy above us. Long icicles hung forebodingly from the bony branches, collecting the light of the full moon.

We came to the first greenhouse, a semi-transparent strip doming over the frozen ground. It was slightly warmer inside as Aramis beckoned me to walk ahead of him through the rows of hanging vegetation and colorful foliage. Tags lined each pot and dirt bed, and I thought of Nonna and how much she'd love such a garden of assortments. My thoughts drifted to her as I followed my brother in silence, hoping she was still clinging to the tether of her family tonight.

"What is all this?" I looked at him over my shoulder, but his attention was on his feet.

"Just various shit they use for their alchemy. Don't touch anything. Most of it's toxic without a carrier oil."

I buried my hands further into the cloak, eyeing the strange plants more suspiciously. "What do they use for glint?"

"A little of all of this, I suppose, but the key ingredient comes from the south. It can only grow in the marshes. The weather here is too volatile, even in the controlled space of a greenhouse."

I nodded, tucking the information away for later. We came to the end of the long greenhouse, and my brother shushed me, telling me to wait where I stood.

"I'm going to go relieve the current guards of their post so we can sneak in the back entrance. The front is better guarded, but they'll not be expecting partygoers to sneak out this far. Hang tight until you hear my whistle."

I nodded in agreement because what else was I supposed to do? I was at the mercy of everyone else until the guards were gone. Aramis patted my shoulder, and the touch was so unexpected I nearly jumped.

"Stay here, Milla." His tone was softer than usual. It should have been a comfort, but my brother was never one to be so tactile. He slipped out of the greenhouse without another word.

My hands dug into the deep pockets inside the cloak, desperately seeking some warmth—even in this glass cage shielding the harsh riverside breeze. There was something in the pocket, my fingers wrapped around cold metal. A key by the feel of the serrated teeth and circular handle. I kept it concealed in case whoever the coat belonged to needed it later.

Too many minutes seemed to slip by. The moist ground slipped into the satin of my flats and numbed my toes. Just when I questioned running to his aid, a short whistle pierced the night, a high-pitch wail like the wind when it passed through a crack.

The Firenzes' lab was a towering warehouse made from windowless brick walls and a mesh of tangled pipes weaving from the side of the building to dump into the river. Chimney spouts jutted out from the top, billowing a grey smoke against the black sky. A gas light flickered, desperately trying to stay alive, near the door my brother was currently posted. He cocked his head toward the back entrance.

"It's clear," he said as I approached. "No one's inside yet, but we should make it quick before that changes."

"Do you expect it to change?"

"I always expect something bad to happen, and things have gone too smoothly so far."

I had to agree. Either the Firenzes weren't worried someone would infiltrate their wares, or we had planned this night to perfection. I was more inclined to think the alchemists were just being negligent.

The inside of the lab was a glorified version of Delilah's Orbitarium. Worktables were pushed to the walls and arranged around the room to keep the center clear. A sky light illuminated the large room, the clear glass collected the first flakes of snow.

A rickety metal staircase ascended the far wall to a second level, where a long window overlooking the main floor interrupted a walled-off section. A walkway of similarly rusted means extended from the offices, over the entire floor, and to the configuration of pipes and gears that ran the machinery in the lab.

Aramis went straight to a chalkboard covered in strange images. A table stood next to it, supporting stacks of notebooks. "I'll look through these. You search the assistant's desk in the corner there."

He pointed to a shameful setup next to the boiler—a so-called desk with boxes of files piled on top of a worn varnish. I look ed instead to the second level. "I think I'll try the offices, actually. I doubt Felix would leave something that important to an *assistant*."

Aramis glanced up at me when I said the word. With his mask now removed, his glare was obvious. "Suit yourself."

The rusted stairs groaned with every step I took, and my brother's shoulders tensed an inch more with every step I took. "Feet of a fucking crueger," he said in a whisper-shout. "Keep it down!"

I made it to the top without the guards outside coming to investigate. The floor was still unsteady, but my steps weren't as obvious. I reached for the door handle, but it barely twisted as I jiggled it. Locked.

"Where's the key?" I asked him.

He shrugged, still looking through the books. "How should I know?"

"You're supposed to know everything about this place."

Aramis snorted before moving on to the next table, opening and closing drawers in a rush. I huffed a breath in frustration. I didn't sneak all the way in here to be blocked by a bloody door. If it was locked, then that meant something valuable was inside. I slipped off my glove, ready to use my power to corrode the lock, when a thought occurred to me.

Removing the key from my pocket, I slipped it into the door handle—and it slid in without resistance.

I didn't know a single woman in the Firenze family. Their wives and daughters stayed out of the family business. So whose coat could this possibly belong to?

Hells, I could think about it later. For now, I tentatively pushed the door open in case there were any alarms and searched the dark office with only the bare illumination from the skylight to guide me.

The place reeked. A putrid smell wafted from a set of beakers filled with dark liquid. A burner had been left on. The bright orange flame immediately grabbed my attention, as did the notebook sitting next to it, but a quick flip through the leather journal informed me this wasn't the book we were searching for.

A weight edged into my bones, turning my limbs into lead as I neared the workbench. It didn't hit me until I saw the various weapons hanging on the wall in the light of the burner. Their tips glowed red—as did all the Niner blades coated in poison. This must have been where they conducted their experiments and dipped their weapons.

A thank-you note was thrown half-folded beside the burner, and I recognized the stationary.

A letter . . . from Vanya.

Dread unfurled in my stomach, understanding then that Vanya had been in contact with the Firenzes—and not for Nico, but for herself. The note detailed her appreciation for supplying her father's guards and her hopes to establish a union between their families very soon.

Cursing beneath my breath, I set the paper over the burner and the words of a liar turn black—then to ash.

My fingers shakily skimmed the wall for a switch, flipping on the gas lamps. They flickered alive to reveal a steel door cracked open to a connecting room. The smell intensified as I neared, pushing it open with the toe of my flat to find . . .

Cages.

My chest seized, unable to breathe as the pungent stench hit me immediately. The lamplight poured from the doorway, gleaming over crudely bent metal bars nailed into a large stain on the floor. My gaze followed the dark spill towards a mass enclosed in the cages.

And two glossy, black eyes staring back at me.

I yelped, stumbling back, tripping over the length of my skirts and landing hard on the splintered floorboards. By the time I was on my feet, Aramis was halfway up the stairs, meeting me as I darted from the office.

"What's wrong?" he asked.

"There's a dead man in there," I whispered on a shaken breath. "*Hells*, Aramis. I think this is where they tested on those poor descendants."

"I'm sure that was a shock to see," he mumbled. "But a lot of bad things have happened here, Camilla. Isn't that why we're looking for the book? To make sure we stop the Firenzes from doing this to anyone else?"

My breath settled some as he grabbed my hands, bringing me back to the reality of our situation. *Right.* The book. We needed to find the book. But something more urgent gnawed at my nerves.

"We need to go back to the house, Aramis. I think I know who this coat belongs to, and if I'm right, Nico is in trouble."

His forehead creased with a curious look. "What are you talking about? We need the book—"

"To hells with the book, Aramis! We can come back later, but I need to warn him before it's too late!" Shoving past him on the stairs, I lifted my skirts to run towards the entry we used before—the only one unguarded that led to the greenhouses.

"Camilla, wait!"

I wasn't listening. My heart hammered in my chest, throbbing like the dull ache in my bones that the fumes of the Niner's poison had triggered. I pushed on the door to open it—but it was jammed.

"What?" I gasped, trying again. It was no use. The door wouldn't budge no matter how hard I pushed it. The handle barely jostled, barred from the outside.

I tried to call on my power, but it was blocked as well, silent in my blood as my pulse danced beneath my skin. Flustered and spiraling, a choked sob spilled from my panic, and I turned to find something to use to pry the door open just as the lights of the warehouse flickered on one by one, shining across large symbols painted on the floor—ones I recognized but barely understood. Aramis stood near the switch in front of the opposite pair of doors.

He was not afraid as I was. There was no surprise striking his features. His lips were flat, eyes downcast to the arcane images. No, he was not caught off guard—because he knew this would happen.

"No . . ." The word broke apart in my throat. "Aramis, *no*."

Those blue eyes that reminded me of our father, that sometimes looked at me with hope, squeezed shut. Any connection we once salvaged was severed. "I'm sorry, Camilla. I never meant to hurt you, I promise."

The lights inside must have been a signal, for as soon as the lab lit to life, the front doors opened. Felix and his cadre sauntered inside. No coats, guns ready, and laced knives glowing inside their sheaths.

"Aramis," I spat his name through my teeth. "What have you done?"

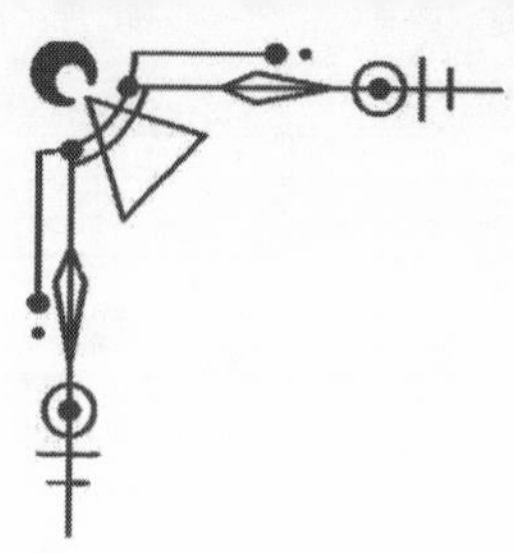
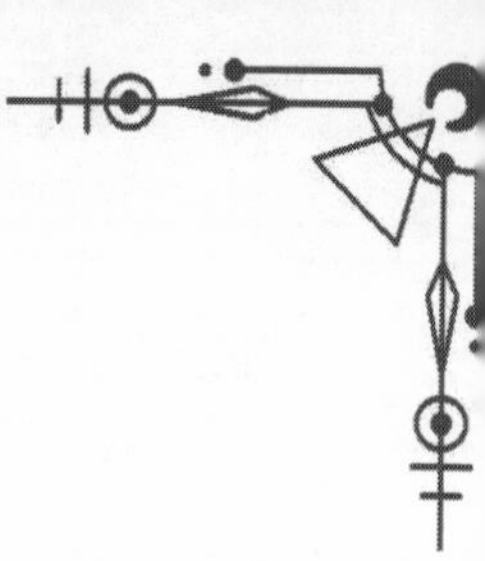

CHAPTER 47

NICOLAI

Neal opened a box that sat at the end of the table and removed an item wrapped in a velvet sleeve. Handing it to a member seated nearby, he instructed him to pass the contents around for our observation. Just the mention of the Arcane had every member of the Nine on the edge of their seat, eager to see what was inside. It wasn't the first time they'd heard it mentioned, it seemed.

"How will the Arcane help us?" I dared myself to ask. The identities of the Nine families remained hidden behind their masks, but I felt their eyes shift in my direction.

Neal didn't answer right away. Instead, he waited for the man next to me to open the sleeve and remove a small, jagged stone. Cut from a larger source, based on the polished sides and the sharp, angled cuts. But I knew that obsidian shine anywhere. Had been trapped by it for nearly five years of my life.

"As some of you may not know, Hightower was not just a prison, but a research facility," Neal started. A quiet rage simmered

in my blood for the confession he once blatantly lied about. "The previous inspector discovered the island and realized it was composed of something supernatural. A gift from a divine."

He offered the stone to me, and I flipped it over in my hand a few times, pretending to examine it. "It is fabled that when the Creator made our realm," Neal continued, "he used that very matter of the void to create everything in existence. So, with the help of the Firenzes and their expert alchemists, we studied it to better understand its properties. This stone wasn't a stone, but a blank slate. A resource for us to create, waiting to be molded into its purpose."

This. This was their Siphon then, as Vesper had called it. The source they drew from.

"Like pressing charcoal into ink, we melt this down and use it similarly. With the Arcane and the codes we've gathered from the remnants, we can create the same power the Creator gifted the saints. The possibilities with the Arcane are infinite, we'll have an advantage—and the upper hand for those willing to pay for it."

The woman on the other side of me cleared her throat, insisting I pass on the stone, but I was fisting the rock to hide the tremble in my hand. "Pay for it?" she asked them.

"Well," Lavern teetered as he waved his hand to dismiss her concerns. "We cannot just grant abilities to everyone, now, can we? This type of power must be carefully distributed. First, to our Nine families and loyal supporters. From there, we will open the procedure to anyone the OIC deems acceptable and responsible for such a gift."

"The wealthy then," I spilled the words before I could catch them.

Lavern quirked his brow, glancing my way. "The price will be quite more than the middle and lower classes could afford based on their annual salaries, but anyone willing to work hard and save can find a way. There will be requirements, of course, to qualify regardless of income."

"What do you mean by procedure?" a member across the table asked.

The old man looked to Neal, who was rolling the sleeve of his shirt up over his elbow. The inky image of a scorpion crawled down his forearm, curling its stinger over its head in a striking pose —a familiar.

"We've used familiars for decades to carry certain long-term medications, formulas to ward off the effects of a remnant, those such things. They are difficult and complex to create, which makes them expensive and exclusive, but otherwise they're the perfect conduits to hold magic."

Everyone spoke at once, discussing the possibilities. Mindless chatter filled the room—what remnant and familiar they would choose, how they would use it to their advantage, the opportunity to have more than one familiar.

"Could we acquire multiple conduits?" a woman asked.

Neal shrugged. "The descendants have polypotentias. Why shouldn't we?"

Because divine ordinance had blessed us with such power. Because we didn't buy our gifts; we were born with them, had learned how to bear the responsibility that came with harboring a powerful remnant. We certainly didn't acquire remnants from multiple *different* saints like this Niner suggested. Combining Blood with Bane . . . what was stopping them from accumulating them all besides money and the favor of the Firenzes?

Descendants in the Row were taught from the day we could summon our power as children how to use it fairly and justly, and though I wasn't one to speak from the moral high ground on the matter, I never used my remnant against a man without cause or reason—no matter how much my uncle would disagree.

This wasn't about protecting themselves from our influence. The Firenzes didn't truly care about evening the score between our sides of the city. This was about control, about manipulating natives so that they believed they were truly powerless without what the Firenzes offered to the exclusively qualified. The ones they conveniently would also deem qualifiable or not.

This pernicious organization selling power and status under the pretense of protection was solely concerned with the monopolization of magic.

Napkins scattered across the table as my remnant slipped in my fury. My fist curled into my palm, channeling the anger and causing me to lose focus into something less exposing. Thankfully, no one at the table noticed the draft.

Milla was right. We needed to get that book at the very least and destroy their research if we could. Doing so might buy us some time before this business plan sunk its teeth into the city—into the entire Isle. But first, I needed to get out of this room.

"What is your conduit, Inspector?" I gestured to the creature on his arm.

He glanced down at the animated tattoo, as if still trying to get used to its presence. "As the head of the Watch, it was important to choose a gift that would make me an asset to my country. I acquired the remnant of Blood."

Neal's lips tightened in a hard line, appearing as if he held back something unsettling. Which meant the Vex Veritas had triggered, but which of his claims had been a lie? His remnant, or the fact that it was his choice?

"Well, no one should be able to outrun or outmatch our inspector, then. I've heard Blood remnants are incredible hunters." Neal smiled before I asked, "Have you had any of the urges? You know the *cravings.*" I dropped my voice to a loud whisper at the word. The Niners stopped their discussions to listen to our conversation.

"I—" His brow furrowed, the corner of his lips pulling down. "That's a very personal question, Mr. Blavatsky."

I raised my hands in mock defense. "I just would like to know if there are any undesirable side effects to this kind of science."

He cleared his throat with a loud cough. "If you must know, not at all. There have been no *cravings* as you mentioned."

Neal mustered a brave face before promptly turning to vomit all over the hardwood floor. A metallic stench stained the air, and I didn't need to look at his mess to know he'd most likely thrown up a decent amount of blood. An incriminatory choice of power, choosing that of a bleeder.

"Inspector, that's very unfortunate for you. I'll go find an alchemedis . . . and a maid." I was out of my seat before I finished, before anyone could stop me.

"Mr. Blavatsky!" Lavern called out. I didn't turn to answer him. The guards made a move to block the door.

"Is something wrong, Mr. Firenze?"

He opened his mouth, but I let my remnant slip beneath the table to shove his cane out from beneath him, sending the old man toppling to the floor near the sullied part of the rug. The guards instantly abandoned their post to rush to his aid, and while everyone was concerned with Lavern, I snuck away.

It was a cheap shot, pushing over an old man who likely had broken something due to his emaciation—but better Lavern than me.

"We need an alchemedis," I told the few guards standing outside the room to further pull their attention away from my swift exit. A few of them sprang into action, running inside to assess the situation while I fled back down the stairs and into a busy hall.

A hand snatched my left hand—my metal one—halting my escape.

"What's the rush, handsome?" Narcissa said softly, a smile curling her blood-red lips. My heart—which had nearly stopped from the fear of being exposed—found relief at the sight of her. She wore no mask, only paint that swirled around her eyes and cheekbones to mimic the look of one.

"I need to lose the guards," I whispered as bodies brushed passed. "Mind escorting me somewhere private?"

She laughed, throwing her head back like she was drunk. All part of her show. She hooked her arm around mine. "I have a place we can get away, lovey."

This side of the house was dedicated to darker deeds. A smoking parlor was pushed down at the end of a wide gallery featuring elegant paintings of generations of Firenzes and the occasional sculpture commissioned by a long-dead artist. The gallery had a lack of admirers, as everyone lingered in the parlor.

Groups of men and women blew smoke around tables crowded with drinks. A full bar was busy serving drinks into chilled glasses crowding a server's tray. My escort snatched one of the crystal coupes as she passed by and sipped it as we approached a den behind the smoking parlor, this one guarded not by watchmen, but by Narcissa's guards.

They let us pass into a dimly lit room filled with the haze of cigarillo smoke. Three courtesans sprawled themselves over velvet chaises. When one of them stood to approach us, Narcissa shooed her away. "Sorry, sweets, he's *not* a customer." She then patted my arm, which she finally released. "You're safe from the guards here. Though I can't speak for the girls."

For the first time all night, I removed my mask and wiped away the sheen of sweat that had formed from the revelations of the meeting. The mask was confining, leaving me unnaturally anxious. Satisfied I was out of the way of the Watch for now, I turned to the girls.

"Would one of you mind fetching a man for me?"

LUTHER THREW off his mask the moment he saw me pacing the length of the den. "Where the hells have you been?" A nervous shake disrupted his voice, like he'd been worried about me.

"There's no time to explain," I murmured. We had already wasted enough of it waiting on the girls to find him. Meanwhile, Milla and her brother were alone somewhere on this property, and I despised the idea of letting her out of our sight for this long. "Any more word on the tracks?"

I didn't like the look he gave me, liked his words even less. "There's been a tip. A few of the guards from the front were reassigned to the Wet District. Finn saw the station in their thoughts—"

"*Fuck.*"

"We have one car past the station, but the second will be approaching soon. If they get caught . . ."

"There will be no chance for the last car," I finished. One or two out of three wasn't good enough. It was all or nothing. We needed all the product on those cars, or I was as good as dead.

"Is there anything I can help with?" Narcissa came to my side, her presence oddly comforting, considering our history.

I shook my head. "No, I don't think so. You've done so much for us already, Narcissa."

Her brows furrowed in reaction. "What do you mean? I only got you away from the Watch. That's hardly worth mentioning."

"I mean everything. Giving Aramis the intel you stole from the guards—"

She shook her head quickly. "Nico, I haven't spoken to Aramis since that day you summoned me at the Industrial Station."

All the blood drained from my heart. "Are you saying Aramis never contacted you?"

Another shake of her head, and then I felt it—what I'd been suppressing all night, and it barreled into me with all the force of a freight train. I didn't think I'd ever felt a fear so withering as the kind I faced now.

If Narcissa hadn't been feeding Aramis his information, where had he learnt it? How did he coordinate this night without her help? And *who* the fuck was he getting it from instead?

The answer stared me plain in the face. That bastard was working for the Firenzes. He'd never *stopped* working with the Firenzes. He'd been scheming against us this entire time—and I'd let him pull all my strings like his fucking puppet.

"Boss?" Luther spoke my title cautiously.

"Will you go for me? To check on the tracks." When he hesitated to reply, I added, "Please, Luther. I need to find Camilla."

"We're better as a team, cousin. You can't fight those bastards by yourself." He shook his head. "I've never disobeyed an order, but I will if I must."

I cursed under my breath before bracing a firm hand on his shoulder. "If we don't get those cars through the city, Luther, I will *die*. It will take one word from the dealer to return my shadow to the void and kill me instantly. I know you don't want to do this, but you must, for my sake. I cannot be in two places at once."

He grimaced, at war with himself. "Don't make me regret this."

I couldn't make such a promise, not while Milla was in danger. "There's no one else I'd trust with my life, cousin."

Narcissa snapped at her girls. "Take our carriage. They'll take you to the car and show you the shortcuts through town."

My cousin nodded and stepped out of my embrace before offering his arms out to them. "Much obliged, ladies. I'll pass by Finn to grab him." He turned one last time to look back at me. "Give the Marchese bastard all our fucking wrath, boss."

Aramis would get much worse than that from me.

Repositioning my mask, I stormed through the silver ribbons of smoke and returned to the party. Clinking glasses and obnoxious laughter blurred into a dull roar. My posture as my steps devoured the path through the house must have spoken for the hidden look on my face, based on the way crowd parted for me on my way to the door.

It wasn't long until I ran into Vanya's concerned stare in the gallery. She seemed to be everywhere tonight. A couple stared at us as they lingered in front of a marble hearth in the center of the room.

"They're looking for you," she whispered, coming close. Through a slit in her skirt, she pulled out a small pistol and handed it to me. "They found the real Blavatsky drunk in the courtyard. You need to get out of here."

I glanced at the doors on opposite sides of the wide hall. "I *need* to get to the lab, where Aramis brought Camilla. Any ideas?"

She thought for a moment, biting her lip. "The side entrance would be the best, but we'd have to cross the main entrance. They'll remember your mask."

I turned to the man standing near the fire. "Give me your mask," I demanded.

He scoffed, like I was joking. "Fuck off."

I cocked Vanya's gun and aimed it at his chest. "I won't ask again."

He threw his hands up in defense, glancing between me and his date for the evening. "Seven hells." He reached for the claps of his face mask. "Fine. No need for threats."

"Obviously." I snatched it from his hands and shed my coat, shoving it into the fire without a proper place to hide it. With a few simple wardrobe changes, any notable feature I'd brought attention to upstairs was exchanged. The couple quickly made themselves scarce, most likely before I asked for anything else. And I let Vanya escort me through the house without drawing a second look from the guards.

"Your wife," Vanya said as we crept down a quieter hall. "Is she alright?"

I shook my head as she glanced back at me. "I don't think so. Which is why I need to hurry."

"Of course. Just through here."

She shoved me into a small foyer dedicated as a catch-all for the side entrance. Searching the coat rack, she cursed.

"What's wrong?"

Vanya shook her head, hugging her bare arms to her middle. "I can't find my coat. You'll have to go alone."

That was preferable, anyway. She gave me vague directions leading to the lab, nearly splitting her bottom lip the way she kept gnawing on it.

She took a slow step back in the direction we'd come from.

"When I shut this door," she whispered, "they will come after you. Don't let them find out I didn't glint you. Play the part."

"Vanya . . ." A weight like lead smothered my chest as I spoke. "What do you mean, they'll come after me?"

She winced. "You're the best shot I've got at getting rid of them. I'm sorry, Nico. Please remember, you have more allies in this city than you think."

"Vanya!"

She slipped through the door, slamming it shut before I could lunge. The sound filled the hollow entrance, and just as my fingers skimmed the locked handle, the Society flooded the small space.

They knocked me out before their gloves burned too much.

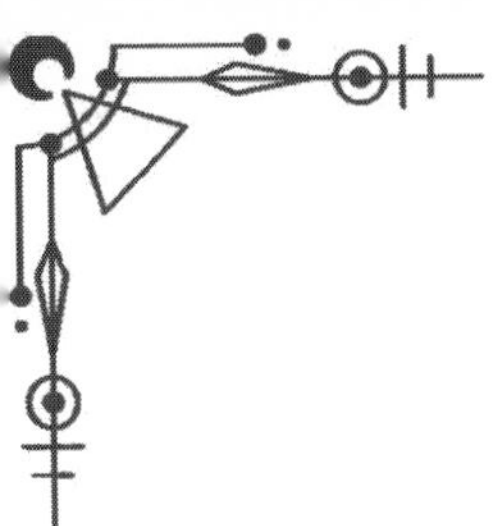
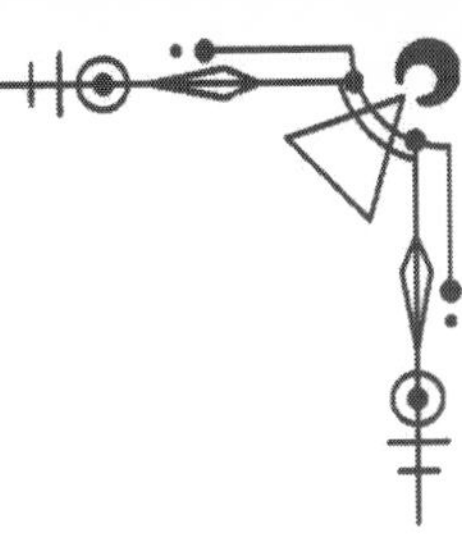

CHAPTER 48

CAMILLA

The scars beveling my skin burned awake for the first time since Delilah drew the strange symbols on me. I tore off the coat, discovering the pinkish flesh that had healed over now glowed once more. My breath hitched, choked in my throat as I swallowed down a cry of pain.

Felix and his men surrounded the barrier. It was a scene I knew before with different faces taking the place of the ones in my memory. Instead of Delilah and her assistant, it was Felix and my brother.

"What are you doing to me?" I managed to ask between breaths.

"Felix is going to fix this," Aramis said, his tone attempted to be reassuring. "Once Chaos is destroyed, everything can go back to normal—"

A hollow laugh took the place of the tears pressing behind my eyes. "We will *never* go back to normal. When will you understand that this is who I am? You cannot remove the parts of me *you* don't

like. There is no science or magic that will change me enough to fit your mold."

"I'm not trying to change you, Camilla. I'm trying to help you."

I scoffed. "If you think I'll forgive you after this . . . Hells, after all the times I defended you, Nico was right all along. I should've walked away from you when I had the chance."

He didn't flinch, his face hard and still as any mask. "You'll soon understand, it was the only way."

Hot tears broke free, spilling down both of my cheeks, and I didn't know if I cried for the pain of the runes or his betrayal. Both stung worse than any wound.

"I trusted you."

Aramis looked at the floor, where old stains discolored the concrete. "I know. Which is why this worked so well."

Felix stepped beside him, catching my attention. "If only you knew the sacrifices your brother was making on your behalf, you wouldn't be so unkind. Is this really the last conversation you'd have with him?"

He was right. If that were the case, if these words were my last, I'd make them count. Make them hurt.

Aramis continued to avoid my gaze, though I was certain he could feel the way I drew daggers with my glare. He removed his jacket and stripped down to his bare chest while another alchemist, the only person here not in armor or a party gown, came behind him. She held a bowl filled with a thick, crimson liquid.

"What are you doing?" I asked. The symbols across my skin burned incandescent as she dipped two fingers in the bowl and dragged them across my brother's back. Just as Delilah had done when she *connected* us.

"He's taking your remnant," Felix answered me, to my surprise.

"So that when we open Oblivion, you will not have access to your full power. It was our deal."

"Why would Aramis want my remnant?"

"Because despite being the child of Chaos and everything the Orders fought to destroy," Felix spat, "he loves you. This was our deal. That he would bring you here, but we would not kill you."

It wasn't quite what I'd consider love. Love was honesty and trust. It was unconditional and lacked requirements. Impossible to earn, even more so to lose, the truer its form. Love was what I had with Nico and his family, and I wondered if Aramis even knew the word. Whatever pity remained for him in my heart ached.

"I told you, Camilla," Aramis said. "If there was a way to take this from you to give you a normal life, I would. And I found a way."

Dread dipped its icy fingers around my chest. They weren't going to kill me—not if I no longer had a remnant. Aramis would take my place.

"Where the hells are they?" Felix asked a guard. "He should be here by now. I sent Vanya to retrieve him."

"Who?" I asked, still looking at my brother. "*Who*, Aramis?"

The swing of the front doors replied for him. A pair of watchmen carried a man between them. His boots dragged against the stone floor, his head limp between broad shoulders. Dark hair fell from the wax hold styling a harsh undercut. They propped him up in a chair in front of the boundary without binding him. Felix and Aramis stood beside each other, leering at their new victim.

Nicolai.

I lunged for him, but my hands ran into the edge of the boundary, crackling an unseen energy through an invisible wall. I winced as twin currents of electricity jolted through my palms and pushed me back. Nico sat just out of reach, beyond the milky line of the arcane border. He roused when I shouted his name. Sleepy eyes blinked open.

"*Milla.*"

I didn't need to look at his hand to know he was powerless. The watchmen wouldn't be so careless as to not give him a dose of glint. He made a clumsy attempt to stand, but the click of a revolver spinning a bullet in the cylinder ceased his movements.

"You actually did it, Marchese. I'm impressed," Felix murmured as he slung the gun around his finger.

If Aramis was pleased, he didn't show it. "You got the Attano, you have the codes, you have my sister's remnant. I did good on my end. I expect you to make good on yours."

Felix used the barrel of the gun to tip Nico's chin up, forcing his gaze to lift to him. But my husband didn't take his eyes off me, nor did I him as we listened to their exchange.

"And if I don't?" Felix asked him.

"I have ensured you will regret such a thing," Aramis replied dryly. "You are not the only one who has connections in this city, Firenze. Double-cross me and your family will burn."

A lengthy pause followed, snagging my breath. The alchemist slid his tongue between his teeth before his lips stretched into a wide smile, laughing in that deranged way of his. "I bet you have. But I'm a man of my word, Aramis. I'll restore your family name and fortune. I'll make sure the Marcheses—what's left of them—get back the house and the property, the shares and the riches." His oily stare slid to me—over me. "Your sister will be taken care of."

Nico's neck thickened with tension; his shoulders rose as he took a massive breath. "Don't you fucking touch her—"

His head snapped back then, like someone had snatched him by the hair, his throat exposed to Felix's revolver. He was doing something—using magic to control him. Felix had occult power like the watchman who'd compelled me to submit at Sabina's docks.

His height, his build, that *laugh*.

It *was* Felix who'd led the legions of watchmen against the bleeders.

"Felix, please," I begged as his finger slipped over the trigger. There had to be something I could barter with for Nico's life, but I had nothing. My brother had stripped away all my power, stole all my moves, left me with nothing to offer the alchemist in exchange for my husband.

"I have been waiting to finish this job for a long time," Felix whispered. "You thought you could take everything from me, Attano. The train, the girl, the power. You just couldn't stay on your fucking side of the city." Felix swallowed hard, teeth gritting. "When I'm through with you, I'll hunt down the rest of your kin one by one, until the Isle has been purged of bender blood."

My eyes slammed shut as the gun went off, and my heart was ripped in two as if thrown into the path of the bullet. The acrid scent of spent gunpowder penetrated the boundary of the circle, the loud bang from the shot ricocheted off the bare walls of the warehouse, all followed by Felix's curse.

"What the hells, Marchese?"

My eyes flew open, breath stuttering in my chest as my pulse skipped with it.

The gun was no longer pointed at Nico, but in the air. The bullet had busted through a skylight, spilling moonlight and broken glass around the pair. Aramis gripped Felix's arm in a last-minute attempt to redirect the shot.

Nico's chest rose and fell rapidly, eyes wide, shocked, knowing he'd been spared.

"Not like this," Aramis spoke firmly. He released Felix to reach into a sheath tucked against his hip—one the watchmen checking at the front doors had conveniently missed. A red blade—a Niner blade—slid out, and he let the tip graze Nico's chest. "He deserves to die slowly, knowingly. Just like his mother."

"*Fuck you,*" Nico hissed.

"No, Attano," he said. "I've been planning this day since the moment you stepped into my courtyard. Even then, with the union between our families, I saw a glimmer of opportunity for revenge. The only reason I let you have my sister, *Bender*, the only reason the Firenzes didn't retaliate after the stunt you pulled, was because we were playing a very long game. One you didn't even know you were a part of until it was too late for you."

"Then finish this," Nico snarled. "Be done with it. Do what I couldn't, Marchese."

"Aramis, don't!" I shouted, but he wouldn't listen. He never did. My words fell on the deaf ears of the man who had controlled my whole world since it mattered, who had destroyed it with the fall of a blade.

Aramis plunged the Niner dagger into Nico's side, sealing his fate.

Nico cried out, a grunt to hide the shriek of pain. Even as my brother withdrew his weapon, the poison on the blade had begun to eat at him from the way he couldn't even bear to look at me any longer. His eyes smashed shut, his teeth bared, as if holding any evidence of his pain hostage.

"*What have you done?*" I cried at Aramis. Disregarding the sprints of pain it caused, I slammed my fist against the boundary, beating fist after fist into the opaque veil that separated us. Nicolai was dying, and I couldn't even touch him. Couldn't hold him as the poison from the blade cleaved his future from mine. My time left with him drained like sand in an hourglass, and with Magrahel bringing the void so near to the weak and dying, I feared there weren't many grains of sand left in the vessel.

"Just . . . just hang on, Nico. Let me reach you at the very least —" Another fist to the barrier shot a current down my spine, sending me to my knees.

"Milla, stop," Nico gasped, looking at me at last—steel-grey and steady despite their glossy glare. "You're hurting yourself. Save your strength for when it counts."

"*Let me out*!" My voice burned in my throat as I repeated the demand, each one followed by a swing of my fist against the boundary.

The pain in my flesh—in my heart—quickly shifted to something more useful. Anger swept through my blood until I was full of it. Desperate to bleed my wrath on my brother and these men, who were circling the boundary as the markings worked on my remnant. The circle didn't dull my power. It was still there, filling my fingers with dark magic. But the symbols glowed against it, obeying another master.

I glared at the Firenze and his men through the dark strands of loose curls that had fallen over my face. "You are all cowards," I told them. "You know you stand no chance against me, so you lock me away like you do anyone who threatens you. Suppressing what frightens you because you know beneath your money and your codes and your fucking poisons, you are *powerless*. And so you hunt those who would prove it so to your city and undermine your influence. You steal what makes them special, not because you hate them, but because you hate yourselves for not possessing their gifts. You"—I glanced at them all, distributing the shame—"are the most pathetic kind of evil."

Felix paced the warehouse slowly behind Nico, watching me torture myself by beating down the barrier. He said nothing to contest my accusations, not that it mattered. He had won. No matter what happened tonight, I'd lose my husband, and there was no victory, no vengeance that would justify his death.

I looked to Aramis then, my voice breaking. "I *love* him."

He nodded, swallowing hard. "I know."

"And I will *never* forgive you for taking him from me."

My brother looked like he was going to be sick. "Good. Hate me. It'll make this next part much easier for you."

The alchemist returned to finish her work, to transfer my Chaos for them to destroy. Nico grunted, catching my attention. The way he looked at me, like he was studying me, like it might be the last time before we were separated forever—it split me in half.

"Don't let them take your fire, Milla."

"But you are my fire, Nico." The well in my heart was empty of tears, but my lips trembled. "I can't do this without you. I need you here."

The corner of his mouth tilted. "You never needed me, my love. You're enough all on your own. It's time they all realized the same."

Tendrils of shadowed flame swirled my fingertips, gathering from their summons. It filled the circle, building on every bracing breath that left my lips. Heatless in its form and yet more destructive than any earthly fire, it lashed around the barrier, seeking something to sink its malice into. With nothing to devour, it grew and gathered and wrapped my form in a void-like darkness.

"Hurry!" Felix's voice was muffled over the hiss of fire. "Finish the runes!"

The place where the demon marked me long ago burned with a fresh fire, though not unpleasantly. Beyond my wrath-filled form, in the dark where the flames danced and threatened, something came to existence. A tear, obvious by an arch of stillness that contrasted the endless churn of swirling fire. This darkness was not mine, nor familiar.

A void. That abysmal black called me into its calm and granted me a way out.

"I'll come back for you," I whispered my last promise to him before slipping through the thinning veil of Magrahel.

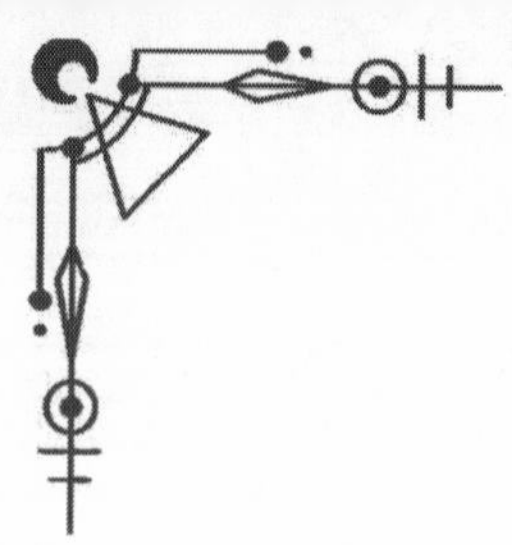
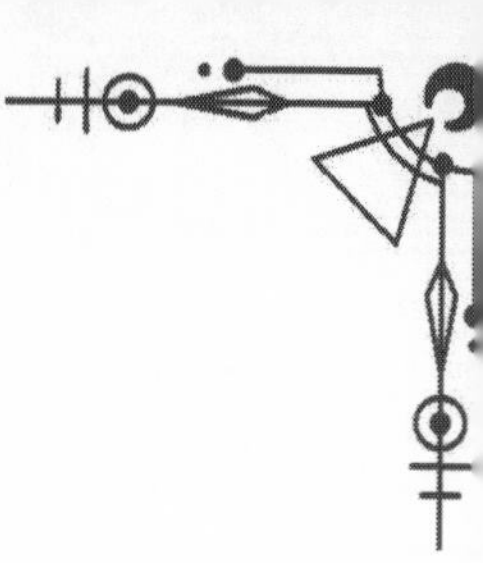

CHAPTER 49

CAMILLA

Little was known about the void that filled the realm behind the stars, other than what had been passed down between generations. It was said to be a place beyond life, where the Creator was born, where the hells stored our souls while our shadows returned to the darkness to keep it so.

As I stepped through a parted place in the veil, my feet hitting soft and shifting earth, I saw no hell nor god—only a vast world of burning plains. A place I'd been to before. The same place I'd retreated when the demon struck me.

Oblivion.

I'd torn open the void and ended up here. A portal to a place only my power could lead. A place I'd never intended to go. The mark on my back from the demon was sore, like a splinter had been removed. And though I couldn't see the mark myself, I knew it was gone from the flash of pain that had split through my spine as I crossed over.

I stood alone in the center of a scorched patch of earth. In the

distance I found what appeared to be a willow tree without leaves, perched on a rolling hill. Its drooping limbs skimmed the tips of the dancing fire.

Taking a testing step, my presence pushed aside the fire and allowed me to walk amongst the flames untouched. My lower back pinched in retaliation, but I pressed on up the hill, searching for a way out—if there was one.

The top of the hill led to an embankment. On the other side was a black river thawing from a frozen state. A man stood on the shore, facing out over the frozen water. His chest was bare, his back covered in strange symbols that neither glowed nor moved, remaining a dull black. They marked the length of his spine, branching over his shoulders and down his arms, which were crossed in front of him as he watched the patches of ice float downstream.

Sabina had once said Oblivion was empty, but if that were true, who was this man and why was he here?

Sensing the prod of my attention, the man looked over his shoulder, his arms slacking some. I took a retreating step, but he raised a hand to stop me. The markings, I noticed then, ran all the way to his palms.

"Wait!" he called, his tone deep and thunderous. "Do not be afraid. I have no power here."

Strange he would lead with that.

His voice interrupted the eerie silence thick in the air. I surveyed the area, but there was no one else accompanying him. "Are you alone?"

He tilted his head, looking me over. "I've been alone for hundreds of years. Yours is the first face I've seen here. How did you . . ." His eyes fell to the party dress I still wore, to my hands, which were still filled with dark power. "I see."

I approached him cautiously, careful to keep space between us. "How did you end up here? Who are you?"

His gaze snapped to mine, eyes like bright gold coins to match the golden sheen of his long hair that skimmed his shoulders. He was handsome, but unnaturally so. Something about his face was too symmetrical to be a product of nature, too perfect to be anything but deliberately designed.

"I haven't thought about my name in a very long time. It is a forgotten thing. As for how I came here, I think about it often. I was tricked and locked away." He glanced at my hands once more. "It was strange. This river was completely frozen. Then you showed up, and the fields caught fire, the starlight winked, and the river thawed. Almost as if you brought the fire back to Oblivion."

I swallowed to unravel a tightness knotting in my chest. "Why were you locked away?"

The man looked down at his hands, at the inky symbols covering his skin. "I tried to save the world before it was ready to be saved. But that was eons ago."

"Are you a demon?"

Thin lips tipped into a smirk. "There are no demons left in Oblivion. Only us."

That was hardly a comfort. "How do we get out of here?"

He gestured to a low hanging fog that settled over the far side of the river. "Oblivion has been sealed since I was put here. The most conformable way out is through the mist, though you'd fall asleep if you entered it and would be pulled back to shore. It's impossible to cross."

"What do you mean, most conformable way?"

"You must have formed an opening somewhere, if you came here on your own."

I squatted in the sand, staring hard at the dark waters lapping gently against the coast. Whatever tear in the void I'd walked through hadn't followed me *here*. The burning fields showed no signs of a rift. If what this man said was true, and I'd think he'd have even more motivation to escape if he'd been here as long as he'd claimed, then I needed to find a way down the water.

Swimming was out of the question. I hadn't done so in over a decade and even then, I'd stayed in the shallow parts of the Narrow Sea where my feet could touch. The water was still cold from the thaw as I tested it with a finger. But as I did so, they skimmed across something solid.

A chain.

"There's something tied down here," I muttered aloud. My inky hands dipped into the river and gripped a metal chain that was tied to a sunken post. Whatever it was attached to didn't budge. I dug my flats into the sand and heaved.

"Allow me," he offered.

I reluctantly stepped away to allow him the space to pull up whatever was buried below. He barely struggled, effortlessly pulling the chain until the coils made a small pile in front of his feet until a boat broke through the water's edge.

It made sense, if the river was the way through Oblivion, that there would be a method of transportation. It was a narrow dinghy, no larger than a rowboat. The wooden slats were stuffed with sand from its rest at the bottom of the river.

The man turned to look back at me. Something malicious flashed in his golden eyes.

"There's only room for one."

I glanced behind him at the boat pressed into the shore. He was right. There would only be room for one of us, and I had a strong feeling he'd do anything to claim that seat.

Unfortunately for him, so would I.

He snapped the chain from the hull and swung it side to side. "I've been here for hundreds of years. Out of the two of us, I deserve to take the boat."

"And you'd be here an eternity if I hadn't showed. I'm taking the boat, and there's nothing you can do to stop me."

Fire flooded my fingers. Nico's image flared through my thoughts. The contortion of his face when my brother stabbed him, the blood on the floor, the poison staining his veins. I was running out of time to get to him before the blade claimed his life.

He whipped the chain in his fist with inhuman speed, so quickly I had no chance to duck or brace myself for the impact. The heavy links struck the side of my face, shooting incredible pain through my left eye and flickering my awareness. It knocked me to my knees, and I fought to stay awake, to deny the pain the pleasure of shoving me toward a more tolerable slumber.

I clawed at my power, scraping every bit branching through my nerves to prime it ready as he grabbed me by the shoulders and lifted me from the sand. Blood dribbled along the line of my jaw, my head flopped to the side, staring at the cocked image of his face. Fire wove itself between my fingers.

No longer was I hesitant to use this flame inside me. The approval of who I was, the parts I loved and resented, was not up to anyone else. It was my choice, and that choice to accept what I'd received unbidden and unasked gave me all the power I ever needed. Trusting myself and my abilities, knowing that I was in control of not only my heart and my mind, but my remnant as well.

I devoured his body in dark flame and watched as the fire of Oblivion, my remnant, descended from my mother, a saint made mortal, tore at flawless skin. His grip on me didn't loosen as I predicted. Unlike the other times I'd used my remnant, he was unscathed.

Never had I seen that before. No one was immune to my fire but me . . .

He laughed as flames whirled, clawed at his face. No more penetrable than the shadows they were made from. "You cannot kill me with your fire, daughter. I have no power here, but neither does yours work against me. The Creator wouldn't give us weapons to use against our siblings, after all. That's why we used mortals."

My power dissipated, and I stared into his golden eyes, perplexed by his words. "Siblings?" I gasped.

In one smooth motion, he flipped me against his chest. A hand buried itself into the crown of my hair, the other wrapped my waist while simultaneously pinning my arms within his constricting hold—and it crushed my chest. Pain lanced my skull from the repercussion of the chain and the yank of my roots from my scalp.

He brought us to the river. My lower half burned as he shoved me into the water and pushed my face just above the still surface. Ripples calmed into a flat plane, revealing our reflections on its wavering canvas.

But the man who looked down at me was not the one who I'd approached before. Gold eyes were now bright red, glowing from large orbits on a sagging face. The thing behind me smiled, revealing rows of sharpened teeth. Terrifying even as the details were obscured by the unsteady surface.

"What are you?" The words shook from my throat. Two faces . . . What creature in the world had two completely different faces. One beautiful and soft, the other emaciated and cruel. The answer hit me just as he plunged my head under water.

This was not a man, but a Saint. The gold of Giver and the decay of Greed.

The deity used both hands to hold me under despite my thrashing. The shock of the river's temperature stole what little breath I could manage before it was too late. My chest burned, the pound of my erratic pulse the only sound beneath the water's edge. Just as my lungs began to shrivel out of desperation, he pulled me out.

Blessed air filled my chest once I emerged. The saint fisted my hair to arch my back, pulling me flush against him. "I am the Order of Creation, the laws that give meaning and life to the world. I am the destruction of evil and free will. I am the undoing of Chaos and her children." Marble-like fingers pinched my airway. "I am everything you should fear because I am the only one who can put out your fire. You might have brought the flame back to Oblivion, but you will never be free again."

"I didn't bring the flame, Giver." My voice was coarse as the sand shoved beneath my fingernails. "I *am* the flame."

My remnant shot from my palms, felt it devour the hard frame of his body still pressing mine against him. He hissed, a pained sound, before finally releasing me to cease our connection. I didn't check to see if I'd killed or harmed him. Instead, I ran to the boat, struggling against the drag of my skirts through the knee-high river, and tossed myself into the vessel.

By the time I reached for the oar, Giver was on his feet, though after experiencing my flames, he appeared more like his alternate form. Half his face was the man I'd met, the other his reflection in the water. Both regarded me with a rage that could kill if wrath was a weapon, but he had no power here. Had admitted so himself.

My mother was Chaos, and she'd created this place for her disorder to thrive. Oblivion answered my call, not his. He had time to take one step off the shore before I reached a hand into the water and let my flames spread across the surface, where they covered the river with flickering shadows. He dared not enter the shallows, because though my flames hadn't destroyed him like the others they'd claimed, he didn't seem to enjoy them either.

"You cannot kill me on your own," he mocked. "Your power is not whole, Remni. You are but a piece of her, not enough to break all of me."

"Maybe not," I spoke through my teeth. "But you'll still burn all the same. Get in the water if you're so certain I cannot hurt you."

He didn't move, and I smirked as I pushed the oar's end against the riverbed to find the current. Only then did I drop the steer, letting the vessel float in a river of my chaos. When I was certain the saint could not follow, I sunk to my knees in a soggy pile of brocade and willed the boat to move faster. The strength in my body was giving out as the flow pulled me further from Oblivion.

I didn't know where it would bring me exactly.

Truthfully, I no longer cared.

The man who'd become my home and my forever was dying and I couldn't stop it no more than I could go back and change all the ways I'd failed him. I'd carry the blame of his death more than I'd blamed my brother, more than the Firenzes. Because I'd seen the warning signs in Aramis and still believed the best of my flesh and blood. He'd shown me time and time again he wasn't on my side, but after losing so much, I'd only wanted to keep the little I had left of my family.

And that child-like foolishness had cost me everything.

"I will find a way out," Giver's voice echoed against the beginning of the mist. "You've opened Oblivion, daughter. There's nothing holding me here any longer."

I'd unlocked what had been sealed. I'd been given what Delilah had searched for. The mark on my back, the mark the demon left on me, it wasn't the fire—no, I'd carried that all along.

It was the key, as if the messenger knew I'd someday require it. Like I was meant to open this place all along.

My thoughts pondered the meaning of it all as the dark mist covered the narrow boat, and I fell into a dreamless sleep and thoughts of home.

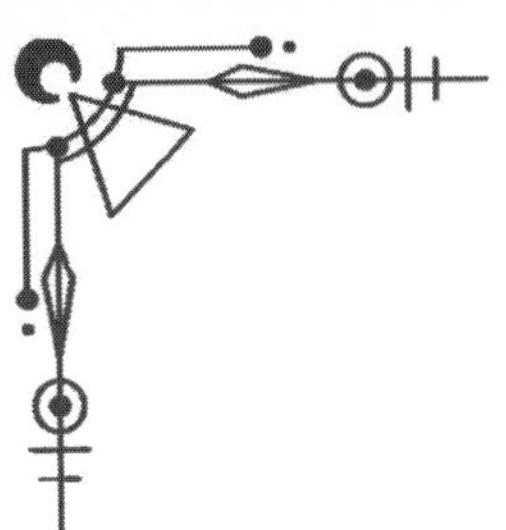
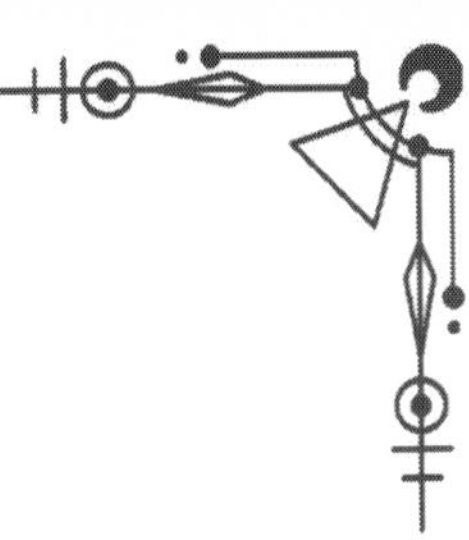

CHAPTER 50
NICOLAI

She was gone.

Camilla's fire had disappeared, taking her along with it. Darkness had once swirled in a violent cyclone within the barrier, and then suddenly it settled to reveal an empty circle. Even with the hole in my side and the burn of the Niner poison beginning to take effect in my blood, I worried only for her.

Felix was equally concerned, but for entirely different reasons, frantically pacing around the circle like he could make her reappear. "What the hells, Aramis? Where is she?"

The idiot balked. "I . . . I don't know! She's never done that before!"

Felix was dangerously quiet for a time. The symbols the alchemist had painted on Aramis faded into a dark color, no longer glowing without the connection to Camilla's remnant.

"I don't believe you, Marchese. Stay here while we go look for your sister."

My chair was shoved forward, tipping over as the legs caught

on a crack in the floor. I crashed hard on the other side of the line, within the barrier's containment. The wound in my side pulled, and I braced my hand against the site to hold it together.

It wasn't as deep as the amount of blood on the floor had suggested. My shirt clung to the site, but there was no fresh blood soaking the area. Oddly, of all the times I'd been stabbed, this wound was the most merciful.

Felix glared at me as he barked orders. "Watch the Attano until we get back. I want eyes on the river and the house and everything in between. Wherever she's gone, she'll come back for the bender. *Find her*!" His men followed his lead out the door.

"Find who?"

In his rage, Felix hadn't noticed the warehouse doors open. Inspector Neal Caldwell filled the doorway with a group of watchmen behind him—and Vanya on his arm.

She didn't even glance my way, even as I begged her silently to look at me, if only so she could see the consequences of her choices. Whatever her motives were, however pure or self-concerned her intentions, her betrayal had been the most blindsiding. My blood boiled as I stared at the place she clung to Caldwell.

"Inspector!" Felix startled. "We were just about to . . . what are you doing down here?"

"We've had word on the missing mirkwood. There are a series of unmarked cars being pushed through the city. Two have already passed over the viaduct, the last is about to reach the Main Station, where we have guards posted to catch the smugglers."

"I told the inspector you'd need to be informed immediately since the mirkwood is your most important ingredient for glint production," Vanya said, slipping her hands off her escort. "You've been looking for this stock, haven't you?"

She glanced at me finally with wide, purposeful eyes.

"Yes, well—"

"And if you lose this stock," she continued, "there would be a very good chance that your entire glint business could go under, leaving the rest of us without any protection whatsoever from remnants besides the laws my father so diligently worked to have passed? Just to be crystal clear."

Felix was seething silently, and sweat beaded across his brow. "Yes, Miss Vanya. It would be devastating to lose the mirkwood."

Vanya hummed. "Seems important to check on then."

Caldwell's gaze fell to me, trapped behind the barrier. "Where is the girl?"

"She escaped," Aramis told him. "She must have used the key you lot didn't want her to know about."

Felix shot him a look made of daggers.

The key? If she had found a way to use the key, then that meant . . .

"You let her open Oblivion?" Caldwell's face shifted then from composed to outraged. His strides ate the distance between him and Felix. The men the alchemist had surrounded himself with lowered their guns, hesitating in the presence of their inspector.

"You were supposed to destroy her remnant, Felix. You vowed you had this under control!"

"It's his fault!" He jutted a finger at the Marchese. "He wanted to take her remnant so that he would die instead. It was our deal. Aramis would bring her to us, far from her lines of protection. In exchange, he'd die in her place, I'd have rid ourselves of the Attano problem, and we'd have the key and a world without Chaos."

Aramis scoffed. "How is any of that my fault?"

"You were supposed to keep her drugged, Marchese," Felix growled. "She wouldn't have been able to escape had her fire been sufficiently medicated."

Had Aramis intentionally not given her glint—just as Vanya hadn't drugged me? Or had Milla just refused, like the previous times he offered? He was too unpredictable to figure out, but I still tried. Even while he feigned confusion in front of the inspector, pretending to be a piece on Felix's shifting gameboard, I had a feeling he was the one holding the dice.

"All I know," Caldwell said slowly, "is that you've managed to lose Chaos *twice*, and this time, she has torn through the veil and *possibly* opened Oblivion. Do you understand how vulnerable you have made us?"

"Inspector—"

"Enough." Caldwell paced. "They will not be pleased with you or your family, Felix. They'll call for your head, then mine. And I sure as hells won't end up like the last inspector that fucked up because he put his faith in the Firenzes."

"She might come back," Felix offered. "She can't stay in the void forever—"

"You better hope she comes back," he spat. "Because if Order returns too soon, while she still lives, he too will be vulnerable for the first time in history." He glanced at me again. "Why is *he* here?"

"A loose end finally taken care of," Felix replied without looking at me, as if I were already dead.

Caldwell assessed Aramis then, staring at the markings on his skin. "You were transferring the remnant to him like they tried in the tower?" When Felix nodded, his brows pinched. "Why are some of them beginning to glow?"

Aramis's eyes widened.

"She must be returning already." Felix blabbered something about getting the men back in position. I didn't hear him, too focused on the Marchese, whose boot was inching closer to the nearest arcane rune constructing the barrier.

I slid to the opposite side of the circle and stripped off my vest and shirt, trying to draw the attention of the guards in the room away from what he was doing—*if* he was trying to disrupt the symbol. Using a dry end of the sleeve, I used my right arm to tend to the site, feigning a grimace that wasn't necessary.

Either Aramis had terrible aim, or he intentionally missed anything important.

"Can you feel her?" the inspector asked Aramis. "Can you lead us to her?"

Felix answered in his place. "The spell tethers them temporarily. He should be able to feel the pull of their connection."

"The Society will take it from here, Felix," Caldwell said coldly. "Vanya, please go back to the house and put the property on lockdown. No one leaves. I'd hate for anyone *else* to get hurt tonight."

The smallest of smiles flickered across her cheek. "Yes, Inspector. Felix, should I inform the Nine—"

The bang of a gunshot ambushed the warehouse.

The room went still. We were all spooked animals, too afraid to draw the attention of the hunter while the shot still echoed in the air. The pistol in Felix's hand was smoking.

Vanya was the first to scream, snapping me from a trance. "What the hells have you done, Felix? You shot the inspector—"

"*Quiet*!" The alchemist trembled. Whatever control he had over the room was slipping. The guards inched back, their weapons only half-raised as the head of their unit lay dead at the hands of the one who paid salaries.

Inspector Neal Caldwell had been murdered, and everyone in this room was now a witness. I didn't think even Felix could get out of this mess if the truth got out. My uncle had always warned me there was a consequence for every stolen life, that killing was a last resort. Had it been Felix's? The tide was shifting back in our favor if he'd been desperate enough to turn on his own man.

Aramis and I crossed gazes. His chin barely dipped in a confirming nod before tearing his gaze back to the dead man in front of him.

What was he up to?

Felix dragged my focus back to him as he resumed his shouting. "You will shut your mouth, Vanya, and refrain from being the insufferable gossip you are until this is handled."

She straightened as he looked at her, undoubtedly using the conduit Caldwell described to control her mind like he had done to me. "You will go back into that house and lock it down. Make up any excuse besides the truth if anyone asks what happened."

He pointed to the guards that escorted her here. "You all will follow, and similarly not breathe a word. I know your names and faces, and I know where you pull rank. If you enjoy your life and privileges, you'll forget what happened here. My truth is the only truth that matters."

A docile expression crossed Vanya's features; her shoulders drooped slightly. "Okay," she murmured, obeying the mind-controlling abilities of a Mirth remnant, before turning on a heel to walk back to the estate, her guards in tow.

"Marchese." Felix snapped toward the door. "You will lead me to your sister, or I'll spare neither of you. We're going to finish this *now*." The alchemist turned, starting toward the door.

Aramis looked at me again. A startling understanding bridged itself between us—and then he smudged the arcane rune with the toe of his boot.

He set me free.

"If you care about her like she claims, you'll get those cars out of the city," he whispered, before sneaking out the warehouse behind Felix like his dog.

Could I do it? Could I leave Milla behind by the order of her brother—the same man who already betrayed us once tonight? What Vanya said had stuck with me. If this missing stock was the same stuff on my cars, and if I could keep it out of their hands, I'd have finally taken down our enemy. If the Firenzes truly meant to industrialize magic, they had to be stopped before it was too late.

The decision truly depended on if I meant my words, if I meant what I'd said to her earlier. She didn't need me. She didn't need anyone else to protect her. Aramis, in his oddness, was actually right. If I truly cared about her, and I loved her more than this life, I'd make sure she was safe when I was gone.

I could make this city safe for her at last, weakening the Firenzes with a critical blow to their business. Their house would fall, the Nine and the Watch would suffer without their biggest investor, and there would be no more glint for an unforeseeable future.

I could give my family everything—could give Milla the life she deserved. I'd just have to let her go first.

Letting go of forever was much more painful than the hole in my side—incomparable to the chasm she left in me. But I stood despite the pull of the wound and limped to the nearest horse.

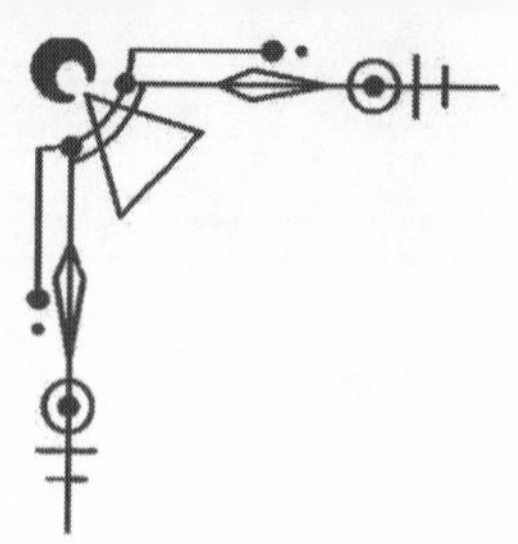
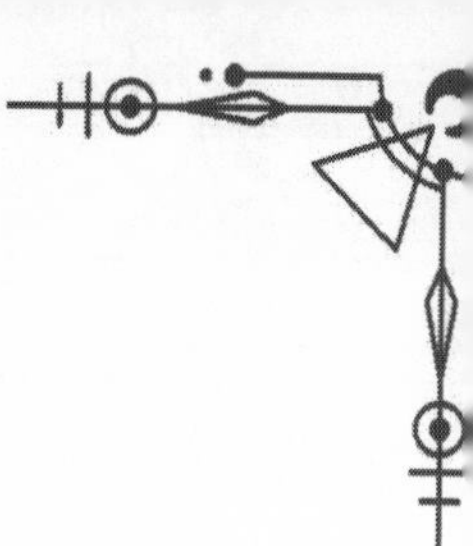

CHAPTER 51

CAMILLA

It was snowing.

I woke on a frozen bed, skin burning from the ice pressing into the exposed places of my dress. The numb pain forced my eyes to open, and I looked up through the snowflakes gathering on my lashes, staring through freezing fog and into a flurry-filled sky. A clock tower chimed an early hour in the distance, singing the same tune I'd heard for twenty-one years.

I'd returned to Lynchaven, then. Be it coincidence or fate, I spent little energy worrying over the reason and more on where exactly I'd ended up—in the middle of the River Ada.

The ice was solid, though I could feel the rush of the current beneath. Like walking on the second floor of an apartment, it was sturdy enough to stand and walk across, but with a hollowness to insist it might not remain that way.

The biting nip of the wind skirted over the river, and the rush of it beat my skirts wildly and practically turned the blood in my veins to slush. My gown was no longer wet, my

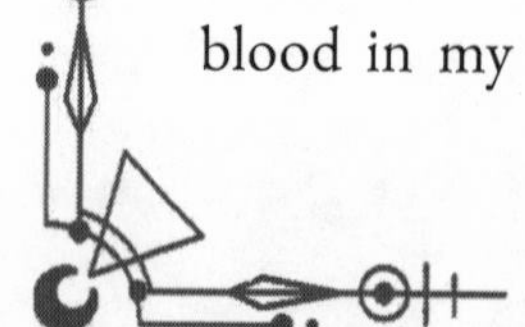

hair similarly dry, and sand no longer weighed down my flats or clung to my fingers—like the entire thing had been a dream. Whatever part of Oblivion I'd collected had remained there.

But my head throbbed from the gash on my face where Giver hit me with his chain, a painful keepsake to ensure my time beyond the veil had been anything but a dream.

The Wet District was close. From here, I could smell the ash floating from their chimneys, the sounds of a distant party. Through the whirl of snow and fog, something glowed from the riverbank, approaching quickly. The form of a man decorated in the symbols they'd painted on him earlier.

Aramis.

I took controlled breaths to cool the rising flame licking my throat. I was furious with him, straddling the border into hatred territory. It hadn't fully processed in my head what he'd done to Nico. It didn't make any sense. My heart couldn't catch up to all I'd seen tonight, and I was left just . . . angry. Just hurt and hollow and fucking *angry*.

Felix appeared behind him, too close now for the misty wall to hide him. Before they got any closer, I drew a line they couldn't cross, melting the river with my remnant and splitting the ice into two sides.

"*Leave no name forgotten*," I whispered to Nico, to the place in my heart he'd remain forever. "*Give no easy death*."

My brother shook from the wind beating his bare chest, still fighting the urge to look at me. Felix didn't appear as satisfied as when I left. That smug smile had gone at last, replaced with a fierce glare that tempered some when he neared.

I'd sink him to a cold ending for what he did to my husband.

"Camilla," Felix said softly, like we were standing in my courtyard six months ago. "You'd never believe me, but this isn't the way I wanted to do things."

I scoffed. "What exactly wasn't a part of your plan? Me rejecting your offer of marriage or the consequential death of most of my family?"

A muscle in his eye twitched. "What does this have to do with your family? Blood remnants murdered Giles and Jasper. I wasn't the one who tore out their throats, and yet you blame me over those monsters—"

"They were under your orders!"

"They had choices," he hissed. "We did not. You gave everything to the Attanos after we made a *deal*. Your family screwed us over and tried to run from it, so your family dealt with the consequences of their betrayal."

But it was my betrayal, not theirs. I dragged my stare away from the alchemist long enough to linger on Aramis, give him his fair share of my loathing.

"Then why are you working with my brother again?"

Felix smiled. "Because he came to me and explained how you were seduced by Nicolai Attano and that you alone made the choice to give him your company. That you—and I quote him —*fell in love*." A snide laugh filled the silence between his accusations. "Aramis reached out to me the day after you were taken, and we made a deal. I'd forgive you for what you did to my family and my company, and in exchange, he would deliver the Attano to me and help me destroy your remnant."

My limbs were freezing stiff, but I still needed him to show his last card. "Why does my remnant matter in a world where magic can be controlled and managed? Why not take it for yourself like you and your family has done for generations with other remnants?"

"Because Order, Camilla, cannot exist alongside Chaos." His voice fell on the next part, as if afraid the wind would carry his words to unwanted ears. "Did you open Oblivion? Did you free him?"

My hesitation answered for me as the two-faced saint nudged into my thoughts.

Felix nodded slowly, his gaze set on something far away. "*Damnit.*" He looked to Aramis. "You understand now, why I cannot let either of you live."

He shivered violently. "But we had a deal!"

"Deals change with the circumstances, as you should know all things considered," the alchemist replied. "Especially one made in a verbal agreement."

Hells, I'd tear him apart right now—peel the flesh off his bone and grind his skeleton into dust—if I didn't want that fucking book. The wind matched my wrath, tearing the loose ends of my hair from their pins and whipping it across my face. Flurries blurred the riverbank until all I could see was the faint glow of light coming from the windows of the warehouse.

"Where is the book?" I asked him outright. The weather alone was lethal enough in Lynchaven without anyone making threats. Yet still, the snow came down thicker, the breeze howling between us.

Felix reached into his coat, but instead of the book I sought, he pulled out a gun.

Before he could shoot either me or my brother—because a stupid, stubbornly loyal part of me still wanted to protect the bastard despite how much he broke my heart—I fisted both my hands above the ice and, when I opened them, released Chaos.

My power splintered through the glaze over the river. Black lines cobwebbed between Felix and me, him and Aramis, me and my brother, until all of us were separated on our own block of floating ice. The cracks ran deep enough, far enough, that the entire sheet over the river shifted and moved, beginning to float downstream.

Felix was a wide-framed man, stocky and sturdy, yet incapable of moving at any sort of speed. The jolt through the ground set him off-balance, and he dropped the gun to catch himself. My brother leapt across the widening crack to snatch it.

"He's got a knife!" I shouted at Aramis as a flash of iridescent blue appeared in Felix's hand.

Aramis grabbed the hilt of the gun and—tossed it to me, and I nearly didn't catch it, expecting him to use it to defend himself. Just as the revolver left his fingertips, Felix's came down, slashing at his outreached arm. The knife sunk into my brother's shoulder, tearing through pale skin, deep flesh, and arcane rune.

The scars on my body ceased their glow.

"Aramis!"

He stammered something between a curse and a cry of pain, and it cleaved something inside of me, separating the person I loved from what he'd done. Tears leaked down my cheeks as I stumbled with the gun, my fingers numb and stiff and poorly pliable. The ice beneath the pair quickly stained red.

Regaining control, I shifted my power from fire to destruction, aiming my focus on the knife in Felix's fists, already high over his head, ready to strike again. Shadows swirled at my silent command, dismantling the fabric of his knife until it reached his fingers.

I took those too.

Felix screamed, snatching his arm from my Chaos to his chest —his eyes gaped where nothing but a cauterized wrist remained.

"Move, Aramis!" I shouted so I could finish Felix the way I

wanted to, careful where I stripped. If he had the book still in his possession, he needed to stay whole until I had it in my hands.

Aramis shifted his weight, throwing Felix on his back and sending the block of ice teetering in the rippling current. River water slipped over the ice, slicking the surface as the pair wrestled for control.

"For my brothers," Aramis hissed as he grabbed Felix by the throat and squeezed. "And for Sera. For taking every last thing I wanted and the life you made a living hell. I'll fucking drag you to the bottom of the river myself."

It was the first time he'd spoken of their deaths, the first he'd said her name. I wondered if he'd been holding them back for this moment—until he had the power to do something about his silent mourning.

Felix threw a connecting punch with his remaining hand to Aramis's jaw, following his temporary stun with a boot between them to kick him back. Aramis stumbled off the side of the ice platform and onto another, collapsing across the plate. It took him too long to stand, as Felix was already on his feet, wiping blood off his lip.

It was just me and the alchemist and no one left between us. The wind wiped away my tears, replacing them with the urge to finish this once and for all.

I opened the chamber of the gun and emptied all the bullets. All but one. Felix watched me as I carved his name into the lead with my remnant—and popped it into a random slot. My thumb spun the chamber before snapping it shut.

"You have six chances of dying, Felix." I aimed the gun at his head. "And you have six chances to save yourself. Are you a gambling man?"

He sneered, teeth bared and furious. "I don't play games. If you want to kill me, then be done with it."

"I want the book."

His brow cocked.

"The book you stole from Delilah. She took it from my mother. It is mine and I want it back."

"I don't have it."

I pulled the trigger, a tight wince crossed the alchemist's face in reaction, but the slot was empty.

Felix was still for a moment before a cackling laugh bubbled from his lips. "That's what all this is about? A fucking diary?"

Another pull of the trigger, another click without the bullet. I hummed a thoughtful sound. "You're pretty lucky, Felix. Might want to reconsider your profession if you make out of this."

"Why not just finish the rest of me? You have the power. Why not use it?" He held up his wrist.

Because I didn't associate my magic with being powerful like he did. It wasn't about using my remnant to make him do what I wanted, to force his hand. Having magic wasn't equivalent to having power, only the feeling of it. I wanted something better. Something my mother, my father and brothers, my husband, my best friend, something they all deserved.

Justice. The ability to deliver it, to offer it, that was true power.

I pulled the trigger twice to make a point. Both empty, though Felix began to sweat despite the cold.

"Alright!" he gasped, reaching into his jacket. "Alright, just relax. Don't . . . don't shoot anymore. I'll give you what you want."

I waited. The hair on the back of my neck stiffened as a bated breath hung trapped in my chest. A shiver hollowed my spine. Slowly, like a frightened animal, he pulled the book from the inner lining of his coat.

"I know why you want this," he said. "It's why I kept it from you."

"You know nothing of what I want."

He shook his head. "The Sons of Order made the connection a long time ago, Camilla. We know you are the daughter of Chaos. We know how powerful you are, which is why you cannot walk away from this."

"Who are the Sons of Order?" My pointer finger wrapped around the trigger. He caught the movement.

"The Sons of Order have gone by many names over the last century," he said with the beginnings of a grin tipping his thin lips. "The Order of Saints. The Order of Inner Courts." He winked. "But first, we were Sons of Greed."

"Greed?" I whispered. He was speaking of the saint, of the one I'd met in Oblivion—that I might have let out. "Order isn't a thing, is it? Not even something you're trying to achieve. It's a divine."

His smile fell. "It's not really something you'd understand as the daughter of Chaos."

"I'm smarter than people give me credit for."

I pulled the trigger. Felix jerked, but it was empty. One last shot, and this one would kill.

"There are people hunting what you hold, Camilla. I only wanted to provide Order to my city, to my country, but there are those who will bring it to the entire realm once your power is purged from the world."

"You want control," I corrected him.

"Order *is* control," he replied. "Chaos is corruption. Your mother taught me that much." He held the book up an inch higher.

There was too much he was leaving out. Perhaps an entire realm of history he was purposely avoiding to keep me in the dark.

He tossed me the leather-bound journal, and I snatched it midair with my gun still aimed at his chest.

But then . . . he pulled out something else from his pocket. A small, silver orb I recognized from Nico's wares. He must have taken it that day they infiltrated Sabina's.

A bomb.

"They'll kill me anyway if they find out Chaos is free again," he murmured. "At least this way, Order has a chance to return to the realm. If I let you live, you could destroy him."

"Felix . . ." I tried to step back, to pull the trigger, but my body no longer obeyed me. I was repressed from my thoughts. Only a passenger in my head.

"If you would have just married me all those months ago." His teeth gnashed together. "None of this would have happened. Your family would be alive. The Attanos would never have risen to power. Everything would be as it should be. But you are truly Chaos, and I see now why we must destroy you."

"Felix, wait—" My heart raced, panic replacing my foolish confidence. I still couldn't move. Couldn't shoot him. Couldn't run.

He lifted the pin to his lips. "I'll fight fire with fire if that's what it takes. And if I go down, I'm taking you with me, Camilla. Let's see which hell our shadows belong to."

Arms wrapped Felix from behind. The alchemist thrashed once to free himself, but Aramis sent a small knife into his neck, one coated with a faint blue glow—giving the alchemist a taste of his own medicine.

But he had already pulled the pin by the time I could pull the trigger.

Jarred from the kickback of the gun, I watched as blood stained his starch shirt, a glossy saturation spread like a starburst over his chest. The bullet sunk into the space above his heart, giving Felix Firenze a moment to count his last breaths. He used his final one to spit the pin at me before falling to the ice.

"Aramis, he's got a—"

My brother instantly noticed the triggered explosive, palming and tossing it as far upriver as he could, where it exploded in the near distance. Heat brushed our faces, stirred the hair on my neck, and flitted away some of the coldness under my skin.

"Off the ice!" my brother shouted. I followed him, lifting my skirts to run toward the riverbank as the ice beneath our strides shifted. One plunge under the river's icy crown and we'd be swept away in the forceful current.

When I hit solid ground, I nearly fell to my knees in relief.

But Aramis was still panicked, tugging me by the hand he snatched while we ran. "Come on. We need to get to the station."

"What are you talking about?"

"I'll explain on the way, but first we need to—"

Fire scourged the greenhouses behind the warehouse like a flame to a dry wick. We both stopped in our tracks, staring up at a burning wall that seemed to grow higher by the second. A noxious smell hit us immediately from all the herbs decomposing in the heat, and I covered my face with my hand to breathe through the stench.

"You're fucking late!" Aramis shouted at a figure beginning to emerge from the smoke.

Jeremiah walked casually, a cigarillo hanging between his lips. His shirt was half unbuttoned and his face and chest were covered with a sheen of sweat.

"Looks like I'm right on time," he murmured.

"You wouldn't be if this entire night hadn't gone to hell. Where's the carriage?"

"Private drive near the last greenhouse—if the fire hasn't spooked the horses."

My mouth gaped, unsure what was going on. Had my brothers been planning this all along behind my back? First the betrayal, then Aramis had helped me, and now Jer was burning down the remainder of the Firenzes' stock.

My head spun hopelessly.

Aramis pulled me down the gravel drive toward the hidden carriage Jeremiah had mentioned. I planted my feet before I joined them.

"I'm not going anywhere without Nico. Where is he and what have you done to him?"

"I'm trying to take you to him," Aramis growled. "If he was smart enough to heed my words, he's getting those fucking cars to the Row, and we need to ensure they make it there."

"Why?" I asked. "You stabbed him with a Niner blade. He's as good as dead!"

Aramis threw open the door. "Because the Niner blade will not kill him, Camilla. Now please get in the car before the Watch comes to investigate the fire. I'll explain it all on the way."

"He's being honest, Milla. For once, I'd listen to him," Jer said softly beside me. He jumped in the driver's seat and readied the horses.

Reluctantly, and lacking other options, I joined my brother—if only to learn his secrets at last.

"HE'S NOT GOING TO DIE?"

Aramis shook his head, seated across from me. "The Niner

poison only works by tearing a shadow from a person, which is why it's a torturous death. Remnants have different kinds of shadows, allowing the poison to be more selective in nature. But Nico"—he canted his head—"doesn't have a shadow to poison. He'll be fine once it leaves his bloodstream."

"And you knew this all along?"

He nodded. "One of my deals with Felix, in exchange for your life, was to bring Nico in so he could end him, but I couldn't do that to you. I couldn't save your life just to take the one good thing you've ever had. Hells know I've done that enough recently." His gaze fell to the floor in thought. "Thankfully, Nico solved that problem for me by taking the deal with Desmond, and all I had to do was make sure Felix left *me* in charge of killing him."

Relief and rage battled for dominance in my heart. "How do you know Desmond?"

Aramis cleared his throat and glanced nervously at the windows. "We've crossed paths several times. He works out of the Vasilli downtown."

"*Are you—*"

"No," he replied curtly. "I have nothing to do with whatever Nico's transferring. In the days before I sought out Nico, I crawled back to the Firenzes to see if there was a way I could barter with them to keep you safe. It turned out Felix didn't know his men had taken you. They must have left Felix out of the deal, less men to split your bounty." He shook his head. "Anyway, I had an advantage, information to give them to gain their trust. They thought Chaos was dead and the key was gone. Sera's act had been most convincing."

"Sera should have never—"

"Sera was a very good friend to us both," Aramis said. "She

didn't deserve what happened to her, but she's the reason this city hasn't gone to hell yet."

"You miss her," I stated the obvious.

He swallowed hard. "It doesn't matter what I feel. If Vanya was right, and the stuff on the cars is the missing mirkwood the Firenzes are expecting, we'll have finally beaten them. There won't be anything available until next spring, far too late for the Firenzes to bounce back. Especially after everything that happened tonight.

"When I learned Nico was part of the deal and what he'd traded, I figured it was all for the best. He'd find a way to get the stuff past the Watch, take the Firenzes most lucrative ingredient for their glint, and he'd be protected when I inevitably delivered him to Felix."

So, it wasn't betrayal—but a blinding white lie. It made me feel a fraction better he wasn't trying to kill my husband, but the weight of this—what he'd kept from me—formed a scar of mistrust that might not ever heal completely.

"Who is this client and how did they take such a thing out from under the Firenzes?" I asked aloud.

Aramis shrugged. "No idea. But when we find out, and Nico hopefully completes this deal and all is well, we need to burn the stuff. Client or not."

"I can help with that," I said, only jesting at first. My hands fell open in my lap, letting go of the book. Chaos magic still clung to my fingers, yet it didn't spread on its own accord. It listened to me, obeyed me in a way it never had before—like it recognized something new in my voice.

My fingers still stung from the kickback of the gun, and I folded them together, reminded of the life I took tonight.

"He deserved it, Camilla." Aramis noticed my fidgeting. "It was him or you."

"I know." He read my body wrong if he thought I was concerned about Felix. I'd have traveled to the void just to shoot him again for all the pain he'd caused my family. "Nico doesn't know about the Niner poison and his shadow, does he?"

Aramis shrugged. "I suppose not."

I bit my bottom lip in thought. "So, he still thinks he's dying."

He nodded slowly, his brows kissed in confusion.

"Does not having a shadow keep you from dying at all?" I asked, my voice shaking.

"No," Aramis replied. "The shadow and the body are two separate entities, either can die on its own."

I breathed a curse and urged Jer to drive faster. "If Nico thinks he's a dead man walking, he might do something to get himself killed. *Hells*, he'll be even more reckless than usual. We need to reach him before it's too late."

"We'll get to him, Milla. He can't be that far ahead of us."

I clutched the book, fingering the frayed pages nervously. I'd be more confident in his calculations if the man in question couldn't control the actual time.

Looking down at the journal, a seed of guilt blossomed in my throat, and I choked back a sob before Aramis could hear me cry. I'd gained a piece of my past . . . and it might have cost me the rest of my future—and my forever.

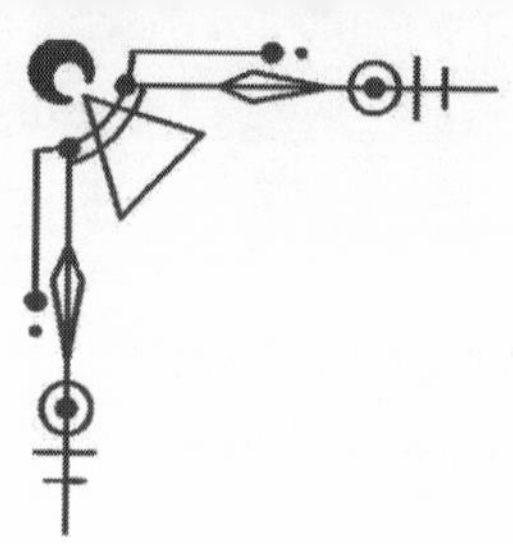
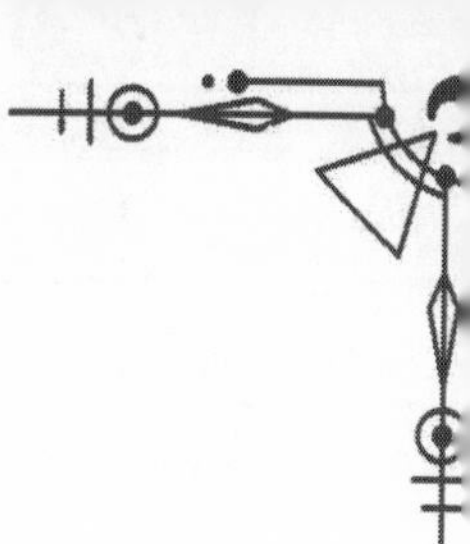

CHAPTER 52

NICOLAI

It took some time to find the railway tracks.

Fog collected over the greenspaces, hiding the car as it moved silently through the city without a single tremor through the rails to betray its location. Lights from the street lamps glowed through the mist, partially illuminating the way with the help of a full moon.

My borrowed horse ran hard, following the slanting earth scarring through the Districts. I was numb to the sting of the wind, the frozen fog, the open wound in my side. Feeling nothing but anxious, I was tempted to use my remnant to pause the time, to give me more to find them, but for my plan to work until the very end, I'd need every scrap of power left available in my bones.

The last car finally broke through the hazy morning.

"Stop!" I shouted. The benders pushing the car only used their remnants to push it faster, speeding further away.

"*Fuck*," I muttered, forced to bend the time to catch up.

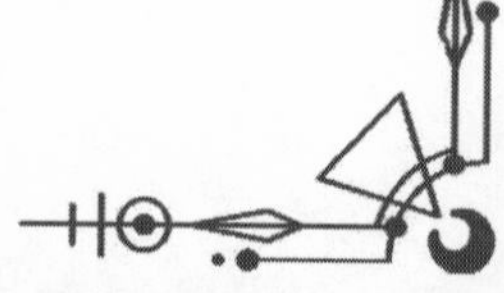

Pulling the steed to the side of the tracks, I stopped it when we came beside the car and climbed the backend where two benders were working.

They nearly fell off when I let go of the second.

"We've been caught," I told them. "I need you to stop the car and get the hells off."

"But sir—"

"That's an order," I barked, the word echoed over the city. They changed the direction of their wind to slow the car to a rolling stop, and I sighed a breath of relief. The bender on the front acting as a lookout climbed down to meet us, and I waited until he joined us before explaining.

"Up ahead," I said, "is a legion of watchmen waiting for this car. It's all a trap. If they catch you, they'll arrest every single one of you and saints know what else. Take yourselves back to the Row and wait for further word. And stay out of sight on the way."

My men—who'd been more than just hired hands on a payroll—almost looked as if they'd defy an order for the first time. Men I trusted in a world where that word held more power than any monetary amount. Each of them was just a year or so younger than myself. A life ahead of them I did not have. It was better this way, for me to handle things from here.

"You take orders from Camilla Attano from now on. Do you understand?"

They didn't. Not fully, but they nodded anyway.

My hands fisted the edge of the guardrail, staring down at the empty tracks. Without looking at either of them, I dismissed them. "Good. Now get the fuck out of here."

They left without further inquiry, and I was alone with nothing but a car full of my rival's biggest profit and a freshly rolled cigarillo in my pocket. A year ago, I would have reveled being in this position, but the circumstances soured the sweetness from the moment.

I reached into my pocket to retrieve the cigarillo to have one last smoke and a picture. The same one Sabina had gifted me months ago that I'd kept close for no reason at all other than to peek at it when Camilla wasn't at my side. It felt so unfair, the entire situation. Out of all the time I'd loved her, had gone through hell for each other, we'd never get our ending like the stories promised.

I kissed her picture for good luck and took a moment to accept the end for what it was—ours.

The last plumes of my father's favorite blend burned and replaced the bitterness in my heart with an impossible kind of peace. But something disturbed the frost covering the ground beyond the reach of the light, footsteps padding quietly as if to hide their steps. Sparks exploded near my face as a bullet hit the wall of the car behind me.

Without another choice, I bent the time, slowing it to a stop.

"*Fuck.*"

We weren't far from the station, but I had no idea how long my remnant could hold the time. Had never been eager to challenge the depths of my power out of fear of reaching the bottom. Tonight, however, that was no longer an issue.

I slipped off the back of the car to steer it from the front, to make sure the tracks were clear on the way back to the Row. Milla was right, once I got the car moving—with an assisting shove from the wind to nudge it along—it was easy to pull, even alone.

A light pulse fluttered through my bones, reminding me how much bending the time stole from the well, but I ignored the warning. Became as numb to it as I did rest of me and pulled the car away from the residential areas of the Steam District.

The marshaling yard. That's where this would end. I just had to make it that far, and then it would be done.

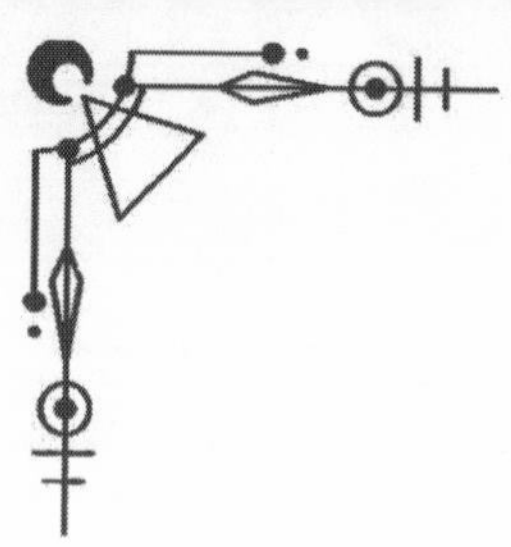
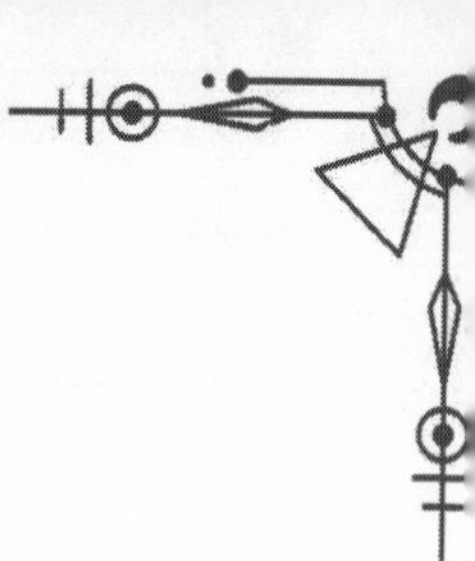

CHAPTER 53
CAMILLA

Jeremiah parked the carriage outside the Main Station, the wheels skidding to stop.

"Camilla, wait—"

Before Aramis could complete his warning, I was already out the door and running up the brick paved steps to the boarding deck.

The station was draped in snow and thick ice that gleamed in the streetlamps still flickering in their orbs over the cobblestones. Ice made the steps up to the entrance perilous, but I slipped a little fire in front of my path, still unfortunately wearing nothing but my flats and the party dress—which had held up considerably for what it had been through. Far more than I could say for my nerves.

Nico was nowhere to be found. The place was empty, and yet there were footprints covering the platform, pressed into the light dusting of snow that had blown in from the exposed loading deck.

"He's not here," I called to my brother through the archway. "You said he'd be—"

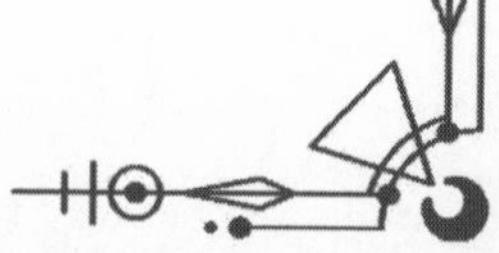

Something sharp sunk into my neck, and my power went quiet in my blood. Shots fired from behind—Aramis eliminating the watchman that drugged me. He fell to my side with a solid thud that tremored through the platform.

"Camilla, get down!"

Before I could take cover behind the ticket booth nearby, a man popped out from behind the door and shoved me off the platform. I fell onto a bed of sharp rocks, only to be dragged by two guards across a set of tracks while Aramis took the offensive for me. And if I heard correctly, there were two guns firing from the depot. Jeremiah must have finally found his fight.

"Do we kill her or take her back?"

"Let Halloway decide."

The men dragged me behind an abandoned railcar and pinned me against the side, the layout of the yard similar to how we'd left it the night we rescued Regulus. A man dressed in a fine suit, like he'd just left a party, appeared from around the corner with more guards trailing behind him.

His large hand wrapped my neck, canting my head to view every angle of my face. A grin stretched his cheeks. "You're the Attanos' little treasure. Nicolai's whore of a wife." He released me quickly, like I revolted him. "We will have fun with you. But first, we take care of the car."

"Where is he?" I spat through my teeth.

He ignored my question and stalked off, leaving me with two guards. The gunfire continued, more joining the chorus of bullets splitting metal and brick, and I worried for my brothers trying to fight back with so little coverage. I needed to get out of their hold quickly—before something terrible happened to either of them.

There was a sudden blur of movement, the flicker of silver and the slice of wind preceded a guttural sound from both watchmen.

Their grasps simultaneously loosened, slinking to the ground in a pile of loose flesh and black armor.

Solomon Attano stood in front of me, wiping the blood from a double-edged sword on one of their uniforms. He returned it to the base of his cane, where it connected to appear like a normal walking assistant.

"Camilla, are you alright?" He touched my face. "What's happened? Brief me quickly!"

I shook my head, the weight of every fear pressing on a single point over my chest, making it difficult to breathe, much less explain. He took me under his arm and spoke in my silence. "My mother woke up a few hours ago and pulled the truth out of Gideon and Adler. The minute we heard about the deal with Desmond, we came."

"We?"

"The family. Caught Luther red-handed at the Industrial Station and he filled us in on the way here."

"Sol, if you've given Nonna a weapon—"

He chuckled. "Nonna, despite her initial arguments, decided to sit this one out. Now, what's the plan?"

"Right, what's the plan, boss?" Gideon asked, approaching with Adler and Esme from behind the nearest railcar. She smiled, though it didn't quite fill her face as it usually did.

I sighed, trying to think straight. "We need to get the last car over the viaduct, but I can't find Nico. The only other place he could be is perhaps helping the men push the car. But I'm worried he's going to do something . . . drastic."

"Drastic is his nature," Sol murmured. "Should we clear the yard, then? Give him a clear path?"

There had to be nearly twenty watchmen, twice as many of us. Some of which had Niner blades tucked in their sheaths. But

Solomon Attano did not consider spilling blood lightly, and my threshold had lowered significantly to the idea as well.

"We can try," I said, feeling breathless. Because what else was there to do until Nico showed himself? He could be suspended in the second for all we knew.

A thought struck me. If the Attanos had come from the industrial park, then Nico had never made it. He'd do anything to get that last car through the city, knowing the contents would shift the scales. Anything—even if it drained him of magic.

"I need you to cover me while I wait on the tracks," I told the cousins.

"Milla, that's out in the open. You'll be target practice—"

"I don't think Halloway wants me dead just yet. Besides, it won't be long if my theory is correct."

"And if it's not?" Esme asked. "What will we tell Nico when we give you back to him full of holes?"

I grabbed a pistol from one of the dead guards and checked the chamber, thankful it was full. "You'll tell Nico that I loved him enough not to let him destroy himself."

I SHOT at anything with a cape that moved until I stood on the center track, blocking the way back to the Row. Staring down the south end of the station, I willed the car to appear. Something to emerge from the misty end of the marshaling yard.

Bullets whirred past like the irritating buzz of a fly, but I denied them a reaction. They were missing on purpose, knew my value enough to heed their commander's order. The family behind me shot down any head that peered around a railcar, keeping me protected despite the risk of standing out in the open.

"Ceasefire!"

Halloway appeared then, hands raised above his head, along with his gun. He came to stand in front of me, blocking my view of the south entrance. Smoke curled in the dead space between our forces from the wasted bullets, and a strange silence returned over the yard.

"Camilla," Halloway spoke loudly. "You're going to get everyone you care about killed, including your husband. Surrender yourself and the car and no one else will be punished tonight. That's more than fair."

"Fair?" I laughed. "You think what the Niners are doing is fair? What Felix did to those he tested on? What the descendants went through in Hightower? This has nothing to do with justice or laws or doing what is right. It's about the Nine's incessant preoccupation for Order."

"You cannot stop us, Camilla."

I shook my head slowly, buying a few more seconds of time. "I already have."

The car appeared behind him, too late for anyone to do something. The speed of the abandoned railcar coming down the tracks was enough to thrust the rusted end of the coupler through the unaware man standing in front of me—unaware until it was too late.

Halloway's mouth gaped open in shock, and the car, without anyone pushing it, slowed to a stop mere feet in front of me. With glazed eyes, he looked down at his chest and the protruding metal, then looked back up at me.

A lazy arm lifted, and I was suddenly looking down the barrel of a gun.

"Milla!"

I hit the ground before the shot went off. Sharp rocks dug into my temple as Nico's arms slid over me. "*Seven hells*, Milla! What were you thinking?"

He was trembling violently all over. I shoved off the ground to sit up, stroking every mark on his face as I assessed him. Dark circles hung beneath bloodshot eyes. He breathed heavily, like he'd just finished a sprint, but his skin was ice-cold. A deeper chill than the weather could penetrate.

Dread curled beneath my ribs. "Nico, did you drain your remnant?"

"I . . ." He gasped. "I don't know. Perhaps."

But I couldn't focus on him long when the watchmen emerged from their shelters and ran for the car in front of us. Nico noticed the guards trying to take back the stock and shouted at his family. "Adler! Burn it!"

"No!" I tried to nullify the command, but the cousin didn't question an order from his boss. The air around us suddenly dropped even colder, ice crawled over the tracks as the heat bender stole the remaining warmth left in the world around us to light a blazing inferno inside the railcar, burning anything and everything within it. Burning Nico's last chance to get his shadow back.

The watchman cursed, looking at each other, looking at their dead commander, calculating their odds against the Attanos, before eventually deciding better of retaliating. I felt their disappointment for different reasons. We both had failed.

"It's alright, my love," Nico said, pulling me into his cold chest. His heart fluttered against my temple. "It's better this way."

"No, you impulsive fool!" I beat a fist against that weakening heart. Cursing every skipped beat. "We needed to get that car to Desmond to finish the deal."

"The deal doesn't matter if—"

"You're not going to die!" I screamed at him. He went still, his lips parting in question. "Not by the Niner blade. Aramis explained to me how the poison works and, since you don't have your shadow, you weren't going to die from it." But now . . . without the final part of the delivery . . .

Realization hit Nico hard. His features crumbled, and I'd never —*never*—seen him defeated. Not as he was now. "*Shit.*"

We sat there, holding each other as the flames stretched into the night until the heat from the flames became too much. My brothers helped us back onto the platform where the Attanos had already gathered. I explained to them in as few words as possible the events at the party and the implications of destroying the stock —leaving out my trip to Oblivion. It wasn't time for that yet.

Adler cursed, angry at himself.

Fran dismissed her tears with a stealthy swipe of a gloved hand across her cheeks. "This is not the end of it. We are Attanos. We will find a way. Where we fall, we rise."

"*Un cancidamus orbitur*," Luther's voice carried across the station, and we turned to find him and Finn trailed by one of the Canary Boys. "We'll find this fucking client and make sure they agree to a compensation. If they accept the offer, the dealer should be appeased as well. We'll start right now if we must!"

"What do you want to do, Nico?" Sol asked his nephew.

Nico leaned against me slightly, wavering on his feet. He didn't seem interested in finding the client, or anything else for that matter. "I want to go home."

I squeezed his hand and put on a mask, pretending my heart wasn't breaking. "I left something in the carriage. Let me go get it first."

He nodded mechanically, joining me as I led us outside toward the driveway. Waiting in the loop of the drive, however, was not just our empty carriage. There were others, including the least likely person I expected to turn up here.

Vanya Hartsong.

"Sorry it took so long," she said wistfully. "It took a while for Felix's compulsion to wear off so I could leave the party. Fortunately, everyone began to vomit viciously all over the place. Thank hells I didn't host." She winked at us. "Looks like I made it just in time."

"Vanya, we—"

She held up a gloved hand to silence me. "There's no need for an explanation. Let me take a look to see how I can help."

"You can't help this time, Vanya," Nico whispered.

She smiled at him softly before pushing past us. "I'm offended, Nico. After all I've done, even you underestimate me. Let's just see the damage."

The Watch was more than eager to explain to Vanya the events of the evening, with her official title as Head of Public Affairs and the latest inspector dead, she was next in line concerning lawful leadership.

She could've had Nico arrested right there and then for illegally transporting unauthorized stock through the city. Vanya, however, failed to see a crime present. Even as she assessed the state of Halloway's body, grimacing at the grotesque scene.

"As far as I can tell, there is no illegal stock. Just an empty car of ashes," she said. "As for Halloway, it's tragic, truly, what happened to him." She looked at the nearest guard. "Now, did anyone see one of the Attanos push him on the coupler?"

"No miss, the car rolled by itself—"

"And he was standing on the tracks with his back to it? Well, I'd consider that a terrible accident and quite negligent on his part.

Standing on the tracks is dangerous at any time, especially at night with all this fog. Wouldn't you agree, Captain? Or should I say, Commander? A position *is* open, after all."

The guard's mouth slapped shut. "I suppose that's an accurate assessment."

"Indeed," Vanya said, smiling. She looked up at Nico and me, gesturing with her chin to follow her down the platform, away from the guards.

"Vanya, I appreciate this, but you don't—"

"With all respect, Nicolai, please shut up." She braced a hand on his shoulder and patted it lightly. "I suppose, considering everything that's happened between us, I could work something out with Desmond."

My mouth fell open, unsure if I heard her correctly. "You know Desmond?"

"Of course. I'm his most valued client." She let that sink in a moment, a smirk carving into her cheek. "If you haven't worked it out by now, I am the client that asked the Demon Dealer to move an unholy amount of mirkwood through the city. It shocked me to learn that you of all descendants took the job, though it worked out well enough for the both of us."

Nico blinked several times, processing what she was saying. "You mean you'll approve the deal with Desmond? I'll get my collateral back?"

"If he wants to continue working in the city, he'll do whatever the fuck I tell him."

We both released a long breath, and I watched a wide smile stretch Nico's cheeks. A bit of life returned to his eyes and added coloring to his face. "But why? Why would you even . . ."

"Have him move it for me in the first place? Simple. The Firenzes were after my family as head of the Nine Crowns, and I needed them taken care of. I took them down where it hurt financially, trusting you to finish the rest. I'm sorry, by the way, I hated leading you to them tonight, but it was the only way I could plant you both close enough to destroy Felix for good."

Nico scrubbed his face with his hand. "You could have told me your plan, Vanya. This would have been a hells lot simpler."

"I didn't know it was you who took my deal until Camilla mentioned something about it when we met, and let's face it, it was far too late at that point. It took a bit of planning on my feet, but we did it. We removed the threat on the city, and now we can move forward. I hope to continue what we started tonight, Nicolai."

"It won't be easy," he said.

"No." She looked at me then. "But none of us are doing this because it's easy. The people want change. They want peace. The only way for that to happen is if everyone, regardless of which side we belong to, feels safe enough to be who they are here."

I smiled. "Well, you have my vote whenever you decide to run for office."

Vanya barked a laugh but waved a dismissive hand. "I'll let my father have his time, though he knows I'm gunning for his seat. One day, he'll realize I deserve it. Until then, sisterhoods and socialites will have to be enough."

She held out a hand to Nico, and he shook it firmly. "Thank you, Vanya. Always a pleasure."

"Thank you, Nico. Thank you, both. Now get out of here before the rest of the Watch shows up. I'll send word to Desmond immediately to get your shadow back."

"I think that's wise. Looks like the rest of them are eager to get back as well." Nico nodded to my brother, who grabbed the book I'd gone back to retrieve.

When I started to make the long walk toward the viaduct, Nico pulled me back, anchored in place. "Something wrong?" Stupid question. He'd nearly reached the bottom of his remnant and felt like shit, there was plenty bothering him.

"It's morning." He gestured with his chin toward the horizon. The sky cleared over the east side of the city, disrupting the dark sky with gradients of golds and pinks and the hope of a new day.

He pulled me into his chest, his false hand slipping beneath the jacket Gideon spared for me, and I suppressed a chill from the coldness of the metal and the familiarity of his touch. "I love you, Camilla Mercy Marchese-Attano. I don't know how many mornings I have left to keep that promise I made you, but I do. I love you."

My throat nearly shut under the weight of those words. "I love you too, Nicolai Attano. Forever, however long that is."

He kissed me like forever depended on it, and his hands were everywhere at once. Pinching my waist, clawing at my hips, cupping the slope of my neck until his fingers tangled in my hair. He kissed me until the sun rose above the rooflines in the distance and soaked the marshaling yard in a golden glow.

I broke from his lips. "Nico?"

"Yes, my love?"

"I don't want to move out."

His fingers twisted around the hair at the base of my head, tugging them sharply to cant my head and expose my throat. "That's fine. We can stay if that's what you want."

I sucked a breath as he kissed the hollow of my throat. "It is," I managed to say. "I'm ready to tell you everything, Nico. I want you to know the parts of me I hate most, even if you hate them too. Because every piece of me loves you, and I'll not give you anything less than my entire self for the rest of our lives."

"I'm your selfish bastard, Milla." Cold lips grazed my wild

pulse, speaking to the flutter of my heart. "I'll take whatever you give me, as long as you'll have me."

The crunch of footsteps came from behind us, and Nico loosened his embrace on me enough to look over his shoulder. Luther approached, covering his eyes with one hand, and feeling the way with his other.

"Everyone still got their clothes on?"

"So far," Nico replied. "Make it quick, though."

Luther sighed, shaking his head despairingly. "I just wanted to tell you the family is heading to the pub to grab a celebratory round. Thought you might want to join us unless you've got—" He cleared his throat. "Other plans."

"Our plans can wait." I smiled and looked at Nico. "I could really use a drink."

Nico placed a kiss on the hand he held and looped it around his arm. "You're the boss."

We ventured back to the Row together, to a corner establishment I'd avoided for too long. Where they poured ale straight from a tap and the owner had a private apartment right above the pub, who let me drink for free and left me drunk on his kiss. A quiet place on a quiet street where my entire life had fallen into place because of a single dance and a few drinks on the house.

We started our next story how we started our last—at the House of Bane.

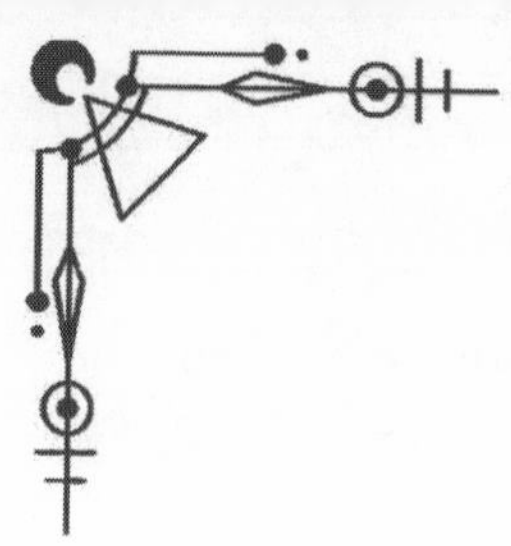
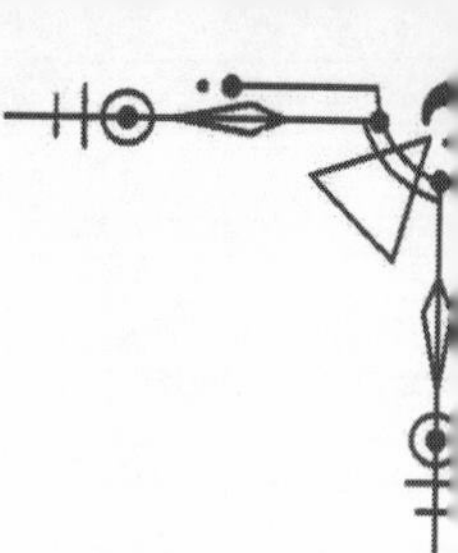

CHAPTER 54
CAMILLA

The city settled into a strange new pace in the weeks that followed Magrahel. The Society had disengaged and was replaced with the working idea of integrating descendants into law enforcements to diversify the system. Halloway's death had been ruled an accident, and the Firenzes went utterly quiet as their business sunk without their supporters or their glint to keep them afloat.

Felix's body was never found, and I was never charged or even suspected of killing him. Especially not after Vanya claimed to have witnessed him murder the inspector and a host of other accurate accusations that tarnished the Firenzes' reputations further. There wasn't much for the alchemists to come back from after that, and they reduced their business model to medicinal tonics and tinctures. Which—from what I'd heard through Vanya—wasn't as profitable as their previous gains.

Thanks to Vanya, Nico had his shadow returned, or rather, delivered. A woman named Sinthia arrived the very next day

following the party with a box of darkness in her hand. Only when I saw his silhouette stretch across the floor did I truly feel the weight of the world lift at last.

Things were changing in Lynchaven under Hartsong's new agenda. Now that the High Overseer had full power without the threat of the Nine, the cabinet added more chairs to the table to allow descendants a voice. Nico became a speaker for the Row, using his influence in a way that didn't involve extortion or blackmail. He was, as I teased him, completely legitimate now. The model of a true gentleman, despite how he acted behind closed doors—but that was for my benefit only now.

My brothers went home, returning to the Marchese Manor after Vanya returned it personally from the city's ownership. I still hadn't gone back—but I would. For now, there were too many ghosts that haunted the halls, and I was too busy preparing for the future to face the past just yet.

Aramis and I were cordial. I never doubted his motivations in the end were to help me, but some hurts lingered no matter how many times they were justified, and while my head had forgiven him, my heart was taking a bit longer to fully trust him again.

He'd still accepted my invitation tonight, to my pleasant surprise.

"I must admit," Nico said. "I thought I loved you in red, but you're a vision in white."

"Don't get used to it." I smiled at him through the mirror, glancing over the cream-colored silk dress that tapered from a fitted bodice. It was simple, with minimal detailing. All the attention went into the structure of the silk and how it cascaded off my body in ivory waves. A brief train draped the floor behind me. "I'm only wearing this for the tradition."

He left his false hand ungloved, dragging a metal finger over the pressed waves of my hair as it fell over my shoulder. "I have your ring, by the way. It finally came back from getting sized."

Talk of jewels distracted me long enough from my reflection to follow him to his desk. From a locked drawer, he removed a velvet box and held it between us before opening it. "I should warn you, this isn't what you picked out."

"What do you mean? What did you get me?" He'd taken me ring shopping weeks ago after he'd proposed properly at the pub. We were both drunk, and Nico's uncle was less than thrilled with the impulsivity of the moment, but it all worked out in the end.

I was wearing *white* after all.

"You told me a long time ago you didn't like diamonds, so instead of buying the one you picked out, I used the opportunity to get your real ring sized." A flush crawled his neck. Was he nervous?

"Nico." I wrapped the box with my hand, forcing him to look at me instead. "I married you once without a ring. I'd marry you without anything."

He quirked a brow. "Even without any money?"

My grin tightened, and I patted his hand lovingly. "Let's not get too hasty."

"Camilla!"

"I'm kidding!" I laughed. *Sort of.* "Please, just show me the damn ring already."

"Spoiled little heiress," he murmured, shaking his head. But then he lifted the lid from the box and revealed what he'd chosen, and my jaw dropped at the size of the ruby.

"*Seven hells*, Nico . . ." I gasped. "It's . . . it's beautiful."

"It was Nonna's," he said. I was speechless as he took my left hand and slid it over my ring finger. It fit perfectly. Every cut in the stone refracted the light in the gas lamps, glittering as I angled my hand.

"I was supposed to give it to you a long time ago, but things got in the way. We used it to make a portal when we broke into Hightower. The other side is in Esme's garage, where she has vowed to protect the mirror until the end of her days." He scoffed at the idea.

"If you're ever far away, Milla," he emphasized, "and you can't find your way back, it'll bring you home. The portal still works if you twist the diamond at the bottom and activate the shadows inside."

It wasn't just a ring, then. It was a piece of his home—our home—I could carry with me always, an heirloom they trusted me to pass down, and a reminder of where I belonged. I cleared my throat before I started weeping. It was far too early in the night for all that.

"I don't plan on ever being far from home, Nico, but the sentiment is beautiful."

He took a step back and sighed, his eyes falling to our bed. "I thought we promised not to keep anything from each other?"

"I'm not—" I followed his stare to the book lying open on top of the covers. I'd read it through nearly a dozen times, had tabbed the parts I thought important. My mother's words hadn't just told her story, they warned me of what was to come.

I just . . . hadn't talked to my husband about it all yet.

"I read it when you were busy," he said. "Why didn't you tell me your mother was alive?"

I swallowed a knot in my throat and fumbled with the newfound weight on my finger. "I just wanted to be sure of all the facts before I came to you."

"Milla," he said my name quietly. That knowing tone made me grimace. "Sabina said she saw your mother leave, *alive*, and the book confirms it. She practically begs you to come find her. Why not see where it leads?"

"Because, for once, we're all finally happy!" I lifted my skirts to gain some distance, pacing the room. "You have responsibilities here and a family that loves you. I cannot take you from your home just for the slim chance my mother is still out there."

"But her warning—"

"Was written twenty-one years ago," I cut in. "Yes, she technically told me to find her when I was ready. But I'm *not* ready. I'm not willing to upend everything we have—"

"I want to go."

My heels nearly caught on the lining of the rug. "What did you say?"

He stood there with his hands in his pockets, looking too casual for this conversation. "I want to go to the Continent. I want to help you find your mother. You saw the saint she trapped in Oblivion when you opened it, and if what he threatened was true, Chaos might be the only one who can help us if Order finds his way out." He stared me down, completely serious. "I think you need to find her, Milla."

My stomach wrung itself and I shrugged. "I wouldn't even know where to start."

"Vesper and Callow are leaving at the start of spring, when sailing conditions are better. Perhaps, with their connections, we can find someone who can help."

I didn't know if I was relieved or terrified to hear him suggest it. Part of me had entertained the idea while the other half didn't think it plausible. We'd be leaving everything we worked for to venture to a land that might as well have been another realm, the differences in our worlds.

"Don't think about it too much tonight, my love," he said.

"We have the rest of the winter to decide, but I think you should give it more consideration."

"There's no certainty we'd ever come back, Nico."

He shook his head, unbothered. "Is there a single certainty in tomorrow, Milla? I'll take the risk if you take it with me."

A knock came at our door. My brothers were here to escort me to Sabina's, who had dedicated her warehouse for our wedding. I smoothed down the skirts I'd disheveled with my pacing. "We'll discuss it more later. For now, don't breathe a word to anyone."

Nico nodded. "Of course." He crossed the room in confident strides to answer the door, though his hand hovered a moment. "You are my family now, Camilla. I go where you go, till death takes me."

"Still betting how many years I'm going to shave off your life?" I jested, but my smile was fleeting.

"No," he said. "You've saved me too many times for that to hold true." He opened the door to reveal my brothers in their finest suits waiting on the other side.

Nico leaned against the door. "Ready for another adventure, princess?"

I lifted to my toes to kiss his lips.

"I'm ready."

ACKNOWLEDGMENTS

There are some stories that change your life and stick with you for a long time. It's why we read. Why we constantly chase the next world, the next hero, the next happy ending. That feeling of finding the perfect story, it's the closest thing to magic we'll ever experience in our world. And sometimes, if you dabble in the chaos called writing, you get to write the story that changes your life, and I'm really proud to say this was the one that changed mine.

To my amazing husband, Kennon. You've been my rock when the publishing world was unsteady, when sales were never promised, when the future was misty. Somehow, you knew I could write before I even picked up a pen. You consistently remind me of my worth and value in our little family and encourage me to make scary choices, knowing those same decisions will push me closer to my dreams. Thanks for being just as crazy as I am and going on this journey with me.

To my editor, Brittany Corely, for being incredibly thorough with the developmental edits and helping me polish this story to its shiniest splendor. We all have that person who changed the trajectory of our lives with a simple, encouraging friendship. Thanks for being mine, and for continuously agreeing to put out the flames of my dumpster fires.

To my agent, Emily Forney, who has in our short time together been an incredible champion for this story already. Thank you for seeing not only the potential in House of Bane, but for seeing something in me. I'm so grateful to be able to work with you on this project and all the stories yet to come!

To my friend, Brittany B., for meeting me over margaritas and listening to me rant about literally everything. You've helped keep me sane over the last few years, and I am so grateful for our easy friendship.

To my sister, Britni (I have a lot of Brits in my life, I know), for introducing me to the fantasy romance genre when I started reading again. I wouldn't be here without you, I'm sure of it. Thanks for reading every book I write and for not telling mom about the deplorable parts.

There are so many people in my life that make writing not only possible, but an option for me. Thank you to my family and my village for helping me wear all these hats, and occasionally borrowing one for themselves when the stack gets too tall.

And lastly, to my marvelous readers for letting me do this again. Thank you for every tag, review, picture, video, message, email, and kind word you've sent me over the last year while I completed this duet. Your love for Camilla and Nico is so inspiring, and I'm humbled to tears by your unyielding support. Thank you for patiently waiting for this book, for taking a chance on me, and for allowing me to live my dream. And thank you for changing my life forever.

IF YOU ENJOYED CITY OF MIRTH AND MALICE

TRY THE ASHONERA SERIES BY DEANNA HILL

SOME ARE LED BY DESIRE. After the mysterious death of the kingdom's queen ushers in a deadly plague, Carnaxa, Princess of Antalis, is promised to a rival kingdom. As ancient prophecies unfold, not only is Carnaxa in danger, but the fate of her kingdom as well.

Meanwhile, Anara, a gift of sorts and nothing more, was taken from her homeland. She didn't realize giving her heart away would keep her emotionally shackled, mirroring the physical chains she wore.

OTHERS ARE LED BY DUTY. Captain Thylas has guarded Carnaxa since the day he washed ashore. When he's asked to accompany her to marry another, he finds himself torn between serving his kingdom and the desires of his heart.

Ereon, the Prince of Shaston, was raised in blood and battle. Faced with an uncompromising demand, he must choose between his birthright and his destiny.

WHEN DESIRE AND DUTY CLASH, LEGENDS ARE MADE.

Made in the USA
Middletown, DE
23 August 2024

59634965R00309